THE DEVIL'S IN THE DIVA

For more drama:

Entrances and Exits

Show, Don't Tell

drama

THE DEVIL'S IN THE DIVA

Includes

The Four Dorothys

Everyone's a Critic

Paul Ruditis

Simon Pulse
NEW YORK LONDON TORONTO SYDNEY

This book is a work of fiction. Any references to historical events, real people, or real locales are used fictitiously. Other names, characters, places, and incidents are the product of the author's imagination, and any resemblance to actual events or locales or persons, living or dead, is entirely coincidental.

SIMON PULSE

An imprint of Simon & Schuster Children's Publishing Division

1230 Avenue of the Americas, New York, NY 10020

First Simon Pulse paperback edition December 2010

The text of this book was set in Weiss.

Manufactured in the United States of America

2 4 6 8 10 9 7 5 3 1

Library of Congress Control Number 2010928196

ISBN 978-1-4424-1444-0

ISBN 978-1-4424-1679-6 (eBook)

These titles were originally published individually by Simon Pulse.

CONTENTS

The Four Dorothys

☆ For Jean and Tim ☆

Anything Goes

It was a drag queen's worst nightmare.

There were four of them onstage . . . high school girls, that is, not drag queens. Though I guess some people would say there wasn't much difference between the two.

Each girl was in a pale blue gingham dress and a pair of bright red ruby-esque slippers looking like Dorothy from *The Wizard of Oz*. If they had been drag queens and all four of them showed up wearing the same outfit, looking like their icon, Judy Garland, in her signature ingenue role, I can just imagine the catfight: gingham, sequins, and little stuffed Totos flying *everywhere*.

It was no accident that these girls were dressed (more or less) alike. They were at the final costume fitting for the Orion Academy Spring Theatrical Production of *The Wizard of Oz*. It was the first time the director had a chance to see them all onstage in costume. I suspect he was as surprised by the result as I was. Even though the girls were each playing the same role, they looked nothing alike. Each costume was dramatically different from the next.

But that was the *least* of the issues we were dealing with on this show.

"Bring up the spotlight," Mr. Randall, the drama teacher-director-choreographer, yelled to the stage manager at the back of the auditorium.

Within moments, the Thomas Reed Spotlight lit up the Scott Vanowen Stage in the Saundra Hall Auditorium. My school is big on naming things after people, especially people who are big on making monetary donations to the school. Which is how we wound up with an auditorium that we refer to as Hall Hall.

Maybe someday when I'm a famous alumnus I'll pay to have something named after me. Like an extra wing on the school. Or maybe an entire building. Then again, knowing my luck, there would be a paperwork mix-up and they'd wind up cutting the ribbon on the Bryan Stark Janitorial Closet.

That's me, by the way: Bryan Stark. I tend to think of myself as a supporting character or a background player. My friends take the starring roles. It's not that I plan it that way. It just happens. In the cast list of my life, my name would be somewhere near the bottom.

Don't get me wrong. I don't really mind being in the background when it comes to the day-to-day. Who wants the harsh spotlight of teen drama shining brightly on him, anyway? In the background, I get to watch . . . and critique. I mean, what's the fun of seeing your friends' lives spiral out of control if you can't get in a snarkastic comment or two along the way?

Judgmental? Yes. But I'm okay with that.

That's enough about me for now. I think it's time to set the scene.

Orion Academy is the ultraexclusive (unless your parents have enough money to make it a bit *less* exclusive) high school that I go to. The student population is a little over two hundred of the best and the brightest from the livin'-is-easy beach community of Malibu, CA. We're only thirty minutes from Hollywood, but light-years away from reality.

My school is as much a character in this little drama as the flesh-and-blood cast members I'll be introducing shortly. In many ways, Orion is like any other school in America and yet, totally unique at the same time. I mean, how many other schools were built by a student of the famed architect Frank Lloyd Wright and have—among other interesting features—a waterfall in the lobby? How many have a fully functional observatory on campus? Sit on the edge of a bluff overlooking the Pacific Ocean?

Actually . . . forget what I said about Orion being like any other school in America. That was folly. Pure and utter folly.

Usually, I try to ignore the perks of our school and focus on the realities. Like at that moment the *reality* was the show was opening in one week and we were nowhere near where we needed to be.

The spring production is usually one of the highlights of the year. An amazing performance showcasing some of the best student work this side of the Great White Way. (*Aside:* That's Broadway, for those of you not in the know.)

This year? Not so much.

First of all, you should know that the Orion Theater Department is kind of famous. It helps that the sons and daughters of the biggest movers and shakers in Hollywood go here. That's not to say that they're *all* great actors. Far from it. But when the children of the glitterati decide to follow in Mommy's and Daddy's footsteps . . . well, it's the only school show that regularly appears on *Entertainment Tonight*. The acting may not always be Oscar material, but the buzz is worth its weight in platinum.

This production was different from the regular extravaganza of past years for a few reasons. First off, there was the play.

Now, don't get me wrong, I'm a big fan of *Wizard*, but doesn't that seem a bit more middle school? Or elementary school, even? Shouldn't high school students be over dressing up like a lion, a tin man, or a scarecrow by now? Aren't there, like, a hundred more mature plays to perform?

Grease, at the very least?

The problem was that last year, Mr. Randall, took the spring semester off for a sabbatical. So, a guest director was brought in. Things kind of went all farcical from that point on.

Being Orion Academy, we couldn't just have *any* substitute teacher. The headmaster invited former Tony Award nominee Grayson McDonough in as our sub. Mr. McD (as he forced us to call him) is the same man who produced a revival of the musical *1776* where acrobatic circus clowns played the roles of our forefathers. The resulting show largely consisted of clowns doing backflips on trampolines while singing about the sovereign colony of Virginia. When Mr. McD came to Orion, he was still trying to live down the resulting scandal.

For our spring show, he chose *Marat/Sade*. If you've never heard of the play, it might help to know that the full title is: *The Persecution and Assassination of Jean-Paul Marat as Performed by the Inmates of the Asylum of Charenton under the Direction of the Marquis de Sade.*

A far cry from munchkins and flying monkeys, wouldn't you say?

The show was amazing. I have never seen a production like it on a high school stage. I only played a background lunatic, but there were times even I forgot we were onstage. I was so lost in everyone's performances, I actually believed we were in an insane asylum. It was *that* frighteningly real.

You can imagine how the parents reacted. Seeing their little darlings writhing onstage as inmates of an asylum. There was outrage over the raw nature of the production. Not to mention the underlying message of class struggle that more than a few of our Fortune 500 parents took personally. But mainly everyone was upset over the fact that *Marat/Sade* wasn't a musical.

The Orion Academy Spring Theatrical Production is *always* a musical.

Mr. McD was forced out of Malibu in disgrace . . . *and* with a three-picture deal from Warner Bros. It's amazing how often scandal leads to success out here in La-La Land. So, while

Mr. McD is prepping the film version of the David Mamet children's play *The Revenge of the Space Pandas*, we're left behind to deal with the *Marat/Sade* repercussions for this year's musical.

Repercussion #1: At the beginning of the year, Headmaster Collins handed Mr. Randall a list of musicals that no one could have a problem with. It was a very short list, highlighted with *The Sound of Music* and *Oklahoma!* All very good plays, but the kind of stuff we did in the third grade.

From that list Mr. Randall picked *Wizard* because it didn't include Nazis or focus too much on a Red State. Therefore—he explained to a few select students—it would be the least offensive choice to the surrounding community of liberal Hollywood elite.

Okay, there was Tasha Valentine's Wiccan parents who took issue with the stereotypical portrayal of witches. But everyone knows the Valentines only follow Wicca because it's trendier than Scientology this year. Making a stink about the Wicked Witch just makes them seem all the more *out there*.

Which is my very long way of explaining the choice of play. But not why there were four girls onstage.

That requires even more exposition.

Little Women, The Musical

"Okay, Heather, find the light," Mr. Randall said to Dorothy #3. She was standing on the edge of the wash from the spotlight.

"But I'm *in* the light," Heather said with her customary deep sigh of exasperation (aka The Sigh That Launched a Thousand Fits). Heather's sighs are so impressive that I'm constantly surprised she doesn't drop from lack of oxygen by the time she's done letting them out.

Now, while it was true that the light from the spot was in the general area of the stage where Heather was standing, she wasn't technically *in* it. Mr. Randall had Jimmy, the stage manager, focus the spotlight like that on purpose. Half the cast still didn't notice when they were standing in total shadow onstage.

"You're close," Mr. Randall said with a diplomacy that comes from years of experience. "But you need to be in the hot spot, where the light is brightest. So please, Heather, find the light."

"It's a *spotlight*," Heather insisted. "It moves wherever the person behind it points the thing. Shouldn't the light find me?"

"Technically, that's true," Mr. Randall said with continued diplomacy. "But you need to know this for all the lighting instruments. You're not always going to be in the spotlight, Heather."

I'm sure Heather would disagree.

Heather gave another sigh that could be heard back in the cheap seats. She then moved a small step stage left and stopped.

"That's closer," Mr. Randall said.

"Here, lighty, lighty, lighty," I whispered softly.

I guess it wasn't soft enough because Mr. Randall shot me a look from his seat one row in front of me.

I shrugged my apology and focused back on the lost Dorothy.

Your typical spoiled Hollywood brat, Heather Mayflower used to go around telling everyone that her family actually owned the original ship that the pilgrims came over on. That is, until back in middle school when poor, clueless Mrs. Sharpe—who was rather dull when it came to understanding a social order wherein thirteen-year-olds were more powerful than teachers—made "the Mayflower Mistake." She mentioned in class that "Mayflower" was actually a common name for boats around that time in history.

Mrs. Sharpe didn't last the full school year.

"Is this better?" Heather asked with a huff.

"Yes," Mr. Randall said. I was the only one who heard him add, "Close enough."

Heather isn't the talented Mayflower in the family. That's her sister, Holly. The younger Mayflower has been working the commercial route for years, has an agent, and has already booked small roles on *The Vampire Diaries* and two of the *CSI*s.

In March, Holly had been cast as one of the lead kids in the pilot for a family sitcom that filmed in April. Rumor had it the show was a good bet to be picked up for the next season. We'd all find out the next week. Because of scheduling conflicts with her burgeoning TV career, Holly wasn't free to do the school play this year. And with Holly out of the picture, all it took was one phone call from Daddy to get Heather cast.

I mean . . . her stellar audition cinched the role for her.

Riiiight.

"Jimmy, put the light on Cindy!" Mr. Randall called out to the spotlight operator-stage manager-all around tech maven.

"Cynthia," Cindy quickly corrected.

I stifled a laugh and Mr. Randall stifled his own exasperated sigh as the light hit Dorothy #2, the stunningly beautiful, semiprofessional model *Cynthia* Lakeside.

Which brings us to repercussion #2.

With four Dorothys (or is it Dorothies?), you'd think that would indicate we had four different performances, right? One Dorothy per show. Or maybe we were simply well-stocked in the understudy department?

No. That would make too much sense.

To explain, we need to go back a bit in history. Stick with me now. I had to learn all this for school. I figure this is probably the only place I'm ever going to be able to use this information in my lifetime.

And now we shall enter the Wayback Machine for a brief history of Orion Academy. . . .

The Orion Institute for Astronomical Studies was originally built as a scientific college back in the 1930s. As the name indicates, the college focused solely on the study of astronomy. I think they even found a couple new stars or something. The school's founder, Lewald Merryweather, was one of the foremost scientists in the field. Considering his interest in Hollywood stars rivaled his work studying the stars in the sky, it wasn't surprising that he wanted to set up shop near what was quickly becoming the entertainment capital of the world.

After about two decades of intensive study of both kinds of celestial bodies, Mr. Merryweather was caught in the kind of Hollywood scandal that the current school administration prefers to gloss over during our history lessons. Let's just say it gives new meaning to the big bang theory and leave it at that. As a result, Mr. Merryweather was forced out of the college he had created and run out of town faster than the speed of light.

The college managed to stay in business for another decade until funding eventually dried up. The school and observatory were closed and abandoned. Since nobody likes the look of vacant property—especially in a ritzy beach community—a bunch of parents got together in the early seventies and formed a private high school to make use of the space. In tribute to the original school, they decided to keep the name. Thus, Orion Academy was born.

During those many, *many* decades the college and high school were already in existence, a residential neighborhood grew up around the campus. And now, today, the fine residents along Breakwater Lane don't like all the traffic going through their winding road at night. After an agreement with the neighbors, Orion Academy is now only allowed to have a dozen nighttime events per school year.

Even though everyone freely admits we were here first.

After parents' nights, stargazing nights (we are still called "Orion" Academy for a reason), and other events, that leaves one night of one-acts in the fall and two nights for the spring show. With our growing theater reputation, our shows sell out faster than tickets to the Super Bowl.

Traditionally, our spring show is double cast. The juniors and freshmen perform on Friday night, and the seniors and sophomores perform the same show on Saturday night. But this year, due to an unfortunate aligning of the stars (literally), we were forced into an extra stargazing night, which meant we had to cut one of our shows.

This wouldn't really be a huge problem except that while in the *Marat/Sade* tailspin, the headmaster also buckled under parental pressure over the fear that little Hilary and Bryce might not get a part in the show and decreed that every student who tried out would get "a role of substance."

Translation: No one was going to be Tree #3.

Granted, Trees #1 and #2 are fairly substantial parts in this play—what with the whole apple-picking scene. But Tree #3 just kind of stands around. No lines at all. And it is *far* better to have a stage full of Dorothys, Scarecrows, and Wizards than to have even *one* student with a nonspeaking role.

As a result, we had four Dorothys: two seniors, two juniors. And one performance.

"Cynthia, did you happen to . . . I don't know . . . maybe . . . *alter* your costume ever so slightly?" Mr. Randall asked.

If you ask me, it was fairly obvious she had taken a pair of hedge clippers to the thing. It had about one quarter of the material as the other costumes. Breasts were bursting out on the top, and panties were peeking out on the bottom. And it was all centered around a considerably bare midriff. She was, by far, the sluttiest-looking imitation Kansas farm girl I'd ever seen.

Not that I'd seen many Kansas farm girls in my life.

"What?" Cindy asked with well-practiced innocence. "I thought it would be good if we all looked a little different. So we can stand out some."

Yes, she looked a little different, all right. And, yes, parts of her were standing out, too.

"Somehow, I don't think the audience is going to confuse you girls with one another," Mr. Randall said. He wasn't kidding either. We had quite the selection of Dorothys.

Cindy wasn't the only one who had made some alterations to her costume. Or, more likely, who'd had the maid do some alterations. Three of the four Dorothys had taken a new approach to the familiar outfit. Cindy's modifications were just the most . . . *prominent*?

The aforementioned Heather was wearing a slinky silk

number. Certainly not something any Kansas farm girl would wear to slop the pigs.

The costume award, however, had to go to Suze Finberg, Dorothy #4. Suze chose to add rather than subtract, starting with fringe on the bottom of the dress and capping it off with some crazy beadwork around the neckline. She probably did it herself because she's all kinds of crafty. I figure someday she'll have her own clothing line and maybe even be a guest judge on *Project Runway*.

Once the spotlight moved onto Suze, the beadwork really popped in the light. It sparkled as much as the ruby slippers, but still managed to look subdued so that Suze wasn't overwhelmed by the outfit. It was an amazing balancing act. Not quite appropriate for a farm girl living in the dust bowl, but with this show, we had all given up on appropriate long ago.

Besides, I knew Suze didn't really care about the play. She hasn't liked being onstage since our kindergarten production of *Babes in Toyland*. And yet, there she was. One of the four leads that most of the girls in the show would have killed for.

At this point, you're probably noticing most of us have a history. Ultraexclusive schools tend to feed into one another. With the exception of unexpected bankruptcies and/or being forced to flee Malibu in disgrace, most of my classmates have been through the same educational track starting at Adamson Elementary School, moving on to Pacifica Middle School, and ending where we are currently: Orion Academy.

Every now and then we get a new kid who is seamlessly absorbed into the status quo. On exceedingly rare occasions we get a standout like Dorothy #1: Sam—don't *ever* call her Samantha—Lawson.

Sam blew into the school last year like a Kansas twister and immediately made herself known as a force to be reckoned with in the drama department. And in my life as well.

Sam is the most talented actress-singer-dancer-mime at Orion Academy. Actually, I'm fairly certain that she's the only certified mime on the school roster. She trained with a world-famous mime for a summer during elementary school. Not that I'd ever heard of this "world-famous mime" before she told me about him.

You're probably wondering what it is about all these hyphens I'm using to describe people. For people living in the L.A. area, life is all about the hyphenates. It's how we rate levels of success. I think it all started back when some singers wanted to start acting and actors decided they were singers. That evolved into actor-producers, singer-songwriters, and writer-directors. Nowadays, it's quite commonplace to see business cards that list a person's job title as body double-dog walker.

A triple hyphenate, Sam would easily have been the lone Dorothy for the junior production any normal year. Her costume was the least altered of the bunch. She prefers to use her actual talent to make herself stand out.

Before she started here, Sam went to school in Santa Monica—a nice but not nearly as pricey area south of Malibu. Sam doesn't exactly come from "the other side of the tracks," but we are talking two slightly different childhoods. The tooth fairy used to leave a dollar under her pillow. I always found stock options under mine.

To this day, I don't have a clue what a stock option is.

Sam's only here because her mom teaches English at Orion. They can afford the tuition thanks to some money her grandparents left her, combined with the discount teachers get for their kids to attend. Sam's the only teacher's kid to go to the school. The discount really isn't that much of a discount if you don't have an inheritance to back it up.

"Is it time for my close-up?" Sam asked as she expertly stepped into the hot spot of the light. "Because, I'm ready for it, you know."

"Yes, Ms. Desmond," Mr. Randall said with a wry smile. "How very *Sunset Boulevard* of you."

Sam clasped her right hand to her heart while reaching out to the spotlight with her left. "What light through yonder window breaks?"

"That's the guy's part," I yelled out.

She shot me a look that told me I would later be receiving a lecture on modern gender roles in theater. Then she changed character. "I would like to dedicate this performance to all the little people out there."

"Who are you calling little?" I called to her. "I'm, like, a whole foot taller than you."

"You look to me like a munchkin from up here," Sam shot back with a laugh.

"Are you two quite finished?" Mr. Randall asked. "Because I'd like to get this over with today."

"Sorry," we both muttered.

Now, you might be wondering what I—a guy—was doing at this costume fitting for the four Dorothys.

The reason I gave Mr. Randall was that I wanted to photograph the costumes for the yearbook. But, honestly, I just had nothing better to do.

There was a soccer game going on at the same time, and *everyone* in school was there. It was the reason we weren't having an actual rehearsal even though we sorely needed it with only a week to go before the show.

Everything at Orion Academy shuts down when there's a soccer game. The entire student body makes its way to the soccer field. Even the teachers—who usually can't wait to get out of here on a Friday afternoon—stick around. But with the show only a week away, Mr. Randall needed to fit in the fitting.

Hence my excuse for the photo op. I'll find almost any reason to miss a soccer game. Besides, I was there because I'm friends with Dorothy #1. Best friends, in fact.

Sam is the Dorothy to my Scarecrow . . . the Sandy to my Frenchy . . . and the other half of my vampire pact.

Vampire pact? you ask.

Sam and I have solemnly sworn to each other that if either of us is ever turned into a vampire, the first thing we'll do is turn the other one. What better way to spend eternity than with your best friend? If we had to be tortured souls like in some Anne Rice novel, there's no one else in the world I'd rather share that bleak future with. Besides, wouldn't it be totally cool to have supernatural powers? Extreme strength? Powerful night vision? Able to leap onto second-floor garden balconies in a single bound?

We've also sworn to use the powers for good. We'd only drain the life from criminals or terrorists or people who talk in movie theaters.

More than a fair trade for an immortally tortured soul, if you ask me.

"I think we're good," Mr. Randall said, really stretching the definition of "good," as far as I'm concerned. "You can all get to the—"

"Heads!" Jimmy screamed from the back of the auditorium.

All heads looked up to see a metal lighting instrument dropping from above. It was falling toward the stage—and the Dorothys—below.

The Boy from Oz

I could swear the lighting instrument was falling at seventy-six frames per second. (*Aside:* That's movie talk for slow motion.) And yet, there was nothing anyone could do to stop it.

The speed of the world around me slammed back to normal as the lighting instrument crashed onto the stage only a few small feet from Sam's small feet.

Then there was silence.

That lasted about three seconds. Then the screeching began. First Heather, then Cindy (I mean, Cynthia), and finally Suze.

I'm proud to say that Sam did not get all screechy. She simply stared down at the twisted metal and glass shards that settled around her red-sequined shoes.

"Is everyone okay?" Mr. Randall asked as he bolted out of his seat.

"I think I found the light," Sam replied as she pointed down to the shattered glass and twisted metal.

Leave it to Sam to break the dramatic tension.

Almost.

Jimmy raced past me and leaped onto the stage before Mr. Randall could even get out of his row. When properly motivated, that kid can *move.*

Jimmy is our passive-obsessive stage manager. He can usually be found buzzing around behind the cast and crew, looking over their shoulders to make sure everything meets with his detail-oriented eye. He never quite criticizes anyone directly, but you can always tell when he wants to get in there and do things his way. That's just on a normal day. During emergencies like these—or on opening night—there's no metaphor created that can properly describe his frantic behavior.

Me? I was still at my seat. But I wasn't exactly doing nothing.

Once it was clear that Sam's wit had survived the accident, I started snapping pictures of the aftermath with my trusty digital camera. Not only would the near disaster make front-page news for the school paper, *The Orion Star*, but the shots of the Dorothys freaking out would provide hours of entertainment for Sam and me.

"Okay, Bryan. You've got more than enough pictures for the lawsuits," Mr. Randall said as he gently pushed my camera down. (I hadn't even thought of that!) "Besides, the lighting instrument landed on the *other* side of the stage."

I saw that Mr. Randall's look of concern had been replaced by that same wry smile I so rarely see from other teachers. He must have realized that my camera was aimed at Heather, who was cowering behind the stage-right curtain. She looked like she was afraid the lighting instrument was going to jump up and bite her.

(*Aside:* We rarely refer to lighting instruments as "lights." Technically they're called "lamps." But I didn't want you thinking I was talking about some cheap, plastic desk accessory from IKEA. These things have heft.)

Once the dust settled, Mr. Randall joined Jimmy and the Dorothys up onstage to examine the fallen lamp. As there was nothing I could do but add a well-timed quip, I sat back in my seat. Sam already had the quip quotient quite covered. (Say that five times fast, I dare you.)

"I'm guessing the fitting is over?" Sam asked. "I'd say it was a smashing success."

We both groaned over that one.

"Yes, Sam," Mr. Randall said. "You can all change out of your costumes and get over to the soccer game."

"Thanks," Sam said as she fled the stage, quickly followed by the other Dorothys.

Not that Sam had any intention of going to the soccer game. We aren't big on hanging out with the masses who flock like sheep to the soccer field. We are very much our own people, with lives full of excitement way more interesting than some high school sporting event.

Even though we didn't have any other plans for that particular afternoon, we'd come up with something eventually.

With the shrieking Dorothys gone, I decided to hop up onstage myself and check things out. That's the kind of thing menfolk do, you know. While the girls are off changing outfits, the guys stand around examining the broken equipment, trying to determine what caused the accident.

Maybe we'd even call in the Malibu CSI team.

"So, what do we think happened here, fellas?" I said as I moseyed up to Jimmy and Mr. Randall. I would have spit some tobacco into a spittoon had either been available.

Actually . . . no, I wouldn't.

"I think that, maybe, the clamp could've rusted through," Jimmy said, pointing to the metal clamp that usually hooked around the pipe grid up above. "I mean, obviously, it rusted through . . . see all the rust . . . and the *through*."

Jimmy doesn't always make the most sense when he speaks. But he was right about the rust. The metal was brown and holey and missing the all-important top part that hooked it to the pipe. (That's about as technical as my terminology is going to get here.)

"I keep telling the headmaster we need to replace this equipment," Mr. Randall said, shaking his head. Suddenly, I had a stellar idea. I'd ask my parents to make a contribution. The Bryan Stark Light Grid has a nice ring to it.

Or, maybe not.

"What about the safety line?" I asked. Each lamp is supposed to be clamped tightly to the pipe. But in case something goes wrong, an aircraft cable is looped around the bar to make sure if the clamp goes, something like this doesn't happen.

Jimmy was silent. This in itself was an amazing feat. Jimmy

is never silent. Not even backstage during a performance. Even his whispers are loud and agitated.

"Jimmy?" Mr. Randall asked.

"I can't . . . umm . . . I could've . . . ," Jimmy said. "I mean . . . I might . . ."

It was clear to me that Jimmy didn't want to admit that he could have missed attaching one of the cables. He tends to freak over little mistakes like that. Though, in this case, I guess it wasn't a *little* mistake.

"I'm sorry, Mr. Randall," Jimmy said. "I should have paid more attention. You're always telling me not to rush so much. And I usually listen. I *try* to listen. But there's just—"

"It's okay, Jimmy," Mr. Randall interjected, laying a calming hand on Jimmy's shoulder. I was glad that Mr. Randall stopped him because it looked like Jimmy was on the verge of breaking into tears.

Jimmy is equal parts sweet and intense, with a small dash of scattered in the mix. In spite of that, there's no one else I'd want to have in charge on show night because when he's *on*, he's on *fire*. Unfortunately, the flip side is also true: When he screws up, it tends to be noticeable. Still, he's loyal like a Labrador, doesn't have a mean bone in his body, and is kind of adorkable in his own way.

While Jimmy and Mr. Randall cleaned up the mess, I grabbed a seat in the front row to wait for Sam. It really wasn't a three-person job. I'd probably get in the way.

Besides, I'm incredibly lazy.

I just realized I've been babbling for quite a few pages now.

I never really introduced myself, you know, *properly*. This is the problem with not being a main character. You tend to get lost in the introductions, even when you're the one doing them.

So . . . who am I, anyway?

As I wrote earlier, my name is Bryan Stark. I can't be sure, but I think my last name should be longer. My dad changed it, either for business reasons or because we're in the Witness Protection Program. I honestly couldn't tell you. I think the full last name was something like Starkinovichskysteinenberger . . . or something like that. Though I guess if we were in the Witness Protection Program, he wouldn't have just shortened the name. He would have changed it entirely, to something like Smith or Jones or someone else who starred in *Men in Black*.

I think I may be Jewish, too.

At least, part Jewish. I don't really know much about my dad's family. His parents died before I was born, and I guess he was an only child. I know my mom used to go to some church. I'm not sure which one. We do celebrate Christmas every year, though.

Let's stick with what I do know about myself.

I'm on the periphery of popularity in a school with no losers, slackers, or geeks, but a ton of Future Media Moguls of America. I'm surprisingly grounded (if I do say so myself) considering that I've rarely been lacking for anything in my life. Not that I'm spoiled, but I've never had to worry about my college fund.

I haven't quite figured out my hyphenate quotient yet. If pressed, I'd say I'm an actor-photographer. But photography is really more of a pastime than a lifestyle. Let's just say I'm half-a-hyphenate on a quest to complete myself.

Oh, I like that.

I've been acting pretty much for as long as I can remember. I blame my grandma Millie for that. She used to be a Radio City Music Hall Rockette and had small parts in a bunch of Broadway shows in the fifties. I doubt you would have heard of her, but she was scandalous at a time when scandal wasn't nearly as commonplace as it is today. Since I started going to school I've been in at least one play a year. I kind of take after Grandma Millie since I haven't really broken out with any major roles yet myself, but I'm getting there.

Wizard is my first leading role. I play Scarecrow #2. Figures the first time I get a good part I have to share it with someone else.

As for how I look . . . picture if Brad Pitt and Colin Farrell had a love child. That child would look absolutely nothing like me. But it's fun to imagine, isn't it?

Me? I'm kind of tall and kind of skinny. *Lanky*, might be a good word to use. Not by me, mind you. I'd never call myself that, but other people have. They were all born before 1950, but it's been said.

I tend toward a paler shade of pale, which is somewhat annoying because I do live in the beach community of Malibu. What can I say? Credit my father's Eastern European skin tones. Having jet-black hair only makes me look paler than I really am, too. Even my eyes are gray.

Grandma Millie says I look like a young Cary Grant.

Sometimes I wonder if she means that I look like I belong in a black-and-white movie. She's always talking about how handsome ol' C. G. was back in his early movies from the thirties, like *Sylvia Scarlett*.

You ask me? I think I look more like Cary Grant as he is today: dead for over two decades.

But that's only my opinion.

(*Aside: Sylvia Scarlett* is not a particularly great film, but it was the first time Cary teamed with Katharine Hepburn, which makes it interesting from a historical perspective alone. In the movie, Kate dresses up as a boy for reasons defying explanation and falls in love with a man while in her drag king disguise. And the movie came out in 1935!)

By the way, Grandma Millie's the one who usually calls me lanky. I'm pretty sure she means it in the kindest way possible.

I could go on about myself but, believe it or not, I'm not my favorite subject. Okay. Don't believe it. But, in all honesty, this story isn't really about me anyway. Think of me as the Greek Chorus. I'm here to comment on the action, but rarely do I get involved.

Okay, I may get *involved*, but I'm not the star. That would be Sam. And though you might think that the story began when the lamp fell, you'd be wrong. As far as I'm concerned, the real inciting action occurred when Sam came back from the dressing room, held her hand out to me like a proper English gentleman, and uttered the following line:

"Shall we go to the game?"

After the Fall

"The *soccer* game?" I asked for the sake of clarity.

"No. *The Pajama Game*," she said, taking full aim with sarcasm.

"Cool! Will there be pillow fights?"

"Come on, it'll be fun."

"Fun? *Really?* And how are we defining 'fun' nowadays, 'cause I'm not seeing it."

Sam gave a Heather-worthy sigh and plopped down in the seat beside me. She looked at me with exasperation that matched her sigh. Like I was the one who had suddenly gone all crazy high schooler, like Kim McAfee in *Bye Bye Birdie*.

We *never* went to the soccer games. It was our thing: total apathy toward all school sporting events.

We watched as the other Dorothys came back from the dressing room. Heather and Cindy were walking together, chatting about something and nothing at the same time.

They pretty much ignored us as they made their way up the aisle. The two naturally unnatural blondes were both dressed in a collection of designer names and logos that I won't even bother to list here.

As for my clothes, there was nary a logo in sight. I had on a pair of black vintage jeans and a nondescript T, covered by a midnight blue button-down shirt (untucked, naturally). I'm sure each of these items has a name of some kind on them, but I really don't look for that when I do my shopping. I'm mainly focused on clothing that doesn't emphasize my lack of musculature.

I do know that my shoes were Skechers. But that's because I only have one pair of those. The company tends to make shoes with really thick soles that usually add an inch to my already tall stature, so it's rare that I buy them.

And, okay, the underwear was Calvin Klein, but we all have to pamper ourselves sometimes.

I topped off the look with my grandpop's black fedora. The hat is true vintage and in pretty good shape considering it's way older than me. I wear it as much as I can. Not because it's a statement or anything, I just like it.

While I'm at it, Sam was wearing a designer label–free, cream-colored peasant top, no-name jeans, and comfortably worn sandals. In the small patch of skin at the base of her neck rested a small silver unicorn hanging on a chain.

I can't speak for her underwear. And I wouldn't even if I could.

The last of the Dorothys, Suze, exited the dressing room in

some name-brand jeans with a silver scarf tied around her waist like a belt. She also wore a blue blazer that she had added silver piping to for effect. Given that the school colors are blue and silver, we didn't have to ask what she was dressed for.

Suze paused for a second to look at the remains of the lamp before heading out with a "See you at the game" directed toward Sam and me.

Which was weird, because *everyone* knew we never went to the games.

"It's not like you don't go to rugby games all the time on weekends," Sam said.

"That's different," I said. And it was. The rugby games I go to are played by adults with a love of the game, not high school kids looking to prove their freakishly active brand of superiority.

Not that I'm bitter, or anything.

And don't think it has anything to do with the fact that I'm a spaz on the field . . . any field. Soccer. Football. Baseball. Badminton. You name the game and I've made a complete and utter fool of myself trying to play it. But my refusal to go to a high school game was for a totally different reason. Well, *mostly* different.

"When did you turn into one of the sheep?" I asked.

"It's not sheeplike to go to one game," Sam insisted. "Besides, Hope doesn't miss a game. You don't call her a sheep."

"Extenuating circumstances," I replied, in reference to our other best friend, Hope Rivera. "Besides, I've got *other* issues with her over that."

"You have so many issues that I sometimes lose track."

"It's part of my charm."

But Sam wasn't buying it.

"Are you coming or not?" Sam asked as she stood up. "Because I will go without you."

"And who are you going to sit with and make fun of people?" I asked as I reluctantly stood too.

"Hope," she said with a look of satisfaction.

"She's not half as vicious as I am."

"True," Sam said. "So, you're coming?"

"Like I have a choice?"

"I like to at least give you the illusion."

Together, we left Hall Hall, dropped our books off at our lockers—which are conveniently across from each other—and headed out the school's back exit.

Even though I've lived in Malibu all my life, it's still amazing to push open a set of doors and be greeted by a view of the Pacific Ocean stretching out into forever. I could stare at the endless blue endlessly, and have spent more than a few afternoons lost in the waves. If only this could be one of those afternoons.

The cruelest part of the design for our school is that none of the classrooms actually face out to the ocean. Instead, all the hallways open up to this amazing vista. That student of Frank Lloyd Wright's must have really believed in form following function. Even when this was a scientific college, he knew that the students would spend half their classes staring out at the waves if they could.

Sam slipped off her sandals once we hit the dirt path off the courtyard. She prefers to go barefoot whenever possible. I can't imagine it was comfortable for the short hike past the parking lot and the observatory.

"Are we doing anything this weekend?" Sam asked as we made out way through the trees beyond the observatory. Our campus would be a lot smaller if it weren't for the fact that there was a small forest in between the main campus and the sports fields.

"You want to come work at the store?" I asked. "Mom guilted me into helping with inventory."

Sam was kind enough to act like she was considering before she said, "No thanks."

I couldn't blame her. It's not that I am embarrassed about my mom's job, but it isn't something I go around bragging about either. My mom owns a boutique on Melrose Avenue called Kaye 9. And if you can't guess by the cute name, she's in the business of designing and selling doggie duds along with her best friend and business partner, Blaine.

Every six months she cons me into helping inventory her stock of crazy creations like diamond doggles—jewel-encrusted goggles for your pooch. I've yet to figure out why any dog would need glasses. They aren't even prescription.

"Let me guess," Sam said. "While you and Mom are doing inventory, Dad is off to Colombia for a major drug score."

"No," I said. "Syria for an arms deal."

"I was close."

My dad's job is somewhat less eccentric than my mom's.

In fact, it's so boring that I don't really know for sure what he does. Since he's always traveling the globe for work, Sam and I like to make up wild stories about what his true work is, such as him being an international arms dealer or the head of a major drug cartel.

In reality, he's probably just bringing democratic office supplies to China.

We don't much talk about Sam's father since he up and left her and her mom back when Sam was five. She hasn't heard from him since.

"And you?" I asked as the trees started to open up ahead of us.

"Study, study, study," she replied.

I should have figured. Sam is in constant struggle with her grades. The girl can learn all of her lines for a role in a matter of hours, but has the hardest time with memorizing things for tests. Her grades are good enough—mostly B's and maybe a C or two—but that won't win her a scholarship. She's going to need some kind of help paying for college since her inheritance went for Orion.

As we reached the clearing, a rousing cheer came up from the crowd watching the soccer game.

"For me?" Sam asked demurely as if anyone in the student body had actually been aware of our arrival. "Oh, that's so . . . I'm speechless."

"That's a first," I said, looking out over the Charles E. Martin Bleachers. Yes, our soccer field has bleachers. I told you we take the sport seriously here. "How are we ever going to find Hope in all this?"

"She should be sitting on the end," Sam said, heading us around the field.

"BAAAA!" I said in my best, and loudest, sheep imitation.

She ignored me and tromped over to the stands in her bare feet.

What could I do? I followed.

Baaaaa.

The soccer field is in the middle of a huge clearing in the trees. Two sets of bleachers line either side. The fans from St. James Academy were sitting in the shoddier, metal bleachers, while our fans had the permanent stands built into raised concrete. Between the trees and the opposing stands I wouldn't even be able to stare out at the ocean during the game. I was going to have to watch it.

Fortunately—or unfortunately, depending on how you look at it—Hope was easy to find. She kind of stood out at the end of the second row, dressed all in black, from the bottom of her steel-toe boots to the top of her black beret. A huge plastic purple flower was pinned to the hat. This is pretty much how she looks everyday: all in black, with a burst of color somewhere on her body. She calls the look Goth-Ick.

The only other color that Hope displayed was her amazingly violet eyes. They were contacts, but still pretty cool.

Everything about Hope is pretty cool, in my opinion. She's a writer-actress-free spirit-. As you can see, she's kind of a double-triple hyphenate. I leave her an extra hyphen at the end because she can be anything else she wants to be on any given day.

As if to mock my paleness, Hope has this incredible light brown skin that looks great with her short black hair. Her secondary hyphenate, if you will, is that she's half-Mexican-American and half-California-Blonde (although the California-Blonde part is more a recessive gene).

Hope was quite pointedly sitting on the opposite side of the bleachers from her full California Blonde stepsisters, Anorexia and Bulimia . . . I mean, Alexis and Belinda. Hope's father married their mother about six years ago, and their daughters have been on opposite ends of the bleachers ever since.

"The girls and I saved you seats," Hope said with barely a glance from her notebook. She picked up her bags to clear two seats for us on the bleachers beside her. Maybe it's my suspicious nature, but the fact that she had saved seats made me think that maybe Sam's decision to go to the game wasn't all that spontaneous.

By the way, the "girls" Hope referred to weren't other friends of ours or her long-distance step-sisters. They were Hope's breasts.

Back in middle school, Hope was among the first to develop. We're hoping she's finally stopped. Her chest has become quite formidable. She's always sure to mention the girls as much as possible, if only to beat everyone else to the punch line.

"What's the score?" Sam asked as she slid in next to Hope.

"Score?" Hope asked, still not looking up.

"Of the game?"

"Game?" Hope questioned.

"Never mind," Sam said as she tapped Jason MacMillan on the shoulder in front of her.

"Tied, four–four," Jason replied without taking his eyes off the game. His right arm was locked with his girlfriend, Wren Deslandes.

"Hey, Scarecrow," I said to Jason.

"Hey, Scarecrow," he answered back.

He and I were Scarecrows #1 and #2 respectively. As it so happened, Hope and Wren were Glindas #1 and #2.

"Go, Comets," I deadpanned as I sat. "Rah."

Hope shot me a playful grin behind Sam's back. Even though Hope was busy writing, I knew her head was totally in the game too. Considering her on-again–off-again-boyfriend, Drew Campbell, was one of the players, she wouldn't miss a second of the action. Though I doubt she wanted it to look that way.

"Never thought I'd see the day," Hope said to me.

"Neither did I," I replied.

Hope has known of my hatred of school sports—especially soccer—for way longer than we've even known Sam. I've actually known Hope almost all my life, but we didn't really become friends until she and Sam became friends. Now I don't know why we didn't hang out together sooner.

A shout reflexively pulled my attention to the field. The ball was getting perilously close to the St. James goal. Everyone on our side jumped up to cheer, except Hope and me. When the goalie caught the ball and sent it in the opposite direction, I felt vindicated for not bothering to move my butt off the bleachers. I'd rather expend the energy on an actual score, if at all.

I saw a look pass from Hope to Sam when she returned to her seat. I was *definitely* out of the loop on something.

Hope caught me catching her look. "What's a good rhyme for carrion?" she quickly asked.

"Carry on?" I asked. It was hard to hear clearly over the crowd noise.

"No, *carrion*," Hope repeated. "You know, rotting flesh."

"Oh," I said. "How about Marion?"

Hope shook her head and looked at Sam for a more useful suggestion.

"Bulgarian?" Sam guessed, refusing to turn her head away from the game.

"You guys are no help." Hope went back to her notebook. It looked like she was onto something. "Scratch that," she said as she started scribbling. "You did give me an idea."

"Marion the carrion?" I asked. "She used to be librarian."

Hope ignored me as she finished her work.

"How's this?" she asked. *"The darkening moon sets upon the sea, as pain and grief wash over me. My beloved, Daisy, is carrion. With me to only carry on."*

"Brilliant!" I said with more excitement than I had managed to express for the game so far.

"Best you've written in a while," Sam added, holding out both her hands for a double-pumped thumbs-up.

I guess we didn't realize how loud Hope was, because Wren turned to look at the three of us like we were full-on Medea.

(*Aside:* Medea is a character from Greek mythology who goes all crazy and kills her sons to get back at her husband. She has a whole play about her and everything.)

Lest you (like Wren) think we lost all sense of artistic criticism, I assure you Hope is a really amazing writer. *Really.* She's got reams of poetry and prose a billion times better than anything you'd find in your average teen's blog of despair. But Hope only shares those works with the inner circle, namely Sam and me. The journal she was writing the bad verse in is her *Book of the Dead Puppy Poetry, Volume Six.* The book—and its five predecessors—were created back when she was eleven, on the day after Hope's stepmother and two stepsisters moved in . . . and the moving van backed over Hope's cocker spaniel, Daisy.

Hope was understandably devastated. She wrote about it in her journal as any eleven-year-old might do. Naturally she blamed the entire thing on her stepmother for moving in on her and her dad. The next day, Hope's private journal somehow came up during a session with her therapist. That was when Hope realized that her private writings were no longer her own. From that day on, the only writing her family has ever seen her do is to lament the passing of her poor Daisy. You'd be surprised the number of ways she can fit the phrase "pushing up daisies" into a poem.

"Now that that's done," Sam said, "why don't you watch your boyfriend?"

"Please stop referring to him as *my* boyfriend," Hope said politely. "He's got an identity of his own. We do not subscribe to labels. I do not own him. He does not own me."

"Hope, he's got the ball," Sam said. "Cheer."

"Fine," Hope said as she rose from the wooden bench. "GO, DREW! SHOVE IT DOWN THEIR THROATS!"

Such a dainty little darling, isn't she?

Drew must have heard her, because he stumbled slightly. Probably from shock. I doubt she was usually this vocal during a game.

Drew recovered and took the ball downfield. He weaved in and out of his opponents as he made his way toward the goal.

Soon everyone on the Orion Academy side—except me—was on their feet along with Hope screaming encouragement. The noise was way louder than anything I've ever heard from a theater audience.

Yet another reason why I hate sports.

"Go, Drew!" Hope screamed with genuine excitement now. "Come on!"

I was forced to stand to see what was going on. It was a clear shot to the goal. Drew was going to score. I checked the scoreboard. There wasn't much time left in the game. It could be the winning goal.

"Kick it in!" Hope yelled. Her brassy voice carried out over everyone else's in the stands.

Just as it looked like Drew was going to score, a St. James player came out of nowhere and stole the ball away. Drew looked even more shocked than everyone watching.

The Orion fans—except me—let out a collective groan as we all sat back down.

"Well, that yelling clearly served no purpose," Hope said as she opened up her notebook again.

"No, wait," Sam said. "Eric's got the ball."

Oh, great.

Eric Whitman is Drew's best friend and, in my humble opinion, a total asshat. He's also the star of the soccer team and the only junior on the starting roster. And if you must know, he's a soccer stud-surfer boy-class president-blond god-total asshat.

I could build up the suspense here, but I'm not a member of the Eric Whitman fan club, so I'll keep it simple: He took the ball back down the field, scored a goal, and won the game.

Go, Comets.

Blah.

Desire Under the Elms
(Well . . . They Could Have Been Oaks)

Sam unilaterally decided that we would hang with Hope while she waited for Drew to finish up. To be honest, I didn't much mind. Everyone who was leaving the bleachers was heading for the parking lot. If we left with them, it would take, like, a half hour to get out the one exit.

So we waited. While the soccer team shook hands with the guys from St. James. While they went through their cooldown stretches. While they had their on-field, post-game wrap-up.

We weren't the only ones waiting either. The personal fan clubs of the players were also waiting. Sam, Hope, and I sent a few silent glances back and forth as we watched Heather Mayflower standing on the sidelines. She was waiting for her boyfriend, Jax, to get off the field. Even in the open air, her award-winning sighs were audible.

Sam's mom was at the game too. She was sitting in the

middle of the stands with the faculty contingent. I doubt they were waiting for any of the players on the field. They were probably sticking around until the parking lot cleared too.

We would have gone over to say hi, but we prefer to treat Sam's mom like a teacher as much as possible while we're in school and keep the mingling to a minimum. Even when we're all just sitting around with nothing else to do.

Finally, Coach Zachary dismissed the team.

Jax was the first player to make it to the sideline. He clearly knew better than to keep Heather waiting any longer than necessary.

Before he even had the chance to kiss her hello, Heather was regaling him, and everyone in the vicinity, with the death-defying tale of the falling lamp. This was one of the best performances I'd ever seen from her. It had heart, drama, and actual pathos. Not to mention that it was even more of a fantasy than a play about a wizard, munchkins, and a magical world over the rainbow.

My personal favorite part of the story was when she "valiantly pushed the other Dorothys out of the way, putting [her] own life at risk to save her less talented costars."

I *so* wish I were kidding about that.

"Are you okay?" Hope asked Sam when she heard the story.

Sam let out a derisive snort to let Hope know it was nothing.

In the meantime, I was so busy trying not to overhear Heather's conversation that I totally didn't notice that Drew and Eric were walking right toward us. They were all sweaty and dirty from the match and, quite frankly, not that fun to be around even at their cleanest.

Not that Eric looked bad. Eric *never* looks bad. He's a prime example of the beach blond perfect specimen that you see in every movie set in California since the dawn of color film. You know, the kind who doesn't actually exist in real life, except for the one walking toward us with his sculpted abs, playfully tousled hair, and typical dimples. It was enough to make me want to puke.

And then there's Drew. He's not the textbook pretty boy that Eric is, but that's what makes him even more attractive, in my opinion. Sure, Drew has great, sandy brown hair, a tall, non-lanky body, and incredibly muscular legs. But it's the imperfections that work for him. He's got this little crescent-shaped scar on his chin that he's had since he was eight, a slightly crooked smile, and no dimples whatsoever to speak of. He has what I call "attainable good looks." The boy can definitely turn some heads, but he's not so perfect that he's entirely out of your league.

"Hey, Sunshine," Drew said as he gave Hope a kiss. Even I can appreciate the irony of calling her Sunshine when she wears black almost exclusively.

"Good game," Hope said. "And, you stink."

"Thanks," Drew replied, taking her into a full-on hug that looked more pleasant than it probably smelled.

"Hi," Eric said to Sam.

"Hi," Sam said back.

Sam's toes were digging into the ground. Eric was trying to put his hands in nonexistent pockets.

Me? I guess I disappeared for a moment. Because no one even *bothered to acknowledge my presence!*

"Did you watch the game?" Eric asked, with his eyes glued to Sam.

Considering there was no other reason for us to be at the soccer field, I found it to be a fairly obvious question.

"Caught the end," Sam replied. "Saw you score."

"Yeah," he replied, and actually kicked his foot into the dirt.

I think I may have laughed or snorted or something, because Sam shot me a look. I guess I was kind of staring, too.

"Can I talk to you?" Eric asked, motioning with his head that they should walk away.

"Sure," Sam said a little more eagerly than I thought the question warranted.

Eric led Sam off to the trees. He walked with a confident swagger that, I guess, comes from scoring the winning point at a game that cinched Orion a spot in the finals. Next Friday, while two other teams fought it out for the final spot in the finals, our guys could relax until the actual game in two weeks.

A couple fans high-fived Eric along the way into the woods, but he didn't even slow down to bask in the glory. He and Sam stopped at the edge of the tree line. Even at a distance, their conversation wasn't looking any less awkward than it had when they were standing right next to me.

Since it wasn't like I was going to stand there openly gawking at them, I turned my attention back to Hope and Drew.

That? Was a mistake.

"Did you hear me cheering?" Hope asked.

"Yeah," Drew replied. "Didn't you see me trip?"

"So what? I shouldn't have cheered?"

"No," Drew said. "It just caught me off guard. You've never done that before. You've never taken your head out of that book at a game before."

"No wonder," Hope said. "Considering the kind of appreciation I get."

"What are you talking about?" Drew asked.

"Never mind. I need to talk to Mr. Telasco about something." Hope stormed off to speak to the art teacher.

Leaving Drew and me there alone.

"So," I said.

"So," he said.

Since neither of us had much more to say to each other, I turned my attention back to Sam and Eric. It looked like they were no longer having any trouble coming up with things to talk about. They were smiling and laughing, and her hand was resting on his arm.

"What are they up to?" I asked. Unfortunately, I asked it out loud, and for some reason, Drew thought I was talking to him.

"Who?" he asked.

"Over there." I pointed. "My best friend . . . your best friend. What are they doing?"

"Getting friendly?" Drew said.

"Very funny," I replied.

"Didn't expect to see you here," Drew said.

"Didn't expect to be here," I said.

"What did you think?"

"Of the game?"

"No," Drew said. "Of the new uniforms."

"The blue clashes with your eyes."

"My eyes *are* blue."

"See what I'm saying?"

Drew looked me over with disdain. "Rarely."

He walked away, shaking his head.

His stride didn't have nearly the same swagger as Eric's, yet I couldn't take my eyes off him. Or, more specifically, I couldn't take my eyes off that part of the body where he would swagger if he could. Just above those incredibly muscular legs, those soccer shorts only managed to accentuate Drew's best asset.

Pun fully intended.

In case you haven't figured it out by now, my interest in guys tends toward something other than just friendship. Not that I have many guy friends. But I do have guy *interests*.

This isn't something new. I've kind of suspected it my entire life. It's not like there weren't signs growing up. Certain leanings, as they say. Nothing definite, but definitely something.

Those leanings grew pretty hard to ignore when I was about fourteen.

My growth spurt was more like an explosion. I'm currently six feet tall, and we're not sure I've stopped growing. I started shopping in the men's department early.

Finding clothes has never been a problem for me. I have very specific tastes. I know what I like and what I look good in. That is, anything that camouflages my wiry frame. But shopping trips have always been in and out with an armload of bags in no time flat. That's why I was so surprised when it would take forever to pick out the right underwear. I would just stand there comparing the boxes for boxers, briefs, and boxer-briefs.

Eventually I realized the dilemma: I wasn't nearly as interested in the underwear as I was the pictures of the guys on the packages.

But don't worry. This isn't one of those angst-filled books where I'm struggling to come to terms with what it all means. I've long since accepted it. I'm gay. I'm over it. There will be no endless, teary-eyed, internal dialogues. No tormented, sleepless nights. I am 100 percent at ease with who I am.

Except for the fact that I haven't told anyone yet.

In my defense, none of my friends have announced to me that they are straight. Until they do that, I don't see much point in making some grand declaration of my own. Besides, I've got more important things to worry about.

"Eric asked me out."

"What?" I asked. I think I may have actually done a double take as Eric walked past us toward Drew and Hope.

"Eric asked me out," Sam repeated with something sickeningly close to glee.

"When?"

Sam looked at me like I was the one acting like a fool. "Just now."

"No. When did he want to go out?"

"Oh. Tomorrow."

"And you said no, right?"

For some reason, she looked at me like I was twice the fool. "*No.*"

"He asked you out? For tomorrow night? And you said yes?"

"Now you've got it!"

I gave her a similar "You're the fool" look. "Who asks someone out one day in advance? Couldn't he at least give you *some* notice?"

"Who are you? Miss Manners?"

"At least I *have* manners," I mumbled.

"Oh, my God!" Hope shrieked as she ran up to Sam. "I just heard."

And now, I swear, they both giggled.

Giggled!

I'm sorry, but we do not giggle.

Hope and Sam were acting so girly that I had to tune them out. I still couldn't believe she said yes. It is incredibly rude to ask someone out for the next day. And, if you ask me, it's also a little desperate to accept so quickly. Hadn't Sam ever heard of playing coy? I know we tend to make fun of girls who play coy, but this would be different. This would have been playing coy with a purpose.

"Are you in?" Hope asked me.

"Sorry?" I hadn't heard a word of what they were saying.

"We're going to hit Rodeo tomorrow and find something perfect for Sam to wear," Hope said.

Suddenly we'd gone from being coy to being materialistic. It was quite possible I had stepped into some kind of alternate universe.

"I don't know," Sam said. I suspect she was mentally going over her finances.

By the way, "Hitting Rodeo" is code for shopping the outlets in nearby Camarillo. We don't ever shop on Rodeo Drive in Beverly Hills. First of all, no one around here does. That place is for our parents . . . or tourists. Not to mention that Rodeo Drive is somewhat outside of Sam's budgetary constraints.

"I'm sure I've got something that will be fine," Sam added in a tone that didn't sound certain in the least.

I've seen Sam's entire wardrobe and she has *plenty* of outfits that would be more than fine for a date with Eric Whitman.

"We don't need *fine*," Hope said.

Don't say it, I silently pleaded.

"We need *super*fine."

She said it. And Sam bought it. They were going shopping.

"That's settled," Hope said, then turned to me. "Wanna come?"

"Can't," I said. "I'm going to be busy gouging out my eyes this weekend. But your plans sound almost as fun."

"So I thought," Hope said dismissively. "Hey! We can look for prom dresses!"

"Prom shopping, too? You're just trying to make me jealous," I said.

Now, don't get me wrong. I love to shop. I can't think of a better way to spend the weekend than by hanging out at the mall with my friends. The problem is, my friends are girls. Most of the time this fact doesn't really come into play in our relationship. Sometimes, however, they're *really* girls. And that's the kind of shopping trip they had in mind. All day trying on outfit after outfit to find the most perfect of the perfect, while I wait outside the dressing room for hours, leaning on the racks, trying to stay awake.

I could probably hang out in the dressing rooms with them, but we really prefer to keep that area of our lives separate.

"If you're going shopping for a prom dress, I would like to remind you that I look good in blue, green, and especially gray," I said. "So, those are good colors to match your dress to . . . you know, my vest or tie or whatever."

"Noted," Sam said. "Are you sure you don't want to come?"

I reminded her of my work commitment at my mom's store.

"Then I guess we won't see each other till Monday," Sam said.

I would have reminded her that a weekend has two days in it, but I knew what she meant. We had that history test on Monday. She was planning to spend all day Sunday cramming for it. You'd think we could study for the test together, but Sam's cram sessions are a solitary practice. This is more out of respect for our friendship than anything. The one time we tried to study together, I dared to take a moment to make a snack before we started and she nearly killed me.

Hope and Sam were already busy putting together their game plan for their shopping trip.

"So who needs a ride home?" I asked.

"Drew's going to take me," Hope said.

"I'm waiting for Mom," Sam said.

"Oh," I replied as I realized there was no reason for me to be there at all.

The Suppliants

My weekend was fairly uneventful. I spent most of Saturday at Kaye 9 inventorying stuff like doggie vests, shoes, and lingerie (ew!). I studied a bit for the history test. I didn't even bother trying to call Sam on Sunday since she wouldn't have answered the phone.

Truthfully, that's not the reason I didn't talk to her. I wasn't interested in hearing all about her date with Eric. By the time Monday morning rolled around, I can't say I was any more intrigued about what they did and did not do. Conveniently, with all thoughts on the test first thing in the morning, there was little time for gossip. Which brings us to . . .

Lunch.

It was turning out to be another beautiful Malibu day. There was no need to wear a jacket while eating at the Kenneth Graham Pavilion. That's our version of a lunchroom. It's not so much a room as it is a wooden deck at the north end of the school. The pavilion was built in an octagonal shape with a wood roof that rises to a peak like a circus tent. There are no walls, just beams holding up the roof. Heaters in the ceiling keep us warm on chilly days, and plastic blinds come down on the sides if it's windy and rainy.

Contrary to popular belief, it does rain in Southern California. We just prefer to contain all of our rain to a few months—usually February and March—and spend the rest of the year with dry, sunny skies. But we are by the beach, so it can get chilly on occasion.

Since the pavilion juts out from the main building we have an unobstructed view of the ocean, the observatory, and the courtyard. That beats cinderblock walls painted institutional gray any day.

I grabbed two chicken soft tacos and dropped them onto my tray. Since I wasn't much hungry for anything else, I pulled a fruit juice from the refrigerator and made my way to the pavilion. That is another reason we don't call it a lunchroom. There are no facilities to actually make lunch. No ovens or stoves. Not even a lunch lady or a hairnet. The administration contracts with restaurants in the area to bring in food every day. The school calls it a "catered lunch." I call it pretentious.

If the pavilion were a typical lunchroom in a typical school, this would be the point of the story where some character would discuss the social structure of the lunchroom seating. The character—in this case, me—would direct your attention to the tables with the jocks and cheerleaders, the brains, the arty crowd, the potheads, and the slackers. Then he'd (or I'd) go on to explain how the social groups were strictly defined, rarely mixed with one another, and all that junk.

Yeah, we've got none of that here.

With only two hundred students in the entire school, we have a fair amount of overlap. The jocks are all brains. The potheads, too. We don't *have* any slackers. No cheerleaders either. The only real organized sports we have are boys' soccer, girls' volleyball, and mixed-gender swimming. None of those sports really call for cheerleaders.

Surprisingly, we don't have any cliques of any kind at Orion Academy. We all pretty much hate each other individually and equally. We all *like* each other in much the same way. The pavilion is one big melting pot of friendship, with a large amount of passive aggression stirred in.

Except for my table, that is. Sam, Hope, and I regularly dine at the table reserved for the Drama Geeks. Please note that this is a self-proclaimed title. A badge we wear with pride. We're the outsiders. The ones who don't follow the status quo. You know the type: the people who randomly burst into song in between classes for absolutely no reason whatsoever.

We're the closest thing to an arty crowd around here, except that we are fairly mainstream when it comes to our entertainment choices. None of that overwrought, overblown, independent film junk. *Unless* it stars a really hot actor trying to break out of his typical big-budget film roles.

Not that I'm talking about Colin Farrell again. I'm just saying.

Sam, Hope, and I make up the regulars at the table. As do Jimmy—who's usually pounding down a few bottled

Frappuccinos—and Tasha, the resident vegan true-Goth chick. (Hope usually runs all of her Goth-Ick looks by Tasha to make sure she's not being offensive to the actual spirit of the movement.)

Otherwise, the rest of the Drama Geeks filter in and out depending on the day. We also have non-drama students pop by the table from time to time, but the less said about them the better.

As I reached the table, the only other people there so far were Sam and Hope.

Today, Hope was sporting a red belt with her all-black outfit, highlighted by these flaming red contacts. She did look a touch demonic. It was especially odd, considering she takes the whole concepts of demons and religion more seriously than most people I know. She refuses to take part in my vampire pact with Sam. Hope subscribes more to the Buffyverse definition of vampires, seeing them as soulless demons only interested in killing. She won't even *consider* the possibility that being a vampire could be all cool and romantically tormented.

She has, however, promised to stake Sam and me if it turns out that she's right and we're wrong. And really, what more can you ask from a friend than for her to kill you to save you from an immortal life as a demonic creature?

"So, how did you do on the test?" Sam asked before I could even sit.

"Failed horribly," I said. "You?"

"Miserably," she replied.

"Oh, shut up," Hope said. "You both did fine like always."

I was pretty sure I did, but I could tell Sam was genuinely doubtful.

"Now that you finally got here," Hope said to me, before turning to Sam, "Sam can tell us all about her date."

I chose not to say anything.

"I knew I wasn't going to get through lunch without the inquisition," Sam said. She may have been protesting, but she was also leaning into the table so no one else could hear but us.

"What's the story, morning glory?" Hope sang as she leaned in to match Sam. She grabbed my sleeve and pulled me forward too, so Sam could start with the storytelling.

I'll save you all the gory details. You can thank me later. Sam and Eric went to dinner at CPK—that's California Pizza Kitchen, for the nonnatives—and then to some movie. Honestly, I wasn't much listening, so I couldn't tell you which movie. Apparently it wasn't worth seeing. I think it starred Ben Affleck.

Anyway, the story on the date itself wasn't important. It was what she said when she finished the story that you need to know.

"If it's okay with you, Bryan."

I have *got* to start listening more when I'm part of a conversation.

"What?" I asked.

"Bryan!" Hope said, smacking me in the shoulder. She does that a lot. For someone with such a sweet disposition (*cough-cough*), she has a nasty left hook.

"Sorry," I said, seeing my excuse walking in this direction. "I was distracted when I saw the matching Abercrombie & Fitch–ness of your *boyfriends* coming this way."

Sam quickly turned in their direction, then, just as quickly, turned back to share a bug-eyed look at Hope. Then, even more quickly, she swung her attention back to me.

I swear all that happened in, like, point-zero-five seconds.

"He's not my boyfriend," Sam said. "But that's kind of what I was just saying. Now don't get mad."

Never a good opening.

"I know we always said we'd go to the prom together if we weren't seeing anyone," Sam said, reminding me of our oft-discussed agreement. "It's not like Eric and I are officially *seeing* each other or anything, but he did ask me."

"To the prom?" I asked as I watched Eric and Drew approach. I swear they were walking in slow motion across the cafeteria.

"Yeah," Sam said. "But I won't go with him if you don't want me to. We did sort of promise each other."

"It wasn't really a *promise,*" I said, trying for magnanimous, but probably sounding a bit whiny. Eric and Drew were almost at the table.

"Whatever," Sam said. "Is it okay?"

What was I supposed to say? It *wasn't* okay. Sure, we hadn't technically promised each other we would go to the prom together. But we had been talking about it since forever. Now I was being all rushed to make a decision because asshat Eric was coming to the table.

Oops! Too late. Already here.

Arsenic and Old Lace

"How's it going?" Eric asked as he put his tray down on our table.

Here's the problem with not having well-defined lunchroom cliques: Anyone feels that he can just sit wherever he wants.

Drew came around the table and slid in between Hope and me. He gave her a little kiss on the cheek as he pushed his way in. On the other side of the table, Eric sat beside Sam. Neither one of them seemed too sure if they were supposed to kiss or not. They both settled for some weird shoulder-bump thing that—in my opinion—could not possibly have been what either one had intended.

"And what's the lunchtime topic today?" Drew asked. "Not us, I hope, Hope."

"Not *you*, at least," I said as I took a bite of my chicken soft taco.

"Prom," Hope quickly said.

Sam's eyes about bugged out of her face this time.

"Really?" Eric asked, looking directly at Sam. "And what were you saying about it?"

You know how cartoon characters look the moment they realize they've walked off a cliff and there's nothing beneath their feet but a huge drop? Yeah, Sam looked very much like that. She clearly did not want to get into a discussion about the prom in front of me until we got over the whole "implied promise" thing. At the same time, she didn't want to be totally rude and ignore a direct question from Eric either.

She looked somewhat like her head was about to explode.

As her friend, it was my job to come in and save her.

"Um," she faltered. "Well . . . it's like . . ."

Notice I didn't say, "*Rush* in and save her." I felt it wasn't entirely out of line to let her struggle for a bit first. Not to be harsh, but we had gone from total trio to fifth wheel scenario in one weekend. I wasn't about to make this any easier on her.

Okay, maybe I was being a tad harsh.

"Prom!" Sam blurted out as if it answered Eric's question.

At this point, I could bear no more. "Sam told us you guys are going together," I said.

"Did she?" Eric asked, smiling this disgustingly large grin as he looked directly at Sam. "She hasn't told *me* that, yet. All she said was she'd get back to me."

Sam definitely got points for that.

"Well . . ." Sam started to look like she was hanging off that cliff again.

"Wait till you see my dress," Hope jumped in, speaking to Drew and me. "We got it this weekend at this great vintage shop. It's this black—"

"Naturally," Drew and I said in unison. Purely unintentional, I assure you.

This time, Hope smacked Drew, not me.

"Lace Chanel evening dress in a kind of forties couture style with a bolero jacket," Hope continued. "It was originally made for Shelley Winters before she gained all the weight."

I started to say something, but stopped myself. There was no polite way to ask the question. And I didn't want to get smacked again.

"Who's Shelley Winters?" Eric asked.

It was all I could do not to snort with derision. No. That was *not* the question I was afraid to ask.

"You know," Hope said, "the actress from the original *Poseidon Adventure*."

I could see in Eric's eyes that he had no clue what she was talking about. "Nope," I said. "Try again."

"The hillbilly mom from *Pete's Dragon*," Sam tried.

"Disney musicals? Not a chance," I said, turning to Drew. "Your turn."

Drew didn't bother to look at me when he said, "The grandmom on *Roseanne*."

A look of relief washed over the girls' faces as Eric finally got the reference. *Thank God for Nick at Nite.*

"Oh," he said, "but she was—"

"Quite the voluptuous stunner in her younger days," Hope said threateningly.

"Yeah," Drew said, "but even then, she didn't have . . . never mind."

"Go ahead," Hope said threateningly to Drew. "Say it."

"Say what?" Drew asked, taking a bite of his taco, then speaking through his food. "Don't know what you're talking about."

"Can you please not do that?" I asked, wiping a piece of spit chicken off my tray.

Drew held up his hands in what I guess was some lame form of an apology as he chewed his food. Once upon a time, Drew used to have manners. I guess things like that all depend on the company you keep.

Obviously, Drew and I had had the same thought about Shelley Winters and vintage Chanel. I'm glad I wasn't the only one who wondered how they'd both fit in the same dress. Now, don't get me wrong. Shelley Winters was never a stick figure. She came from a time when beautiful women in Hollywood were judged by their curves, not by how many ribs you could see peeking through their dresses. Her body type was originally quite similar to Hope's.

But not entirely.

"What did I miss?" Eric asked.

I didn't see Drew's face, but I could tell it mirrored mine.

Mine was silently saying, "Shut up, idiot."

But Hope saved us both at her own expense. "Okay. Fine. It does have to be let out a bit in certain areas."

"Let out?" Eric asked. "Oh! You mean the chest!"

Drew and I shoved the rest of our tacos in our mouths simultaneously. We were having no part of this.

"Can they even do that with lace?" Eric asked, showing a far better grasp of fashion than I ever thought he would possess.

"I'm sure my mom's people can," Hope said. Her mom, Natalie Ellis, is one of *the* top designers in the fashion world. She has design houses in Los Angeles, New York, and Paris, and her work can regularly be seen on the red carpet at all the major events. Since she has to split her time evenly between the three design houses, Hope lives with her dad and steps.

"But I hate asking them for favors," Hope said. "Alexis and Belinda do it all the time and they're not even *related*. Why do my parents have to get along so well?"

"Bitter divorce is *so* the way to go," I said. Not that I know anything about that subject. My parents are still firmly together. There's nothing bitter about their marriage either. It's hard to work up the bitterness when my father's out of town so much and my mom's too easily distracted by puppies to have any abandonment issues.

"You should ask Suze," Sam said as Dorothy #4 was passing with her tray. "She'd probably listen to what you want more than one of your mom's flunkies."

"That's a great idea," Hope said. "Hey, Suze! Hold on a sec!"

Suze dropped her tray at the next table and came over to ours before Hope could even get up. Suze is one of those girls who bounces around the lunchroom, eating at a different table every day. She is equally friendly with everyone, which makes half the girls in school hate her, naturally.

"What's up?" she asked as she knelt on the end of the bench beside Sam.

"A project," Hope said, with a gleam in her eye. "If you're interested, that is. It's a fashion emergency."

"My favorite kind," Suze said as she slid down to sit on the bench.

Hope pulled her cell phone out of her bag. "Check this out." As she passed it to Suze, I caught a glimpse of a black dress on the screen.

"Hope, we're not supposed to have cell phones in school," Drew needlessly reminded her as he quickly looked around the pavilion. Sometimes he can be incredibly annoying with the worrying. There wasn't a teacher in sight. Not a surprise, really. All the teachers *hate* lunch duty, and usually find some way to be late.

"I'm not using it to call anyone," Hope said.

"Not like she could if she wanted to," I added. One of the problems with having a school built halfway up the side of a mountain is that we have lousy cell phone reception. Even if we were allowed to have them in school, they would be utterly useless.

"I see," Suze said as she scrutinized the image. She reminded me of a doctor examining a patient. That's how intensely she looked at the photo of the dress.

We were all so focused on Suze studying the dress that we didn't notice Jax lumbering up to the table until it was too late.

"Yo, Drew, what's—" As Jax leaned across the table to give Drew five, or bump fists, or whatever it is *some* guys do, he spilled his soda all over Sam's shirt.

"Jax, you idiot!" Eric yelled as he jumped out of his seat. Drew was also up in a flash. I would have jumped up too, but the other guys looked like they had matters well in hand.

"Geez. Sorry," Jax said. His hands were rubbing at the quickly setting stain on Sam's top.

Sam grabbed the moving hands and pushed them off her. "It's all right," she said through clenched teeth. Honestly, she was handling it far better than I thought she would. Though, that could have something to do with the fact that as soon as Eric yelled out, the entire pavilion had gone quiet. Everyone was looking at our table.

"You'll want to put some vinegar and water on that," Suze suggested.

"I'll be right back," Sam mumbled as she left the pavilion. She was in such a rush that she left her sandals under the table and ran out in her bare feet.

I couldn't help but notice that all heads were turning to follow her. I was really annoyed to see Jax's girlfriend looking like she was enjoying the whole thing. But that's Heather Mayflower for you. She specializes in taking pleasure in other people's pain.

"Idiot!" Eric said again.

"Dude, I said, *sorry*," Jax said as he moved off to join his girlfriend.

While Eric and Suze wiped the remaining soda from the

table, I continued to watch Jax and Heather. The kiss she gave her boyfriend made me suspect that the accident wasn't so much of an accident. What a petty little Dorothy she could be.

Heather was totally jealous that Sam got to sing "Over the Rainbow." Cynthia was too, but she at least acted like it didn't bother her. It didn't help that Sam is a junior. All the seniors in the play thought the best number should go to a senior. Meanwhile, everyone else in school thought the best number should go to the best singer.

Besides, Heather wasn't supposed to even be one of the four leads in the first place. Everyone knew that part was supposed to go to Wren Deslandes. If it weren't for that well-timed call from Heather's father, she would have probably been the head flying monkey. But when Anthony Mayflower says, "Jump," Orion Academy says, "How high does your checkbook go?" And thus, Wren gets to be Glinda #2 while Heather hacks her way through the play in ruby-esque slippers.

"So, what do you think?" Hope asked.

At first I thought she had noticed the intensity of my gaze over at Heather's table. But Hope had already moved past the assumed accident. She was talking to Suze about her dress.

"Chanel?" Suze asked as she looked over the image on the cell phone screen.

Hope nodded.

"I'd say, late forties," Suze added. "Maybe early fifties."

Hope rolled her eyes in my direction. We both knew that Suze was showing off for us.

"Can you do something with it?" Hope asked.

Suze shut the phone and handed it back to Hope, drawing out her response for utmost dramatic effect. "But, of course."

"Great!" Hope said, trying not to look as excited as I knew she felt. Hope has a horrible time finding dresses, but she has an even worse time asking her mom's employees to do her any favors. Having a friend who is was as talented as anyone her mom hires came in handy.

"Let's go shopping for materials right after school," Suze said. I think she was even more excited than Hope.

Did I mention that Suze *loves* fashion?

"We've got rehearsal," Hope reminded her.

"Oh, yeah," Suze said with a fair amount of disappointment, if you ask me. "Then I have piano lessons. We'll have to hold off till the show's finally over."

"And I'll pay you whatever you want," Hope said.

"Just cover the materials," Suze said. "That's fine."

"No," Hope said. "I insist."

"It's fine," Suze said. "I love these projects."

"But I can't take—"

"Show your mom a picture of you in the dress," Suze said. "And be sure to tell her who altered it for you. That's enough."

Hope's face broke into a smile. It was a smile I had seen many times before. Some ingenious plan just popped into her head. "Sure," she said as she dropped her phone back into her bag.

"Miss me?" Sam asked as she slipped in between Eric and Suze.

I could tell Eric and Drew were as surprised as I was to see

Sam slide into her seat. We were so busy watching the painfully cheery nonnegotiations that we hadn't noticed she had come back into the room wearing a new shirt.

One of the perks of having a mom on staff is she tends to keep things on hand for these kinds of emergencies. Sam had probably done a quick dash to her mom's room and pulled something out of her "book" closet, which was much closer to the pavilion than Sam's locker.

"That was fast," I said about Sam's return. I wasn't sure if the need for speed was because she wanted to get back to Eric right away or she wanted to make sure I wasn't left unsupervised with him for too long. Like I would do anything to jeopardize this burgeoning relationship.

If only I had thought of that sooner.

"My lunch is probably getting cold," Suze said as she popped up off the bench. "How about getting together Sunday for materials?"

"I'm free after church," Hope said.

"Perfect," Suze said. "Brunch and then materials shopping."

"Book it," Hope said.

Suze bounced across the aisle to her table and joined the rest of the junior prom committee. Considering the dance didn't take place until the end of the month, prom season seemed to be starting sooner than usual this year. Pretty soon it would be all prom all the time.

Oh, fun.

"What'd I miss?" Sam asked.

"An exciting discussion of fashions of the late forties,"

Drew said. This got him a smack in the head from Hope. "Ouch."

"You should know better by now," I said.

But does the boy learn? Nope. He started reaching in Hope's bag for her phone.

"Come on," he said. "Let me see the picture."

"Not until prom," Hope said, deftly keeping the phone away.

"What, is it, like, bad luck to let your date see the dress before the prom?" he asked.

"No," Hope said, swatting at his hands. "But I like to tease you."

"So we hear," Eric said through a mouthful of taco.

"What!" Hope shrieked. Suddenly, the playfulness stopped as we all wondered exactly how detailed Drew's conversations with Eric were.

"He's making a joke," Drew said as the table did a quick shift and Eric sat straight up. I suspect that Drew just kicked his best friend in the leg.

Drew quickly turned to me. "Don't *you* want to see what the dress looks like?"

"I'm sure she'll show me later," I said, both getting in a dig and getting myself out of the middle of their pending argument.

But Drew wasn't done with using me as a shield yet. "Who are you going to the prom with, anyway?" he asked.

I swear if I ever *do* become a vampire, Drew is the first person I'm putting the bite on.

The uncomfortable silence that followed was interrupted when Suze sprang up from her bench across the way, clutching her throat. Her face was turning a rather deep shade of red. I wish I could say that I had never seen her do that before, but I had. And I knew that it wasn't good.

Appointment with Death

You know how they say that your life flashes before your eyes when you're about to die? For some reason as I stood there watching Suze look like she was about to die, her life flashed in front of *my* eyes. It wasn't her entire life that flashed. Just one very specific moment: the Big Bee Sting Blowup of Freshman Year.

Suze has massive allergy issues. She's been like this for as long as I can remember. She follows a strict diet, avoids being outdoors at certain times, and visits the allergist regularly for shots. Even with all those precautions, a single bee sting had sent her to the hospital for a month at the start of freshman year.

Now, as she dropped to the floor gasping for breath, she looked exactly like she did on that day. Apparently, I wasn't the only one stuck in flashback mode. Everyone else in the lunchroom was standing frozen like me as Suze clutched at the air.

Surprisingly, Jax was the first to react. Springing into action, he dashed across the pavilion and fell to his knees at Suze's side.

Someone yelled, "Her purse!"

Eric ran over to Suze and started rooting through the purse. Meanwhile, Jax ripped open her shirt, popping off buttons and exposing a satin blue bra with beading that matched her outfit so well that I assumed she must have made it that way. It was an odd time for Jax to be copping a feel, but I was still too stunned to actually comment on it aloud.

Eric pulled something out of the bag and handed it to Jax. I couldn't see what it was until Jax lifted his hand above his head, preparing to plunge the thing into her chest. He was holding her emergency injector of epinephrine.

"STOP!" I yelled. With my adrenaline rushing, I stepped up on the bench and bounded over the lunch table in a giant leap, landing at Suze's side.

Dramatic, no?

Truthfully, I was still frozen in place. What actually happened was, I yelled and Drew—having already moved to the other side of the table—grabbed Jax's hand.

Jax looked more confused than usual.

"This is not *Pulp Fiction,*" I said as I finally found motion and quickly moved to the other side of the table. Drew took the EpiPen out of Jax's hand and gave it to me. Suze's face was turning blue as I knelt beside her.

Sam was on her other side, holding Suze's hand and keeping her calm.

"You *do* know what you're doing?" Drew asked.

I looked at him. "Everyone get back."

"You heard him!" Hope yelled to the gathering crowd. "Give her some room!"

I looked at the needle in my hand. It was filled with what I hoped was enough epinephrine to stop the vicious allergy attack. I raised her skirt slightly up her thigh, not wanting to add to the humiliation of already having her breasts exposed to the junior and senior classes. Then, I stuck the needle in her thigh.

As the medicine went into her body I saw a look of calm relief wash over Suze's face, replacing the fear that had been there a moment earlier.

"For anaphylactic shock," I said to Jax (and for Drew's benefit as well), "you have to inject the medicine in the thigh or you could cause a cerebral hemorrhage."

Did I mention that the Big Bee Sting Blowup of Freshman Year happened at my birthday party? Having one of your guests nearly die is not something you soon forget.

I could hear Suze's breathing go back to normal. Her face was returning to its typical lightly tanned hue. The crowd—who hadn't bothered to move back at all—looked as relieved as I felt.

"What's going on here?" Mr. Clark, the teacher on duty, asked as he pushed his way through the students, rushing in too late to actually do anything useful. I can only imagine what he thought, seeing a student lying in the middle of the lunchroom with her clothing ripped open and a crowd gathered around her.

Sam quickly pulled Suze's shirt together, and Mr. Clark

scattered everyone for real. He sent Jimmy out to get help and within minutes the nurse, headmaster, and assorted administrative personnel were in the lunchroom.

Nobody reacts after-the-fact like the Orion Academy staff.

The students were eventually shooed out to the courtyard to finish our lunch. Normally, we aren't supposed to take food outside—for fear of a stray wrapper littering the grounds—but we were granted a stay on that rule due to the extenuating circumstances of Suze nearly dying.

"That was crazy," Eric said.

"Total Ophelia," Sam agreed.

"Forget Ophelia," I said. "That was a full-on Hamlet."

"Really?" Hope asked. "You think Hamlet was crazier than Ophelia? Most of that craziness was an act to prove his uncle's guilt. And it's not like there weren't extenuating circumstances. But Ophelia was driven to madness about as quickly as Suze's reaction escalated."

Hope did have a point. "How about . . . it was all Lady Macbeth in a full-on sleepwalk?" I asked.

"Exactly!" Hope and Sam agreed.

"You guys are so weird," Drew said.

"Thank you," the three of us said as we all settled on a patch of grass around the William Foster Reflecting Pool and took a seat.

Sam's sandals were off before she hit the ground. "I knew Suze had allergies, but that was intense."

"Not as intense as the first time," Drew said before turning to me. "You remember that? At your birthday party?"

"Why do you think I knew what to do with the EpiPen?" I asked as if it wasn't obvious. Because it *was*. And, by the way, it was a *surprise* birthday party. My mom made the guest list while unaware of certain social realities of the time. Like the fact that having Drew and Eric at my birthday party was the last thing I would have wanted. Even worse, they both showed up like they didn't think anything at all of coming when they totally should have known that they weren't welcome.

"Did anyone hear what caused it?" Hope asked.

Sam had been the nearest to Suze when the nurse arrived, but she hadn't heard anything. No one else had either.

"All we had were the chicken and veggie tacos we have every week," I said. "If she was allergic to anything in those, that would have happened long ago."

The school menu rotates daily, but remains the same week in and week out: Soft Taco Mondays, Burger Tuesdays, Salad Wednesdays, Sandwich Thursdays, and Pizza Fridays. Every day we have veggie and vegan options for the noncarnivores. Other than that, there's really no deviating from the menu. It's weird that Suze would react that way all of the sudden.

As we were about to resume our lunch, we heard sirens approaching. Everyone in the courtyard stopped what they were doing to watch the ambulance drive right up to the pavilion and the EMTs rush out to check on Suze.

Hope looked at what was left of her taco. "Suddenly, I've lost my appetite."

"Me too," Sam and I said in unison, putting down our food as well.

"Hey," Eric said. "Why don't we all grab dinner after practice and rehearsal?"

Not exactly a natural segue when people have just finished saying they aren't hungry.

"What do you say?" Eric persisted, directing his question to Sam. "Your appetite will be back after rehearsal for sure. We can all go."

Sam immediately looked at me.

"We can't," I said. "Toto shopping."

Drew gave me an odd look. "Is that some kind of code?"

"Yes," I said. "It's code for 'We have more important things to do this afternoon.'"

That shut him up.

Okay, I was being childish, but I really didn't care. Thankfully, Sam wasn't saying anything. We didn't actually have *formal* plans for that afternoon. Sam had agreed to go on a props run with me sometime this week. This was the first mention that "sometime" had become "today."

You'd think that, at a school that loans out free laptops at the beginning of the year, we'd have more of a budget for our school show. Yeah. Not so much. To offset the fact that we don't charge for tickets, the budget is kept pretty bare bones. So there's not much money to get stuff with.

It's true that most of us can buy our own props and costumes, but we have far more fun being resourceful about it. It's kind of a tradition. We even give out an award for the best costume or prop found from an unlikely source. So far it looks like this year's award is going to go to Gary McNulty.

He's the tenth grader who plays Nikko, the head flying monkey. He's using one of his mom's old fur coats for his monkey costume.

We hoped Tasha's parents won't throw a can of red paint on him in the middle of the show.

Since my mom is all hooked up in the animal world, I offered to pick up some stuffed dogs for our Toto. Mr. Randall wanted four identical dogs so each Dorothy could have her own to work with during the week. Fleischman Brothers Animal Emporium, one of my mom's suppliers, gladly offered to donate the stuffed animals for the show. The only problem is that the Fleischman Brothers work on an appointment-only basis. And they are really hard to pin down for an appointment.

I still hadn't managed to get one.

"Was that today?" Sam asked, like she had forgotten something we both knew I never told her. Thankfully, she didn't call me on it. I suspect that was her way of making up to me for blowing me off about the prom.

"Sorry, Eric," she said. "But I promised. Maybe another time."

"Cool," he said.

I tried not to feel like dirt while Sam covered her look of disappointment.

"I'll be right back," I said as I got up to head to the bathroom.

Once I was out of their sightlines, I made a dash for the school phones. Now, I *really* had to get that appointment.

The Tempest

Mission accomplished!

After trying several numbers my mom gave me for the Fleischman Brothers' workshop and cell phones, I managed to get the senior Fleischman on the phone. He said that he and his brother would be in the studio that afternoon. Sam and I were welcome to come look over their inventory.

Whew.

By the time I hung up the phone, I was more than ready for my next class. It had been a surprisingly eventful lunchtime.

I'm sure you can imagine what the talk was for the rest of the day. More than a few people came up to tell me how cool it was that I, "like, saved Suze's life and all." These were mostly freshmen and sophomores who, I suspect, only wanted to hear what had happened from someone who was there.

Who was I to keep the story from them?

I wasn't entirely comfortable with the sudden fame. Our

school's not large enough for anyone to disappear in a crowd, but I do tend to keep to the fringes. I know it's odd that a Drama Geek doesn't like the spotlight, but that's just me, I guess.

I especially didn't like the spotlight when it found me in Headmaster Collins's office at the end of the day. At first, I thought I was going to get some award for my quick thinking. Maybe a special assembly for heroically saving the life of another.

What? It could happen.

But that idea went out the window as soon as I stepped into the headmaster's office, literally with fedora in hand.

"Please have a seat, Mr. Stark," Headmaster Collins said stiffly as he glanced up at me over his silver-frame glasses.

"Yes, sir," I said, taking one of his guest chairs. I kept my fedora in my lap, not sure if it was rude to wear a hat or not in the headmaster's office. I figured removing it was a "better safe than sorry" move. Besides, it gave me something to twist in my hands as Headmaster Collins spoke to me. For some reason, he always makes me incredibly nervous.

The headmaster drummed his well-manicured fingers on his desk. I swear, Headmaster Collins and his wife are two of the most beautiful people I've ever seen in my life. And I live in a place where beauty is appreciated over anything else. I'm not saying that the two of them have come about this by a natural process. They have both been bronzed, trimmed, sculpted, and injected to within an inch of their lives. So far as I can tell, neither of them has gone under the knife yet, but the amount of money they must spend on teeth bleaching alone could fund a small nation. And don't get me started on their wardrobes.

Maybe that's where the budget for the school show goes.

"You've never been in my office before, have you?" Headmaster Collins asked.

"Not since the admissions interview," I said. That was four years ago, but the place hasn't really changed. Same mod—and thoroughly uncomfortable—furniture. Same trendy artwork on the walls. Same plastic, though intimidating, headmaster.

"You've never been summoned here before for any disciplinary problems."

"No, sir," I said, not entirely sure if it was a question. I just focused on my hat.

"Now, don't get me wrong," he said. This is *never* a good conversation opener. "What you did this afternoon, with Ms. Finberg, is likely to be much appreciated by her family. I suspect they may even wish to show that appreciation in some way. I am sure your friends have probably been patting you on the back through the halls all afternoon."

"I—"

He raised his hand, politely informing me to shut up. It was a good thing too, since I wasn't sure what I was going to say, anyway. I didn't really care if the Finbergs got me anything. And no one had actually patted me on the back since my grandpop died three years ago.

"I know this may appear confusing," the headmaster continued, "but what you did this afternoon, while appreciated by many—including, I'm sure, certain segments of the school faculty—I regretfully have to tell you, was not the best course of action in this case."

I had no idea what he just said.

I mean, really.

Even after I pulled apart his sentence in my head, I still wasn't sure what he was getting at.

"Did I do something wrong?" I asked, looking up from my lap.

"While some might say no," he said, "I am going to have to say, yes."

Let's try this one more time.

"So, I *did* do something wrong?"

"It is against school policy for students to administer any form of medication to one another," he said, clearing up some but certainly not *all* of the reasons I had been summoned.

"But, it was an emergency," I said.

"That is understandable," he replied. "You reacted in the heat of the moment. But have you ever administered epinephrine prior to this afternoon?"

"Well . . . no," I said. "But I saw it done once before." I think the only way I could have sounded any lamer was if I'd added "on TV" to the end of that sentence.

"And did you stop to think for a moment that you could have made things worse?" he asked through a smile that was so bright that it was intimidating on its own.

"I did stop Jax from pumping it straight to her heart," I said weakly, offering up some sort of defense.

"I have already spoken with Mr. Klayton," Headmaster Collins said. "We are discussing *your* actions at the moment."

Considering that we all study in the Klayton Library, I can

imagine *that* conversation had been a little less intimidating. I really need to talk to my parents about buying something around here. Maybe that new light grid. It would certainly make my education considerably less stressful.

"What should I have done?" I asked, going for a more pro-active approach.

"Found a teacher and reported the incident so the school nurse could be summoned," he said.

I really didn't want to get Mr. Clark in trouble for not being at his post, but it was either him or me. "There weren't any teachers around at the time."

"Then you should have gone for the nurse yourself," he said. "Or sent one of your friends while you waited with Ms. Finberg."

"But she could have died in the time it took someone to get to the nurse and back," I said.

"She could have died from you administering the drug into her system incorrectly," he said.

"But she didn't."

"But she *could* have."

I guess he took my stunned silence as an apology, because he got up from his seat—brushing the nonexistent wrinkles from his silk suit—and went to the door.

"I knew you would understand," he said as he opened the door.

Still painfully confused, I got up and walked out.

"Please see that you don't do anything else that would have you sent to my office," he said.

"Okay," I replied after the door had shut behind me.

I promise not to save anyone else's life during school hours.

Sam's mom, Anne, was standing in the outer office. At first, I thought it was odd that she was standing right by the door when I came out. It wasn't entirely clear what she was doing there. She certainly wasn't standing around talking to the headmaster's secretary, Mrs. Bell, even though Mrs. Bell was obviously interested in what was going on. You could tell by the way she was leaning forward and staring straight at me as I left the office. Mrs. Bell? Not one for subtlety.

"I had a feeling this would happen," Anne said to me.

I was still pulling myself out of the stunned silence. I think I managed to blink a couple times.

She threw an arm around me, took my fedora out of my hands, and gently placed it back on my head. Usually she refrains from outward signs of affection during school hours, but I suspect she knew I was in some shock. "I'm guessing that Headmaster Collins expressed some concern over what you did this afternoon," she said.

"Kind of."

Anne pulled me out to the empty hall. I guess she didn't like it that Mrs. Bell was still obviously eavesdropping. The woman didn't even bother to hide the fact that she was leaning even farther across her desk. I was afraid she was going to fall out of her seat.

"He thinks he has to say that," Anne said once we were out of earshot. "It's a cover-his-butt type thing. Don't let him make you think you did anything wrong."

"He said I should have gotten the nurse," I said.

"The only thing she's empowered to do is hand out aspirin,"

she said. "Bryan, Suze is going to be perfectly fine. And that's all because of you."

"Really?" I asked.

"Really."

Sure, I had been talking about saving Suze's life all afternoon, but I never really *believed* it until Anne told me I did good.

"Thanks . . . Ms. Lawson," I said. I'm not supposed to call her by her first name at school. "Does anyone know what caused the reaction?"

Anne looked down the hall to make sure no one could overhear. "The headmaster would prefer that this information not get out. So please don't tell anyone," she said. "But there was a mix-up at the restaurant that catered today. A shrimp taco was accidentally sent with the regular order."

"Wow," I said. "Talk about a lawsuit in the making." Shellfish is on the top of the list of things that Suze is allergic to. A fact that Suze's mom had made sure the school knew about back when we started here.

Anne walked me the rest of the way to Hall Hall. I considered asking what she thought of the whole Eric Whitman situation, but decided against it. It was too early to play that card. I wanted to see where this thing was headed before I had to bring in the big guns. She might not even know about it yet. With Anne being a teacher here, Sam already has so much overlap between her school life and her personal life that she doesn't always rush to tell her mom everything.

"I hear I owe you," Anne said. "Sam said I could go home early today."

Sam must have told her about our shopping trip. Anne usually has to wait around until the end of rehearsal to take Sam back to Santa Monica.

"All I ask is that you remember this when I'm in your class next year," I said smoothly, coming out of my headmaster-induced stupor.

"Naturally," Anne said, not meaning it at all. In the world of owing favors, I'm sure I owe her a lot more than she owes me. "Tell my daughter I said hi."

"Will do," I said as I went for the door, leaving Anne out in the hall. I would have asked if she wanted to come in, but I knew better. Sam gets totally flustered when her mom comes to rehearsals.

I checked my watch. Mr. Randall hates it when we're late for rehearsal. I was glad that I had a good excuse, but quickly realized I wouldn't need it. I knew my late entrance would easily be overlooked as soon as I opened the door and heard the chorus of girls' voices in heated discussion. I slipped in totally unnoticed.

Sam and Hope were sitting on the edge of the stage. They were practically the only girls in the cast not encircling Mr. Randall. The chattering girls were all talking over one another so much, I couldn't make out what any of them were saying. Poor Mr. Randall had obviously given up on control. All he could do was stand in silence while they let loose.

"So what are we doing here?" I asked, pointing at the commotion as I joined Sam and Hope onstage.

"Well." Sam leaned in so she could be heard over the noise.

"Since Suze is going to be out for the rest of the week—"

"She's out for the whole week?"

"At *least*."

"You know her mom," Hope added.

"That means we're down a Dorothy," Sam continued. "So Mr. Randall promoted Wren into the role."

"That's great," I said. "Dorothy #4 dances the jitterbug number. Wren is an amazing dancer. Perfect match."

(*Aside:* "The Jitterbug" is a song that was cut from the movie. Check out the two-disc special-edition DVD if you ever want to hear it. It's a really great song.)

I looked over to the seats and saw Wren was already running lines with Jason. I knew she appreciated the part more than Suze had. It was nice that someone in the cast was finally getting what she wanted and deserved. It was also nice that she and her boyfriend were already getting down to work. Considering I was the act two Scarecrow, I would have to offer my services later since Wren would be working with me onstage and not Jason. But Wren and Jason looked like they didn't want to be bothered at the moment.

Those two are an interesting couple. No one would have ever guessed they'd get together. Not because he's Irish and she's Jamaican. This is Malibu, after all. It's because she's a senior, and he's a junior. It goes totally against the rules of high school dating that they'd be a couple. Sure, it's fine for a senior guy to date a junior girl . . . or even a freshman girl. But for some reason, the reverse is not true at all. People would be more scandalized by the age difference if we all weren't pretty sure they'd break up as soon as Wren graduates. They totally have the feel of "High School Couple" about them.

"So *that's* why Heather and Cynthia are so mad," I said, going back to the commotion.

"They probably thought we'd all get more lines," Sam added. I suspect she had expected the same thing.

But that didn't explain the rest of the girls. Most of them were freshmen and sophomores. They couldn't have possibly expected to be a Dorothy. Leads only go to seniors and juniors since everyone else has two or three more chances for a starring role before they graduate.

It didn't take long for me to do the necessary cast calculations to realize what at least part of the commotion was about.

"So, if Wren is now Dorothy #4, who's playing Glinda #2?" I asked.

Hope smiled at me and waved with a smug kind of joy.

"You get to be Glinda in *both* acts?" I asked.

She giggled for the second time in a week. At least this time she was doing it on purpose. Hope was now the only cast member who would appear in both acts of the play. Not even the stuffed Totos would get to do that.

"That's why all the *other* girls are complaining," Hope said. She looked quite pleased with Mr. Randall's decision, and I couldn't blame her at all.

Toys in the Attic

Mr. Randall eventually got the situation under control and started the rehearsal. Since Hope and Wren were new to act two, we began there and worked our way backward.

The difference in dynamic was totally noticeable with Wren in the role of Dorothy. Suze is an amazing actress. She's got this innate talent that I would die for. The thing that really kills me is, she doesn't care. She has no interest in being on the stage at all, so she pretty much walks her way through the scenes. I'm not saying she purposely doesn't try, but she does kind of phone it in.

Wren, on the other hand, worked for every moment. You could actually see her connect with the nuances of her character. She really gave you something to work off. The first time Wren said to me (as the Scarecrow) that she'd miss me most of all, I totally believed it.

And you should see her move. We like to joke that

she's been dancing since before she could walk, but I honestly wouldn't be surprised if that was true. We were moving through the second part of the second act rather well with Wren in the role. I don't think the same could be said for everyone else.

There were actually several rehearsals going on at the same time, one per Dorothy. While we worked on the end of act two with Mr. Randall, Sam and Cindy worked on their scenes with whoever was available. Meanwhile, Ms. Monroe, the music teacher-assistant director, tried to coax vocal talent out of Heather.

From what I could hear, Ms. Monroe was failing.

Miserably.

Eventually Mr. Randall called an end to the main rehearsal because he needed the stage to work on the jitterbug dance number with Wren. Since he now had a trained dancer in the part, he wanted to try out some new choreography. Luckily, he didn't want the rest of us in the scene to stick around. Sam and I had to get to the Fleischmans.

After the tragic lunch earlier, our spirits were so lifted by the rehearsal that Sam led everyone in a rousing rendition of "We're Off to See the Wizard" as we left the theater. There is nothing like the sound of two dozen Drama Geeks' voices raised in song, echoing through the empty halls in the late afternoon. I guess Headmaster Collins felt differently, because he hurried out of his office to quiet us down right when we got to the "because, because, because, because, becaaaauuuse" part.

The group quickly dispersed and I was alone with my two best friends, who were still stuck on what I had told them earlier about my last run-in with the headmaster.

"I can't believe he had the nerve to act like you did something wrong," Hope said as we left school together.

"Yeah, but I'm over it," I said nobly (in my opinion). "I'm more concerned about Suze."

Hope shook her head sadly. "Nearly killed by a rogue shrimp taco."

"Talk about a lawsuit in the making," Sam echoed my earlier comment.

See why we're such good friends?

Let me interject for a moment to clarify: I knew when Anne told me not to tell anyone about the shrimp taco earlier, she meant anyone *other than* Sam and Hope.

"You sure you don't want to come with us?" I asked Hope as we hit the parking lot. "The Fleischman Brothers are a kick."

"You know how I feel about riding on the freeway in your death trap," Hope said.

"Hey! Not so loud. She'll hear you." I played being insulted, but I had expected that response.

"It's not like she doesn't know how I feel about her," Hope said as we worked our way through the student parking lot. Filled with Hummers and hybrids, it was like an ecological battleground of trendiness. With one notable exception:

Electra.

"Hi, sexy," I said as I reached my baby, safely parked along the far edge of the lot, away from the masses.

Electra is a red and white 1957 Ford Fairlane Skyliner with a silver streak running down the sides. She's even got a convertible hard top, although the top hasn't been able to convert since before I was born. My grandpop left Electra to me when he died. True, she's not the most *ecologically* sound car in the world, but she's got style. Even Hope appreciates that and loves to be seen tooling around Malibu in her.

Hope's problem with Electra is when I take her out on the freeway. Since Electra is so . . . mature of age . . . she was born at a time before seat belts were standard. That coupled with the fact that Electra takes some time deciding whether she wants to brake or not makes Hope a little nervous.

Can't imagine why.

"I'm going to hitch a ride with Drew," Hope said as she veered off toward the soccer field. Since we got out of rehearsal early, they still had a half hour of practice to go.

"Tell him we said hi," Sam said.

I waited.

"And Eric, too," Sam added.

I did a very good job at not gagging as we boarded Electra and headed on our way.

The Fleischman Brothers' studio was in Burbank, which is a straight shot down the 101 to the 134. Considering that rush hour in the L.A. area runs from three o'clock to sometime after seven, we were hitting the freeway at the height of the traffic. It took us close to an hour and a half to get there. This is why I don't understand Hope not wanting to come with us. How bad of an accident could we get into going four miles an hour?

We used the car time to run the second act since I didn't exactly have it committed to memory yet. Memorization isn't one of my strong suits. It's even more difficult when your best friend already knows the entire play, including the parts she's not in. By the time we pulled into the small parking lot behind Fleischman Brothers Animal Emporium, I had a much better handle on my part.

"This is it?" Sam asked skeptically. We were outside a small warehouse in an industrial section by the train tracks and the 5 freeway.

"You know what they say about a book and its cover," I said, getting out of the car.

There was a sign beside the door that asked us to ring the bell for service. I pressed the button, looked at Sam, and we both went, "Who rang that bell?" like the doorman from the Emerald City. Then we broke down in the kind of hysterical laughter that probably would have annoyed everyone we know, except Hope.

"Bryan! So good to see you!" the elder Fleischman Brother said as he opened the door. "How's your mother?"

"She's fine, Mr. Mariano," I said. As we entered, Sam gave me a weird look.

"Tell her we're working on the fall line of stuffed dogs and should have a preview for her soon," he said.

"Will do."

"And who is this lovely young lady?" he asked, eyeing Sam.

"This is my friend Sam," I replied.

"Hello, Mr. . . . Mariano?" Sam asked.

"Please, call me Tony," he replied, taking her hand. While he was still holding her hand, Tony leaned over to me and said in a rather loud whisper that Sam could easily hear, "Is she a *special* friend?"

"Just a friend," I said with a smile. We get that a lot.

"Well, now, any friend of Bryan's . . ." Tony turned and pushed open the double doors to the showroom.

"Wow!" was all Sam could say.

"See what I meant about a book and its cover," I whispered.

"It's . . ."

"Yes," I said. "It is."

I knew exactly how she felt. I was six the first time I was in the Fleischman Brothers' showroom and I still remember the overwhelming feel of it all. True, a stuffed animal palace would impress most six-year-olds, but I've been back to the Fleischmans' place numerous times since then and I have still never seen anything else like it in my life.

Imagine a bright-white car showroom with a sparkling marble floor. All along the floor, where the cars would be, stand nearly life-size lions, tigers, bears, and other stuffed animals too big to fit on any shelf or hug while asleep. The white walls are filled with lit cubbyholes showing off smaller stuffed cats, birds, and more styles of teddy bears than you could ever imagine. Now, triple the size of the showroom you've imagined and you'll start to have an idea of what the reality is like.

"It's amazing," Sam finally managed to whisper loudly enough for us to hear.

Tony was beaming proudly.

The Fleischman Brothers are known throughout the world for the stuffed animal creations they've been designing for decades. They really are works of art. All the prototypes are made by hand, then sent to their factory in Minnesota for mass production before being shipped all over the world. The small Burbank warehouse is where it all starts.

"Jacob, don't be rude!" Tony yelled—quite loudly—into the back workroom. "We have guests!"

"In a minute!" Jacob yelled back.

Don't think the yelling was simply because they were calling to each other across a large room. Or the fact that they are older men and hard of hearing. The Fleischman Brothers can hear just fine, they just like to yell at each other. I guess that comes from being in business together since World War II.

"I swear, Jacob is going to be the death of me with his horrible manners," Tony said—loudly—to me. Then he yelled back, "At least say hi to Bryan and his young lady friend."

"Hi, Bryan and his young lady friend," Jacob echoed back.

"Hi, Mr. Miller!" I called back, trying not to laugh.

"Hi!" Sam yelled. She looked at me with the same confused face she had earlier. "Um . . . who's Mr. Fleischman?"

Tony and I shared a laugh. I would have explained it to Sam earlier, but the Fleischman Brothers do so love telling their story.

"We're both Mr. Fleischmans," Tony said. "Except we're not."

"Okaaay," Sam said, clearly clueless.

"Mr. Fleischman is our father-in-law," he explained.

"*Was* our father-in-law," Jacob corrected as he came out of the workroom. "And he was no father-in-law of mine."

"He was too," Tony said before turning to Sam with a conspiratorially loud whisper. "Jacob's mad because Papa Fleischman liked me best."

"That old man didn't like nobody," Jacob said. "'Specially not the two men who dared to marry his little angels."

"That's kind of true," Tony admitted.

I had met both their wives a few years back. They are just as loud as their husbands. I can only imagine what their father was like.

Much as the faux Fleischman Brothers were enjoying their routine, it *had* been a long drive to the showroom and I was getting hungry. I tried to hurry things along. "Mr. Fleischman Senior started Fleischman's Animal Emporium back in the twenties."

"He was one of the first to mass-produce stuffed animals on an assembly line," Tony said with pride.

"And the first to price-gouge on kiddie toys," Jacob added, with considerably less pride.

"He took us on as kids," Tony explained. "That's how we met our wives. When he passed, he left us the business."

"And gave us the business too, if you know what I mean," Jacob said. "Man couldn't manage a budget to save his life. We brought this company out of near bankruptcy, stabilized the pricing, and made it the success it is today."

"Mom only buys her dog models from the Fleischman Brothers," I said. Tony and Jacob both beamed. "Which is why I knew they'd be the perfect guys to go to for help with our play."

As we say in L.A.: Flattery can get you free stuff.

"Right this way," Tony said as he led us across the showroom. "Not everybody gets to go up to the stockroom, you know. It's only 'cause we've known you 'bout near all your life now, Bryan."

"I'm honored, Tony," I said, and meant every word. So honored, in fact, that it took me a moment to realize that we were heading to the workroom. I think my feet were the first to notice, because they stopped in their tracks before I reached the doorway. I could feel the blood run out of my face. "We have to go in *there*?" My voice trembled with fear.

"That's the only way to get to the storeroom," Tony said calmly as he passed through the Threshold to Hell.

I grabbed Sam before she could follow. "Whatever you do, *don't* look at the room. Look at your feet. Look at the ceiling. Keep your hand at the level of your eyes. Whatever it takes. Just *don't look*."

Sam laughed. *She laughed!* "Bryan, knock it off."

"I'm serious. Trust me."

"Sure," she said. "Whatever."

I didn't think she was going to listen.

Still laughing, Sam crossed into the workroom. *Oh, the horror.* I took a deep breath and followed, keeping my eyes squarely focused on my shoes the entire time.

I had only been in the Fleischman Brothers' workroom once before. When I was eight. I still have the terrifying images burned into my brain. There is nothing in the world that can prepare a child for the absolute horror of dozens of very real-looking stuffed animals with their innards spilling out onto the tables and floors. The severed limbs and tails and ears scattered about the room are enough to make you lose your lunch. It's worse than any horror movie I've ever seen. Following my last visit, I had nightmares for months. I haven't been able to enter a Build-A-Bear Workshop since.

But that's not the worst of it.

The truly horrific part is the eyes.

Step by step, I made my way through the workroom, looking at nothing but the floor. I could feel the empty beaded eyes of the rows and rows of decapitated animal heads watching me from the shelves.

This would be one of the downsides of having an overactive imagination.

Eventually, we made it through the room and into the small stairwell beyond. Even though the Fleischmans had been the only ones talking while we were in the workroom, I knew that Sam hadn't listened to me about not looking. I prepared myself to be there for my friend when I finally looked up from my shoes to see her face.

Surprisingly, the mask of fright I had expected was not there. I thought it was possible that she had been simply too stunned to react.

"Are you okay?" I gently asked.

"They were stuffed animals," she said with no quiver in her voice whatsoever. "Seriously. Not that scary."

"But . . ."

She put a hand on my shoulder, "Come on, Tarzan."

"This way," Tony said brightly as he took us upstairs.

I shook off my confusion as Tony and Sam led the way, leaving Jacob and me to bring up the rear. In much the same way his brother-in-law spoke in a stage whisper, Jacob asked, "So, is this young lady a *special* friend?"

I could see Sam's back rising and falling in front of me as she held back the laughter.

I echoed what I had told Tony, but stopped short once we reached the stockroom. I was literally struck speechless. The showroom was one thing, but this stockroom was unimaginable.

It ran the length of the entire building, and the ceiling was twice as high as the first floor. Hundreds upon hundreds of shelves rose up from the floor all the way to the roof. They were piled with stuffed animals that must have dated back to Mr. Fleischman's early days. There was row after row after row of everything from tiny toys to larger-than-life-size replicas, including two horses rearing back in front of the doorway as if they were guarding the sanctum.

"Dogs are two rows down." Tony waved to the right. "The stockroom is divided by animal and then by breed. You'll find terriers about three quarters of the way back. Take whatever you want."

"Thank you so much, guys," I said.

Sam and I started toward the dog row, but Jacob grabbed me to hold back for a second.

"Just so you know, the ladies love it with all the stuffed cuties," he said. "The wife and I have had many a romantic interlude up here."

Okay . . . *eww*!

"This is the most adorable thing I've ever seen," Sam said as she grabbed onto a stuffed collie and hugged it like it was a real dog.

Apparently, Jacob knew of what he spoke.

And . . . *ewww* . . . again.

"What do you think of Toto being a collie?" Sam asked. "You know, considering we have four different Dorothys and all. Who would complain?"

"I think it's quite possible that if we come back with anything other than a dog that looks like Toto as Mr. Randall imagines him, we might make our teacher cry."

Sam put the collie back on the shelf. "Good point."

We continued down the row past the dachshunds and dalmatians, the German shepherds and poodles, until we finally reached the terriers.

There were terriers of all sizes and colors. The organizational system was impressive. We found a great selection of black terriers easily at a shelf that was eye level. It was a good thing too. I didn't want to have to climb one of the ladders to get to the top shelf all the way up by the peaked roof of the warehouse.

"This is too perfect," Sam said as she grabbed at the dogs.

"Do I know where to go, or what?"

"You are the doggie master," Sam said.

I wasn't quite sure how to take that.

We grabbed four terriers and made our way back down to the showroom. This time, I forced myself to keep my eyes open and focused ahead of me as we walked through. I figured if Sam could do it, I could too. Honestly, I was still a little freaked by the disembodied heads, but it was not really as horrifying as I remembered. They were only cloth, beads, and stuffing, after all.

Once we got back to the showroom, we saw that Tony was holding a plush white unicorn with a silver horn. He had a huge grin on his face. I mean Tony, not the unicorn.

"For the little lady," Tony said. "To match your necklace."

"Oh no, I couldn't."

"'Course you can," Jacob said. "A little something special for Bryan's special friend."

This is what I don't get about some people. I've told them twice that Sam isn't my "special" friend. But here they are trying to put us together. With cute little stuffed gifts, even. Now, imagine for a moment that I was, in fact, straight. And imagine I had some secret crush on Sam. And further imagine that she had no interest in me at all.

I know that last one is a lot to imagine, but stay with me here.

Don't you think it would be kind of hurtful to keep pushing her on me?

Sam took the toy. "Thank you."

"Now, you two kids get going," Tony said. "The night is young."

I didn't bother to remind them that the night got a little older when you factored in the drive all the way back to Malibu and Santa Monica. Sam and I left, but we hit the food court at the Burbank Town Center Mall before getting back on the freeway. I'm not usually big on fast food, but any meal that doesn't include Eric Whitman is a five-star dining event as far as I'm concerned.

The Front Page

"Did you ever feel like you're really close to figuring something out but there's, like, this wall that's in your way? You know there's an answer on the other side, but you can't get to it at all," Hope asked as the two of us went out to the courtyard.

"Every day," I said as I took a seat on the grass beside her. So far, lunch hadn't been nearly as eventful as the day before. Not one person had come close to dying.

Eric and Drew had joined us once again. Drew's been dating Hope on and off for—well, it seems like *ever*—and this was the first time he'd eaten with us two days in a row. And he probably wouldn't have if Eric hadn't suggested it.

I was concerned that Drew was the wall Hope was talking about. The two of them were cute together, but I just didn't see this as the greatest love of all time or anything like that. There just didn't seem to be a romantic connection, a spark. But I wasn't ready for *that* conversation.

Thankfully the guys didn't follow us out to the courtyard. Sam had to talk to her mom about something, so Eric and Drew went off to work on some project, leaving me and Hope to talk about whatever was bothering her.

"I hate this play," Hope finally said as she pulled out her script.

I tried not to look relieved that she wasn't planning to have a more serious conversation.

"Having trouble finding your character?"

"Glinda's such a smug little priss, don't you think?"

"The script just says she's a good witch," I said. "Doesn't mean she's nice."

"All along, she has the way for Dorothy to get home," Hope ranted. "Who is *she* to withhold that information? The poor girl is worried about her family, but all Glinda cares about is teaching Dorothy a lesson."

"Well, it *is* a dream," I explained. "Glinda could represent Dorothy's conscience. Dorothy knew she was being whiny before the twister and she has to learn to appreciate what she's got."

"And these song lyrics," Hope went on. "There's no such thing as a ding-a-berry! I looked it up!"

Somehow, I don't think Hope was really that upset about the play. Maybe she *had* noticed Drew's sudden interest in eating with us was suspiciously tied to Eric's interest in Sam. Drew isn't always the most sensitive when it comes to other people's feelings. It's not like he's intentionally cruel, just oblivious. Trust me. I know what I'm talking about here.

Hope was waiting for me to say something. "Look . . . I . . ."

Yeah. I had nowhere to go with that. Hope and I don't really do *serious*.

"Sorry," Sam said as she arrived, saving us from a real conversation. "Mom stuff."

"You were gone, like, three seconds," I said, dramatically checking my watch. "I think we can manage without you for that long."

"Shut it," she said with a smile.

"Although some people obviously can't," I added.

Yep. The Abercrombie Zombies, Eric and Drew, were heading our way in their almost matching ensembles of khaki shorts and faded T's. The only difference between the outfits was that Eric's shirt was maroon, while Drew's was this really amazing shade of blue that totally made his eyes pop. I was having a hard time not staring right into them.

Not that I noticed.

"Don't you guys *ever* separate?" I asked as they plopped down a few feet away from us and opened up Eric's laptop.

"Don't you?" Drew asked, looking over at Sam, Hope, and me.

"Point taken," I ceded.

"Didn't you want to go over lines?" Sam asked Hope in an obvious attempt to break the mounting dramatic tension.

Hope held up her script. "Please."

We quickly ran through the end of the play a couple times so Hope could try some different things with line reads and such. I shared Hope's script, but Sam waved us off. That whole being off book thing was starting to get annoying.

(*Aside:* As the name indicates, "off book" means when an actor no longer needs to read from a script.)

We were doing fairly well at first, but Hope's line reads got more and more intense the further along we read. It was clear that Hope hadn't quite found her character yet. She had a real problem committing to the sugary sweet character made famous in the movie. When she finally yelled, "Yes! And Toto, too, you spoiled, selfish, whiny little baby!" we figured it was time to take a break.

"Isn't that the end of the play?" Eric asked as soon as we stopped.

"Yes," Sam replied.

"But, aren't you just in the first act?"

"Yes."

"You memorized the whole play?"

Sam blushed.

"Wow."

What*ever*.

"I like to work with the whole script," Sam explained. "Get down my character's motivation."

"It's *The Wizard of Oz*," I reminded her. "Dorothy's motivation is to get home."

"You know what I mean," she said, without even looking back at me.

Sam takes acting very seriously. Just because it was a high school show with four girls sharing the same part didn't mean she wasn't going to work it like it was Broadway. I've always thought that was impressive, with maybe a little side of obsessive.

"I apologize, dear thespian," I said with my best British accent. "And I tip my fedora to you." And I did just that.

"Is there some reason you can't just call it a hat?" Drew asked.

"Peasant." I shot him my most withering glare, the one I save for people who are seriously beneath contempt.

"What's wrong with your face?" he asked. "Don't tell me you're having an allergic reaction, too."

I could feel my teeth clenching. Drew is well aware that it was my grandpop's fedora, and how much it means to me. We do not make fun of the fedora.

"Anybody hear how Suze's doing?" Sam quickly asked before I exploded.

Eric and Drew took the question as an invitation to slide over and merge our two groups. They were still working on the computer, but their focus wasn't really on their work. It was on Sam and Hope.

Once again I got the feeling that I had disappeared.

While they talked about Suze's health and well-being, I checked out what was going on in the courtyard. There was a sudden flurry of activity as people ran from group to group talking animatedly about something. I noticed more than a few laptops seemed to be the focal point.

"Suze's home from the hospital," Hope said. "I'm bringing my dress over to her this afternoon so she can get a feel for what she wants to do with it."

"That's okay?" Sam asked. "After yesterday?"

"She's already bored out of her mind," Hope said. "She's dying for something to do. Sorry. Bad choice of words."

"But she's not allowed to come back to school?" Sam asked.

Hope simply shrugged. That was typical of Suze's mom. The woman is a smidge overprotective.

I wasn't really paying attention to the conversation. All that movement and mumbling had suddenly stopped. The place had gotten very, very quiet.

I scanned the courtyard more closely. Now, everyone was huddled in groups around their laptops. I doubted that they were looking at breaking world news.

"Oh. My. God," Drew said.

Both he and Eric were staring at the screen of the iBook with pretty much the same look that everyone else around us had. I guess Sam and Hope also caught up with what was going on, because they looked at me like we were the only ones out of the loop.

Which, I guess, we were.

The three of us quickly slid over so we could see the screen of Eric's laptop. The guys shifted slightly out of the way so we could get a peek. Needless to say, we weren't quite expecting what we saw.

Let me back up for a second.

Every student is loaned a laptop at the beginning of the school year. Our school is a WiFi hotspot, and all the computers are programmed to open up on the school's home page when we go online. Naturally there are "safeguards" in place to catch us if we ever use the school computers to surf for porn.

Apparently, there's nothing in place to stop the porn from coming to us.

Because, looking at the screen, we were all shocked to see a slideshow with naked pictures of Cindy Lakeside on the school's home page.

I'm sorry . . . *Cynthia*.

"Wow," I said in awe.

"Bryan!" Hope and Sam yelled at me, then slammed the laptop closed.

"I can't believe you," Sam said.

Hope smacked me on the shoulder.

"They were staring too," I said, in my own defense. What? Like I wasn't supposed to have a reaction when one of the most beautiful girls in the entire school was splashed naked on a computer screen in front of me?

Okay . . . actually, the "wow" was more in reference to the shots themselves than Cindy's naked body. What little I saw was pretty amazing. The balance of light and shadow was subtle enough to kick Cindy's natural beauty up to stunning. The pictures were clearly taken by a true artist.

My attempt to get Eric and Drew in trouble along with me was all for naught, because, at that very moment, Cindy came strolling out to the courtyard. From the way she was laughing and carrying on with Wren, she had no clue that she was the new online pinup girl.

It only took her a moment to realize that every head in the

courtyard was staring at her. Then looking at their computer screens. Then staring at her again.

And here's why Cindy impresses the hell out of me.

She took it all in.

She came to a conclusion.

She pushed her way into the nearest group to look at what they were ogling.

A brief flicker of shock crossed her face before she went totally emotionless.

Then she stood up tall and strolled out of the courtyard without looking back.

That's when the silence of the past two minutes erupted.

How to Succeed in Business Without Really Trying

"I can't *believe* Mr. Randall thinks the play is cursed," I said as we left the theater.

"I can't *believe* he canceled rehearsal," Hope said as we fell in step on the way to her locker. The play opens—"

"And closes—"

"On Saturday."

"But he needs to work with the Dorothys," I reiterated his reasoning. "I'm sorry. But *I* still haven't gotten the new choreography for the jitterbug."

"And *I* still don't know how he wants me to make my entrance in act two!" Hope said as we reached her locker. "This is ridiculous!" She punctuated her statement by slamming her fist into her locker.

We spent a moment glaring at each other.

"Feel better?" I asked.

"Yeah," she said. "You?"

"Much."

No one had seen Cindy since lunch. Various reports had her storming off campus in tears or throwing a fit in front of Headmaster Collins. Personally, I couldn't see Cindy doing either of those things. The rumor I *did* believe was that she was so mortified by the nude pictures that she wasn't planning on showing herself around here for the rest of the week. At least, that's what Mr. Randall had been told.

The result: a new shift in the Dorothy roles.

"I can't believe Mr. Randall gave Sam all of act one," Hope said.

I shrugged. It made perfect sense to me.

Mr. Randall was busy turning the jitterbug number into this huge dance exhibition for Wren. It was almost like he had given up on the entire play and was focusing on nothing but that dance. He certainly wasn't going to expand Heather's role any. He'd want to keep her total suckage to a minimum to lessen the damage to the play. That left the first act to Sam.

Of course, the other girls in the cast weren't exactly happy with that plan. Especially when Mr. Randall canceled the afternoon's rehearsal to work with the Dorothys. Actually, nobody in the cast liked that part. We were nowhere near ready for Saturday's show, but instead of doing whatever we could to fix that problem, we were all sent home.

Just use the time to go over your lines, he had said.

Hope tried to open her locker, but it was jammed shut.

"Guess it doesn't like to be hit," I said.

She glared at me through the narrowed slits in her eyelids as she reworked the combination.

"I thought the rest of the girls were going to freak when Randall said he wasn't promoting anyone else to a Dorothy," I said.

Hope pulled at her locker again. It opened slightly, but not all the way. "We can't keep changing everyone's roles," she said. "At some point we've got to lock this thing down so we can be ready for tech."

She was right. Our all-day technical rehearsal was two days away and we still hadn't had a single run-through of the entire play from start to finish.

Hope finally yanked her locker open all the way. "Maybe the play *is* cursed."

"You don't really—"

"Stranger things have happened."

"Sure," I said. "Maybe the lamp falling, and Suze accidentally eating a shrimp taco when she's deathly allergic . . . okay . . . *those* could be accidents. But someone went in and put those naked pictures of Cynthia on the school website. That wasn't any curse. That was just cruel."

"True," Hope said.

"Someone did that on purpose," I added, not liking where this line of thought was taking me.

Apparently, it was taking Hope to the same place. "You don't think someone is sabotaging the play."

"*Or* sabotaging the Dorothys," I said, coming to that conclusion on the spot.

"That's ridiculous."

"And having four girls cast in one role *isn't* ridiculous," I said.

"That lamp could have killed someone," Hope said. "I doubt anyone would go that far."

Maybe I *was* being a bit overly dramatic, but it was weird that these things kept happening to the Dorothys.

"What was up with those photos, anyway?" I asked.

I hadn't expected an answer, but Hope had a look on her face that told me she had clearly done some research. I'm not embarrassed to admit that a shiver of excitement ran up my spine over the potential gossip. "What's the tale, nightingale?"

"Well," she said, "according to Wren, Cindy had them done on her eighteenth birthday. I guess she was keeping it a secret and hoping that someday in the future when she got famous, the photos would accidentally come out and cause all sorts of scandal."

"Thus making her even more famous," I added.

"Exactly," she said. "Some guy named Leonard Brock took them."

"That's why they looked so good," I said. Brock is *the* hot new guy on the fashion photography scene. My mom nearly went into hysterics when he agreed to shoot her doggie designs for a spread for *ELLE* on supermodels and their dogs.

It figures that Cindy would only go to the best for a scandal.

"You going to see Suze now?" I asked. "I'm sure she's dying to hear about what happened today."

"Right after I pick up her homework," Hope said. "Anne collected it all for me."

"Mind if I tag along?" I asked.

"I was hoping you'd ask. I could use a lift." Hope had no problem riding in Electra as long as we kept to the back roads of Malibu.

"Glad I can help." I felt for Hope. Especially since I had been in her situation not so long ago. California has this stupid law that for the first six months after getting a driver's license, underage drivers can't drive with their friends in the car unless there's an adult present. They can drive alone fine, but what fun is that?

My six-month probation ended about six weeks ago. Since Hope had been in Paris for the summer over her sixteenth birthday she didn't have a chance to go for her driving test until winter break. She's still got more than a month to go before she can drive with her friends in the car. Since she can only drive by herself, the steps get first dibs on the spare family car. This leaves Hope stuck with bumming rides from people.

Hope slammed her locker shut. She had to do it twice before the lock caught.

"I have to swing by my locker." Which was in the opposite direction. "I'll meet you at Anne's office."

I watched Hope head down the hall for a moment before I turned to go to my locker. She was right about the lamp falling. It was too dangerous for someone to have done it on purpose. Not to mention that Suze's reaction to the shrimp taco could have killed her too. No matter how intense the children of the rich and famous get around here at times, no one would actually commit murder over the school show.

Then again, it's not like people around here actually think anything through. I can imagine any number of my beloved classmates who would drop a lighting instrument on someone entirely unaware that it could do serious damage.

Heather, for instance.

That last thought was running through my head as I went for my locker. It didn't stay too long because as soon as I turned the corner, I saw Cindy at her locker. I was surprised that she was still around.

She probably didn't want anyone bothering her, but I was dying to know about those pictures. "Hey, Cindy."

She tensed up visibly. "Cynthia. Please."

"Sorry," I said. "I've been calling you Cindy since grade school. It's kind of hard to switch it like that."

"I know," she said. "But I'm trying to book modeling gigs. I don't want people thinking I'm a little girl anymore."

I'm guessing the naked photos will help with that.

"How are you?" I asked.

"Saw the pictures, huh?" She let out a forcibly lighthearted laugh. "Who am I kidding? The whole school saw them."

"It's not the end of the world, you know," I said. "Nothing to quit the show over."

"Right. Like I'm going to walk onstage in front of everyone after they saw me like that."

"It's not as bad as you think," I said. "The pictures were actually quite beautiful. The way the light reflected off your skin. It was like you were glowing. And you looked so comfortable . . . so natural. It's honestly some of your best work . . . I mean, you know . . . not that I . . ."

"Thanks," she said, saving me from my embarrassed stumbling. "But I'd rather spend the next few days hiding out at home. Let it all blow over."

Honestly, I couldn't blame her. If naked pictures of me—okay, you know what . . . I'm not even going to let my mind go there.

"How did they get on the site, anyway?" I asked. I figured if someone was sabotaging the Dorothys, Cindy—Cynthia—might have a clue or something.

"Damned if I know," she said. "I was keeping the CD with the shots in my locker so my parents wouldn't find them at home."

"Who knows your combination?"

"Doesn't matter." Cynthia shut her locker, turned the lock, and reopened it without bothering to put in the combination. "It's been like that since I got it."

Not surprising. Half the lockers around school are just as bad.

"Of course, now my folks know all about the photos," she said.

"What did they say?"

"They were cool," she said. "Actually, my dad thought one or two of them might be good to include in my portfolio."

Am I the only one disturbed by that statement?

I chose to lock that concern away in the part of my brain I try not to visit often. Instead, I focused on the positive. "See?

Your folks are fine with it. Everyone around here probably is too. It's hardly any worse than that bathing suit you wore to the end-of-the-year picnic last year."

"I *did* look good in that," Cindy said. "It was La Perla." She had this fond look of recollection on her face that was so perfect, I was pretty sure she had practiced it in a mirror.

"You can't go into hiding," I said. "You're letting the person who put up those pictures win by forcing you out of the show. You are so much better than that."

Cindy looked at me for a moment. Then she gave me a smile that probably would have filled most guys' dreams.

"You are *so* not like normal guys," she said.

I can't tell you how often I get that particular *compliment*. "Thanks."

"No, I mean it," she said, adding insult to the . . . well . . . insult. "I ran into Jax earlier and he was all 'Hey, nice rack.'"

I tried to ignore the fact that she considered Jax a *normal* guy.

"Okay, look"—she checked the hall to make sure we were alone—"if I tell you something, do you promise not to tell anyone?"

I couldn't wait to hear where this was going. I knew Sam and Hope would love whatever it was when I told them. "Sure," I lied.

"I'm not really going into hiding," she said.

"Then—"

"Somehow, a booking agent saw the photos on the web."

Somehow? A booking agent? Saw photos on our school website?

"Victoria's Secret is flying me out to New York tomorrow for their next catalog," she said. She was bouncing up and down on the balls of her feet in excitement. "Did you ever think you'd see me in *Vicky's Secret*!"

I could honestly say that that thought had never crossed my mind. Unlike, I'm sure, many of the *normal* boys at our school.

"I just had to come back for the original CD," she said as she took the disc with what I assume had dozens of naked photos of her on it out of her locker. Oh, the number of guys who would kill to have a few minutes with that disc. "The photographer wanted to match the look."

"But why the act?" I asked. "Why don't you just tell everyone the photos don't bother you in the least?"

"I've already used up more than my share of excused absences for modeling gigs," she said. "If I miss any more school, I'm going to have to make up work over the summer."

Suddenly, the dawn came. "And this way you can use the fact that Headmaster Collins probably feels horrible over pictures showing up on the school website to cut you some slack on the unexcused absences."

"Exactly," she said with a happy little shrug. "Besides, Sam totally deserves to get act one to herself. It's not like she has all that much going for her besides her talent."

It was amazing how Cindy could be both condescendingly thoughtful and totally self-serving at the same time. I immediately stopped worrying about her. Cindy would be perfectly fine. *Cynthia* would see to that.

"Congratulations," I said.

"Thanks," she replied. "And thanks for being so . . . not typical."

I shrugged my shoulders. What else could I do?

"Later, Bryan," she said as she moved down the hall with a spring in her step. Obviously, she had been rehearsing her runway walk.

"Later, Cind-ithia."

Design for Living

"Bryan Stark, you get in here this minute!" Mrs. Finberg said as she pulled me in the front door and gave me a hug that cut off the circulation to the lower part of my body.

"Good to see you, too," I said. Though it came out more like, "Moom mo mee moo moo," considering how my face was smashed into her shoulder at the time.

"Hi, Mrs. Finberg," Hope said, temporarily forgotten in the doorway.

"Hello, Hope." Mrs. Finberg finally released me. "I'm sorry you both came out here, but Suze isn't ready for guests yet."

"I wanted to return this dress she loaned me," Hope said as she held up the outfit that she had bought over the weekend. We had rehearsed this bit in the car, so I waited for my cue.

"Please don't tell me that's another one of her creations," Mrs. Finberg said. I could hear the disdain in her voice. "I swear, that girl has got to learn to make better use—"

"No," Hope jumped in. "It's something she picked up at a consignment shop. It was for a scene we were doing in drama class. She thought it would look better on me."

"Oh! A scene? What play?" Mrs. Finberg asked, ignoring the fact that Hope's body would have a difficult time fitting into any dress her daughter would get for herself. Any talk about Suze doing any kind of acting set her mom's heart aflutter.

Mrs. Finberg could give Mama Rose a run for the money in the stage mom department.

"*The Miracle Worker*," Hope said.

Mrs. Finberg's eyes lit up with excitement. "Come in, come in!" She ushered us into the huge living room and took a seat on the couch. Hope and I remained standing. We didn't want her to think we were staying. At least, not in the living room.

"Suze never tells me about her scene work," Mrs. Finberg said, literally sitting on the edge of her seat. "Which part did she play? No. Don't tell me. She had to be Helen Keller. Such a challenging role. Not that I don't think you could play it, dear. But Suze is much more the ingenue type, don't you think?"

I took that as my cue. Hope would probably have killed Mrs. Finberg if she went any further. "Since we're here," I said, "are you sure Suze can't see anyone? Even for a few minutes?"

"Doctor's orders," Mrs. Finberg replied.

I've known this family long enough to know the "doctor" here was actually Mrs. Finberg. She worries incessantly about her children. Although, considering a tiny insect is a threat to Suze's very life, I guess I can't blame her for being over-protective.

"I understand," I said with a pout. "I was just concerned. You know, I haven't seen her since I gave her that injection. I just wanted to make sure she was okay."

"She's doing wonderfully," Mrs. Finberg said happily, to ease my mind.

"It's just . . . it was so scary," I said, pouring it on even thicker. "Seeing her like that. Are you sure we can't pop in for a minute?"

"Well . . ."

"We'll keep our distance," I quickly added. "And if she starts to look tired, we'll leave immediately."

"I guess I can trust you with her," Mrs. Finberg said. "After all, you did save her life. But only for a few minutes."

Hope and I shared a smile as Mrs. Finberg got off the couch and took us back out to the foyer. I had been to Suze's house many times before. We didn't really need her mother to take us all the way upstairs, but she wasn't about to let us go unannounced . . . or without instructions.

Mrs. Finberg gently tapped on the door to Suze's bedroom. She spoke in a voice that I didn't think would even carry through the thin wood. "Suze, you have some visitors. Can we come in?"

"Yes, Mom," Suze said with a raspy voice. I immediately felt sorry for coming over. Hope hadn't said that Suze sounded so horrible when they had talked on the phone earlier. Even though I was curious about what had happened to her, I didn't want to totally impose.

At least when Mrs. Finberg opened the door Suze didn't

look as bad as she sounded. If anything, she actually looked pretty good for someone who had gone into anaphylactic shock the day before. She was sitting up in bed, but she didn't seem all that comfortable. Her head was kind of tilted back over the pile of pillows. It was like she had stuffed one too many of them behind her back.

Last time I was in Suze's bedroom must have been in the fifth grade, when we were making posters for her run for president of our elementary school. I was her campaign manager. We ran a great campaign, getting funny quotes from all my mom's famous clients to endorse Suze on the posters. Sadly, she lost the election. Holly Mayflower—Heather's sister—bought the vote with gift baskets from Snookie's Cookies.

Suze's bedroom hadn't changed much since then. It was a vision in lavender and lace. Imagine if an issue of *Martha Stewart Living* threw up and you'd only start to have an idea of what the room looked like.

"Hope, you didn't need to return the dress today," Suze squeaked out. She was almost lost in a sea of bedding and frills in her lavender and white canopy bed.

"Well, we both wanted to see you," Hope said. Her voice was oozing with concern.

"I told them they can only stay a few minutes," Suze's mom said from the doorway.

"Thank you," Suze replied with a slight cough. "But could you close the door? There's a draft."

"Sure, darling," Mrs. Finberg said.

As soon as the door shut behind Mrs. Finberg, Suze sat up straight and started pulling at the pillows behind her.

I rushed over to help. "Here, let me."

"That's okay," she said, waving me off. Her voice sounded perfectly normal. The raspy tone was gone.

Suze pulled a large sketchbook out from under her pillows. She opened it and checked the design I assume she had been working on when her mom knocked on the door. "I didn't have time to get this hidden comfortably," she said.

The sketch was pretty amazing. It was an updated version of Hope's dress. I couldn't believe that Suze had remembered so much detail from the small picture on Hope's cell phone screen, especially considering all that had happened right after Suze looked at it.

"You sure you can't make it back in time for the play?" Hope asked. "We could really use that kind of acting talent in the show. I honestly thought you were on death's door."

"Years of practice," Suze said. "Mom isn't happy unless I'm near terminal."

"But you *are* okay?" I asked.

"Fine," Suze said. "I could go back to school tomorrow, but you know Mom likes to keep an eye on me. It's actually funny this time, because of the show. She was all torn up, trying to decide if my starring role was worth risking my health. Ultimately, the hypochondria won out over the stage mothering. I think it's because I'm splitting the role with three other girls."

"Who knows if that will be true by the end of the week," I said.

The questioning look Suze gave me pretty much confirmed that no one—including Hope—had filled her in on the events of the day. I brought her up to speed, embellishing a few of the facts for dramatic effect. Hope didn't bother to correct me. She knows the healing properties of really good gossip. While I went through the story, Hope was busy taking the dress out of the garment bag and strategically hiding it in Suze's closet.

Since I knew I could trust Suze, I even filled her in on the part Cindy didn't want anyone to know. How could one possibly keep Victoria's Secret a secret? Especially from someone who needed cheering up.

"And I thought Cindy's bathing suit at the summer picnic was revealing," Suze said when I finished the tale.

"Oh, it was," I said, remembering back to the string bikini she had worn to the beach last June. "It was La Perla, don't you know?"

"I do, I do," Suze said, playing along. "Only Cindy would pay so much for so little material."

"Are we still on for shopping Sunday?" Hope asked. "I'd understand if you're not up to it."

"Oh, *I'm* up to it," Suze said. "I'm not sure my mom is. She's going to have to let me go to school on Monday if I'm going to pass finals. Maybe we can go sometime next week."

"Will that give you enough time before the prom?" Hope asked.

"Plenty," Suze replied. "I've already done my dress. Now I just need someone to go with." She looked at me. "I assume you're going with Sam?"

"Nope," I said.

"Oh, I thought . . ."

She wasn't the only one.

There was a soft tapping at the door. This time, Mrs. Finberg didn't bother to announce herself. Suze dropped her sketchbook on the floor and I helped out by pushing it under the bed with my foot.

"Just checking in," Mrs. Finberg said in a singsongy voice that subtly covered up the fact that she wanted us gone.

"A few more minutes, Mom?" Suze pled. "We haven't gone over my homework yet."

And I still hadn't asked what I wanted to know.

"One more minute," Mrs. Finberg said as she closed the door.

"We'll have to keep it quiet," Suze said softly. "She's waiting outside the door."

Seriously. There's overprotective and then there's *overprotective*. I can't imagine living with a parent who hovers like Suze's mom does. I bent down to retrieve the sketchbook from under the bed. It took me a second to find it, considering all that was going on down there.

"It's like this is the place where old sketchbooks go to die," I said as I pulled out the one I was pretty sure she had been working on.

"Yeah," Suze said with a resigned sigh. "I can't keep my sketchbooks out in the open. Mom prefers the performing arts over the visual ones. She keeps telling me how I deserve to be on the red carpet, not designing outfits for it."

Hope and I shook our heads. Having an incredibly talented daughter isn't enough for Mrs. Finberg. Suze has to be incredibly talented in the right way to make her mother happy.

Hope pulled Suze's books out of her bag. "Here's your homework—oops!" She dropped it all on the floor.

I bent to pick them up.

"That's okay," Hope said, pushing past me and nearly knocking me into Suze's nightstand. "Didn't you have something to ask Suze?"

Suze patted the bed for me to sit beside her.

"About the accident," I said as I sat.

"Accident?" Suze asked. "You really think it was an accident? The one person in the entire school who's allergic to shellfish just happened to get the one taco filled with shrimp?"

My thoughts exactly!

"So you think it was on purpose?" I asked.

"Don't you?" Suze said. "Isn't that why you're here?"

"Well, I'm here to make sure you're okay," I said quickly. "But yeah, that too. Any idea who had it in for you?"

"Half the cast," Suze said.

"Yeah, but none of them would want you dead," Hope said from the floor. She was taking an awful long time to pick up two schoolbooks and a few papers.

"Who said they thought I'd die?" Suze asked. "Everyone knows I carry the EpiPen. Besides, they probably figured the taco would make me break out in a huge rash like when that peanut M&M got mixed in with the regular ones at Mr. Whitman's Christmas party."

I had forgotten about that happening. The rash popped up within moments of her eating the peanut M&M. She had been in a green dress at the time. We all—including Suze—had joked at how the red rash was a perfect match for her Christmas dress. Suze's allergic reactions weren't always life threatening.

"Who could have switched out the tacos?" I asked. "Was anyone suspicious around your food?"

"Could've been," Suze said. "I was sitting with you guys for a while. And we were all distracted when Jax spilled that soda all over Sam."

"That's right!" I said. It was more than a simple coincidence that Heather's boyfriend had caused a commotion around the time that someone might have been replacing Suze's taco. Something was fishy, and it was Heather Mayflower who smelled like the mahimahi.

"All right," Mrs. Finberg said as she burst into the room. "Time to go. Suze needs her rest."

Hope quickly popped up from the floor and handed over the books. She was holding her garment bag closely to her chest.

"Thanks for coming by," Suze said as Mrs. Finberg quickly ushered us out of the bedroom.

Hope and I hurried downstairs, keeping ahead of Mrs. Finberg every step of the way. We quickly bypassed the living room, hoping Suze's mom wouldn't ask us to stay and talk more about Suze's fictional scene work. We managed to escape the house without further discussion.

"Crazy about that taco," I said to Hope as we walked to Electra. "Someone obviously must have planted it."

"It is a mystery, all right," Hope said as she opened the passenger side door.

"You know what's another mystery?" I asked as I got in the car.

"What?"

"Why you stole one of Suze's sketchbooks up there and hid it in your garment bag."

Hope looked at me with mock surprise. The look of glee on her face told me that she knew she'd been caught and she didn't care. "Yes," she said. "That is a mystery too."

Doubt

"Okay, Jimmy," Mr. Randall called offstage. "Let's see if this works."

"Just a second, Mr. Randall," Jimmy yelled back.

Poor Tasha looked nervous enough standing in the oversize basket. It was torture to make her wait any longer. I bet she never suspected that when she had been cast as the Wizard her life would ultimately be in the hands of Jimmy Wilkey.

"How you doing, Tasha?" I asked from my spot beside the basket. She forced a smile, but I could tell she was worried. I knew how she felt. If the contraption that Jimmy had rigged didn't work, that basket could fall off the platform and land on top of me.

After spending half the weekend checking out the light grid to make sure that none of the other clamps were rusted through, Jimmy and Mr. Randall had also re-rigged the fly system. They added a series of pulleys that could accommodate the basket of the "balloon" that would take the Wizard away from Oz. It was going to be the showstopping effect of the production. We expected it would even get its own applause.

If it could get up off the ground.

The Jordan Myers Fly System had been donated years ago to help lift set walls up above the stage for faster scene changes. We had never used it to lift anything with a person on it before. Thankfully, Jimmy's father asked one of the crew guys from the movie he was producing to help out with the rigging. There's no way the school would have let a student in the basket if Jimmy and Mr. Randall had been the only ones to work out the logistics.

The basket had already worked while it was empty. It had worked when we added books to simulate dead weight. But this was the first test with an actual person inside.

"Here we go," Jimmy said.

Tasha reached for the rim as the basket gave a little lurch. She was trying to look calm, but from where I stood I could tell she was shaking.

The basket lurched again, and then it started to rise straight up into the air. Slowly, it inched its way up off the platform. The movement was jerky at first, but the ride eventually smoothed out.

Tasha threw out her arms and looked out to the auditorium. "Second star to the right," she shouted, "and straight on till morning!"

It's not every day you see a girl with multiple piercings quoting Peter Pan while rising above a stage in an oversize wicker basket.

I *so* wish I had my camera at that moment.

To continue with the *Pan* homage for a moment: *She was flying. Flying!*

Tasha went right up into the rafters. She even stopped before she collided with the ceiling. Everyone in Hall Hall gave a cheer that was equal parts excitement and relief. It was the first thing that had gone right all week. Not bad considering it was still only Wednesday afternoon. Maybe we could get this show off the ground before Saturday.

"Good job, Jimmy," Mr. Randall yelled to the backstage area. "Bring her down!"

"Just a second!" Jimmy yelled back.

"Bryan," Mr. Randall said. "Can you go get Hope so we can run through the scene?"

"Sure," I said. I hopped off the stage and onto the house floor. I couldn't help but feel a twinge of optimism. Things were starting to look up. Literally.

Wednesday also marked the first day that nothing scandalous or life threatening had happened at lunch. Granted, Sam, Hope, and I had eaten with Anne in her classroom. Sam would have preferred to spend that time with Eric, but once I told her about my suspicions of Heather, she knew that being with her mom was the safer way to go. The pavilion and courtyard area had become a dangerous place for Dorothys this week.

With our three remaining Dorothys, we had split the afternoon rehearsal into three groups to maximize our time. Mr. Randall ran the technical blocking onstage, while Ms. Monroe handled musical numbers in the back of the auditorium and a third group worked on their own out in the lobby. From what I could tell, everything was starting to click.

"No, Heather," Ms. Monroe said in exasperation. "You can't bump fists with the Tin Woman. It's not correct for the time period."

I said, *starting* to click. I did not say *perfect*.

"What's wrong with updating this play a little?" Heather asked. "My dad has made a bundle updating old music with new talent. You could learn a thing or two from his business model."

"Even so—"

"Why don't we see what Mr. Randall says?" Heather didn't even wait for a reaction. She just stormed up the aisle.

Ms. Monroe looked at me as if I could do anything to help her with Heather.

I just shrugged. "I'm looking for Hope," I said.

"Outside," she said. I could tell Ms. Monroe wished she were outside as well.

I left the theater and went out to the foyer, where Hope and Sam were standing amid a group of ninth-grade munchkins.

"Hope, Mr. Randall needs to see you onstage," I said.

"But I'm working on my first entrance," Hope said.

"And he's working on your last entrance," I said. "Go figure."

Since flying the Wizard out had worked so well, Mr. Randall wanted to try flying Glinda in. Personally, I think he was being rather ambitious, but I didn't want to say anything about it. The poor guy had enough on his plate with this show. If he wanted to string up a few students, who was I to get in the way?

If only he had taken suggestions on which students to string up.

"You'd better go before someone offers to take your part," Sam said.

"Someone already has," I said. "Actually, three someones, so we should get back before we're both recast."

"Pretty soon we're going to run out of students," Sam joked.

No one laughed. Not even the munchkins.

Hope gave a dainty curtsy to Sam, which I assume meant she was still working on finding Glinda's character. Then she took my arm and went for the door.

"Bryan, wait a second," Sam said.

Hope and I both stopped. I suggested that she should go join the rehearsal. Mr. Randall could do without me for a minute. It's not like he was really in a position to start recasting the male roles now.

"What's up?" I asked.

Sam pulled me away from the group to stand over by the waterfall.

"I can't do a thing with the munchkins," she said in a whisper. The sound of the rushing water was a good cover for what she was saying.

"There's a sentence you don't hear every day," I said. "What's the sitch? Boozing and womanizing? I hear that was the problem with the original munchkins too."

"More like laziness and apathy," Sam said. "It's like they don't care."

"I guess I can't really blame them," I said. "Imagine you grow up around here with everyone talking about how great the Orion spring show is, then you finally get here and you're cast in this farce."

"Good point."

"Promise them that next year will be better. Then threaten them that Mr. Randall will remember how they all acted here when he casts next year's show."

"A little sugar and spice," Sam said. "I like it. How are things going in there?"

"Not horrible," I said. "Well, except for Heather."

"She hasn't tried anything?" Sam asked.

"Not yet," I said as I saw a very determined-looking Headmaster Collins storming our way. "But this looks promising."

The headmaster continued past us, heading into the auditorium. Anne was right behind him in full-teacher mode. She gave us this look that kind of said "Stay out of this," which made us so curious that we simply *had* to follow.

We weren't the only ones.

The munchkins were right on our heels.

Within moments, Headmaster Collins was leading a parade of our cast down the center aisle.

"Mr. Randall, I'm sorry, but I need to interrupt your rehearsal for a moment," Headmaster Collins said.

Mr. Randall looked out at the gaggle of students behind the headmaster and Sam's mom. He shook his head with resignation. "Headmaster Collins, I believe you already have."

"Be that as it may . . . Ms. Mayflower, may I speak with you for a moment?"

Heather looked around like he had been talking to someone else.

He wasn't.

"What is it?" she asked.

"Can you come down here?" Headmaster Collins said from the floor.

Heather did as she was asked and walked down to what would be the orchestra pit, if we had an orchestra.

"Can we take a look in your purse?" the headmaster asked.

Heather looked at Sam's mom, then back at the headmaster. "No."

"Ms. Mayflower," Headmaster Collins said with a measured calmness that I assume meant he knew Heather's father was out of the country at the moment.

Maybe he was meeting with my dad.

The headmaster continued: "We need to see the contents of your purse."

At this point, Anne noticed that pretty much the entire cast was leaning in to watch what was going on. "I think we should take this to your office, Headmaster Collins," she said quietly.

"This is ridiculous," Heather said, getting all dramatic for no apparent reason. She moved to the third row and grabbed her bag. "The play opens in three days. I don't have time for this." She handed her bag to the headmaster.

"Here. Don't blame me if you have to dig through feminine hygiene products."

Headmaster Collins's face went bright red. He held the purse out to Sam's mom. She didn't take it. "I'm uncomfortable going through a student's personal possessions," she said. I didn't blame her. She knows a potential lawsuit when she sees one. With Suze and the shrimp taco, that could be two lawsuits in one week.

That doesn't come close to the record around here, though.

"Fine." Heather grabbed the bag and walked over to the stage.

She began pulling out the contents. I couldn't quite make out everything that she was holding, but it was clear when she got to the bottom of the bag that there was something there that surprised her. She quickly closed the bag.

The headmaster held out his hand. "Ms. Mayflower."

She handed over the bag. "I don't know how that got in there."

Headmaster Collins opened the bag and pulled out a CD. He showed the CD to Anne, who nodded her head.

"Ms. Mayflower, we now need to go to the office," the headmaster said. "Mr. Randall, I think you should come along as well."

"Headmaster, we really do need to be rehearsing for the show right now," Mr. Randall said.

"This won't take long," Headmaster Collins said. "And the show is involved as well."

It was clear that Mr. Randall did not like the sound of that. "Let's hold off on flying Hope for the moment."

"How 'bout we cancel that idea altogether?" Hope asked. Did I mention she has a thing about heights?

Mr. Randall ignored her and kept giving out instructions. "Ms. Monroe, please continue with your group. Sam, take your people back out to the lobby and work the opening. And . . . Bryan, can you go over the ending onstage for me?"

"Sure," I said.

Like there was a chance any of us were going to be doing any work while he was gone.

Once the doors to the theater shut behind Headmaster Collins, Anne, Mr. Randall, and Heather, the cast broke out in numerous conversations at once. Poor Ms. Monroe didn't even have a chance at maintaining control. Eventually she gave in and gossiped along with the rest of us.

The cast spent the next fifteen minutes trying to figure out what that had been all about. Most people thought Headmaster Collins had pulled out a copy of the CD containing the nude photos of Cynthia. But that didn't explain why Sam's mom was involved.

The conspiracy theorists in the group suggested that it could be a CD containing a secret school budget that Headmaster Collins didn't want anyone to see for legal reasons. Most of us ignored them. They're the same ones who insist FOX rigs the voting on *American Idol* to provide them with the most marketable stars.

There were several other theories floating around the room, but none of them sounded plausible to me. Sam was the only one not offering a suggestion. I think she was thinking about how Heather's departure could affect her. If Heather was out of the play, then we definitely had a chance to salvage the show. But that would only leave two Dorothys, and with three days before curtain, anything could happen.

Once Mr. Randall got back, we heard the full story.

"Heather is no longer in the play," he confirmed our suspicions without bothering to brace us for the news.

Hope was the first to regain her voice. "People come and go so quickly here."

Nervous laughter filled the auditorium.

"She was found in possession of Ms. Lawson's final exam," he continued.

"She took the test?" Jason asked.

"Heather claims that she is innocent," Mr. Randall said. "She said someone planted it there."

"Was she expelled?" a munchkin asked.

"No," Mr. Randall said in his most official, "Don't gossip with me" tone. "Since the headmaster could not immediately disprove her claim, he could not take such drastic action."

"But he could kick her out of the play," Sam said.

"Extracurricular activities are discretionary," Mr. Randall said. "Now, that's all we're going to say on the subject. We have a lot of work to do. Sam, you're still going to be Dorothy for act one. Wren, you've now got the entire second act."

At that announcement, several girls converged on Mr. Randall to repeat what they had been putting him through since Monday. Like there was really time to keep shifting roles in the next two days.

"So much for your theory on Heather being behind Suze and Cindy getting kicked out of the play," Hope said.

"I haven't changed my mind," I said.

"But she's not in the play anymore either," Sam said, not sounding all that disappointed.

"This is *Heather*," I reminded them. "The girl who, in one phone call, got Lady Gaga, John Mayer, and Shakira to perform at the fall dance for free." And the call wasn't even to her dad. "She's up to something."

Neither Sam nor Hope said anything. I wasn't sure if they agreed with me or thought I was crazy. But I had known Heather long enough not to underestimate the girl. She was behind all this. I just couldn't figure out this latest stunt.

But, more importantly, I was worried. There were only two Dorothys left. One of them was my best friend. So far we had gone through near death, total embarrassment, and possible expulsion. This was serious whether or not Heather was behind it.

Oh, but Heather was behind it.

Of that, I had no doubt.

Just because she was caught up in her little plan didn't mean she wasn't the one pulling the strings. Heather's pretty good at this manipulation thing. She's had a lot of practice. I didn't count her out yet.

Now, gentle reader, before you go thinking I'm all paranoid and suspicious for no reason, let me make one thing very clear: As far as I'm concerned, there's no mystery in this mystery. There isn't going to be one of those meaningful life lessons with a heavy-handed moral on making assumptions about people. This is the real world . . . or as real as it can get in Malibu. Things are pretty much the way they look around here.

Simply put: Heather is evil.

And I'm going to prove it.

The Rivals

Since the rehearsal had already run longer than usual, Mr. Randall dismissed everyone but the two remaining Dorothys. I guess he wanted Sam to work with Wren since she was now performing all of act two. He also asked Hope to stick around to see if they could try to work out the rigging on her, bringing new meaning to the phrase, "High Hopes."

This meant that I was free to go. But since I had nothing better to do, I was planning on sticking around to watch . . . until Sam came up to me with a look in her eyes that clearly spelled trouble with a capital T, and that rhymes with E, and that stands for . . . you can see where this is going.

"Can you *please* do me a favor and tell Eric I can't make our date?" Sam asked. They were supposed to go out to dinner together. On a school night, no less. Has that boy learned anything about asking a girl out yet?

"He'll figure it out eventually," I said. "You know. When you don't show up and all."

"Bryan!"

"You do realize this is the second time in one week that I've had to walk all the way over to the soccer field because of you," I said.

Sam pushed out her bottom lip in a pout. She wasn't playing the girl card, she was making fun of me. "Poor baby. Besides, they'll be back in the locker room by now. No need to risk fresh air and exercise."

"In that case," I said, then turned and walked away.

"Thank you!" she called after me.

I waved back at her over my shoulder, successfully managing not to storm off like a spoiled four-year-old. This is the problem with not having cell phones at school. When Mr. Randall decided to call that extended rehearsal, Sam had no artificial means to blow off Eric.

She needed me to do it for her.

Normally, I'd have no problem with telling Eric that Sam had to bail on him. Heck, it could probably even be fun. But there was nothing enjoyable about doing it in front of the soccer team.

First of all, there was the locker room. I've never felt particularly welcome in the locker room. Not for the reason you think, either. I'm not afraid of the locker rooms or anything. It's kind of like the school dressing room. I'm sure the soccer guys wouldn't feel comfortable in the dressing room either.

Like I said earlier, we don't have defined cliques. There's a lot of overlap. The jocks are brains and all that. But there are two groups that simply don't mesh: the soccer team and the Drama Geeks. Or, I should say, the soccer team and the *male* Drama Geeks. More and more of the girls in drama seem to be dating soccer players these days.

It's not that the personalities don't click. It's not that one group of guys thinks it's better than the other. It's just that the spring show rehearses all during soccer season. Girls can play volleyball or swim in the fall and winter. Guys can swim too, if they want. But the only things that really overlap are soccer and the spring show. That means the choice is one or the other for guys. You're either in the show or on the soccer team.

That's why I was standing outside the locker room waiting for my best friend's new boyfriend instead of going in and finding him. Well, maybe it was because of that other reason a bit too. I never quite know where to look when I'm in a locker room. All those guys in various states of undress. At the same time, I don't want to look like I'm not looking. But then I don't want to overcompensate by looking too much so it doesn't look like I'm not trying to look when all I want to do is *really* look.

You know what I mean?

Thankfully, I didn't have to wait long out in the hall. Jax was the first guy to come out of the locker room. "Yo, Stark. What are you doing hanging around the locker room?"

So many answers came to mind at that moment. Obviously, I couldn't use the actual reason. Saying "I'm here to break a date for Sam" probably wouldn't go over too well. Didn't want to go messing up my street cred by looking like anybody's errand boy.

What? Stop laughing.

Lacking a better plan, I simply changed the subject.

"Uh . . . Jax, have you heard about Heather?"

"What happened now?" he asked with an exasperated sigh that wasn't nearly as impressive as his girlfriend's abilities in that area.

I quickly filled him in on the latest news. Even though I didn't have much to say, I'm pretty sure it was the longest conversation that he and I had had ever had. By the time I reached the end of the tale, Jax looked even more shocked than Heather had.

"How did that test get in her bag?" he asked.

"Beats me."

"The headmaster doesn't really think she'd cheat, does he?"

"I don't know."

"Is she still here?"

This time, I just shrugged. "I honestly don't know anything more than what I told you."

I guess he found my lack of information annoying, because he bolted down the hall without another word. I assume he was going to the headmaster's office. I couldn't begin to imagine what he was going to do once he got there.

Slowly the rest of the team filed out in dribs and drabs. Most of the guys said, "Hey, Stark," and kept walking.

No one snubbed me.

No one stopped to hang out with me either.

Finally, Eric came out, along with Drew.

"See," he said to Drew, "you can't hold back on the field. You see a guy coming at you, don't flinch, don't slow down. Just keep barreling. . . ." He trailed off when he saw me waiting.

"Are you in the wrong place?" Drew asked.

"Undoubtedly," I said, then turned my attention to Eric. "Sam has to cancel on your date tonight."

Eric quickly covered up a look of what could have been disappointment. Even more quickly, he adopted what could have been described as a macho posturing attitude. "And she couldn't tell me herself?"

After a quick roll of the eyes, I filled him in on the latest school gossip and how it affected Sam and, by default, him.

"Can't she go out after?" he asked.

"Not on a school night," I said, sounding exactly like I knew Anne would.

"Can you ask her?"

"Do I *look* like a messenger service?"

"Actually, yes," Drew chimed in unnecessarily.

"Was I *asking* you?"

"Nope," he said. "Just saying."

"Dude," Eric said to me. "What's your problem?"

"I don't have a problem," I lied.

"Do you like Sam?" Eric asked. "'Cause if you do, you need to take it up with her."

What an idiot. "I am *not* interested in Sam," I said with complete and total honesty. "Why would you even think something like that?"

"Because you've been on my case since I asked her out."

I wasn't quite sure how to answer that. Other than Sam and Hope, people don't often call me on things.

Luckily, Drew came to my rescue.

"Dude," he said to Eric. (Again with the "dude.") "That's not true. Bryan's been on your case since long before you ever went for Sam."

My hero.

Not.

"You're right," Eric said. "Why is that? Jealous of my good looks and natural athletic ability?"

Again, my eyes did a roll. Like he didn't know why I couldn't stand him. But we weren't here for that conversation. "That must be it," I said. "Now, if you'll excuse me, I've got to get back to rehearsal."

"Hey," Eric said as I started to walk off.

"What?"

"Seriously. Can you ask her to call me when she gets home?"

"Fine," I said as I continued walking.

I didn't really have to get back to rehearsal. All I was going to do was sit around. I could have gone home, but all I'd do is sit around there, too. At least at the rehearsal I'd be able to keep an eye on Sam in case any other mishaps happened.

When I got back in the theater, Hope was yelling at Jimmy because the rigging had ripped her shirt. At this point there wasn't a doubt in my mind that Mr. Randall's dream about having Glinda the Good Witch float in and out of the play was not going to come to pass.

While Hope abused our poor, defenseless stage manager, I pulled Sam aside to pass along Eric's message. I briefly toyed with forgetting to tell her that he had asked her to call later, but I figured that was pointless. She'd eventually find out about it.

Then she'd be all "Why didn't you tell me?" and stuff.

Then I'd have to defend myself.

Then we'd get into a fight.

No . . . if I was going to sabotage this thing between her and Eric, I'd have to be much sneakier about it than that.

But first, we had to get through the play. I wasn't about to try anything with Sam's life—or at least her role—potentially in danger. There were only two more rehearsals to get through before we were in the clear.

The scary part was that one of those rehearsals—tomorrow's, in fact—was our all-day tech rehearsal. That meant a whole school day fraught with potential danger for the remaining Dorothys.

And I still wasn't entirely off book yet.

The Taming of the Shrew

What can I say about the All-Day Rehearsal?

You know how everyone says that the band continued to play as the *Titanic* sank? Well, the all-day rehearsal was kind of like that. First the "wind machine"—which was nothing more than a couple fans we "borrowed" from the computer lab—couldn't even create enough wind to blow a piece of paper across the stage. Then, Jason got stuck on the Scarecrow's post and couldn't get down. But the highlight had to be when Gary McNulty got a little too *into* his part as the lead flying monkey and took a header off the stage. He was okay, but we had to stop the rehearsal while the nurse checked him out and gave him a couple faculty-approved aspirin.

But, through it all, the band sounded great! That wasn't much of a surprise, since we only used prerecorded music for the show. At least the music was clear as it came out of Mr. Randall's iPod and was piped through the auditorium's sound system.

The rehearsal ran to the end of the school day. We all wanted to stay longer, but Mr. Randall had said that we'd done enough. Actually, he said that he'd *had* enough, but . . . same thing.

Tired and dejected, we all took seats so Mr. Randall could go over notes with us and tell us everything we did wrong. That took about a half hour. The past few days of rehearsals had been so focused on the Dorothy drama that we'd hardly been able to work on the rest of the play. So, *everyone* got notes.

The munchkins were stepping all over one another's lines.

The Tin Woodspeople were having makeup issues.

And *everyone* needed to find the light at one time or another.

It went on for a while. We got notes as groups and as individuals. Hope was still having problems settling on her motivations for Glinda. I dropped a few lines that were kind of important to the plot. Sam got surprisingly few notes considering that most of her part was new. In fact, she got the least notes of anyone in the show.

The same could not be said about Dorothy #2. Nobody could really blame Wren. She'd only had the part for three days. I'm sure Mr. Randall was considering giving the entire role to Sam, but there was no way in the world—or at least in the world of Orion Academy—that he could do that and still keep his job.

Once the notes were done, I guess Mr. Randall figured it was time for the old inspirational speech to the saddest group of actors I'd ever seen. You know the speech: the old, "You want fame? Well, fame costs." That kind of thing.

I don't know if it was intentional or if Jimmy was just

working on the sound system, but throughout Mr. Randall's monologue the prerecorded "band" was playing "The Merry Old Land of Oz."

Ironic, no?

"Listen, guys," Mr. Randall said, gearing up for his load of inspiration. "I know this week has been tough. I know you've all put in a tremendous amount of work on a show that—let's be honest—none of us wanted to do in the first place." Not quite the Saint Crispin's Day speech from Shakespeare's *Henry V* (*Aside:* Act IV, Scene iii), but the guy did have a rough day. "And I know that you're all scared about the show opening in two days." The music began to crescendo. "I'm scared too. But in the history of theater there have been more daunting obstacles to overcome. Think of the time when plays were outlawed and actors could be arrested for doing nothing more than setting foot on a stage." He was shouting over the music. "Dare I say it, but the show must go on!"

At this point the music was blaring so loudly that half of us were covering our ears.

"Jimmy!" Mr. Randall shouted. "Can you *please* turn that down?"

"I'm sorry, Mr. Randall," Jimmy yelled from the soundboard at the back of the auditorium. "But something's wrong with the sound system. I'm dancing as fast as I can."

At least, that's what it sounded like he said. Upon further reflection it was probably, "I'm doing the best that I can." Then again, with Jimmy, you never really can tell. Besides, the music was so loud that no one could hear him, anyway.

"Everyone go home," Mr. Randall finally said as the band played on.

Most of the cast took their cue and fled the theater as the music blared. I could tell that it was really getting to Sam, because she was out of there without so much as a "good-bye." Which is kind of rude, if you ask me.

"Need a ride home?" I yelled at Hope as she gathered her things. Those things included a flat cardboard box about the size of the sketchbook that Hope had taken from Suze's room the other day. I would have asked her what she was doing with it, but I was pretty sure she wouldn't tell me, so why bother?

"That's okay," she said. "I'm getting a ride with the steps. They're helping me out with . . . an errand."

"What's that costing you?"

"My dignity," she replied before bolting out of the auditorium.

She wasn't kidding. Since Alexis and Belinda were the primary car drivers—and the car was purchased during Hope's time abroad—the double-mental twins got to decide what car to buy. Their choice? A pink and purple Mini Cooper. A *customized* pink and purple Mini Cooper with a silver diamond etched on the roof, sparkly pink spinners on the wheels, and purple fur covered seats.

In some ways the car sounds like it could be really cool. Trust me. It's not.

Within moments, the only people left in the theater were Jimmy, Mr. Randall, Wren, and me. Wren was trying to talk to Mr. Randall, but it was clear that they were having trouble hearing each other over the blasting music. Finally, Mr. Randall left the auditorium, after motioning wildly for Wren to have a seat and wait for him. Me? I should have left when I had the chance.

As I gathered my books, I felt a tap on my shoulder. When I turned, Jimmy was behind me. "A little help?" he yelled over the still blaring music.

"Why don't you unplug the iPod?" I asked back.

He yelled something about still needing to fix the sound system. I'm not entirely sure what he said because he did ramble on about it for a while. It was pretty hard to hear, even if I *had* been trying to listen.

"What do you need?" I finally asked.

After a few false starts, Jimmy finally managed to indicate that he wanted me to stand onstage while he played with the sound system. If he ever managed to get the sound back to something approaching normal in the auditorium, I could tell him how it sounded onstage. That way, he wouldn't have to run all over the theater to check the sound levels. Having nothing better to do for the second day in a row, I agreed and took a spot onstage.

Jimmy managed to get the music down a couple notches on the stage speakers. I tried to tell him that, but he wasn't looking up from the soundboard. After about a minute of waving wildly at him, I gave up. Wren was starting to look at me funny. You'd think she'd get out of her seat and go tell him. Ultimately it didn't matter because the sound went right back up to deafening.

While we worked I saw the red light on the cordless stage

phone light up. Mr. Randall had left it with his stuff in the front row. The phone usually stays in its base backstage, constantly in silent mode in case anyone needs to call during a performance. The blinking light grabbed Wren's attention as well. Since she was the closest, she got up to answer it. As one would expect, the conversation must have been difficult. Eventually, she hung up and left the auditorium, leaving me alone to contemplate my inner munchkin.

After about five more minutes of an endless loop of "The Merry Old Land of Oz" I was starting to get rather bored. I looked over at the side of the stage and saw the Wicked Witch of the East's backup legs propped up against Dorothy's house. Jimmy being Jimmy, he had an extra pair of mannequin legs ready to be placed under the house in case something happened to the original pair. Between multiple legs, multiple Totos, and multiple cast members, it was beginning to look like we were performing our play on Noah's Ark. Then again, considering how some people thought the play was cursed, I wouldn't have been surprised if a flash flood had come bursting through the theater at any moment.

Since I was effectively alone, I decided to have some fun. I pulled the legs out onstage with me and danced them around to the music. We started out with a little tap and then moved into a few ballet moves for variety and then hit up a kick line. I was really starting to get into it too, when the music suddenly cut out.

"Peace, at last," I said into the silent auditorium, and I put the legs to rest.

"Mr. Randall!" a shrill voice bellowed from behind me. One of the backstage doors slammed open revealing a very angry Heather Mayflower, heading straight for me. "Where is Mr. Randall?" she demanded.

"I don't know," I said. I looked out to Jimmy for help, but he had ducked under the soundboard again. I couldn't tell if he was working on the system or hiding. My bet was on hiding.

"Is he coming back?"

"He left his stuff." I pointed to the front row.

Heather stared at me like she was waiting for something. It was rather uncomfortable. "He could be in his office," I suggested.

"I stopped there first," Heather said.

I looked to the back of the auditorium. Jimmy was still under the soundboard. At that point, I figured it was either him or me. "Maybe Jimmy knows. He's back there working on the soundboard."

I guess my voice carried, because Jimmy's head suddenly popped up. I couldn't tell for sure from the distance, but I could swear he was glaring at me angrily.

"Jimmy!" Heather shrieked as she left the stage and walked up the aisle.

I watched for a minute while Heather accosted Jimmy. The poor guy was trapped behind the soundboard. I couldn't hear what Heather was going on about, but I could tell that Jimmy wasn't able to get a word in.

Logic told me I should stay right where I was. I had successfully pawned Heather off to the stage manager. He would deal with her. That was his job, after all. If only I hadn't been born so naturally curious. Before I knew it, my feet were taking me up the aisle because my ears were wondering what Heather was in such a snit about. If only my body had listened to my brain. By the time I reached Heather and Jimmy, the sound system had mysteriously burst back on again and music was blaring throughout the auditorium.

"Jimmy!" Heather yelled over the music.

He did his best to ignore her while he fumbled with the wiring. "I have to fix this," he shouted back. "Talk to Bryan!"

My body went numb. He was throwing me to the wolf.

I wanted to yell, *Traitor!* But, quite frankly, he was only returning the favor. I had sold him out first.

"You can talk to Randall for me," Heather said as she grabbed my arm. Roughly. "Tell him to put me back in the show. He'll listen to you."

"I don't think it's Mr. Randall's decis—"

Heather wasn't interested in logic. "If I get enough teachers on my side, we can all go to Headmaster Collins."

"I don't know," I said. "Jimmy should—"

I didn't think it was possible, but the music got even louder. With an annoyed glance Jimmy's direction, Heather proceeded to pull me out of the auditorium to continue our conversation. Why hadn't I gone home when I had the chance?

"Please tell me you'll talk to Randall," Heather said, once we were in the silence of the hallway. I swear I heard the music cut out a split second before the auditorium door closed.

I couldn't imagine what Heather expected me to say to Mr. Randall. The school took a pretty harsh stance on cheating.

If it was any other student—that is, any other student with a different father—she would have been suspended. Personally, I was surprised she was even having this discussion with me. With a father like hers, I wouldn't have been enlisting students to help me. Particularly students I could barely even consider a friend. I'd go straight to Daddy.

"My dad's in New York with Holly," Heather said, as if she knew what I was thinking. Now, there's a scary thought: a psychic Heather Mayflower.

Psychotic? Definitely.

"Can't you call him?" I asked.

"And tell him I was kicked out of the show for cheating on a test?" Heather was nearly hyperventilating. "He'd tell me I deserved it and hang up. But first he'd tell me not to bother him while he was working on Holly's career. You heard her show got picked up, right?"

Actually, I hadn't. Holly was in New York for upfronts. That was when all the TV networks decided their schedules for the fall season. It looked like Holly was going to be starring in a new sitcom come fall. The thought of senior year free of Mayflowers brought a smile to my face that I hoped Heather read as happiness for her sister. "That's great!"

That's when the tears started flowing. "No, it's not!" Heather screeched. Mrs. Brown stopped in the hallway to look at us. Once she saw who was doing the screeching, she continued on, not wanting to get involved. I couldn't blame her.

Scratch that. I could blame her. And I do.

"Just one more thing Holly's better at than me," Heather

whined. "She's my *little* sister. Do you know how much that sucks?"

Considering that they were only a year apart, it was hard to think of Holly as all that much "littler." Besides, she's half a foot taller than Heather, anyway. Not having any siblings of my own, though, I couldn't really imagine what Heather was going through. Or why she was being so melodramatic about it.

She grabbed my hand and held it in both of hers. "Promise me you'll talk to Mr. Randall," she hissed.

At this point, she was starting to freak me out. "What do you want me to say?"

"That someone put that test in my bag," she said as if it were the most logical thing in the world. "Remind him that I'm going to be class valedictorian. I don't need to cheat on a test."

She had a good point there. Heather may be lacking a heart, but the girl has more than her fair share in the brains department. As many enemies as she has, I couldn't imagine anyone risking suspension to pull that kind of prank. Especially since it was guaranteed that Heather wouldn't get more than a slap on the wrists. Still, it did get her kicked out of the show, so it wouldn't have been a worthless prank.

I still firmly believed that Heather was the one behind Suze and Cindy finding their way out of the show. I just couldn't figure out how this fit into her plan. And then it came to me: She'd intended to plant the test on Wren, but was caught before she could do it.

Hoisted on her own petard, as they say. Okay, I don't know who really says that. But it's such a great way to say that she fell into her own trap.

"Besides, who wants to see Wren try to act? She has no talent." Somewhere a pot was in the process of calling a kettle black. "And, I know Sam's your friend and all, but she only goes here because her mom's a teacher."

I didn't really see what that had to do with anything. Nor did I see how she thought attacking my best friend was going to bring me around to her side. I stood there in silence because it was clear that I wasn't her scene partner. I was her audience.

As usual.

"I need to be in this show," Heather cried to me. For the briefest moment I could have sworn I saw something approaching a genuine emotion, but it was hastily covered by her histrionics. "It will show my father that I'm just as good as Holly. I know I shouldn't be so petty. But you don't know my father. You don't know how hard I try. Bryan, we've been friends for years and years." *We have?* "You've got to talk to Mr. Randall for me. You will, right? Promise me!" She ended her monologue by collapsing on my shoulder with heaving sobs.

Wow. That was . . . wow.

"Promisssse!"

"I promise," I said, not meaning it at all.

As I stood there, patting her overly processed hair, I was certain of one thing: Heather really was a horrible actress.

Okay, two things: Someone needed a trip to the stylist because her roots were totally starting to show.

Witness for the Prosecution

The thing about a good lie is that it should always be based in some form of the truth. That way, you can always justify it to yourself as being *partially* true and therefore not a *total* lie. At the very least, it makes it easier for you to recall some part of the story if you ever get questioned about it later.

I had no doubt that Heather's underlying story was true. She *was* jealous of her younger, more talented, and—let's be honest—more beautiful sister. That wasn't much of a surprise. Heather may be fairly hot and even more intelligent, but Holly is the star in the family. At least that part of Heather's "breakdown" rang true—overwrought and melodramatic, but true. The real question was why the heck was she telling *me*?

It took me a few minutes to extricate myself from Heather's clutches. I could have gone back into the theater, but I had nothing more to say to Jimmy. He had thrown me to the proverbial lioness, with a smile on his face.

Well, I couldn't swear to the smile, but I suspect it was there after we had left the auditorium. Either way, he wasn't getting any more help from me. Instead, I went to my locker, picked up my things, and headed for home.

As soon as I was in a cell friendly area—my driveway—I tried calling Sam to tell her all about Lady Heather and her theatrics. No one was home at Sam's house, and she's cell free no matter what area she's in, so I was thwarted in my effort to gossip. All I could do was go into my house and wait. And patience is *so* not a virtue of mine.

I went in through the kitchen, hung up my fedora, and didn't bother to call out to tell anyone that I was home. Mom was still at the bow-wow-tique (her word, not mine) and Dad was in some foreign country below the equator, if I remember correctly.

I grabbed a cherry Pop-Tart and pulled up a leather and steel stool to sit at the stainless-steel island in our stainless-steel kitchen. Aside from my room, the kitchen is the only room in the house I'm ever comfortable in. It's sleek and cool and totally to my father's specifications. He's an amazing cook, and the room is the one place that's totally his when he's in country. The rest of the house belongs to Mom.

Dad and I call the rest of the house "the Museum" because of its perfect preservation. My room and the kitchen are the only two rooms where you're allowed to wear shoes. Or drink anything that could stain. Or collect dust.

I pulled out my script so I could run lines while I snacked. The show was in two days. We might not have any Dorothys by then, but I'd be damned if I was going to drop a line.

I read the lines aloud, hoping that reading them and hearing them would count twice toward memorizing them. Hey, it was worth a shot. I'd sleep with the script under my pillow if I thought I could memorize through osmosis.

I managed to get all the way through my act when the doorbell started blowing up.

Not bothering to clean up my plate, I raced to the foyer worried that the world was coming to the end. As the bell continued to ring, I threw open the door to find Sam in a highly agitated state.

"I need you as an alibi," Sam said.

"Gladly," I replied, ushering her into the house. "For what?"

"You haven't heard?"

"Hence the question."

Sam slipped off her shoes and plopped down on Mom's white leather couch in the media room. She tucked her feet in beneath her, trying to get comfortable, but still looking rather manic. "Wren had an accident. She's out of the show."

"Is she okay?"

"Sprained her ankle."

"What? Where? How?"

"Attacked. Observatory. Sabotage."

"Tell."

"From what Jimmy told me," she said, "Wren got this call while the sound system was still malfunctioning."

"I saw that," I said, realizing that I was a small part of the story. "I don't know how she heard anyone on the phone over the music, but she left the auditorium after she hung up."

"Whoever called her pretended to be Mr. Randall," Sam explained. "The person told her to meet him—or her—in the observatory so they could rehearse the jitterbug number."

"In the observatory?"

"They needed a large enough space," Sam continued.

"And Jimmy and I were still working on the sound system in the auditorium," I said.

"Right," Sam noted. "But when she got to the observatory, Mr. Randall wasn't there."

"Please don't tell me she went inside," I begged.

Sam nodded.

I shook my head. Wren was usually smarter than that. Dorothys were dropping faster than flying monkeys in a field of poppies. Why in the world would she go into the observatory because a mysterious voice on the phone told her to?

"She said she heard a noise," Sam explained. "From behind the telescope. Like someone was hurt."

"And she couldn't go and get help?"

"She wasn't sure what it was," Sam said. "So she went to check."

"And she was attacked?"

"Not exactly. You know how the only way to get around the telescope is up on the catwalk?"

"Oh, no," I said, anticipating where this was going. The telescope in the observatory is pretty huge. To look through the telescope, you have to walk up a small metal staircase onto a catwalk about five feet off the ground. That's the only way you can get to the other side of the telescope too.

"She made it to the top step and the tread came loose," Sam explained. "She fell down the steps, backward. Then, the lights went out. She heard someone drop from the catwalk in the dark and saw a body run out the door, but she couldn't tell who it was."

"Is she okay?"

"Just a few bruises," Sam said. "And the sprain."

"Wren can still do the show with a sprained ankle."

"She's a dancer, not an actress," Sam said.

"But she's a pretty good actress," I insisted.

"Doesn't matter to her," Sam clarified. "If she can't do the jitterbug, she doesn't want to do the show. She doesn't even want to go back to being a Glinda."

"Leaving you as the lone Dorothy," I stated the obvious. Then I got a little more obvious. "Until someone decides you were the one behind all the attacks."

"See why I need an alibi?" she asked.

"Actually, no," I said, stalling. I didn't want to tell her what horrible thought just popped into my head. I played a bigger part in this story than I'd originally thought. "What were you doing during the attack?"

"I was alone."

Notice how that wasn't the answer to the question I had asked. It was an answer, yes, but not the one required. "Were you still at school?" I hoped I could back into the truth here.

"Yes."

"Waiting for your mom?"

"No," Sam said. "But that's not important. I need you to say you were with me if anyone asks."

"But you won't tell me what you were doing?"

"I said it's not important," Sam reiterated, which only made it even more important for me to know the truth. "I need your help. You were right all along. Heather's got to be behind this. She'll be coming for me next, and I need to protect myself. And the first thing I have to do is stop her from pinning Wren's attack on me."

"*That's* why she was caught with the test," I said. "Because now she's not a suspect."

"But she's still not in the play."

"I'm sure she's got that covered."

"Which is why I need an alibi."

Which is why she should tell me what she was really doing. And just so you don't go thinking the wrong thing, there wasn't a doubt in my mind that Sam was innocent. She would never hurt anyone over a part. Okay, maybe she would for the *right* part, but not for Dorothy in the Orion Academy Spring Theatrical Production of *The Wizard of Oz*.

As our conversation had already started going in circles, I figured it was time to drop my bombshell. "I can't be your alibi," I said. "I was with Heather when Wren was attacked. Jimmy and Mrs. Brown saw me."

"She could have had an accomplice," Sam suggested. "Heather would never get her hands dirty."

"I don't doubt that," I said. "But it doesn't help you with your alibi problem. What about Hope?"

"She was with the steps," Sam said. "And there's no way we'd get them to lie about being with me, too. They're Holly's best friends. They would never turn on their best friend's sister like that."

"I don't know about that," I said, thinking back to Heather's hatred for her sister. Odds are the feeling was mutual, I'm sure. But we couldn't risk it. Alexis and Belinda want nothing more out of life than to be "sources close to the celebrity" when they grow up. You know the ones. They are the "friends" who run to the tabloids when their close celebrity "friend" is contemplating divorce, or has just found out she's pregnant, or has switched to decaf. Which is just my way of saying they love a good scandal more than the average Malibu teen. And that was saying something.

I had a possible solution to Sam's problem, but I wasn't willing to use it and was hoping to come up with another.

None came.

"What about Eric?" I asked.

"He's on his way to LAX," Sam explained. "He and Drew are meeting with the soccer recruiter for the University of New Mexico tomorrow. I guess they have one of the best soccer programs in the country."

"Really? I get the Eric part, but Drew really thinks he's that good?"

"Bryan! Focus!"

"Sorry," I said, getting back on task. "But why can't you say you were with Eric at the time? Wasn't that, like, over an hour ago?"

"Because he's not here to back me up," Sam said.

"What? He doesn't have a cell phone?" I didn't like the direction this conversation was taking.

"There was soccer practice this afternoon."

Now I knew I didn't like where this was going. Notice she didn't say, "He was *at* soccer practice this afternoon."

"He didn't go to practice today," I said, filling in the blank.

Sam looked down at the couch. Since there was nothing there to look at but white leather, I'm guessing she was trying to avoid my piercing stare. "I felt bad about canceling our date yesterday," she said. "And with him going away the next few days . . . we wanted to spend some time together."

Oh, how *cute*. Blech. But I had other things on my mind at the moment. I did a quick check to confirm she was still wearing her unicorn necklace. See, Sam has this thing about unicorns. In mythology, unicorns only approach girls who are still pure (meaning: virgins). Sam had confided in me long ago that when she finally loses her pure status she would take off the necklace once and for all.

It was still on her.

But that didn't really have anything to do with the issue at hand.

"This isn't the fifties. You don't have to worry about your virtue being intact." Though I was glad to see that it was. "So what? You and Eric were locking lips at the time."

Sam shook her head. "The soccer team isn't allowed to miss practice without an excuse," Sam said. "Eric told Coach

Zach he had to leave early so he could get his medical files for the recruiter. If the coach finds out Eric was with me, he'll be suspended from the finals."

"And the world as we know it will come to an end," I said.

"Bryan!"

"How about this scenario: Headmaster Collins thinks that you're behind the disappearing Dorothys and expels you."

"There's nothing that points to me in this," she said, backpedaling.

"Except that you're the last Dorothy standing," I reminded her. "Even if people don't start suspecting you, you should start worrying about what could happen to you next."

"I can protect myself," she said.

"I don't doubt that," I said. "But Heather's out to stop the Dorothys. And I'm pretty sure she's got one more move in her to take you out of the play and get herself back in. You need to protect yourself. You need to call Eric."

Sam had come to me looking for an alibi. Why was she suddenly more concerned about her relationship with Eric?

"Okay," she said, leading me to false hope. "I'll call Eric . . . if I have to."

"News flash, Sam: You *have* to! Heather will be out for you next."

"Do you always have to be so dramatic?"

"Excuse me? You're the one who freaks out over how every little quiz affects your GPA. And now you're not even worried about being expelled? Not to mention criminal charges. We're talking about two attacks here."

"I see what you're saying," Sam said as she got off the couch and moved to the foyer. "But it'll all be fine. Trust me."

"You, I trust. It's Heather who worries me."

"I'll be careful," Sam said as she slipped into her sandals.

I wanted to say, "It doesn't matter how careful you are." I wanted to tell her she was totally insane. I wanted to say, "Why are you leaving so soon? You just got here." But I knew she wouldn't hear me.

She had Eric on the brain.

Which, believe me, is as disgusting as it sounds.

And Then There Were None

Friday morning started out with a different energy from the rest of the week. It's always like that the last school day before a show. Friday was our last chance to work through the *Wizard* and we knew we'd need all the work we could get.

Nobody really does any schoolwork the day before the show. Not just the Drama Geeks. I mean, the entire school. All the teachers know to keep the lessons light since any number of students can be called out of class at various points in the day to work scenes, get fitted for last-minute costumes, or help finish painting the set.

Or to just skip class. But the teachers don't need to know that.

This year, I expected that it would be like a second all-day rehearsal. With Sam now obviously the lone Dorothy, there was a lot of work still to do.

"What will this day be like, I wonder?" Sam sang the opening lines of "I Have Confidence" as she came up to my locker.

What could I do? I sang back. *"What will my future be?"* Too bad I hit a really sour note on that "be." I guess I'm not destined to play the part of Maria in *The Sound of Music*.

Pity.

"How many classes do you think we can get out of today?" Sam asked, saving me from having to continue a song way out of my range.

"Considering how much work needs to be done on the show? I'd say we could probably get out of classes we don't even take."

"Too true."

I guess we were ignoring that huge white elephant in the hall; the one that was trumpeting the fact that we still had one day of Heather's machinations to contend with. Fine. If she wanted to play that game, I was totally up for it.

Unfortunately, the imaginary trumpeting I heard wasn't an elephant. It was the sound of a parade led by Headmaster Collins and consisting of Mr. Randall and Heather Mayflower.

The wicked witch of Orion was about to strike.

"Ms. Lawson," Headmaster Collins said as he approached us. "May I take a look inside your locker?"

Sam took a moment to size up the situation. Having watched many movies and TV shows with her, I knew she was well versed in drama to know that the moment someone asks to examine your locker, your room, or your intentions, that's the last thing you want to happen.

"What's wrong?" she asked, stalling.

"I need to see inside your locker," the headmaster said.

Sensing scandal, people in the hall started lingering by their own lockers to watch.

I saw Heather looking all smug beside the headmaster. Her reaction gave me a few ideas on what could be in the locker. My mind was racing with ways to distract this little ensemble as well as the crowd who was quickly gathering around us. The only thing I could come up with was yelling, "Fire!" and pulling the alarm. I doubt anyone would fall for it, but at least the sprinklers going off would clear the hallways. None of the girls—and few of the guys—would stick around to let their hair get messed.

"Is there something you're looking for?" Sam asked. She was now searching the halls. I wasn't sure what she was looking for, but I started looking too.

"Headmaster Collins," Heather said. "Sam's obviously hiding something. You should just—"

"Heather, please," Mr. Randall said.

Heather hit us all with one of the deepest sighs she had ever let out. Seriously. I nearly fell over from the force of the wind. The only person who seemed to be actually falling for it was the headmaster. Then again, *he* was the only one it was probably intended for, so the sigh was doing its job. "I turned over my purse as soon as you asked me the other day," she said.

Well, that wasn't entirely true. But I didn't think pointing that out at the moment was a good idea.

Suddenly, it was totally clear to me what she was up to. But in case anyone didn't make the connection, Heather made it for us. "Of course, I never expected to find *her mother's test* in my purse." Thank you, Heather . . . But she continued, "Maybe Sam knows there's something in her locker she doesn't want you to see."

I could practically see the debate raging in Sam's mind. There was nothing she could do. The school policy on locker searches was pretty clear. If Sam didn't open it, the headmaster would be totally free to do it himself.

Just as I was about to yell, "Fire," Sam crossed the hall to her locker. All the students in the area, including me, shifted our attention to follow her. Sam turned the combination, shot a helpless look at me over her shoulder, and opened it.

There was a collective gasp from the gathered crowd. I think they jumped the gun a bit, because nothing looked out of the ordinary from where I stood. The contents of Sam's locker included a sweater, various textbooks, two paperbacks from the Dragonriders of Pern series, her hanging crystals, and wind chimes. None of this was shocking in the least. There did look to be two items on the top of the pile, but it was hard to see what they were from where I stood.

Headmaster Collins stepped up to the locker and pulled them out for everyone to see: a CD marked CYNTHIA in block lettering and a screwdriver. Now, the gasp that came from the crowd was more appropriately timed. The CD would have been hard to explain, but there was no rule against keeping tools in your locker. If only a handful of screws hadn't dropped out of the locker when he removed the items. No doubt the screws would match up with the ones in the metal staircase in the observatory. I was amazed that Heather had enough control not to leave a taco wrapper that smelled of fish, too.

But I wasn't worried about any of that. Sam had an airtight

alibi for when Wren was attacked. All she had to do was invoke the name of Eric-the-perfect and all would be fine.

"I know this won't come as a surprise," Sam said, looking to Heather and then the headmaster. "But I don't know how that stuff got in there."

I focused my attention back on the fire alarm. All it would take was a simple pull and we could delay this discussion until a time when cooler heads could prevail.

Too bad I was frozen in place.

"Ms. Lawson," Headmaster Collins said. "What we have here is potential evidence that you caused an accident that injured another student."

Actually, what we had was some hardware. There wasn't anything that directly tied her to the crime. For that matter, the CD was just a CD at the moment. No one had even seen what was on it. But what's the point of quibbling. We all knew where this was heading.

"Can you explain what these items are doing in your locker?" he asked.

"No," Sam said.

I wanted to scream, "They were planted there by the girl smirking beside you!" but I couldn't get my mouth to work at the moment. I'm guessing Sam was having the same problem, since she was surprisingly silent as well. She was, however, still looking past the headmaster and down the hall like she was waiting for something.

I looked to Mr. Randall for help. I guess he was struck by the same silent bug that was going around. He was about to lose the one shining light in his dismal show, so I would have figured for more of a vocal reaction. Maybe a little disbelief mixed with his disappointment.

It was a shame that Hope's locker was on the whole other side of school. We could have certainly used her at the moment. Nothing ever kept her mouth shut. Her particular brand of chutzpah—see, told you I'm part Jewish—would come in handy to diffuse this situation. But for the moment, we were totally without Hope.

That was when I saw Sam's eyes light up. She found what she had been looking for. I turned in the direction of her gaze and felt a wave of relief wash over me. Hope may have been gone at the moment, but salvation was walking in our direction.

Sam's mom pushed her way through the crowd, looked at Sam, the open locker, the screwdriver and CD, and sprung into action.

"Everyone get to class," she said to the crowd. "First bell is about to ring."

Assorted moans and groans rang out around us, but Anne's glare—backed up by Headmaster Collins once he realized there was a crowd of students watching—sent most of our classmates scurrying.

Most, but not all.

Heather stuck around even though this was none of her business.

I was probably expected to leave too, but there was no way I was about to abandon my friend in her morning of need.

"Ms. Lawson," the headmaster said, addressing Anne this time. "Your daughter—"

"Do you think it's wise to have this conversation in the middle of the hallway, Headmaster Collins?" Anne asked, all sweetness and light. As concerned as the headmaster is about keeping up appearances, he is woefully unaware of how he causes scenes.

"Very well," Headmaster Collins said. "Let's adjourn to my office."

"We'll be right there," Anne said dismissively.

The headmaster clearly didn't like that, but he left, anyway. Mr. Randall followed, but Heather hung around until Anne glared at her. Finally, Heather joined the others on their way to the headmaster's office.

"Okay, Sam," Anne said. "I can pretty much figure what's going on here. Now, you know I trust you completely, but you have to be absolutely honest with me before we go into the headmaster's office. Did you have anything to do with the stuff that happened this week?"

"Anne, don't be crazy," I said, forgetting all about the rules of address while in school.

"Bryan, dear . . . please," Anne said softly. "Sam?"

"No, Mom," she said.

I was about to jump in with Sam's alibi, but Sam shot me a warning look. My first instinct was to ignore it, but I forced myself to stop. Sam may not have told her mom anything about Eric yet. If I went and blabbed about the fact they were dating, that could cross over into one of those unexpected betrayal areas.

Not that Anne would have a problem with Eric. He's one

of the best students in the school. But he *is* a student. And Sam works very hard to keep her school life and her mom's school life separate. It's doubtful that she'd want this news spread from my big mouth. So, we formed our own little three-person parade and went down to the headmaster's office, where I was told to wait outside . . . with Heather.

"I'm glad *that's* over," Heather said as the door closed behind Sam.

I went back into silent mode. The headmaster's secretary, Mrs. Bell, was not at her station, but I've often suspected she has recording devices strategically placed around the office in the event she might miss scandalous events while out for her morning coffee.

"Not that I'm surprised Sam was behind it all," Heather said. "Like I said before, she doesn't really belong here. She's not like the rest of us."

I couldn't help but wonder who this *us* was that she was referring to. I don't exactly count Heather among my inner circle.

"You don't really think Sam was sabotaging the play," I said innocently.

"Who else could it be?" Heather asked, twice as innocently.

Who else?!

We could have one-upped each other's innocent acts all morning. Time to change track. "The thing I don't get is why she had to go all out. Couldn't she have been happy to have one whole act to herself?" I proposed.

"Some people want it all," Heather said. "And some people *deserve* it all."

"You're right," I said. "Sam does have the talent. She did deserve to be in the entire play."

"That's not what I meant."

"Oh?" I said, going back to innocent. "What *did* you mean?"

There was a brief pause while Heather took in the situation. She knew I was onto her. But she also knew there was nothing I could do about it.

"Do you really think you're going to trip me up with your oh-so-subtle questions?" Heather asked. "I've been getting around my dad's backstabbing, greedy, manipulative wives for years. And he only marries the best. So, how much do you think you're worrying me right now?"

If only my parents didn't have such a rock solid—though incredibly boring—marriage, I would be much better prepared to deal with my peer group.

"She's probably being expelled as we speak," Heather said.

"Nobody ever gets expelled from Orion," I said. The school administration works very hard to make sure it only accepts the best. In the rare cases where a student has been "transitioned out," it's only after his or her parents can arrange for an opportunity in a more challenging school environment. We tend to fail upwardly here.

"Right," Heather said. "Because whenever anyone gets close to that kind of trouble, their parents rush in and buy a building or something. What do you think Ms. Lawson can afford? Maybe a stack of outdated encyclopedias for the Klayton Library?"

I stared at her. My mouth was open, yet nothing was coming out. This was the second time today I was at a loss for something to say. And I'm usually such a chatty person.

"You look extremely happy," I finally managed.

"Why wouldn't I be?" Heather said. "I'm going to be cleared of the cheating scandal and now I get to be the one lone Dorothy. All in all, it's been a good day, and I haven't even been to one class yet."

It was killing me enough that she was being so smug about Sam's problem, but there was something else, too. Something more than our little play was behind her joyous expression.

"Oh, and did you hear about Holly?" she asked.

I couldn't imagine what her sister had to do with anything. She was still in New York basking in her burgeoning TV career, as far as I knew.

"You know how her show was picked up for next season?"

I didn't bother to respond. She knew full well that I knew, since she was the one who had told me about it the day before.

"Well," she said. "I guess the network wanted to go a different direction with her character. So, even though the show will be on this fall, she won't. Her role is being recast. It will be in all the trades on Monday. Isn't that horrible?" The bright, beaming smile on her face stood in stark contrast to what she was saying.

Still grinning about her sister's embarrassing and horrible news, Heather spun in her name-brand, ridiculously expensive shoes and bounced down the hall toward the auditorium. I swear I could hear her maniacal cackle echoing through the halls of the building.

Or that could have been my imagination.

Either way, in case you weren't paying attention earlier, please allow me to reiterate: Heather is eeeeeevil.

Ann(i)e Get Your Gun

I stared at the door to the headmaster's office, focusing my mental abilities in the hope that I could see what was going on behind his closed door. Or at the very least, try to hear what everyone inside was saying.

Maybe I shouldn't have been listening so intently because when Hope came into the outer office yelling, "What the heck is going on?!" she came pretty close to giving me a heart attack.

Once the pitter-patter of my heart returned to normal, I quickly filled her in on the situation, highlighting the Eric involvement in the story and my feelings about all that. I gave her a moment to absorb what I told her, figuring she would come up with the perfect plan to convince Sam that she had to play the Eric card.

Imagine how disappointed I was when Hope said, "Yeah, I get that. I don't know that I'd want to get my new boyfriend in trouble either. It's not a good way to start a relationship."

Considering this *relationship* consisted of one date and a make-out session somewhere on campus, I didn't necessarily agree . . . and proceeded to tell Hope as much . . . with expletives, even. I'm guessing the headmaster's door was steel reinforced because he didn't open it to wash my mouth out with soap. No wonder I couldn't hear anything earlier.

"You done?" Hope finally asked.

"For now," I said.

"Good. I know firsthand how hard it is to get someone out of a practice. Especially right before the final game. If Drew had done something like that for me, I don't know that I'd be all quick to turn him in."

"Really?" I asked, thinking about her always shaky relationship. "You wouldn't? Even if you could be expelled?"

"Okay, bad example," Hope said. "But, still, I understand Sam's situation."

"Yeah, but . . ." I didn't have a chance to figure out what I was going to say next because the door to Headmaster Collins's office finally opened. Mr. Randall, Anne, and Sam walked out, each looking more stunned than the next. It was all we could do not to pounce on them.

My heart broke a little when Sam couldn't even look at me or Hope.

"Why don't you go home, honey," Anne said softly. "I can get a ride home after school."

Sam simply nodded and walked out of the room. She didn't even bother to say good-bye. We watched her perp-walk down the hall like she had just been tried and convicted.

Once I was sure Sam was out of earshot, I turned and strained not to shout, "She was expelled?!"

"Oh," Mrs. Bell said as she came in from the other direction holding a steaming cup of coffee. "Did I miss something?"

"No, Mrs. Bell. Nothing at all," Anne said as she and Mr. Randall ushered us out of the office.

"Sam hasn't been expelled," Anne said once we were in the empty hall. "There wasn't enough evidence to prove she actually pulled the prank on Wren or put Cindy's pictures up online. Headmaster Collins wants to let things settle for the weekend, then he'll launch a full investigation next week."

"He's calling the attack on Wren a prank?" I asked.

Anne shrugged. "There's no way to prove it was done intentionally to hurt her."

"In the meantime," Mr. Randall added, "Sam is out of the show." He seemed even more upset about that than we were. If that's even possible.

"But that's not fair," I said.

"You know how easy it is to break into lockers around here," Hope added. "Anyone could have planted that stuff."

"*Heather* could have planted that stuff," I insisted.

"Believe me," Anne said. "I already reminded the headmaster about that. The locker part, not Heather. We can't go throwing around false accusations. Unless you two know anything for sure?"

There was one thing I *did* know for sure. I was about to tell Anne about Sam's alibi when I felt the crushing stomp of Hope's steel-toe boot on my Chucks. (Of all days to opt for the canvas sneakers instead of my hard leather Skechers.)

Even though I didn't say anything, Anne must have seen something in my expression. Pain, mostly. "Do you know something, Bryan?" she asked.

I didn't need to look at Hope to know the expression on her face. "Not really," I said as my toes throbbed.

"If you'll excuse me," Mr. Randall said. "I have to find Heather and start working act one with her."

"She's in the auditorium waiting for you," I said.

"Of course she is," he said as he turned and went down the hall.

"How serious is this?" Hope asked. "Can Sam really be expelled?"

"I can get my parents involved," I said, knowing full well that my mom lived for this kind of fight. And she *loves* Sam to boot. "Heather seemed to think that . . . well, she kind of said . . ."

"Yes," Anne said, "I can imagine what Heather said. And thanks for the offer, but Sam's got more on her side than you might think."

I wasn't sure what Anne was talking about at first, but she quickly cleared up my confusion. Turns out, Sam has something even better than money. She has publicity.

Like I wrote earlier, Sam is the only student here on the teacher-discount plan. She may not have a building named after her grandparents, but that doesn't mean she can't be useful to the school in other ways. Apparently, she is a great press release for equal opportunity education.

Any time anyone went after the school for being elitist,

Headmaster Collins would trot Sam out as an example—the *only* example—of how the school benefits the less financially endowed. It is, quite possibly, the most patronizingly offensive thing I have ever heard in my life. And yet, it's also a great bargaining chip. Because how bad would the press be if Orion Academy's one true charity case—Anne's words, not mine—was expelled without a thorough investigation and actual proof that Sam was behind the attacks?

But that didn't get Sam back in the show.

Considering the stolen test had come from Anne's class, Headmaster Collins felt that clue pointed to Sam's guilt as well. As such, he reinstated Heather as a Dorothy. Correction: The lone Dorothy.

I was wondering if it was too late to return the show tickets. There was no way I wanted my mom to have to sit through the travesty that awaited us all.

"I should get to class," Anne said. "No telling what the sophomores have done to my room by now. You should get to class too. Do you want me to write you a note?"

"No, we'll get excused for rehearsal," Hope said. "That's where Mr. Clark probably thinks we are, anyway."

When Anne said good-bye I could hear the concern in her voice. I still wanted to tell her about Sam's out, but my toes couldn't take another assault. That didn't mean I had given up the fight.

"Is there some reason we couldn't tell Anne about Eric?" I asked as Hope and I moved toward Hall Hall.

"Because it's not our place to say."

"Forgive me if I don't think Sam is in her right mind at the moment. She could be expelled."

"Do you really think she'll let it go that far?" Hope asked. "It's not the end of the world yet."

"It's the end of the show," I said.

"Please," Hope said. "This show was over before the first rehearsal."

"There's that old 'show must go on' spirit," I said. "Mr. Randall would be so proud."

"Like he's not thinking the same thing," Hope said. To emphasize her point, she opened the auditorium door. We were greeted by the shrill sound of Heather's singing.

"If you ask me, Sam's the lucky one," Hope said.

"You have an odd outlook on life."

"Just promise me you won't go making things worse," Hope said.

For the second time in as many days I made a promise I had no intention of keeping. It bothered me more to lie to Hope than it did to Heather, but only a little bit.

Sleuth

By lunch I was beginning to suspect that Hope was coming around to my side. Certainly her attitude was darkening over the whole situation as the day progressed.

"A half dozen people have come up to me already, blaming Sam for ruining the play," she said as she sat at the Drama Geeks' table.

Today we were joined by the regulars, Tasha—who was paging through a book of Edward Gorey's morbid artwork—and Jimmy—who was busy highlighting his prompt book with the music and light cues for the show. Luckily, Wren's boyfriend, Jason, was also there, and he was surprisingly quick to jump to Sam's defense.

"That's ridiculous," he said. "You tell Sam that Wren doesn't think that at all. There's no way Sam would hurt anyone. Not to mention that she doesn't need to. This play should be the least of her concerns. She's so much better than that."

"How is Wren?" I asked.

"Milking it," he replied. Not exactly the doting boyfriend, is he? "It's just a sprain. She could do the play. But since she can't shine as the prima jitterbugger, she doesn't want to do it at all."

"Does she have any idea who *did* do it?" Hope asked.

"No," Jason said, trading his exasperation for real concern. "Once the lights went out, she couldn't see anything." I noticed his hand was squeezing his Snapple bottle in anger. Maybe this relationship would last beyond Wren's graduation. "I don't understand why she would go into the observatory alone after everything that's happened this week."

That was the question of the day for most people. Not me, though. My burning question was, "Who was the saboteur?" The answer was pretty obvious:

Jax.

Heather's boyfriend had the motive. Namely, Heather. He had the means. It wasn't too hard to loosen a few screws. But I kept getting stuck on the opportunity. If it was such a big deal that Eric bailed on soccer practice, the same could be said for Jax. If he did miss practice, wasn't that a way to move his name to the top of the suspect list?

Jax could be the proof that I was looking for. And, unlike his Machiavellian girlfriend, I knew I could trick him into admitting the truth. There was only one problem with my plan.

"What is Heather doing here?" I asked. Because as soon as

I looked over to where Jax was sitting, her blond hair was the first thing I saw.

"She's *here*?" Hope's head swung around in the direction I was looking.

"Nice to know she can take time out of rehearsal to grab a bite with her boyfriend," Jason added. I think my fellow Scarecrow took this play more seriously than anyone in the school. Actually, he generally takes performing more seriously than anyone in the school (with the possible exception of Sam—in spite of her current attitude).

Heather's lunch break made perfect sense to me. Aside from the fact that Heather didn't think she needed all that much work, she probably also didn't want to leave Jax alone at lunch. Especially knowing that I was on the case.

It's possible that she wasn't worried about me specifically, but it was a big risk leaving him unsupervised during the sociable part of the day. Heather had too much riding on tomorrow's show for her plan to fall apart at the last minute.

But I didn't need to force an admission out of Jax to redirect suspicion in Heather's direction. I only needed to prove that he wasn't at practice. Luckily, I had one of the few breaks of the week happen. Coach Zach was on lunch duty.

In light of what happened on Monday, all the teachers had been reporting to duty on time for once. This would eventually start to drop off as we got further away from Suze's accident, but for now I was going to use it to my benefit.

I was about to get up from the table when I heard the opening notes of the song "Defying Gravity" from *Wicked* emerging from Hope's bag. "That's me," she said as she pulled out her cell phone.

"You get reception here?" I asked. *Nobody* gets reception at school. I had to find out what plan she was on.

Hope checked to make sure Coach Zach didn't see her answering her phone. She looked at the caller ID and answered the phone with an unusually cheery voice. "Hi! Did you get it? . . . I told you . . . I know . . . I can do that. . . . That's great! But, I better go before someone sees me on the phone. . . . Love you, too. Bye!"

She closed the phone, dropped it back in her bag, and resumed eating.

"Care to tell me what that was about?" I asked.

"Nope."

I waited for something more, but she just kept eating. I suspected that the call had something to do with Suze's stolen sketchbook, but Hope was still keeping mum on that. I decided to deal with one mystery at a time.

"Be right back," I said as I went to speak with Coach Zach. I knew that I couldn't just come out and ask him if Jax was at practice. That would be too obvious. Coach Zach might try to protect one of his players. No, I had to be crafty about this. And not in the way Suze is crafty. I meant manipulative. I had to be Heather.

Talk about an acting challenge.

"Hey, Coach Zach," I said.

"Hey, Bry," he replied, ignoring my cringe. I hate when people call me "Bry." "Let me guess. You've decided to give up on your dream of acting and come out for the team?"

"Obviously you've forgotten about that baseball game in gym last month," I said.

"I've tried," Coach Zach said as he bent to rub his shin. "But I keep getting a reminder when it rains."

Note to all aspiring players: When swinging the bat, maintain a firm grip. Do not let it slip from your hands. Do not let it fly across the baseball field. And, most of all, do *not* let it hit the person who determines your grade for the class.

Changing subject.

"But I am interested in soccer," I said, hoping that if I got him talking about his team, he might let something slip. "For an article in *The Star*." The odds were pretty good that he didn't know I am just a photographer for the paper, not one of the writers. "About the work it takes to be a soccer player. Like how you run your practices. Take yesterday, for example."

"We didn't have a full practice yesterday," he said. "I had the guys do a cross-country run. Soccer players have to be runners, too, you know."

"You don't happen to run with them, do you?"

Coach Zach laughed.

Yeah, I thought not. So he'd have no idea if Jax took a detour during the run. No one on the team probably would have noticed either. And no one would be able to prove that he had gone to the observatory for the attack.

Hmph. That got me nowhere.

The Wiz

Throughout the rest of the day I tried getting in touch with Sam by calling, e-mailing, and IMing. I even considered carrier pigeon, but where would I get one on such short notice? If only Orion Academy had an owlery.

It didn't matter. Sam would not pick up, reply, or respond. I could only imagine what she would have done to the poor pigeon that showed up at her window.

Driving Electra over to Sam's apartment was an option, but not really a good one. If she wasn't answering the phone, she wouldn't know I was outside the security gate wanting to be buzzed in. It was silly to drive all the way to Santa Monica to do my impression of Stanley Kowalski from *A Streetcar Named Desire*, yelling, "Sam!" from the pavement instead of "Stella!"

I wondered where I could print up some "Free Sam" T-shirts. That seemed to be the only plausible course of action at that point.

I wasn't the only one in a quandary. Mr. Randall had spent the rest of the day—minus lunch—working with Heather one on one. He didn't even bother to involve the rest of the cast. His thought process was that we all knew our parts well enough and we could work around Heather.

Work around the lead of the show, you ask?

Yeah, it was pretty clear to all involved that Mr. Randall had simply given up.

Everyone had lost that "show must go on" spirit.

That's why instead of going over one last polish of the show with my friends after school, I was once again sitting in my stainless-steel kitchen eating a Pop-Tart. This time it was Brown Sugar and Cinnamon, for those of you keeping track at home.

I sat, staring at my Pop-Tart, thinking about the events of the past week. I guess things really did all start with that falling lamp. An accident. It had to be. Even Heather wasn't good enough to simulate metal fatigue. But maybe it inspired her; gave her the idea that she could be the lone Dorothy if other "accidents" happened along the way. From that point, everything else had been her doing.

It really was brilliant, now that I thought of it. Jax had spilled his drink on Sam Monday, sending her out of the pavilion and, more importantly, away from our table. Even though we all knew she was changing shirts, someone else might think it was an opportunity to switch Suze's taco while she was supposed to be out of the room. We were all focused on Hope's dress at the time, so nobody would have noticed.

And that's why nobody noticed Heather doing that very thing.

Tuesday was pure brilliance. Anyone could have had access to Cynthia's locker. Sam wouldn't have even needed to know that the locker was so easy to break into. *Most* of the lockers in school are that way. The mere fact that not every piece of evidence pointed directly to Sam made her look better at covering her tracks. Until the CD turned up in Sam's locker, that is.

Wednesday, Heather took herself off the suspect list by making herself a victim. Notice how she used Sam's own mom to trap her? Out of all the tests she could have stolen, it wasn't merely a coincidence that she had taken the English final.

And we all know what she did to Wren—and me—yesterday. Which brings me to Friday afternoon in my kitchen, still staring at my Pop-Tart.

That left two questions. One: How did Heather know Sam wasn't going to have a usable alibi? And two: How did Jax get the coach to schedule a run to the beach instead of regular practice? Were these things just luck?

Oh, and three: How could I get the answers to these questions before the show opened?

And, of course, one more: Why wouldn't Sam give up Eric as her alibi? Isn't the school show just as important as some soccer game? Aren't her needs as important as Eric's? Aren't hers even more important since she's never going to get a college scholarship with this kind of thing on her record?

Okay, so that was a lot more than two questions. But it was the end of the list that was the most upsetting.

Why *was* Sam not telling anyone where she was yesterday? Honestly, I find it hard to believe that Coach Zach would bench his star player from the finals just for missing one practice. Oh, sure, Eric would have to be punished with some kind of detention, but not in a way that would risk the end of a winning season.

I couldn't help wondering why Sam refused to tell me what was really going on. Or why she was totally ignoring me all day. I had nothing to do with any of this. Well, except for the fact that I was a constant reminder that she had a way out. All she had to do was betray the guy she only recently started seeing.

It finally happened. A guy had come between us. And not in the way I had ever feared.

I dropped my Pop-Tart on my plate. My appetite was gone.

"Hey, Little Prince," a sugary sweet voice with a hint of a giggle said as the kitchen door swung open.

"Hi, Mom," I replied as the woman of the house came breezing into the room carrying a box full of doggie duds. She dropped them on the kitchen table and blew by me so quickly that I knew she wasn't alone. She pulled a doggie gate out of the pantry and locked it into the doorway leading into her pristine museum home.

"All clear," she yelled out.

I turned toward the kitchen door as one of my oldest and dearest friends came barreling in. "Hey, Mal!" I said as a seventy-five-pound black Lab came bounding into the kitchen and jumped up on me. "Who's my favorite girl?" I asked in that kind of baby talk we all instinctively revert to whenever we're around adorable animals.

Mal—which is short for Maleficent—is the closest thing to a cousin that I have. Since both my parents are only children, my family circle includes my parents' closest friends. And no friend is closer to my mom than her bestest friend and business partner, Blaine.

"Hey, kiddo," Blaine said as he came in behind Mal carrying two more boxes of my mom's creations. Mom is the artist behind the business. Blaine is the brains. Even with the bulk in his arms, he managed to free a hand to muss my hair. Leave it to Blaine to catch me without my fedora on.

Just so we're clear, Blaine is the only person in this—or any other—world permitted to muss my hair. Or to call me "kiddo."

I know what you're thinking, by the way. Because his name is Blaine and he's co-owner of a boutique that designs clothing for the prissy, pampered pets of the prissy, pampered Hollywood elite, you've probably gotten this picture in your head. Let me guess: a stunningly tanned, perfectly coiffed, gay man with a lisp, wearing neatly ironed clothes in hues of pink and white?

Wrong.

Blaine is a 250-pound, bald black man who could snap you in two like a twig. But he *is* gay. In fact, he plays rugby on the only straight-friendly rugby team in L.A.

And now you're probably wondering why—if my mom's

best friend in the entire world is a totally well-adjusted and perfectly happy gay man—why then, oh why, am I so reluctant to come out of my own closet?

Good question.

"Bryan. Table," Mom said. She likes to keep the sentences simple when I'm in trouble. I took it to mean that she didn't like the fact I had dropped bits of Pop-Tart on the center island.

I quickly wiped up the crumbs. "What? It's *stainless*."

"Such sass," Blaine said, chucking me lightly on the arm. I say lightly because if he really wanted to hit me, he'd knock me off the stool. "Don't you talk to your mother that way."

Blaine was smiling as he said this because we both knew the response it would get.

First there was the look of wide-eyed horror. Then, the sharp intake of breath. Followed by, "Oh, you know I was just messin'. Eat away!"

Mom prefers to think of herself as a best friend instead of a *mom*. At times, the friend status clashes with her more natural instincts as a neat freak.

"Thanks, Mom," I said, taking a big bite out of my Pop-Tart, not caring where the crumbs landed. Mom can be pretty cool when she wants to be. At least she doesn't make me call her by her first name like so many parents around Malibu force their children to do. It's one thing for me to call Sam's mom by her given name. That's okay, because I think of her as a friend, and *Sam* still calls her "Mom." It's another thing entirely when your own parent expects you to be so informal with them.

"Give me a second," Mom said to Blaine as she climbed over the doggie gate, "and I'll get that thing I promised you."

"The magazine article on the new pet hotels," Blaine reminded her.

"I know," Mom said as she left the kitchen. Part of the reason Mom keeps the house so clean is because it's the only way she can keep track of anything. She's definitely where my artistic side comes from. Luckily, it doesn't also come with her lack of organizational skills.

I gave Mal a good squeeze as she tried to climb up on my lap. Even though there was no room for the two of us on the stool, I didn't mind. She was exactly what I needed. We can't have pets of our own because of my dad's allergies. Not that he has anything near the level of Suze's. I think he's just not a big fan of animals. Which is why when I'm down I usually have to go to Mal. Thankfully, someone knew I needed her today.

"Spill," Blaine said.

I looked back at the counter. "I didn't spill anything. It's all clean."

"Very funny," he said, pulling up a stool. "Now, do you want to tell me what's bothering you?"

Did I mention that Blaine is like scary psychic when it comes to me? He always knows when something's up. Or when I've done something wrong. I think it has something to do with the world maintaining balance. In light of an often absent father and a sweet, but oblivious mom, the powers-that-be have put a person in my life who doesn't let me get away with anything. Ever.

Sometimes, it can be a real pain in the ass.

This? Was not one of those times.

I quickly found myself spilling out the details of the entire week, from the falling lamp, to the aborted prom date, to Sam not talking to me. I doubt most of it made any sense, but Blaine listened quietly, only interrupting for a few clarifications.

Once I finally finished babbling, Blaine sat quietly for a moment. I suspected that he was about to come up with some of his traditional words of wisdom. I waited in silence until he finally spoke.

"Stop being an idiot," he said.

This was no surprise, as his advice often opens up by indicating I had missed the obvious.

"First thing, first," he continued expanding on my alleged idiocy. "You need to get Sam back in the show."

"But she won't—"

He held up a hand that immediately silenced me.

"In my many years of being friends with your mother, I have learned numerous valuable lessons." This was going to be good. "One of the most valuable is when I cannot get what I want *from* her, I often find it helps to go *around* her."

Which is how I found myself sitting on the front steps of Eric Whitman's house the very next day.

Old Times

It was another typically sunny Malibu afternoon. The morning haze had burned off, leaving nothing but a totally blue sky over my head. But that didn't lighten my mood any. Nor did it darken my complexion, sad to say.

Mr. Whitman's housekeeper had told me over the phone when he'd be back. I had expected to get Eric's dad, but I guess he went with Eric and Drew to New Mexico. I was still having trouble thinking of Drew playing college soccer. He's okay enough, but it never really struck me that it was anything more than a pastime. He has been playing soccer for years, but never with the kind of intensity Eric showed on the field.

I had a lot of time to think about this since their plane was apparently late. Either that or they stopped for lunch on the way home.

Eric lives in one of the really, *really* expensive homes down by the water, with the beach as his backyard. For decades the residents on his street had been in battle with the county over that particular stretch of beach. Technically, it was supposed to be a public beach, but considering the neighborhood was built with about a half-foot of space between the houses, it wasn't really conducive to tourist traffic.

Eventually the county won out and opened up a couple throughways for people to get from the street to the sand. Now, on any given day you can see various people tramping across the private driveways looking for beach access.

From time to time, people in unfortunate swimwear would stop by Electra, tap on her door frame, and ask me for directions. But mostly, they just yelled out to one another, "I think we go down this way!" This was usually followed by the sound of an angry dog barking because the tourists had guessed wrong and found themselves on private property.

I spent the rest of the time enjoying the ocean breeze while safely sitting in the shade of Electra and reading the late, great Katharine Hepburn's memoir. The book was a little self-indulgent for my tastes, but, ignoring some of her more outrageous flights of fancy, you have to admit that woman was a heck of a dame.

Two hours after I had estimated they would be home, the Whitmans' tricked-out black SUV finally backed into the short driveway. I could see the surprise on Eric's face through the lightly tinted windshield as I got out of Electra. I assumed the shadow in the backseat was Drew.

"Bryan Stark!" Mr. Whitman said as he stepped down from his oversize vehicle. His perfect smile and even more perfectly sculpted hair were both shining in the sunlight. "What a pleasant surprise."

"Hello, Mr. Whitman," I said as I reached him. My hand disappeared into his as we shook. Mr. Whitman always has this larger-than-life personality that could eclipse anyone in the room. Eric clearly takes after his dad, while his little brother, Matthew, is the introvert in the family. I guess Matthew was at a friend's for the weekend, because he wasn't around at the time.

"Come inside, come inside," Mr. Whitman said, ushering me indoors.

The looks of surprise had not left Eric's or Drew's face as they followed us through the foyer into the expansive living room accented by dark wood and forest green wallpaper. *This* was a room of men. The darkness looked totally out of place against the beach backdrop, but the décor was more of a statement than a lifestyle. The place was very different before Eric's mom ran off with the tennis instructor from their country club a few years ago.

The only thing that saved Mrs. Whitman's exit from being a total cliché was that the tennis instructor was a rather attractive woman named Claire. Eric traditionally spends the holidays and one month out of the summer with them in the Hamptons.

"Have a seat. Have a seat," Mr. Whitman said as he deposited me on the brown suede couch. The man did have a penchant for repeating himself.

"Come in, boys," he said to his son and Drew, who were still standing in the doorway. "Come in."

Eric and Drew looked at each other. There was a definite chill in the room, and I have to admit it was emanating from me. They could tell I was in the mood for a showdown of some kind. Understandably, they didn't have a clue what it was about.

They eventually did as Mr. Whitman instructed, sitting on the two leather chairs at the entrance of the room.

"Look at this," Mr. Whitman said as he held his arms out toward us. "The Three Musketeers, together again."

Hold on! Let me clarify that comment.

There were never any *Three* Musketeers. Eric and I have never been friends, much less as close as Musketeers. Or Mouseketeers, even.

But, Drew . . . that's another story entirely.

A long time ago, we used to be friends. *More* than friends, actually. We were *best* friends. Inseparable since kindergarten. The originators of the Vampire Pact. Except back then it was the Super Secret Agent Pact. We agreed that if one of us was ever recruited by a Top Secret Ultra Black Ops Government Agency, he would insist that the other was also brought in. That way we could be partners in saving the world from foreign powers.

We were the *Two* Musketeers. But somewhere along the way—soccer camp the summer before sixth grade, to be specific—Eric came into the picture and started following us around. Insert image of little puppy dog here, if it so pleases you.

But the status quo hadn't totally changed. For years, it was Drew and me with Eric tagging along. Until one day . . . it wasn't anymore.

It was taking a while for Mr. Whitman to catch on to the new dynamic, so we all had to sit through a round of questions about my family, my schoolwork, and assorted personal details that I'm sure Mr. Whitman would forget the moment I left. That took up a good five minutes before we were both searching for something to talk about.

"It looks like you men have things to discuss," Mr. Whitman finally said. I suspect he caught on to the fact that he and I were the only ones who had spoken since we all entered the house. "I'll be in my study. Bryan, it was good to see you. Good to see you, indeed."

"You too, Mr. Whitman," I mumbled.

As soon as Mr. Whitman left, the room fell into silence. Eric and Drew were waiting for me to say something, but I wasn't even sure where to begin.

"How was the trip?" I asked.

"Fine," they said in unison.

"Are you really thinking of going to New Mexico?" I asked Drew. "I thought you always wanted to go somewhere on the East Coast."

"I'm looking at different places," Drew said. "I don't know what I want. I've got a while to figure it out."

"I get that," I said. I had no clue where I wanted to go either.

I guess Eric wasn't into small talk, because he jumped in with, "Is something wrong?"

"Why would you think that?" I asked, switching to full on attitude. "Just because I visit on a Saturday afternoon? Obviously something must be wrong? I couldn't just stop by to say hi?"

Honestly, I had no idea what I was saying.

"I'm sorry," Eric said, matching my attitude. "Have I *done* something to you?"

"Oh, *that's* precious," I said. "Like you—"

"Hey!" Drew interrupted. "Knock it off!"

That managed to shut Eric and me up. But we still sat seething at each other. This kind of thing has been happening between Eric and me for years. I guess, technically, I'm the one responsible for the attitude. But, can you *really* blame me this time? How many of my best friends does he want to take from me?

"Bryan," Drew said, calmly. "What brings you here?"

"Sam," I said.

"Is she okay?" Eric quickly asked.

"No," I said, reluctantly giving him points for being concerned. I quickly took them away too. "No thanks to you."

"What did I do?" he asked.

"Well, first of all, you couldn't keep your hands to yourself."

"Hey, Sam never said you two were together."

"What are you talking about?!" I can't believe he thought I was jealous.

"What are *you* talking about?" Though I guess I could understand why he might be confused.

Realizing that we were getting nowhere, I stopped the attack and quickly brought Eric and Drew up to speed on everything they'd missed since leaving for New Mexico on Thursday. "And she's doing it for you," I added at the end, driving home the point that I blamed Eric for Sam's situation. "She's giving up her role in the show so you don't lose your place on the team."

I let that last comment hang in the air for a moment. Eric didn't even bother defending himself. He just sat there. Silently. You'd think he would at least say something. But no.

Eventually, he got up off his chair and went to the phone.

"What are you doing?" I asked.

He simply pushed a button and waited. Not even bothering to look at me.

"Headmaster Collins?" Eric said into the phone. "This is Eric Whitman."

Did I mention that most of the school parents have the headmaster's private residence on speed dial?

I sat back on the couch, trying not to look at Drew, while Eric explained to the headmaster why Sam couldn't have possibly attacked Wren on Thursday. Eric even went so far as to take full responsibility for his actions for cutting soccer practice and admitted that he was prepared for whatever punishment the coach felt necessary.

He did it all of his own free will and without any prompting from me.

Lest you think that selfless act of nobility changed my mind about him. Sorry. Wrong. He's still a total asshat as far as I'm concerned.

Well, maybe not *total*.

The Mousetrap

Jimmy handed me a program and I immediately opened it to check my name. It was spelled right, for a change. More often than not, the printer "corrects" the spelling to "Brian," ignoring the fact that "Bryan" is a perfectly acceptable form of the word. Personally, I think "Brian Stark" looks like a third-rate agent specializing in dog acts or people who used to guest-star on *Star Trek*. At least "*Bryan* Stark" has some flair to it.

Or not.

I carefully slipped the program into my script so I could add it to the Bryan stack when I got home. If I was right, the Bryans had finally caught up to the Brians. I then stuck the script in my back pocket because I knew I'd be checking it at least a hundred times before I set foot onstage. I get a little crazy about my lines on show nights.

Still, there's nothing like the excitement of being backstage on opening night. Or on closing night. You can probably imagine how frenetic things are when your opening night *is* closing night. One night to get the show right. To hit your marks. To know your lines. No chance to fix the mistakes or try something new.

One night to succeed or fail.

Then, throw in double, triple, and quadruple casting, add a wild week of losing every one of your leads to the general chaos, and you might start to understand what the Roberta Kittridge Dressing Room looked like with only fifteen minutes to curtain.

Thankfully, we have a fairly large dressing room. The space is divided by a row of folding screens to separate the boys from the girls. The segregating of boys and girls is more of a *suggestion* than a reality. With a cast of dozens getting into costumes and makeup, there really isn't enough space for modesty in the dressing room.

"You've all got your programs. Are you happy?" Jimmy said as he shifted from passive-obsessive to obsessive-aggressive. Show nights always did this to him. "This is your fifteen-minute call. I'll be back for your ten-minute call in five minutes."

"You mean four minutes and fifty-nine seconds," I said, hoping to lighten his mood.

"Four minutes and fifty-eight seconds," Sam added from beside me.

Jimmy glared at us, yelled, "Actors!" and left the room in a huff.

Now, just because Sam was sitting next to me and we were riffing off each other, do not think that all was forgiven. She hadn't managed to speak directly *to* me since she arrived forty-five minutes earlier.

With Eric's confession, it was finally clear that someone had stuck the hardware in Sam's locker hoping to frame her. From there, the headmaster took the logical leap that the copy of the CD with naked photos of Cindy had also been planted. With no real evidence, he was forced to reinstate Sam in the show.

At the same time, there was still no evidence that indicated Heather was the one behind the frame-up. So she stayed as the act two Dorothy while Sam came back in for act one.

The show was now set to open with flair, but end in tragedy.

The jury was still out on what Eric's punishment would be for skipping practice. I could only assume that was the reason Sam still wasn't speaking to me. That made it all the more difficult for us to get ready, since Jimmy had assigned us seats next to each other. And the first rule of show night is do not mess with Jimmy's organizational system.

"Promise you won't laugh!" Hope yelled from the boys' side of the dressing screen. Sam and I were sitting at the long table on the girls' side, already in costume, trying not to look at each other. She was in makeup, but I didn't have to put mine on until intermission.

Without acknowledging each other, Sam and I were already snickering in anticipation. "Promise!" we yelled back simultaneously. What was one more broken promise this week, anyway?

"You're already laughing!" Hope yelled back.

At this, we cracked up. You'd think this shared laugh before the show would bring us together. I thought it would. But when I looked over to Sam, she was looking pointedly in the opposite direction.

Hope is not one to embarrass easily. We could only imagine what she looked like since she refused to let us see her in costume until this moment. Hence the laughter.

"Get out here," Sam yelled.

"Fine."

Hope stepped out from behind the dressing screen.

We both sat stone-faced, willing ourselves not to laugh.

I can't speak for Sam, but it was some of the best acting I have ever done.

As Glinda the Good Witch, Hope was a vision in fluffy pink taffeta on top of more crinoline than in an entire production of *Grease*. She looked not unlike a giant pile of cotton candy. I don't think I'd ever seen her in so much color. And the whole black outfit Goth-Ick look only started when we got to high school.

"Oh, shut up," Hope said, even though we were both sitting in stony silence.

"I think you look . . . *beautiful*," I said, stretching out that last word into way more syllables than nature had intended.

"How did Mr. Randall get you into an outfit that can be found on the color wheel?" Sam asked.

"Oh, I made my little adjustments," Hope said conspiratorially. "I'm wearing a black bra underneath."

"We can see," I said.

"Pink taffeta isn't as concealing as one might think," Sam added.

Hope's eyes bugged out and she ran back to the guys' side. I assume she went behind the privacy curtain for a quick underwear change.

"You didn't see the bra either, did you?" I asked.

Sam smiled at me slyly.

Even when we weren't speaking, we were totally in sync.

I figured this was my opening. "Look—"

"After the show," she said. So much for being in sync. "I need to get into character."

I guess I couldn't blame her. Thirteen minutes and twenty-five seconds to curtain wasn't the best time to have an emotional discussion. As she finished up her makeup, Jason saddled up to our area.

"Break a leg, guys," he said.

"Break a leg," we replied.

Even though I knew this had been Jason's preshow ritual for years, it seemed a little inappropriate for him to be wishing everyone in the cast to break a leg. Considering what had happened to Wren the other day and all.

"Hey, Bryan," he continued. "I just took a peek through the curtain. There's a strange guy sitting with your mom."

"Thanks, Jason," I said as he moved on to wish broken legs to the rest of the cast.

The "strange guy" Jason was joking about was obviously my dad. It was nice of Jason to let me know Dad had made it in time. Not that this was a surprise. No matter where in the world Dad is, he always makes it to a show before the curtain goes up. Since his mysterious business travel began back when I was around nine, he has never missed one performance, one birthday, one holiday, or any other special event. He is great on the big stuff. It's the day-to-day he needs to work on.

Sam was going through her preshow vocal exercises when I heard her stop halfway through. Something must have been wrong, because she never stops in the middle of her exercises. It's a ritual. When I turned toward her, I saw her looking for something.

"Where's Toto?" she asked. It was more of a rhetorical question. She wasn't speaking to me directly, but I took it as an opening.

"Where did you see him last?" I asked.

"Right here." She pointed to the end of the table. "I was working with him before Hope showed us her outfit."

"No worries," I said. "Just go to the prop closet and get one of the spares."

She let out an annoyed huff and went over to the closet. I know she was upset because she had been working with that specific Toto all week, but a stuffed dog is a stuffed dog. Any dog will do.

"The Totos are gone," Sam said. "All of them."

I did a quick scan of the dressing room. The place was packed with people buzzing all over. Anyone could have easily moved the Totos. Accidents happen, especially on opening night. But I knew this was no accident. This was . . .

"Heather," we said in unison.

We looked over at the other Dorothy's station, but Heather wasn't there. We were about to tear apart the dressing room when Sam noticed Heather walking out the door. She had a Toto under her arm.

"That's it," Sam said as she stormed toward the door. "I've had enough."

I hurried after her, grabbing her arm. "Wait. She wants you to follow her."

"I can't go onstage without Toto."

I doubted that anyone would make that big a deal if she pantomimed the dog, but Sam is more serious about these things than I am. I knew we should have told Jimmy and let him handle it. He was back in the dressing room, but he was also clearly in panic mode. I didn't want to be responsible for sending him over the edge.

"I'll go," I said. "You stay here."

"But—"

"Just stay here," I said. I ran back to the makeup table and grabbed my camera. Just in case. Maybe I'd get a nice action shot of Heather up to no good. We could run them in this month's issue of the *Star* along with the pics of the fallen lamp.

We weren't supposed to leave the dressing room once we signed in, but I felt pretty justified in breaking the rules. I was on a mission to save the show. Still, I didn't want to incur the stage manager's wrath, no matter how noble my intentions. After making sure that Jimmy was occupied tormenting the munchkins, I hurried out of the dressing room, but the hall was already empty. I had no idea which way Heather went.

Since the gate was down to block off the rest of the school, there were only two options. Going to the right would take me out to the lobby. As most of the cast had already snuck a peek out the curtain, I knew the theater was almost entirely full at this point. It was possible that Heather was hurrying around the front to save seats for her family. *Because she's that thoughtful and considerate.*

I turned left and headed for the pavilion.

It's always weird being at school when it's closed. Since no one is supposed to be walking around, all the lights are off except for the ones at the entrance to Hall Hall. Passing by the rows of defective lockers totally alone in the dark reminded me of way too many horror movies for it not to be a little unnerving. I was so busy hearing imaginary noises all around me that I nearly missed the two voices—straining to stay at an agitated whisper—up ahead of me.

I walked even more carefully, not wanting to give away my presence. It sounded like Heather was arguing with someone. Definitely a male someone. Probably Jax.

While normally a lovers' quarrel would only be interesting for the ability to generate gossip, I couldn't help but think that this one could be more valuable. I got my camera ready as I tiptoed to the entrance of the pavilion.

"Get going!" Heather whisper-yelled to Jax.

"I thought you were coming," he replied.

"I've got to get back to the dressing room," she said.

"No one's going to miss you. You don't go on for, like, an hour."

"What are you, a baby?" Heather asked. "Just go!"

"This is your dumb plan. You go."

Dumb plan? What could *this* be in reference to, I wonder?

Okay, I didn't wonder at all. I knew.

"I don't even care about this stupid play," he added.

For some reason, I got all defensive about that. How dare he make fun of the school show! Where is his Orion Pride?

But Heather was defending the art form just fine at the moment. Besides, I had other things to worry about. A seemingly disembodied hand reached out of the darkness and grabbed me on the shoulder.

"What are you doing?" Sam—who was attached to that hand—asked. Loudly.

"Waiting for my heart to slow down," I said, urging her to be quiet.

"Why aren't you getting Toto back from Heather? She's right there."

"Apparently, Jax is having problems with her dumb plan . . . and this stupid show."

"He called the show stupid?"

"Sam."

"Can't say I disagree."

"Sam."

"What?"

"They're leaving."

Heather and Jax had stopped their fighting and were heading out to the courtyard, with Toto.

"Go back to the dressing room," I said to Sam as I made my way across the Pavilion with my camera in hand.

"Where are you going?" she asked, grabbing me before I could go out to the courtyard.

"Wherever they're going," I said. "They're up to something, and I'm going to find out what it is."

I pulled myself out of Sam's grasp and went out to the courtyard. Heather and Jax were nowhere to be seen. It didn't matter. Unless they both decided to take a lovers' leap off the bluff—one could hope—there was only one direction they could walk. I went that way too.

The Orion Academy grounds can get pretty dark at night, what with all the trees and stuff. Luckily, there was a full moon, so I could see well enough to get to my destination. Once I made my way across the courtyard and the north wing of school, I was rewarded when I saw a dim light coming out the open door to the observatory. I hurried to the doorway, stopping along the edge to take a peek. Toto was inside, sitting up on the metal catwalk like he was waiting for Dorothy to rescue him from the wicked witch. As I took in the situation, another hand grabbed me.

Correction. The *same* hand grabbed me *again*.

SAM!

"Get back to the dressing room," I whispered through clenched teeth. It was, like, five minutes to curtain. Jimmy would be calling places soon. He was probably freaking out this very minute.

"And let you stumble into Jax alone?" Sam said. "He can beat the crap out of you."

I couldn't argue with that logic, so I didn't try. Our shows tend to start ten minutes late, anyway. (The result of parents who usually take more time to get into makeup than our cast does. And I mean both the moms and the dads.) So, technically, we still had about fifteen minutes for her to get back.

"I found Toto," I said with a nod in the stuffed dog's direction.

"How dumb does she think we are?" Sam asked.

"Well, considering you did follow me out here when you should be getting ready to make an entrance."

"You know, I haven't quite forgiven you yet," she said. "Don't know if now's the time to be making jokes."

Forgiven me for what? I wondered. I got her back in the show. Why was I suddenly the bad guy?

"Wait here," I said.

"Be careful."

Like she could have given me any more obvious advice.

I couldn't see anyone inside the observatory, but that didn't mean that Heather and Jax weren't waiting for me on the other side of the telescope. I carefully slipped into the room with my camera at the ready. I wasn't sure what to expect, but I was prepared to get some photographic evidence.

I made it to the staircase without a problem. It didn't sound like anyone was in the large room. I guess I should have given the place the once over, but Sam didn't have time. I slowly made my way up the steps, careful to test each tread before I put my weight down on it. All of them were firmly in place. Even the top step had been fixed. Once I reached Toto, I turned to see Sam leaning in the doorway.

I was about to wave the all clear, when the lights when out.

"Bryan!" Sam yelled into the dark room.

"I'm okay!" I yelled back.

But it was too late. Sam let out a yelp as someone pushed her inside and slammed the observatory door shut behind her.

No Exit

The observatory lights came back on. Sam had stumbled a few feet into the room. I still had Toto in my hands on the catwalk. But we both knew the door was locked without even touching it.

Off in the distance, I heard Heather's evil laughter echoing across campus.

"Mwa-ha-ha!"

But maybe that was my imagination again.

I ran down the stairs and joined Sam at the exit. It was locked, naturally. We looked out the glass window in the center of the door, but could only see the dark night surrounding us.

"Heather! Let us out of here!" Sam yelled.

"Come on!" I yelled, pounding on the metal door along side of her.

I couldn't believe I was so stupid to let Heather trap us like that. Too bad we couldn't do anything about it at the moment beyond yelling.

We gave up on the noise before our voices gave out. She slid down to the floor and sat in silence while I looked for some other way out. I ran over to the observatory phone, suspecting the worst. It only took a second to confirm. No dial tone. No way to let anyone know we were there. The show would be starting in a few minutes. There was plenty of time before I went on in the second act. But I wasn't about to let Sam miss her entrance. She opened the play.

You might think that Mr. Randall would hold the show for us. He probably would. But Mr. Randall wasn't running things at the moment. On opening night, the show is turned over to the stage manager. And if you think Jimmy can be anal about where we sit in the makeup room, you should see him when it comes to us taking places.

Once he saw Sam wasn't there, he'd pull Heather onstage. Not that it would require much pulling. Then he'd make a quick announcement that the role had been recast and would raise the curtain before Mr. Randall could do anything about it.

I'm sure Mr. Randall would then rush backstage, but the damage would already be done. The show would go on.

Without us.

Hope would insist on sending out a search party. Sam's mom would probably head it up. But who would ever think to look for us all the way out here?

I gave up on finding an exit and sat beside Sam. Hoping

to lighten the mood, I came up with an escape suggestion. "I guess we could find the switch that opens up the roof and extends the telescope. One of us could shimmy up the telescope, drop onto the roof, and then jump to the ground."

"Go ahead."

I did not like her tone at all.

"Still, I have to say, it was an impressive plan," I said, struggling for conversation. "Heather probably knew we'd come here together. She anticipated that one of us would stay outside. So she had to find a way to force us both inside."

"A true criminal mastermind," Sam said.

"On the bright side," I said, "Heather got us talking again."

"Seems like you're the one doing all the talking," Sam said as she turned away from me.

"We're stuck in here," I said. "We might as well get it all out. Why are you so mad at me?"

Sam looked me over, like she was deciding whether or not she wanted to deal with this now. I guess logic eventually won out. We had nothing else to do at the moment. "You shouldn't have gone to Eric," she said.

"Is that what this is about?" I was glad to finally have some context. "I was doing it for you."

"I don't remember asking you to get involved."

"Friends don't have to ask," I said, basking in my own smugness. I had the moral high ground here. I don't know why she refused to see it. Granted, it would have been easier to see if we were standing under the stage lights, but we can't have everything.

"You only went to Eric because you didn't care if he got in trouble," Sam said. I would have been more impressed by her reasoning if my motivation hadn't been so obvious.

"What do you even see in him?" I asked.

She shot back with her own question. "What do you hate about him?

"He's *so* boring."

"To you, maybe," Sam said. "I know plenty of people who find him quite interesting."

"Of course you do. He's *perfect*. So boringly perfect. And normal. You deserve better than normal. You deserve extraordinary."

"Star soccer player. At the top of the class. Looks that could stop a truck. This is normal?"

"You know what I mean."

"Hardly ever, lately."

How could I put it into words when I didn't even understand it myself? Sure, my hatred of Eric went way back and had more to do with Drew than it did Sam. But this wasn't about that. Honestly. This was about something else entirely. "You deserve someone as unique as you are. He doesn't fit in with us. He's so . . . typical."

"You know, I'm getting a little tired of you always talking about how *unique* we are. How we're the Drama Geeks and that makes us different by definition."

"Well, we are," I insisted.

"Are we? Really?" Sam asked. "Your mom designs outfits for dogs that cost more than my entire wardrobe. Hope writes poetry about a pet that died five years ago. Cindy's posing nude and appearing in Victoria's Secret ads. Heather's going around knocking off the competition for the lead in a high school production of *The Wizard of Oz*. You and me? We're the most *normal* people we know."

"But we're the Drama Geeks," I said weakly.

"And at any other school, people would be staring at us when we went down the halls between classes singing show tunes," Sam said.

"Exactly."

"But it's kind of hard to compete when half the people we go to school with think the hallways are their own personal runway where they show the latest fashions Mommy and Daddy bought them when they jetted off to Milan over spring break."

I wanted to argue the point, but I gave up on fighting logical arguments long ago. Sam was right. We *are* normal. Blandly, boringly normal.

Sure, we know how to turn a phrase. And I'd say that we each have a pretty biting wit. At any other school, we *would* be the eccentric artsy crowd. But when it comes down to it, the only thing freakish about us in comparison with the rest of Orion Academy is that we aren't insane.

Although that didn't explain the overriding question.

"But Eric?" I asked.

Sam shook her head and laughed at me. "Aren't you tired of people thinking that you and I are dating?"

"Well . . . yeah," I said. And for the first time, I realized that was a lie. I didn't really mind. Because as long as people thought we were dating, no one was asking me why I *wasn't* trying to date anyone else. "But it's not that big a deal," I quickly added to cover the revelation.

"It is to me," Sam said very gently. I think she was trying to spare my feelings. "I *want* to date someone and turn heads because I'm dating him. Not because you and I know all the words to 'Suddenly Seymour.'"

"We are pretty good on that one," I said.

Well, we are!

"Have you ever noticed that when people around here look at me, it's not because of my acting? Or even our eccentricities?" Sam asked. "I'm reminded that I'm different every day here. Whether it's the girls asking me where I got my outfit, knowing that it's last year's fashion because it came from an outlet. Or if it's the guys who know they can't take me home to Mother because my mom is only a teacher. So, yes, I like the normalcy that comes with Eric. I *crave* it, in fact."

I thought about what she was saying. It took a moment for it to sink in. I had never realized all those times we joked about hitting Rodeo or made fun of girls wearing outfits with designer names emblazoned on them that Sam wasn't enjoying it the way Hope and I were. I never thought that we were all that different. I guess it's easier to be that way when you don't have reminders constantly slamming you in the face.

Suddenly, I heard how Cindy was all "It's not like she has all that much going for her beside her talent."

Or when Heather was talking about how, "She only goes here because her mom's a teacher."

Sam must get that all the time.

"I'm sorry," I said. "I just assumed . . ."

And there it was . . . exactly what I promised wouldn't happen: a heavy-handed moral on making assumptions about people.

Damn.

Wicked

The silence stretched on for a bit. It was probably the longest time we had ever spent together in one room without speaking, except when we were taking a test. To say this wasn't how I expected to spend my evening would be an understatement. The lockdown was one thing, but knowing how much I had unintentionally been hurting Sam was another. There was only one thing I could say in this situation. "You do realize everyone's going to assume you're after his money."

And finally . . . laughter.

"I am sorry," I said. To be honest, I wasn't 100 percent sure what I was apologizing for: giving Eric such a hard time, being clueless to her social status, or using her as my high school beard. I figured I'd leave it at a simple "I'm sorry" and let her attach it to whatever she wanted.

"Thanks," she said. "Now, how do we get out of here?"

"I'm still leaning toward my shimmy up the telescope idea."

Not surprisingly, Sam ignored me. "It's a shame there isn't more light in here," she said. "There's a chance someone could see the light through the window and come out here."

I jumped up from the ground. "That's it!"

"What's it?" Sam asked as she slowly rose.

"Light!" I pulled out my camera and held it up to the window.

"This is *so* not the time for taking pictures," Sam said. At the same time, she struck a pose in her gingham. "Though I do look fabulous in my costume. It would be a travesty if my fans didn't have some record of me in it."

"Tone it down, Madame Egotistia," I said as I took a sample picture of the door. The camera I used had red eye-reduction, so it ran a series of flashes before the actual flash. The bright light lit up the observatory and, more importantly, spilled out the small window.

"Brilliant!" Sam said.

"We have to do this sparingly," I said. If I started going all flash happy, eventually we'd run out of battery and hope. (That's with a lower case-h-hope. Although if the camera flash helped capital-H-Hope find us, that was okay, too.)

I tried to factor out how long the show would run and then calculate how I could burn the flash off at set intervals. But that was just too much math for my brain to wrap around. Considering we had never even run one act all the way through in rehearsal, it wasn't like I had an idea of how long it took. Not to mention how much Heather's fumbling might slow it down. I figured if I put a minute between each shot and made sure to leave enough battery for the end of the show, we might be okay.

"Now, we wait," I said.

"Oh, fun." Sam slid back down to the floor. "As you know, I'm famous for my patience."

I couldn't blame her for being depressed. It was quite an emotional week for her. She went from having a small leading role, to getting the entire play, to losing the entire play in a matter of days. But just because we didn't have an audience didn't mean we couldn't do the play. As Shakespeare said, "all the world *is* a stage."

I slid my script out of my back pocket, careful not to lose my program.

She looked at me and the script. "Don't even."

Undaunted, I flipped to the first act and prompted her on her opening lines.

"You're kidding, right?"

I repeated the line.

"This is crazy," she said. "We don't even have a stage."

Obviously, she wasn't taking Shakespeare's words into consideration. I stretched out my arms to the room around us. "Think of it as theater in the round." I held Toto out to her and hit her with my version of puppy dog eyes.

The wonderful thing about true actors is that they're always ready to perform. Even if there isn't an audience around. I'm sure that to some people, that's the really annoying thing about actors too. But we really don't care about those kinds of people, do we?

Sam took the prompt—and the dog—and started the Orion Academy Spring Theatrical Production of *The Wizard of Oz*, Observatory Version. We ran through the first act with me playing the guy parts and her playing the girls. Not surprisingly, she knew a fair amount of the girls' lines without having to look at the script. That is one way that she *is* freakishly unique.

Every few minutes I would take a picture of the surrounding landscape and allow the flash to go off. It may have been a waste of time, but at least we were entertaining ourselves.

We worked our way through the first act about as quickly as I imagine they were inside. Actually, we were probably faster. We were averaging several camera flashes per scene, with no hope that we'd be getting out of the locked observatory before classes on Monday. We had just gotten to the point where Dorothy, the Scarecrow, and the Tin Man were about to meet the Lion when there was a banging at the door.

"Sam! Bryan! Are you in there?" a muffled voice yelled from outside.

"Mom!" We both yelled as we bounded over to the glass window, where our savior, Anne, was peeking in.

Thankfully, she didn't bother to ask us the silly question of what we were doing locked in the observatory. She just said, "I'll get the key," and was gone.

"Looks like we'll get you back in time for your act," Sam said, doing a rather poor job of covering her disappointment over missing her act. Not that I blamed her.

"And once we explain what happened, Mr. Randall will put you in the second act too," I said.

"So long as Heather doesn't have any more surprises for us," she said. I couldn't blame her for the negativity. With Heather Mayflower, it was always best to be prepared.

Anne was back in a few minutes with the key and Mr. Randall. Sam grabbed her Toto, and we were off. We filled Anne and Mr. Randall in on what happened on our way back to the auditorium. They both believed us, but without any evidence it was going to be hard to punish Heather for any of it. It was just our word against hers. And she spoke the language of her daddy's money.

Intermission had just begun when we reached the auditorium. We wound our way through the crowd of parents, heading backstage. I thought I heard Eric calling Sam's name, but the noise of the crowd drowned him out. It was just as well. We didn't have time to deal with that, too.

Anne peeled off in another direction as we worked our way through the auditorium. It would have been easier to go around through the empty halls, but this was the direction Mr. Randall had taken.

Being actors who know nothing about subtlety, we burst into the dressing room with just the right amount of flourish. And let me tell you, until you've heard a room go from wildly animated conversations to pin-drop silence merely because you walked through a door, you've never experienced a truly dramatic entrance.

The cast was looking at us with various expressions of

relief and annoyance. Clearly some of the cast still believed Sam was a troublemaker who was just looking for more attention by missing the first act.

Naturally, Hope was the one to break the silence. "It's about time you two got here," she said. "Now, would you like to explain what the heck is going on?"

Hope was surely a sight in her pink taffeta and . . . black steel-toe boots?

I guess she saw me looking at her feet, because she smiled brightly and said, "Found my character."

With a laugh, I let my attention drift from Hope to the rest of the room. Heather was sitting at her makeup station, pointedly ignoring us. She didn't even have the class to look the least bit concerned.

I was momentarily distracted when Eric came into the room. I wanted to remind him that non-cast members weren't allowed backstage during intermission, but it seemed pointless at the moment. The way he moved directly to Sam and took her into his arms was certainly melodramatic enough for him to fit in with the Drama Geeks.

Shortly afterward, Headmaster Collins came into the dressing room and took up a position beside Mr. Randall. I guess Anne had told the headmaster what was going on. I took stock of the room one more time and realized everyone was looking at me for some kind explanation.

Talk about performance anxiety.

Anne was still missing, but I knew it was time to get on with the show. I considered opening with the old "I know you're all wondering why I called you here." But considering we were in the dressing room during intermission, where else would everyone be?

My mind was flooded with information. I couldn't figure out the best way to present it all. It wasn't like anyone needed a recap of the week. The events of the past six days were all that we had been talking about lately. It only made sense to skip to the end.

"Heather did it!" I blurted out. I even pointed an accusatory finger in her direction.

I had expected gasps and maybe even a few people fainting from shock. Some *applause* at the very least.

Yeah. They were still silently staring at me.

"Could you be more specific, Bryan?" Mr. Randall gently prodded. "Please explain what it is you are accusing Heather of."

"She did it all," I said. "Everything. Well, maybe not the lamp falling. But everything else."

Oh, yeah. *Much* clearer.

"Mr. Randall," Heather said calmly as she stood. "I don't know what he's talking about."

Take three.

"I'm talking about locking us in the observatory so we would miss the play," I said. "I'm talking about framing Sam for everything. I'm talking about Wren's 'accident,' and posting Cindy's pictures on the school website. I'm talking about nearly killing Suze. All so you could be the lone Dorothy."

I replayed my accusation over in my head. It still sounded stupid. But maybe that was the brilliance of her plan.

"Headmaster Collins," Heather said. "Weren't we through all this yesterday? There's no evidence to prove I did any of those things."

"Mr. Stark," Headmaster Collins said, immediately raising my own tension level. "We are all well aware of those accusations, but we are looking for proof. Can you prove any of it? Can you prove Heather locked you in the observatory?"

"Well . . . no."

"Did you, at least, see her lock the door?"

"Umm . . ."

"Then I'm afraid my hands are tied," the headmaster said. He didn't seem all that upset by it. I assume that's because he knows my parents aren't nearly as much of a threat as Heather's dad.

I looked at Sam. She was looking at me. Neither of us knew what to do.

"However," Mr. Randall added, "since there is still no evidence to indicate Sam's guilt, I don't see why she can't perform the second act. That is, if she is familiar with the second act."

"Oh, she knows it," Hope said.

All eyes turned to Sam. She looked almost shy as she nodded her head.

"Well, that settles that," Mr. Randall said.

"Wait a minute!" Heather stormed over to Mr. Randall. Somehow, I didn't think she considered the matter settled. "I don't see why I should be punished just because Sam couldn't make her call in time."

"Don't even try it," Sam warned, holding out Toto threateningly.

"Like I'm afraid of you," Heather said. She was stroking her own stuffed Toto in her arms, playing up the role of Evil Heather to the hilt.

The two girls stared each other down. As we all braced for Catfight on a Hot Tin Roof, the dressing room door opened and Anne entered with Jax.

Heather's henchman took one look at the room, saw Sam and me beside the headmaster and burst: "She made me do it!"

"Shut up, moron," Heather said.

"Don't you try to pin this on me," he said. "You were the one who wanted to trap them in the observatory."

As everyone in the dressing room let out an audible gasp, Heather dropped her Toto and bolted out the door.

"Where's she running?" Sam asked.

"Fleeing the country?" I suggested with a shrug.

I ran out the door after her, grabbing Toto on the way. (The Fleischmans did me a favor. I wasn't going to repay them by letting one of their creations get all dirty.)

Heather was already halfway down the empty hall when I got out there. I had no clue where she was going, but I wasn't about to give her time to escape so she could plot a way out of this mess. I silently apologized to the Fleischman Brothers and flung Toto at her head with all my might.

He landed somewhere around her feet. But the stuffed dog still managed to trip her up, sending her sprawling to the ground.

Ding-dong, the witch was dead. Well . . . maybe just stunned a little.

Everyone poured out of the dressing room to find Heather on the floor. She glared at me with a level of hatred I suspect she usually reserves for her sister.

Headmaster Collins took Jax and Heather by the arms. "I think we should go to my office." He then looked at Heather. "Then I'll have a private word with your father."

At that, the entire cast broke into applause.

"We got her, my pretty," Sam said to me as the applause died down.

"And her little dog, too," I added, picking up the stuffed Toto.

As we shared a laugh, Hope smacked us both in the backs of our heads.

All's Well That Ends Well

After all that, you'll probably be shocked to learn that the second act started pretty close to on time. It went off nearly without a hitch. The cast kicked it up a notch with Sam in the role. Hope was excellent with her kick-ass Glinda. And Tasha's flyaway exit in the balloon basket got a full minute of applause.

Sam was brilliant, as expected. She had all her lines down and even covered for me when I dropped one. The jitterbug wasn't as much of a dance number as it could have been, but you should have heard the girl sing. All in all, it was a stellar performance.

Nobody seemed to question why Sam was in the second act when she was supposed to be in the first. In fact, my parents later told me that they hadn't even noticed that anything was wrong with the play. Other than Heather's lackluster performance in the first act, that is.

"Lackluster" was their word, not mine. Nor was it anyone else's in the cast. That night at the cast party I heard many other words to describe Heather's acting. Most of them are not printable here. But before we got to the party, there was one more thing that needed to be done.

Sam got a standing ovation during the curtain call. I was glad to see Wren and Suze in the front row yelling at the top of their voices. I guess Cynthia was still in New York in her underwear. Heather's sister, Holly, was right beside them, though. She looked more annoyed than anything. I could understand it. She had had a tough week. Almost as tough as her sister's.

The warm embrace from the audience was almost the perfect way to end the show. But I had a much better idea.

When Mr. Randall got up on stage to give his curtain speech, I pulled him aside to make a suggestion. I wasn't sure if he'd heard me over the noise, but I was hopeful.

Mr. Randall stepped center stage and took up the microphone. "Parents, faculty, students, friends . . . paparazzi," he said addressing the hushed crowd and flashing cameras. "As many of you know, this has been a trying week for our little drama club. But I think we managed to pull off a good one here." The audience went wild again. "There are so many people to thank, and so many things to say right now, but it's late and we all want to get to the cast party." This time, everyone in the audience *and* onstage burst into applause.

During the break in his speech, Mr. Randall looked at me and smiled. He *did* hear me. "But before that," he continued.

"Due to an unusual set of circumstances that would take forever to explain, we did a little switcheroo with casting this evening. And because of that, I feel, we all missed out what could have been one of the highlights of our production. Ladies and gentlemen, if you would permit us to delay the party for a few extra minutes, I'd like to see if we could convince our remaining Dorothy to sing her rendition of 'Over the Rainbow.'"

Sam did an actual double take, from Mr. Randall to me to Mr. Randall again. She didn't even have time to protest before the audience went absolutely insane. I could even see Eric jumping up and down as he cheered. Apparently, Heather had butchered the song during the show, so they were probably looking for a good rendition.

Sam looked embarrassed, but that didn't stop her from stepping out of the crowded cast. And here's why Jimmy is the best stage manager any high school production has ever seen. Nobody even noticed when he left the stage and ran back to the soundboard, but wouldn't you know that as soon as Sam stepped up to the mic, the first few notes of the song were coming over the sound system.

There was only one word to describe the performance:

Flawless.

In theater, there is one sure way to tell when you've captured your audience. It's not by applause, it's by silence. Once Sam let go of the last note, there was not a sound in all of Hall Hall. Not a clap. Not even a breath. Everyone was overwhelmed by the pure beauty of her voice.

Then the entire place erupted.

I would love to stop things here with the happy ending. That would be such an old-school musical way to end things. I would add on a tag to say that Heather and Jax got the punishment they deserved. But this is Orion Academy, not the real world . . . and certainly not a classic from the golden age of Broadway.

Heather's dad was pulled out of the auditorium before the second act had started. By the time we reached curtain call, plans for the installation of the brand-new Anthony Mayflower School Lockers were in place, and Heather and Jax were given a stern talking-to.

Justice isn't swift around here so much as it is negotiable.

The official line was that since there was no actual evidence to prove Heather and Jax did anything other than lock us up in the observatory, they got off relatively easily. Especially considering their crimes included assault and attempted murder. Not that they were really *trying* to kill Suze. I'm willing to give them the benefit of the doubt—and avoid a libel suit—and say that they probably never expected such a violent reaction.

It was more stupidity than felony.

But Suze had already moved on . . . to New York, in fact. That's where she would be spending her summer, thanks to Hope. See, the sketchbook that Hope had stolen from Suze's bedroom? Hope sent it to her mom, the famous fashion designer, Natalie Ellis. The phone call Hope got on Friday was her mom telling her she loved every design in the book. By that afternoon, Suze had an invitation for a summer internship. All she had to do was convince her own mom to let her go.

More than an equitable fee for the work Suze did on Hope's dress.

The other Dorothys were equally agreeable. Wren wasn't interested in pressing charges on the arranged accident since she was suddenly cast as lead dancer in a video for a major star under the Mayflower Music label after her leg healed. And we already know how Cindy—I mean, Cynthia—was reaping the rewards of her "exposure."

Anne was the only one who tried to hold her ground. Heather *was* caught with a stolen test, after all. But Headmaster Collins forced Anne to trade off a failing grade for a punishment of a different color.

Okay, there was one actual repercussion: Heather and Jax were forbidden to attend the senior prom.

And speaking of repercussions, Eric was allowed to play in the soccer finals. Surprise, surprise. There was a lot of talk about suspension from the team or after-practice detention, but it was all forgotten by the time the game rolled around.

The Comets won. The crowd cheered.

Which brings me to the junior prom.

It was fantabulous!

I shared a limo with Sam and Eric and Hope and Drew. Suze came along as my date . . . 'cause I saved her life and all. Even better, she made me a vest, a tie, and a hatband for my fedora to go along with her self-designed cobalt blue dress.

We really stood out among a sea of designer gowns and tuxes, and have the photo to prove it.

Well, there *was* one dress that put our outfits to shame. But Suze had had her hand in that as well. Hope looked positively stunning in her black lace-Chanel designed-Shelley Winters-worn couture dress. Even her breasts looked understated in the classy outfit, beneath the beautiful wildflower corsage in a burst of colors that Drew had picked out for her.

We had a blast. I spent the entire night on the dance floor with Sam, Hope, Suze, and (surprisingly) Drew. I even got in a couple slow dances with Sam as the night wore on and Eric hung to the edge of the dance floor. After all that drama, it turns out that Eric doesn't even know how to dance.

Figures.

The curtain may have come down on the Orion Academy Spring Theatrical Production of *The Wizard of Oz* with me listed as Scarecrow #2, but I guess I was moving up in the cast list of my life. I may not have been the star of this particular drama, but I certainly played an integral part. There's still plenty of time for me to take the lead. This show may be over, but I've still got the rest of my own first act to play out.

And . . . scene.

Orion Academy Spring Theatrical Production

The Wizard of Oz

Cast List

Director

Mr. Terrance Randall

Asst. Director / Vocal Trainer

Ms. Deborah Monroe

Stage Manager

James Wilkey

Dorothy

Sam Lawson A Star Is Born

~~Cynthia Lakeside~~

Heather Mayflower Boo!!!

~~Suze Finberg~~

~~Wren Deslandes~~

Glinda

~~Wren Deslandes~~

Hope Rivera

. . . and her black steel-toe boots!

Auntie Em

Emily Whitsett

Uncle Henry

Hayden Reynolds

Hunk

Shawn Wallace

Scarecrow

Jason MacMillan

Bryan Stark

Hey, that's me! And it's spelled right, too!!

Hickory

Erica Prince

Tin Woodspeople
Trent J. Markus III
Randi Cates

Zeke
Theodore "Teddy" Dougherty

Lion
Jonathan Battles

Miss Gulch
Carol Young

Wicked Witch
Dakota Jane Markus
Linda Robertson

Nikko
Gary McNulty "Monkey Boy"

Professor Marvel
Kirk Weisman

The Wizard
Natasha Valentine

Guard
Madison Wu

Coachman
Van Henderson

Apple Trees
Hilary Huffman
Bryce Tanner

Munchkins
Members of the Ninth-Grade Class

Totos provided by *Fleischman Brothers Animal Emporium*

Everyone's a Critic

☆ For Babe, Amy, and Brané ☆

The Odd Couple

"SOMETIMES, I JUST WANT TO RIP YOUR HEAD OFF, DISEMBOWEL YOU, AND FEED YOU TO THE SHARKS!"

There's a pretty picture.

That dainty line of dialogue was courtesy of Hope Rivera, one of my best friends and banter partners. Hope was in the process of breaking up with her boyfriend and my *ex*-best friend, Drew. Not that this was anything new to them. At last count, Hope and Drew had broken up at least a dozen times. It's just that there was a note of finality in this particular fight. A note that was both sweet and sour at the same time, much like the chicken I was dining on with Suze Finberg as we shared a blanket while trying not to listen. Or, more specifically, trying not to look like we were listening, while we listened. Just like everyone else on our section of beach. Not that any of us could have missed it. Hope's voice does kind of carry.

"DON'T YOU DARE BLAME ME! YOU KNOW I DON'T HAVE A PROBLEM WITH IT. THAT'S ALL YOU."

We hadn't quite figured out what they were fighting over, but apparently it was Drew's issue, not Hope's. At least, if her latest outburst was to be believed.

"ALL YOU, BABY!"

Then again, it wasn't like she was having one of her more rational moments.

"How's the chicken, Bryan?" Suze asked me from our little patch of sand as we took in the unexpected dinner theater.

"Tastes like alligator," I said. "And the quiche?"

"Real men would totally eat it."

"Good to know," I said. The party could use a real man or two as far as I was concerned.

Speaking of not-so-real men, we were sitting on the sand outside of Eric Whitman's Mondo Malibu Dream House for the Start-of-Summer Beach Party. Our host, Eric, was nowhere to be found while his best friend's relationship was going through the wringer. *Nice.* Meanwhile, I was trying to avoid my wondering wanderings since Eric wasn't the only one missing at the moment.

A cute waiter circulated by our blanket, and Suze and I grabbed some vegetable pot stickers and continued to watch the show.

"I DON'T CARE IF EVERYONE CAN HEAR ME!"

That much was apparent.

Hope and Drew had been dating on and off for about . . . well, it seemed like forever, but it had been around three years.

I'd love to be able to tell some meet cute story about the first time they ever saw each other, but that would have happened back when Drew and I met her in kindergarten. The only thing cute about that meet was that I was positively adorable in my first-day-of-school outfit: GapKids from head to toe. Now that I think of it, I looked a bit like ye olde tyme newsboy, complete with strategically distressed messenger bag.

As for how the dating thing started, I'm not really sure. The two of them had never seemed particularly close while we were growing up. Then, one day after Drew and I stopped being best friends, I heard he was going out with Hope. That was later confirmed when I saw them holding hands between classes. Sorry, it's not a more exciting story, but since I wasn't in it all that much, how exciting could it have been?

"[CENSORED]!" (The language Hope was using, however, had gotten *very* exciting. Too exciting for me to even write here. Use your imagination.)

Just so you don't go thinking I'm ignoring Drew's part of the fight by only including Hope's dialogue, you'd be wrong. Drew wasn't saying much during the encounter. And what he had said had been spoken so softly that it was almost impossible to hear. Trust me, Suze and I tried. It wasn't easy. We had only managed to piece together the phrase "I'm putting you under a hex." And that couldn't be right. Aside from the fact that Drew didn't really go in for the occult, Hope was fairly religious and took these things seriously. If he ever tried to put her under a hex, she probably would have hauled off and knocked him out. Nope. They had to be fighting about a more worldly subject matter.

If only we could come up with a word that rhymed with hex.

Of course, our attention was split at the moment. "Try the crab puffs," Suze said as she handed me one.

"You can't eat crab puffs." I needlessly reminded her of her food allergy.

"I know," she said. "That's why I want you to try one. So you can tell me what I'm missing."

I smiled as I popped a puff in my mouth and gave her a thumbs-up. It was a pretty good puff. It was also a pretty good time. I mean, for the two of us. Hope and Drew didn't seem to be having much fun.

"So . . . ," Suze said, drawing out the word like she was trying to figure out how to approach a subject.

"So . . . ," I replied, wondering where she was going with this. Suze wasn't usually one for vague opening statements.

"I've had a lot of fun hanging out since the prom," she said.

"Oh," I replied, knowing *exactly* where this was going.

Seeing how my other best friend, Sam, is now coupled with Eric, and Hope and Drew are—or *were*—also a couple, we'd been spending a lot of time hanging out as a group lately. Never big on being the fifth wheel, I'd been inviting Suze along whenever we went out, which wound up being every single weekend since the prom.

Now, let me be clear about this: I *never* asked Suze on a date. I *never*, in any way, implied that I liked her as more than a friend. I wouldn't do that to her. I wouldn't do that to anyone. It's one thing to not mention the fact that I'm gay to my friends. It's another thing entirely to live a lie and use someone else in the process. I can't help it if she jumped to the wrong conclusion.

Can I?

"ARE YOU DONE?" Drew yelled at a volume that finally matched Hope's dulcet tones.

Whoa. Alert the media. Drew Campbell actually raised his voice.

Heads all over the beach turned in their direction, giving up any pretense of subtle eavesdropping, and stared, open-mouthed, at him. Outbursts like that were out of character for Drew. For Hope, it was second nature. But Drew? It was so shocking that Suze totally ignored me to watch what was happening. I'd have to thank Drew later for that.

"NO. I'M NOT DONE!" Hope yelled back.

"WELL, I AM!" Drew turned and stormed away from her . . . heading directly toward Suze and me.

My body went rigid. Why was he walking toward us? We didn't need to be in the middle of this. More specifically, *I* didn't need to be in the middle of this. I could see Hope readying her death glare. Whatever happened in the next few seconds could determine the entire course of my friendship with her. If she thought for a moment that I was on his side or rendering any kind of comfort, then she'd never speak to me again.

Okay, maybe I'm being a little melodramatic here, but you've never been under Hope's death glare, so don't judge.

Drew was getting closer. My mind was racing with things to say. Ways to make it clear that whatever they were fighting about, I was in Hope's corner. But, as Drew's face came closer,

I could see the hurt in his eyes. It was the same expression he had when he learned the truth about the Easter Bunny. Most kids have a thing about Santa Claus, but Drew had always been into the bunny. Seriously. A cute little animal that brings you free candy? What's not to love? And on that day so many years ago, he rode his bike right to my place in search of solace and friendship.

Why in the world would he come to me for that now?

Drew stopped at the edge of our blanket, looking down at Suze and me. At least, I assume he was looking down at us. I was positively enthralled by the plate resting in my lap. The food we still hadn't tasted appeared to be absolutely delicious. So delicious, I felt it warranted my total and absolute attention.

I guess Suze had a problem with the awkward silence, because she was the first to speak. "Are you guys okay?" she asked.

I think Drew may have shrugged. I'm not sure as I was examining a particularly interesting pair of pigs-in-a-blanket at the time. Or would that be pig-in-a-blankets? Pigs-in-blankets?

"I'm going for a walk," Drew said. I watched his feet move away from us.

I kind of felt like he wanted someone to go with him. Like me, maybe. But I'm sorry . . . just because we'd been hanging out—in a group—a bit more over the past few weeks didn't mean we were buddy-buddy again. He ditched me as a friend years ago. Old wounds don't heal that easily. Providing solace and comfort to Drew was Eric's job now, not mine.

"Do they always fight like that?" Suze whispered once Drew was out of earshot. Hope was standing at the water's edge watching the sunset over the beach in her black one-piece bathing suit and matching black sarong. She had a bright blue flower in her hair. This part of Malibu was south-facing so the sun set over the beach to the right of us instead of over the water. She struck quite an imposing figure with the orange light on her tan skin.

I considered Suze's question. "Do they always fight? Yes. Like this? Not so much."

"Should someone say something?" she asked.

"I guess," I said, knowing that the *someone* she was referring to was probably me. But, to be honest, I didn't have a clue what the *something* would be to say. Getting in between Hope and anyone she was angry with was not something one did casually. Quite frankly, I didn't think it was any of my business. That, and I'm notoriously afraid of confrontation. And conflict. Now that I think of it, I don't like most words that begin with *con*. Except *conquistador*. That's just fun to say.

Conquistador.

"What did I miss?" Sam asked as she came out of Eric's house with her boyfriend following like an itty-bitty puppy dog. Like the kind some girls usually carry around in their purse. That poops on their car keys.

Sam and I had only been friends for a couple years, but she's totally the reason I believe in reincarnation. I don't usually go for that metaphysical stuff, but our bond was so strong from the first hello that we must have been friends in previous lives. Like she was Cleopatra and I was her purely platonic consort who would hang with her as the slave boys fed us grapes and fanned us with palm fronds.

Back in the present, I couldn't help but notice that Sam and Eric had been gone for an awfully long time. Maybe they were conjuring up some hexes. I surreptitiously checked to confirm that Sam was still wearing her silver unicorn necklace. (She once confided in me that she would only take that necklace off after she—how do I put this delicately—lost her virginal status.) I was relieved to see that it was comfortably in place at the base of her neck. Not that I understood why I was relieved. It's not like I'm secretly pining for my best friend. And don't go thinking I'm all in denial about my true feelings or anything. I'm really not interested in the girl. Or any girl for that matter.

And I'm certainly not interested in Eric.

"The end of the affair," I said. "It looks like true love has run its course for Hope and Drew."

"Again?" Sam asked.

"Again and for good, if you ask me," I said. "For really good."

The sun continued to set, taking on deeper shades of red as it dipped behind the houses to the west of us. Hope was actually quite beautiful standing there in profile as the shadows descended around her. I couldn't help myself. I grabbed my camera and took of picture of her in her melancholy.

"Bryan!" Sam smacked me on the shoulder.

"Can I help it if misery makes for a beautiful shot?"

"I better go see if she's all right," Sam said to Eric.

"I'll go check on Drew," Eric replied.

As the two of them walked in different directions, I called out, "I'll stay right here and finish dinner."

"Do you always make jokes in times of stress?" Suze asked once we found ourselves alone in the crowd again.

"I make jokes all the time," I said. "It's easier than dealing with reality."

Suze thought about what I was saying. "And exactly how much reality do you deal with around here?" She waved out toward the beach with the typically indescribable sunset. I guess she was right. Between us and the sunset were a bunch of beautiful Malibu teens frolicking in the sand. They weren't *all* model gorgeous, but they were all acting like they were. Like they were just waiting for paparazzi to show up. Then again, it is possible that some of them were actually expecting cameramen to swing by. They are the children of the glitterati, after all.

"Point taken," I said.

Suze cupped her hand over her eyes and looked directly into the fading light. "Twenty-four hours from now I'll be watching the sunset reflected off the top of the Chrysler Building."

"It's a hard-knock life," I said.

Suze's vacation was set to start the next day. Not that it was going to be much of a "vacation" since she was jetting off for an internship at Ellis Designs. That's the company owned by famous fashion designer Natalie Ellis, aka Hope's mom.

This meant she was going to miss out on summer school with the rest of us.

Not that it was *really* summer school.

Now that our junior year at Orion Academy was over and we were all technically seniors, you'd think we'd get to kick back and relax without having to see the inside of our beloved school for another couple months. Wrong! First we had to get through the Orion Academy Summer Theatrical Program before the relaxing began. A two-week, intensive theater-training course that culminates in a full-scale, no-budget production. *Then*, it would be off on holiday.

Hope would join her mom in New York City. Sam's boyfriend, Eric, would visit his mom and her girlfriend in the Hamptons. At some point my mom and I would meet up with my father and summer on the coast for a week or two. I wasn't quite sure what coast we'd be summering on since my father bounces around the globe for his mysteriously boring job, but we'd have a good time.

Until then, with Suze gone, I'd be back to fifth-wheel status. That is, if both my best friends were still engaged in coupledom. As things currently stood, it didn't look all that likely.

I picked up my camera and started snapping shots of the fading light playing off the ocean. Sam and Hope stood off to the left of me, while Drew and Eric were off to my right. Leaving me stuck—physically and metaphorically—in the middle.

On a Clear Day You Can See Forever

In the summer, it should be illegal for morning to begin before noon. Especially in Malibu. You'd think that living in one of the most famous beach communities in the world, it might be worthwhile to get up early and enjoy the day. Honestly? Unless you're a surfer, there's really no need.

Summer usually begins in the midst of June Gloom. That's when every morning starts off with a low marine layer, encasing the Malibu Colony in fog and cloud cover until much later in the day. And don't let the name fool you. June Gloom happens anytime in the year that it wants to. It's just worst when the beach-going is supposed to be the best. Not that it would make any difference in my case. Even if every day was bright and sunny, I'd still be as pale as the walking dead.

The other thing that should be illegal is going to school in the summer. Even though the Orion Academy Summer Theatrical

Program isn't really like normal school, it still takes place *at* school. So, just when you thought you'd escaped, they pull you back in.

I was the first one in the parking lot. I blame my mom for that one. She agreed to watch one of her clients' Labradoodles. (That's a dog, if you don't know. A cross between a Labrador and a poodle.) Mom owns a doggie boutique on Melrose Avenue called Kaye 9. It caters to the pampered pooches of the pampered Hollywood elite . . . and anyone else who can afford to plunk down a hundred dollars for a dog's T-shirt.

I can't blame my mom entirely, though. You see, Canoodle—that's her name . . . Canoodle the Labradoodle—belongs to the headmaster of my school, Headmaster Collins. Mom had agreed to watch Canoodle while the headmaster and his wife were on a month-long tour of Europe. I doubt Mrs. Collins would have left her baby with us if she knew that Mom never let poor Canoodle past the kitchen and into the rest of the pristine house. We do have a big backyard for her to play in . . . Canoodle, I mean, not Mrs. Collins.

Typically, I'm big on dogs, but this particular Labra gets up at the crack of gloomy dawn to doodle and likes to wake up the entire house in the process. Then again, if I couldn't go to the bathroom unless someone opened a door for me, I guess I wouldn't be all that quiet in the morning either.

Here's the problem with starting your day early at Orion: If you get to school before the teachers, you can't get in. I hadn't known that before, never having started my day before the teachers. I guess that seems pretty obvious, but who can be logical at eight o'clock in the morning during the summer?

All I could do was sit in my car, Electra, staring out the window, wishing she had an iPod connection . . . or a CD player . . . or FM radio. That's the problem with driving a 1957 Ford Fairlane Skyliner that previously belonged to my grandfather: What I get in style I lose out in modern conveniences.

Another car finally pulled into the lot around eight thirty. I silently thanked the driver for saving me from staring at Electra's ceiling any longer. I immediately took back that appreciation when I saw who was behind the wheel.

Did I mention that the Orion Academy Soccer Program runs simultaneously alongside the Theater Program? Well, it does. And wouldn't you know, the first two members of the soccer team to show up would be Eric and Drew.

"This day's not getting any better," I mumbled as they parked right next to me. The *entire* parking lot was empty and they needed to park right beside Electra? I pulled the tip of my fedora down over my eyes and pretended to take a nap. I guess my performance wasn't all that convincing, because I soon heard a tap-tap-tapping at my window.

I peeked out from under the rim of my fedora. "Nobody's home."

Eric ignored my sarcasm. "Hey, Bryan. What are you doing here so early?" His voice was *way* too cheery for eight thirty in the morning. Ever since he and Sam started dating, he kept trying to be my friend. It was *really* annoying. Especially since, if I wasn't nice in return, I'd be the one coming off like an ass. Which, I guess I was being, but whatever.

"Trying to sleep," I replied.

"Why don't you do that at home?" Eric asked with actual concern in his voice. "Is everything okay? Suze's leaving for New York this morning, right?"

"I'm up," I said, lifting my fedora. The last thing I wanted was for this to become a *moment*.

I hopped out of Electra. Now that the rim of my fedora was out of my way and I had access to my full field of vision, I could see that Drew was a mess. Don't get me wrong. He was nicely outfitted in Hollister from head to toe, but he clearly hadn't slept at all since the Start-of-Summer Beach Party the night before.

"Is Sam here yet?" Eric asked me.

I made an exaggerated point of looking out over the empty parking lot. "Um . . . no."

"Did you guys hang out last night after the party?" Eric asked. "After you left with Hope."

I guess I was more awake than I thought, because I was on top of things enough to realize that Eric was trying to pump me for information about Hope for Drew. That was nice. Naive, but nice.

"Nope," I said. "Hope wanted to be alone."

"Oh," Eric said. He wasn't about to give up so easily. "Did you—"

"What are you wearing?" Drew interrupted.

He speaks.

"A shirt," I said. Actually, I was wearing an entire outfit: fedora, jeans, shoes, socks, underwear, and a shirt. But his eyes were focused on the shirt when he asked his question. I could understand why. It's really a great shirt. At first it seems like nothing more than a white T-shirt with this crazy black design covering the entire front and back. But after you stare at it for a while you realize that the design is actually a huge pile of skulls. Hundreds of these tiny skulls. Then, once you've seen the skulls, you can't help but see them every time you look at the shirt. Drew's the only person who's noticed so far.

Heck, I'd already worn the shirt twice before I first noticed it.

"It's . . . weird."

"Thanks," I said. Eric looked at the two of us like we were crazy. Like it was our fault that he wasn't observant.

Fortunately, people started filling the parking lot so we weren't stuck for awkward conversation much longer. Unfortunately, the people were mostly soccer players to whom I had nothing to say, so there was still some awkward standing around for a few minutes until Sam's mom pulled up to drop her daughter off. I hurried over to their car.

"Good morning, Anne," I said to Sam's mom, leaning in the passenger's side window.

"I didn't expect you to be here already," Anne replied. "This wouldn't have anything to do with Canoodle, would it?"

I blinked in shock. Anne was scary psychic on that one.

"Headmaster Collins is always complaining about having to walk Canoodle before the sun's up," she explained. Anne teaches English at Orion, so she knows a lot more about our headmaster than we do. "I guess he left that part out when he got your mom to watch her."

"Must've slipped his mind," I said, not even remotely giving our beloved headmaster the benefit of the doubt.

"I can't get out," Sam said to me.

"And you're telling me this, why?"

"Because you're hanging in my window," she said, giving the door a gentle shove into my torso.

"Allow me," I said, swinging the door open for her.

"Good morning," Eric said, with his hand out to help her out of the car as soon as I cleared the way. Had to give the guy points for being smooth. Don't worry, I was sure I could take those points away for some reason soon enough.

"I've got to get to school myself," Anne said. She was taking summer classes too, going for her master's. "Bryan, you're okay with taking Sam home?"

"No problem," I replied. And it wasn't, really. Sam lives in Santa Monica, which is only a short drive down the Pacific Coast Highway. The drive gets a little longer during the summer with all the beach traffic, but it's not that bad. Besides, the view is pretty nice along the way. Most of the surfers tend to strip out of their body-hugging wetsuits right on the edge of the road for all the world . . . I mean the sparkling azure-blue ocean is beautiful as it stretches out into eternity.

You know, once the June Gloom clears.

As Anne drove out the exit, she waved to the driver of the incoming car. We all recognized the vehicle immediately, but the crazy part was seeing that Hope was behind the wheel. She was finally allowed to drive the family car with her peers as passengers. (It's a silly California law.) Don't ever let her know that I said she was riding with her peers, because she was actually with her stepsisters.

I couldn't tell if the sour expression on her face was because of the steps, the fact that Sam and I were standing near Drew, or the car itself. See, the car was purchased while Hope was out of the country, so she didn't get any say in it. She was *supposed* to be involved in the decision, but her stepmom had decided that her own daughters shouldn't have to wait a minute longer for the car Hope's dad was paying for. The result: a customized pink-and-purple Mini Cooper with a silver diamond etched on the roof, sparkly pink spinners on the wheels, and purple fur-covered seats. Not exactly subtle.

My excitement over seeing Hope behind the wheel of the car was tempered by the fact that she stepped out in full on Goth-Ick mode. That's what she calls her style of dress and the attitude that goes with it. As she squeezed out of the driver's seat, I saw she was sporting a full-on Victorian-style outfit complete with high-necked black lace top and a long black skirt. While it was certainly a good choice for a chilly June Gloomy morning, I couldn't help but think she'd eventually grow to regret it come afternoon when the clouds burned off and the sun came shining out. The ensemble was topped by a black blazer with a violently red rose sewn on the sleeve, which, if I'm not mistaken—and I'm not—was dripping embroidered blood from the petals.

Talk about wearing your heart on your sleeve. And in her eyes as well. As she approached, I could see she was wearing a pair of her bloodiest red contacts. Hope changes eye colors like other girls change shoes.

Hope pushed past us, grabbing Sam's arm and pulling her along.

Ouch. If anyone could kill with her eyes, it would be Hope. She wasn't even aiming at me, but I got hit with the shrapnel on that one.

I hung back to give Sam some time to work the poison from Hope's eyes . . . which left me alone with Drew, Eric, and the steps.

"She's been at Hope-times-ten all morning," Belinda said as we watched Hope try to wrench the locked doors open.

"Word to the wise," Alexis said. "Never get in a car with someone going through a breakup." Then, she actually clasped her hand over her mouth as if she had forgotten that Drew was the one Hope was in the process of breaking up with.

Nice.

Alexis and Belinda are the least identical, identical twins I've ever met. Not to say that they don't look exactly alike, because they do. But they do everything in their power not to. Belinda is all earth tones and shades of white. She prefers flowing dresses and outfits that complement her long blond hair. On the other hand, Alexis prefers loud colors in her clothes, and the tighter the better. Her hair is chopped short and at odd angles that cost a couple hundred dollars at the trendiest salon on Sunset Boulevard. Even at eight thirty in the morning, Alexis was made up for a night on the town, while I've never seen Belinda in anything more than a thin layer of foundation and muted lip gloss.

Guess which one got to pick the custom design of their car.

The one thing truly identical about them is they have the exact same shade of natural honey-blond hair. And they both make Mary-Kate and Ashley look fat. Hence why we've nicknamed them the Twin Twigs of Terror.

"But don't worry," Alexis added, moving closer to the guys who weren't me. "We're totally on Team Drew."

"Alexis," Belinda whispered loudly with a glance in my direction. Like I was going to run and tell Hope what she'd said. Like Hope would even care. Or be surprised.

"What?" Alexis said with mock innocence. "It's a fact of the world we live in today. Everyone has to pick a side. Have we learned nothing from our celebrity friends?"

Now, here's the difference between us and them. If me and my friends had ever said something like that, we'd be going for sarcastic. Alexis was being genuine.

Even though their styles are night and day, Alexis and Belinda are of one mind on the critical subjects affecting the world: the importance of fashion, the power of celebrity, and, most important, the entertainment value of scandal. Which is exactly why they were best friends with the girl in the silver Lexus hybrid SUV careening its way into the parking lot.

Now that I think of it, *friends* may not be the most accurate term; *followers* might be more appropriate . . . or *minions*. Even better. Minions it is.

The driver tore up to the front of the lot, parking diagonally across two spots. This was not a real problem since most of the parking lot would be empty, but it was still rude, if you ask me.

The SUV door swung open, and out came a pair of legs that had all the soccer guys—and a few of the male Drama Geeks—swiveling to look. It wasn't like they hadn't seen those legs before, but being that it was summer there was slightly more leg to see than during the school year. They were the legs of a girl that had dressed in anticipation of the warm sunny day that would eventually evolve from the gray morning mess.

They were the legs of Holly Mayflower.

Twice as talented and countless times more evil than her older sister, Heather, Holly Mayflower had been out of school for most of last semester working on a sitcom pilot. The show got picked up, but Holly did not. She returned to Orion in disgrace and driving a new SUV her father bought to soften the blow.

Holly likes to think of herself as an actress–singer–model–movie mogul in the making. I guess, technically, she is all those things, but I prefer to think of her as a Queen Bee–wannabe TV star–mean girl–daddy's girl who knows how to use her influence to get what she wants. That may be one of the more convoluted hyphenates I've ever put down on paper, but it fits her to a baby-doll T.

Oh, the hyphenate thing? That's how we distinguish people in Los Angeles. The more hyphens, the more successful you are, I guess. Me? I'm an actor-photographer (well, part-time photographer) still in search of my ultimate success and further hyphens.

Holly is just a smidge over one year younger than her sister, Heather. I guess their mom wanted to get all the "unsightly" baby weight out of the way all at once. Heather and Holly: As the story goes, their mother had named them after flowers, in honor of their Mayflower last name. Too bad nobody told the woman that Heather and Holly aren't so much flowers as they are shrubs.

Holly got big hugs from Alexis and Belinda, as if they hadn't seen each other for years, instead of hours. Then she read the awkwardness on all of our faces and turned to see Hope and Sam off by the entrance.

"This is the problem with being fashionably on time," Holly said with a practiced flip of her red hair. She then looked right at Eric and added, "You miss all the good stuff."

Eric cleared his throat. "Good morning, Holly."

"It *is*, isn't it?" She gave another pointed look over toward Hope and Sam. "Or is it? Flying solo?"

"What?" Eric asked. "No. Sam? No."

"Oh," she said. "I thought Drew might have inspired you to . . . know what? Never mind. My mistake." Yeah. Like Holly ever makes mistakes.

She smiled and sauntered off with her minions. As they walked away, all the guys in the area were watching Holly's form-fitting shorts as they hugged her perfectly sculpted butt. Hell, even I was looking.

Once I snapped out of the hypnotic rhythm of her strut, I realized that I was alone with Eric and Drew once again. No matter how much I try, I guess they're destined to be a part of my life.

We were saved from any further awkwardness by the arrival of Mr. Randall, the drama teacher. He let us all into school and then went to open up the gym for the soccer team.

"Holly's in pure form this morning," I said as I joined up with Sam and Hope.

"That's about the only thing pure about her," Sam said.

I turned to Hope. "You okay?"

She cocked her head to the side and shrugged.

"If you need anything," I added.

She nodded and then pointed toward her locker. "I'm gonna . . ."

"We'll meet you back here," Sam said as we turned and headed off in the opposite direction toward our lockers.

"What was that?" I asked.

"I wish I knew," Sam said. "She was like that when I tried to talk to her yesterday, too."

"That's . . . weird."

"I know."

Don't get me wrong. I understood that Hope was going through a breakup and all, but this was different. She'd never been quiet before. The shrugging and the pointing . . . that was just not like her. Yelling and screaming and railing at everyone in the vicinity? That's the Hope we all know and fear. Silent Hope was just . . . unnerving.

No other breakup had ever led Hope to dress in full-on Victorian Matron before either. She looked like she was mourning someone's death. I only hoped the outfit wasn't foreshadowing.

"She won't even tell me what the fight was about," Sam added. "Drew won't tell Eric either."

"Did you ever think that they're not saying anything because they don't want you and Eric talking about them behind their backs?"

"We're their best friends," Sam insisted. "That's what we're supposed to do."

I guess I couldn't argue with that. I spend a fair amount of time talking about Sam behind her back too. . . . Wait. That doesn't sound right.

"I'm worried," Sam said.

I nodded. I was a little worried myself.

We walked the rest of the way to our brand-spanking-new lockers in a contemplative silence. The lockers were the price Heather Mayflower's father had paid to ensure that his daughter still graduated after she had sabotaged the Spring Theatrical Production of *The Wizard of Oz*. Ignoring all the drama that she had caused, it did result in a pretty cool repercussion.

The lockers were totally tricked out. They were twice the size of our old lockers and had electronic combinations that we could program ourselves. I punched in my combo (2-4-6-0-1) and dropped my lunch in the cooler—a nice little add-on to keep our hot food hot and our cool food cool. With the inlaid mirrors, voice recorders for leaving personal messages, and air fresheners, I'd consider moving in if they were a tad larger.

When Anthony Mayflower makes up for his children's mistakes, he goes big. He probably would have upgraded to lockers with refrigerators and microwaves if the school could have afforded to pay the electric bill.

"So how are we going to do it?" Sam asked as she closed her locker.

"Do what?"

"Get them back together?"

Oh, dear.

This was not good. Sam had that scheming look in her eyes. That always meant trouble. Sam isn't the schemer. *I'm* the schemer. Sam usually goes along—unwillingly—with my plans. Our success rate is somewhere around fifty-four percent: slightly better than average, but still fairly sucky. In the end my schemes usually work out, but that doesn't mean we don't wind up trapped inside the school observatory at some point along the way. Sam's plans have even less of a success rate, if you can imagine.

"You're kidding, right?"

"Nope. We're going to rekindle their relationship."

"And what makes you think they *want* it rekindled?"

"You saw Hope this morning," Sam said. "She's miserable. And not the fun kind of miserable act she usually puts on to scare people. This is serious."

I had to agree. I had never seen Hope like this before. But I wasn't entirely sure that getting back together with Drew was the answer. Then again, they did seem to enjoy breaking up and making up in their relationship. They certainly did it often enough.

"As Hope's best friends," Sam continued, "we owe it to her to do everything in our power to make sure that she gives her relationship every chance at surviving."

Thank you, Dr. Phil. "Hope is *not* going to like us getting involved."

She crossed the hall to give me a light tap on the cheek. "Silly boy," she said. "We're not going to *tell* her."

Miss Julie

"I'm dying to hear what you've got in mind," I lied as we walked toward the Saundra Hall Auditorium (or Hall Hall as we like to call it). I kept my voice low as various classmates were hurrying past so they could get a good seat for our first day. I also kept an eye out for Hope because she was the last one I wanted to overhear us. "I'm guessing it's very *Parent Trap*. But the question is are we going with the Hayley Mills or the Lindsay Lohan pre-party-girl version?"

"It's going to be intricate," she said. "Nothing subtle for Hope."

"Will it have multiple phases? Please tell me there will be multiple phases."

"And maybe even a contingency plan or two."

I have to admit . . . I was getting excited. Summer in Malibu can get kind of boring. I mean, think about it. We live in a beautiful beach community with almost perfect weather all year long. Manipulating Hope's life could provide for some entertainment.

Okay, seriously folks. I was worried about the girl. It was possible that she and Drew were meant to be together. I mean, some people like to fight. Isn't that what we've learned from TV and movies over the years? Fighting couples are overcompensating for sexual tension and all that? Not that I ever noticed any sexual tension between Hope and Drew, but I was no expert on these things. Just because I wasn't so sure they were destined to be together didn't mean that they weren't. I've been known to be wrong before. Once or twice.

Besides, what harm could we really do? Hope was leaving for New York in two weeks.

Hope silently fell into step with us as we entered Hall Hall. While we had been at our lockers, most of the rest of the Drama Geeks had filtered into the theater. Students from the sophomore, junior, and senior classes were all mingling together, which was cool. During the school year our classes were broken up by grade so we only worked together on the spring show. This was a chance for everyone to mix things up.

There were quite a number of people sitting almost at the front of the house. Odd that nobody ever wants to be in the first row. It's the same way in the classroom too. Following Hope's lead, we walked right up and filled in a trio of seats in the empty row. I guess she figured everyone would be staring at her anyway. Might as well make it easier on them.

I decided to look back at them as well.

Jason MacMillan was a few rows back, looking depressed.

I suspect that his mood had something to do with his relationship recently passing its expiration date. For the past few years, he had been dating a girl in the grade above us. When his girlfriend, Wren, graduated and went off to film a music video and then attend an early summer session at college, they had decided to call it quits without even bothering to try the long-distance thing. It was like couples were breaking up all over the place lately. I wondered if Sam might take some inspiration from that.

I caught Jason's sad eyes focused in our direction, but he quickly turned away when he saw me looking. It was possible his sad act was just an act and he was already scoping out Hope for a possible entanglement. The only problem with that idea was that his eyes had seemed to be directed toward Sam.

The usual suspects were scattered about the rows behind us too. Tasha Valentine, Goth girl, was sitting off by herself, lost in a world of Emo Rock coming from her iPod. (It was either that or she was listening to the audiobook of *The House at Pooh Corner*. With Tasha, you could go either way.) And of course, our stage manager extra-unordinaire, Jimmy Wilkey, was flitting about the place setting things up. Meanwhile, Holly was holding court over Alexis and Belinda as well as a collection of junior girls who fancied themselves as modern-day Pink Ladies prepping to rule the school once Holly was gone the same time next year.

Mr. Randall, our drama teacher, came out from backstage with a strange woman beside him. (Not that there was anything unusual about her. I just mean we didn't recognize her.) He stepped up to the edge of the stage and cleared his throat dramatically, which was wholly unnecessary as we were already quiet. Strangers do that to us. It's not that we're afraid of them or anything. Seeing strangers at our school makes us incredibly curious. Where other kids might whisper about who she was, we tend to be much more patient gossips at Orion. We knew that we'd find out soon enough. *Then* the gossiping would begin about what a person like her was doing at our school.

"Welcome back," Mr. Randall said. "It's been ages." It had actually been four days. No one laughed since Mr. Randall has opened all the Summer Theatrical Programs of the past few years with that same lame joke. Not even the ninth graders—who, I guess, were now tenth graders—found it funny. And it was totally new to them.

"Okay," he said. "I need new material. As you all know, we've got a fun two-week program ahead of us. But, what you don't know is how much fun it's going to be. I know we usually spend this time doing our impression of Mickey and Judy putting on a show in the barn, but this summer we have a different agenda in store."

Mr. Randall paused while the whispers began. The less-theatrically aware of my peers were wondering who the heck Mickey and Judy were and where this barn was located. (*Aside:* He was referring to Mickey Rooney and Judy Garland, who used to costar in movies where their characters almost always wound up putting on an impromptu musical in whatever arena was available to them—usually a barn.)

"This year," he continued, "instead of taking our two weeks to put on a no-budget show, we're going to change things up a bit and focus on scene work. The first week of the program we're going to work on monologues, while the second week will be all about group scenes."

That announcement was met with a chorus of groans. I guess after the debacle that was *The Wizard of Oz*, people were looking to put on a real show. Even one that we only took two weeks to put together. Personally, I kind of liked the idea of doing real scene work. We usually spend so much time getting ready for whatever show we're working on that we don't always get to work the basics of acting during the school year *or* in the summer program.

"I know, I know," Mr. Randall said in reaction to the groans. "It's all about the show. But how about if I sweeten the deal?" This is one of the things that really drives me crazy about Orion. Mr. Randall is our teacher. He's trying to teach us a valuable lesson. But the only way he can get away with making us do something we don't want to do is by bribing us. I would have called him on it, but first I wanted to know what he had to offer.

"Ladies and gentlemen," he continued. "I would like to introduce Ms. Julie Blackstone." Mr. Randall gave a sweep of his hand in his guest's direction. The beautiful, dark-haired stranger walked to the edge of the stage. Talk about an entrance. It was even more impressive that she had been standing there the whole time.

"Call me Julie," she said.

"Actually," Mr. Randall said. "Call her Ms. Blackstone." He turned to her to explain. "It's a school rule that the students have to address faculty formally."

"Okay," she said with a smile. "Call me Miss Julie."

Most of us laughed at the reference.

(*Aside: Miss Julie* is a play by August Strindberg. The joke wasn't that funny. I think we were overcompensating so the pretty lady would like us.)

Mr. Randall continued, "As you all know, Ms. Monroe is off on her honeymoon right now. And Ms. Blackstone—"

"Miss Julie."

"Ms. *Blackstone*," he insisted. "Will be taking her place."

In a story that could have been titled "Love Among the Arts," Ms. Monroe, our music teacher–assistant director–not quite old maid recently tied the knot with Orion Academy's art teacher-graphic designer-confirmed bachelor, Mr. Telasco. They had waited all through the school year to have their wedding. Rather than postpone things until after the summer program, Ms. Monroe (she kept her name) decided to go on her honeymoon immediately. Can't say I blame her.

We had all been wondering how Mr. Randall was going to get through the program without her. Working with all us Drama Geeks from nine to three every day for two weeks could cause anyone to have a breakdown. Enter our answer: the oddly familiar Ms. Blackstone.

And then, it hit me.

Blackstone.

"Urp!" I said. It was not a pleasant sound. Or one that I had intended to make at all, but the realization hit me so fast that I reacted . . . and at a surprisingly loud volume. I slid down in my chair as Sam and Hope busied themselves by acting like they didn't know me.

"Sounds like someone's made the connection," Ms. Blackstone . . . I'm sorry, *Miss Julie*, said.

"Yes," Mr. Randall nodded with a laugh. "I believe someone has. For those of you a step behind, Ms. Blackstone is the daughter of Hartley Blackstone. She's student teaching with us this summer *and* she has a very exciting announcement to make."

"Hi," Ms. Blackstone said, throwing in a friendly wave. I would much prefer if the school policy would allow us to call her Julie since "Ms. Blackstone" was only a couple years older than us seniors. I decided to go with calling her Miss Julie, like she'd said . . . if only for the fact that it is was technically against school rules.

"I hate being . . . well . . . this is going to sound pretentious, but does everyone know who my father is?" she asked.

Duh!

A sea of bobbing heads nodded yes.

Hartley Blackstone is one of the most famous producer-director-actor-writer-songwriter-choreographers (a quintuple hyphenate!) in Broadway history. He's won a Tony Award in just about every category you can win a Tony Award except costume design. (I hear he's working on completing his set by designing the wardrobe for his next production.)

Which begged the question: What in the *world* was his

daughter doing at Orion Academy? Shouldn't she be at some amazing art school in New York? London? *Anywhere* else?

"I guess you've heard of Dad," she said. Even Alexis and Belinda—who really had no right to be there in the first place—knew who her father was. "Okay, so here's the deal," she continued. "I've got to do the student teaching thing for summer credits. This is all kind of last minute on account of . . . well, let me give you guys a tip: Never jet off to your dad's London premiere without locking in your course schedule first. School bureaucrats can be such a bitch." We were hanging on every word. "So, if I want to get my degree, I've got to complete this little two-week unit and then quietly graduate before anyone starts asking questions." At about this point, I believe Mr. Randall's head was about as close to exploding as it had been during the spring show. "So, I bribed my way into this program—"

"Actually," Mr. Randall interrupted. "We were in dire need of another teacher, and Ms. Blackstone kindly offered to help out."

"That's what I said," she added with a smile. "And since things were dire all around, *Ms. Blackstone* wasn't about to throw things to chance and arranged it all with a little help from Daddy. You've all heard about the Hartley Blackstone Acting School, right?"

Sam nearly ripped the arms of her chair off the metal frame. That would be a *yes*. The Blackstone Acting School is a summer theater program in which Blackstone only accepts the most talented students from all over the world to attend. It's nearly impossible to get into. So much so that no one I know has even tried.

"He's left two open spots this year," she continued. "For one girl and one boy from Orion Academy. And Dad's going to come and pick them himself."

There was an explosion of voices as everyone started talking at once. I didn't know what Sam was saying to me. I wasn't even sure what I was saying to her. All I did know was that I've never seen the Drama Geeks that excited before in my life. And we're talking about a fairly melodramatic group of people to begin with.

In the midst of the excitement, Hope remained sitting quietly, as she had been all morning. If anything, I would have thought that this announcement would have gotten some kind of reaction out of her. The rest of us, however, were reacting all over the place.

Eventually, Mr. Randall managed to get us back under some semblance of control. "It's going to work like this. You'll have all week to prepare one monologue for Mr. Blackstone. He'll be here on Friday to watch you perform. He'll give you what I can only assume will be valuable notes on your acting that you can take and apply to your scenes. Then, next Friday he'll come back to see your group scenes and make his final decision."

This time, there was no outburst, but you could feel the energy in the room. We were about to explode again. It was only a matter of time.

"I could continue talking," Mr. Randall said, "but you guys

aren't really hearing anything right now, anyway. So why don't we take a break and you can pick groups for your scenes."

Pandemonium.

That's the only word that can be used to describe the auditorium. As theater students we can be overly exuberant when we're just greeting one another in the morning, but give us something like this—an opportunity to study under one of the masters of theater?

Watch. Out.

I immediately turned to Sam and Hope. "What scene are we going to do?"

And was met with silence.

"Hello? Anybody home?"

Okay, I get that they were a little stunned. Hope was going through a lot at the moment. And Sam . . . she probably never expected to have this kind of opportunity back when she was going to a poorly funded public school. But everyone was teaming up around us. We had to move fast if we wanted to round out our group with someone who knew stage left from stage right.

"Anyone looking for a fourth?" Jason MacMillan asked as he pushed his way past some overeager sophomore girls who, I think, wanted him to join their group as much for his stellar acting ability as his good looks.

Sam finally came out of her coma. "Yes!" she said with a little more excitement than I had expected. "You *so* have to join us."

"Great," he said, grabbing a seat beside Sam.

"Great," she said, looking relieved.

"Great," I said . . . suspiciously.

Okay, maybe I was overreacting, but Sam seemed way more excited to team with Jason than she did when it was just Hope and me. Jason is an incredibly talented actor. Let's be honest, he was the real competition for the guys. I wasn't deluded enough to think that it was going to be easy beating out Jason for the spot. I'd need to ace my audition just to be considered along with him. Still, it wasn't like I was going to bring Sam down or anything.

"Are you guys already teamed up?" a hesitant voice asked from beside me. I looked up to see Gary McNulty leaning over my seat. It was weird that he sounded so shy since Gary's usually quite the outgoing fellow. He played the head flying monkey in *The Wizard of Oz*. People are still talking about the aerial somersault he spontaneously threw in during the show.

"Sorry, Monkey Boy," I said. "Thirty seconds too late. I think we're full up." As much as I would have liked Gary on the team, any more than four people would seriously cut into our stage time. I could see that Sam and Jason were with me because they were solemnly nodding in agreement. Hope was still looking down at her lap.

"Oh, okay," he said as he walked off. It was a shame there wasn't room for one more. Gary was one of the best actors in the junior class. He was also pretty cute with his curly brown hair and thin silver-frame glasses. Not that I noticed.

I didn't really have time to dwell more on these thoughts, because something much more interesting was sashaying up to us. Holly and the Anorexettes were making their way across the aisle.

This should be good.

"Jason," Holly said as she leaned over me, Hope, and Sam to get to him. "Tell me you haven't already found a group."

My, aren't we the popular foursome?

"Sorry," he said. "But I'm on Sam's team."

Um . . . when did we become *Sam's* team?

Holly gave Sam a look that could quite possibly be described as a sneer. "If you change your mind," she said, "I've got something special in mind for our scene."

"I'm sure you do," Sam said. Her defenses were already raised in ways that Holly's sister, Heather, never managed to evoke from her.

Hope finally looked like she had some life in her. Girl could smell a fight from a mile away. Not that the pending battle was nearly that distant. "Don't go thinking about knocking out the competition like Heather did on *Wizard*," Hope warned softly, but firmly. "I'm watching you."

"I don't need to rely on tricks like my sister," Holly said, "I've got actual talent. More than enough to earn me this spot in Blackstone's program."

With that, she and the twigs turned and stalked off in search of an innocent victim. The worst part about our little exchange was that Holly was right. She does have talent. I was just glad that, being male, I didn't have to go up against her.

On the other hand . . . I looked to my best friend.

"Well," Sam said, "now I *have* to win."

Oh boy.

A Lie of the Mind

Hope and I were among the first to get to the Kenneth Graham Pavilion, which is the Orion Academy version of a lunchroom. It's actually a covered outdoor patio with no lunch-making facilities at all, but a beautiful view of the Pacific Ocean. The sun had finally burned through the clouds. It was shaping up to be a pleasant and warm day.

Hope took off her jacket as we grabbed a table nearest the ocean view. The rest of the Drama Geeks quickly came in behind us, staking out spots for themselves and their scene partners.

The soccer guys hadn't arrived for lunch yet, which was just as well, considering I would be useless trying to deflect Hope and Drew on my own. Sam had stayed behind in Hall Hall with Jason to pump Mr. Randall full of questions about the auditions. Since I knew Sam would fill me in on all that she had learned, I figured I didn't need to hang around. Besides, I was hungry.

What I didn't realize was that this would leave me alone with Hope for the first time since her breakup with Drew.

Don't get me wrong. Hope and I are really close. Not quite as close as Sam and me, but I still consider Hope one of my best friends. It's just . . . we don't do *serious* well. We don't have heart-to-hearts. Ever.

"So . . . ," I said.

She didn't even bother to look up. Not that I blamed her. I wasn't giving her much to work with.

I tried a new approach. "If you ever want to talk about you and Drew."

"I don't."

"Oh, no . . . I get that," I said. "It's just . . . I know a thing or two about how Drew can dump on people."

"Who said he dumped me?"

"No. I meant . . . I didn't . . ."

Hence why she and I don't do this often. We kind of suck at it.

Hope looked at me with her big red eyes, softening. "I'm sorry. I'm tired. I was up all night, writing."

"Let's see." I grabbed her notebook and started flipping through the pages.

"Not there," she said, pulling her necklace out from her shirt and dangling it in front of me. That meant she had been doing serious writing. Her notebook is for her fun writing; really crappy poems in honor of her dog that died five years ago. She calls it *The Book of the Dead Puppy Poetry*. She's already on volume six. But her serious work . . . *that* she keeps safely locked in a flash drive tied to a silk rope around her neck. The work in there is deep and meaningful and she only shows it to friends on rare occasions. Somehow, I didn't think this was going to be one of those times.

"That bad?" I asked.

"It's just Drew . . . he's hopeless."

"Literally," I said, trying to break the mood with my usual bad pun.

Hope didn't even crack a smile. At the very least, I had expected her to kick me under the table for making light of her pain. But nothing. No response whatsoever. Thankfully, we were saved from further discomfort when Sam and Jason arrived.

"Learn anything good?" I asked.

Sam dropped her lunch on the table and took a seat next to me. "Not really. Mr. Randall is staying pretty mum on things so he doesn't get our hopes up."

"Too late," Jason and I said.

"Should we get to work?" Sam asked, scanning the room. "Everyone else is."

The pavilion was abuzz with activity. I guess the soccer team's morning practice was running late because the guys were still nowhere in sight. That was fine by me. We did have work to do. Besides, I wasn't ready to see Eric go through the King Solomon task of deciding who to eat with. If he sat with Drew, that meant he wouldn't be sitting with us. There was no way one poor little cafeteria table could handle the tension of Hope and Drew at the same table. But I couldn't see Eric blowing off Sam either. He'd sat with her (and us) for lunch almost every single day since they'd started dating.

Unbelievable. I actually felt bad for Eric. Welcome to Bizarro World.

Without the soccer guys to get in the way, the drama students had broken up into teams and spread out across the cafeteria. I imagine the same discussion was taking place at every table.

First, we were eyeing the competition.

"I feel bad for Tasha," I said. "She's stuck with Jimmy."

"Girl needs to be more aggressive," Hope said. "That is exactly what happens when you sit back and let the world dictate your life. You get stuck with Jimmy Wilkey and a tenth-grade munchkin."

Just to note, she wasn't insulting the tenth grader by calling her a munchkin. Back when we did *Wizard* and they were ninth graders, they played munchkins. Which is just to say that they only had a couple lines in the play and haven't really acted on our stage before. Jimmy's never acted before either. He usually zips around as stage manager making sure Mr. Randall has everything he needs whether or not he wants it.

After *Wizard* Jimmy got on this kick about learning all aspects of theater to make him a better stage manager, and he asked Mr. Randall if he could try out acting in the summer program. Not that he needed to ask, but it would be against Jimmy's programming to tell Mr. Randall he wanted to do anything. Who knew? Maybe Jimmy would surprise us all with his hidden talents.

Honestly? I wasn't holding out hope.

And neither was Hope, for that matter.

"Didn't see that one coming," Jason said as his eyes turned in the direction of Holly Mayflower and the twigs. They were sitting with Gary McNulty.

"Holly and Monkey Boy?" I asked. I would have thought that he'd team with his best friend, Madison, but it's possible Holly made him an offer . . . he'd come to regret.

"Makes sense," Sam said as she took out her lunch. "Once you harness his natural exuberance, he's actually pretty good. I probably would've gone with him too . . . if I didn't have you guys, I mean."

I looked at Hope to see if she thought she was being insulted too, but she was busy glaring at her stepsisters so I just put it out of my mind. In this world, I've learned that you can choose to read something into everything a person says or just ignore it and assume they meant it in the best way possible. I prefer to go the positive route . . . but keep on alert, just in case I'm being insulted behind my back. Not that Sam would ever intentionally insult my acting, but there was a fair amount of hesitation on her part when we were choosing sides—I mean *teams*—earlier. Then again, maybe I was being overly sensitive. That's often a problem for us creative types.

"I say we go with Shakespeare," Jason said, moving the discussion past the gossiping-about-our-competition stage.

"Isn't that a little obvious?" I asked. *Everyone* would be doing Shakespeare.

"You'd prefer something in the absurdist oeuvre?" Sam asked. "Perhaps some *Waiting for Godot*?"

"Shakespeare it is," I said. Sam knew full well how I felt about absurdist theater, and especially *Godot*.

(*Aside:* I'm sorry. I know it's like supposed to be this work of genius and all, but I just don't get it. The play has no real plot beyond these two freaks waiting around by a tree for some guy named Godot to show up. And he never shows! That's it. Nothing happens! Sorry if I just spoiled the ending, but we're not talking about the mystery of *Lost* here. Everyone who goes to the play already knows what they're getting into from the start. And yet they *still* go to see it!)

"What play do you think we should do?" I asked. "Nothing too obvious."

"Gee, how about *Romeo and Juliet*," Jason said.

The three of us stared at him. Blankly.

"That was a joke," he said. "You should have known that by the fact that I said 'Gee.' Do I ever talk like that?"

"Oh," Sam and I said with a tremendous amount of relief.

"Okay," Jason said, sounding a little hurt that we all missed the joke. "I was thinking more like *Measure for Measure* or *Troilus and Cressida*."

"I'd prefer comedy," Hope said with no measure of jovial attitude in her tone at all.

"Yeah, we can tell," Sam said. "Technically, *Measure for Measure* is a comedy."

"Really?" I asked. "A play about a man demanding that a nun sleep with him to save her imprisoned brother is considered a comedy?"

"By some," Sam said.

"Yeah. We won't be doing that one," I said.

"How about *Twelfth Night?*" Hope suggested, showing her first signs of enthusiasm for the scene.

"Mistaken identity comedy about an identical twin brother and sister," I said. "Sounds perfect for us." We were all familiar with the play already since we'd studied it for a week in English sophomore year. There were a bunch of good characters in it, so I was pretty sure that there'd be some good scenes. "Agreed?"

"Agreed," Sam said.

That left Jason.

"Works for me," he said. "We can figure out which scene later. Now we should choose our monologues since those come first."

Hope and I looked at each other. "We'll save that for later," I said, trying to head off any discussion. I've tried to pick monologues with Sam before. It's not a fun time. She can be somewhat . . . indecisive about these things. To the point where I swear I've seen smoke coming out of her ears because her mind was working so fast at going over all the options.

"The guys are here," Sam said as the soccer team filed into the pavilion. I suspect she said this to prepare Hope for whatever choice Eric—and by default, Drew—made about where to sit.

We all sat in breathless anticipation as we watched the guys file in.

Okay, actually, Sam was the only one holding her breath. I was breathing quite regularly. I figured either nothing was going to happen or we'd get a fun show to go along with our lunch. Jason, on the other hand, wasn't even aware that anything was going on. He had his own breakup issues to work through, anyway. Hope, however, was very pointedly breathing in a relaxed manner. She was sitting with her back to the door and hadn't bothered to turn to watch the guys come in. It was all an act, though. I could see her nonchalantly watching Sam's face for a reaction.

All conversation stopped in our group as the soccer guys found their own empty tables or joined their drama friends. Nobody came near us, knowing better than to look like they were taking Hope's side. The soccer team and Drama Geeks usually blend together rather well—especially the soccer guys and drama *girls*—but we were apparently personae non grata. It was only day one and already people were taking sides.

Great.

They arrived in clumps at first, all hot and sweaty from practice. And I have to say, I didn't much mind them not joining us. Hope's eyes continued to flick up to see Sam's reaction. But Sam remained stoic, going with neutral since she knew she was being watched.

After the initial rush, things slowed down and the guys were entering in pairs with some distance between them. With every new flash of uniform that came around the corner, I watched Sam's eyes register who it was, then focus on her food. It was quite the performance. She was giving nothing away.

Soon, there were longer gaps between the guys as the

stragglers followed. One by one and two by two they found their seats. The noise level had increased in the pavilion, but we were still pretty quiet at our table. Eventually, the stream of guys slowed to the point of stopping. And still, no Drew and Eric.

When it finally became clear that they weren't coming, Sam simply leaned over and took a bite out of her PB and J. I turned to nonchalantly gauge Hope's reaction. "Crestfallen" would be a good way to describe it. Though I wasn't sure if she was sorry that she didn't have a chance to *see* Drew or to *fight* with him.

"Who wants to hit the library after school to pick up some monologues?" Hope asked. Clearly she was in a distraught state if she was going to suggest going with Sam to pick out monologues.

"Can't," Sam said, with her eyes trained on me. "We have plans."

I had no idea what Sam was talking about, but since I had done the same thing to her many times before I just nodded my head like I agreed.

"Doing what?" Hope asked, looking directly at me.

Oh, how I love being put on the spot. Hope knew that Sam and I told her everything that we were up to. The fact that Sam was referring to some ambiguous "plans" instead of just saying what those "plans" were meant she was probably hiding something. Now it was up to me to come up with an excuse or Hope wouldn't trust us. And it couldn't be any old excuse. It had to be believable. Also, important enough that we couldn't postpone it, but not so important that it would be suspicious that we hadn't mentioned it to Hope before. But, most of all, we had to be doing something that Hope couldn't invite herself along for.

This was a lot to ask for in a lie. And while I'm pretty comfortable with the whole lying thing, I've never been particularly good at improv.

"We're helping Mom with a private showing," I said, surprising both Sam *and* me in the process. "Some Beverly Hills trophy wife wants an entire wardrobe for her dog that matches the purses she carries him in. You're welcome to join us, if you want."

"Oh," Hope said. "That's okay." I wasn't sure if she believed me, but she wasn't going to call me on it, either. She'd gone to a few of these private showings before and was miserable every time. I usually try to drag a friend along because they're incredibly time consuming and totally boring to sit through on my own. First, we have to dress up a couple dozen stuffed dogs in samples of Mom's entire line of doggy wardrobe. Then lug them all to the client's house and pull a Vanna White showing off the designs while the client criticizes everything from the color to the fit to the thread count. Hope nearly lost it the last time she went with us when the client asked if we thought an outfit made her Chihuahua look fat.

Seriously.

Sam had this satisfied look on her face, clearly glad that we had pulled that one off. But I was more curious about what she had going on in that head of hers. What did she really have in mind for our afternoon? And did I want to have any part of it?

A Delicate Balance

Sam and I watched as Hope squeezed her extralarge breasts into the Mini Cooper and tore out of the parking lot. Alexis and Belinda were hitting the beach with Holly, so they were off in her hybrid. The soccer team had already cut out about a half hour before us. It wasn't long before Sam and I were the last ones in the parking lot.

I started Electra and waited for the purr of her engine. We always had a moment of silence before we took off, both to appreciate the fact that the car was running and to listen for any telltale signs that she might change her mind and go dead on us. I don't know much about fixing cars, but when you own a classic, you have to at least know what to listen for.

Everything sounded good.

I put my hand on the gearshift. "Where are we going?"

"Turn right out of the parking lot."

Electra remained in park. "Well, obviously," I said. Going

left on Breakwater Lane would take us to a dead end. Literally. We'd go off a cliff.

"I'll direct you," Sam said with a bigger smile than I'd ever seen on her face. Sam's ability to hide things from me is only second to her ability to scheme. Which is my way of saying she can't do either with any discernable talent.

Electra continued to idle. On the bright side, the engine sounded pretty good. "Is there a reason you don't want to tell me where we're going?"

"Because if I tell you, you might not want to go."

"I don't want to go already," I said.

"We're going to get some coffee," Sam said with her gaze focused intently out the passenger side window. What had her attention, I did not know. I assumed she was more interested in looking *away* from something—namely me—than looking *at* something—namely air.

By that point, I was able to put two and two together and come up with something. "The coffeehouse at Malibu Colony Plaza?"

Sam nodded her head.

I rolled my eyes.

The Colony is a quaint little shopping center by the beach. The shops run the gamut from a really nice supermarket to upscale boutiques to a newspaper stand and Subway sandwich shop. It may be small, but it's the place to be and be seen running your daily errands. The Colony gets more celebrity sightings per day than the reception desk at the Wonderland Rehab Center.

It's also across the street from Eric Whitman's Malibu Dream House.

"So, we're meeting Eric," I said as I put Electra in drive. "What's the big deal?"

"I didn't know how you'd feel about discussing Hope and Drew with him," Sam said. "Since you guys have issues or whatever."

"We don't have *issues*," I said. "We just both want to be the only man in your life. Me, platonically, of course. Him . . . well, I think we both know what he wants. Seems to me, you're the one with the issues."

"Funny."

"Look, I don't really have any problems with Eric anymore," I said. "He's never going to be my best friend, but he's your boyfriend. I can deal." And I *could* deal. We had been hanging out together for more than a month without incident. I couldn't figure out why it was such a big deal all of a sudden.

The reason hit me at about the same time we hit the Pacific Coast Highway. We'd never been a trio. Someone had always been with us. Usually two someones: Drew and Hope. And since Suze had been tagging along we'd been a right jolly old gang. But now, with me as the third wheel, we were about to enter a new dynamic entirely.

I could see why she was nervous.

A few miles up the PCH, I turned Electra into the Malibu Colony Plaza and found a spot near the coffeehouse. Thankfully, it was still early in the season. Give it a week or two and the parking lot would be packed with cars filled with tourists hoping for a celeb sighting in the frozen food aisle of the supermarket.

Before we got out of Electra, I flipped on my cell phone to see if I'd missed any calls or anything. I get lousy reception in Malibu, especially at school.

"Suze made it to New York safely," I said, reading her text. "Hey. If we get the spots in Blackstone's program we'll be able to spend the summer hanging out with her in the city. And Hope will be there too."

"And Eric will be a short train ride to the Hamptons," Sam added.

"Oh," I said. "Guess you figured that one out already."

"Yep."

What can I say? Sometimes I'm a little slow. So, in addition to this audition being for one of the best acting programs in the country, Sam had the added stress of being able to spend the summer a train ride away from her boyfriend or being stuck on the other side of the country from him. Yeah. It was going to be a fun week.

We made our way to the coffeehouse, which sat between a boutique that specialized in high-priced baby clothes and an empty storefront with a sign asking us to WATCH THIS SPACE FOR AN EXCITING NEW ENDEAVOR. Sam and I stopped to watch the space for a few seconds.

Nothing exciting happened at all.

The coffeehouse was packed as usual, but Eric and his little brother, Matthew, were saving us spots at one of the small tables. So much for worrying about the three-way dynamic among Sam, Eric, and me. I guess we'd just put that off for some future occasion.

Before we got in line, we swung by the table to say hi. I swear I heard Matthew humming as we approached. And I don't mean he had a song in his heart. It was more like one long, sustained buzzing sound that was far from natural for the usually shy and quiet boy.

"Not again," Sam said as we stepped up to the table.

"Again," Eric said, raising a mostly empty frozen coffee drink to the air. Optimists might say that the glass was half full, but I'm a realist. The drink was mostly empty. Considering the humming that Matthew was doing, I doubted that Eric had been the pessimist that emptied it.

"Hi, Sam!" Matthew said with another frozen drink in front of him. It had barely been touched. "Hi, Bryan. I didn't know you were coming. I haven't seen you since . . . since. . . . It's been a long time. Eric wouldn't let me come to his party or I would have seen you there. You were at the party, right? I wouldn't know because I wasn't allowed to go."

I blinked twice. "Hi," I said. Then I turned and went to get in line. Sam followed.

We weaved our way through the coffeehouse vultures waiting for a seat to open up so they could set up camp. Once we were out of earshot, I whispered to her, "That was more words than I've ever heard Matthew say. *Ever.* And I've known him since before he could even say words. He hardly even babbled much as a baby. Just sort of sat there watching the world go by and silently judging us."

"You thought a baby was judging you?"

"I think *everyone* is judging me," I said. "Besides, I was eight at the time."

"You're weird."

"I know that," I said. "But what's the kid's excuse?"

"Caffeine," Sam explained. "Does it to him every time."

I looked back at Eric and Matthew. The little guy's leg was shaking so much that the table beside them was vibrating. The faux hippie dude working on his top-of-the-line seventeen-inch MacBook Pro looked way annoyed. "Ya think maybe Eric should cut back on the caffeine?"

"He always orders his brother a noncaffeinated drink," Sam said. "Somehow Matthew always manages to switch it on Eric without him noticing."

"Maybe it's time to find another hangout," I said.

"Maybe," Sam agreed as we stepped up to the counter. "This is on me."

"Oh, you bet it is," I said. She ordered a Mocha Java, while I got a Vanilla Caramel Java and I gleefully let her pay for both. Normally, we go Dutch, but I figured that she owed me since Eric was now a part of whatever scheme she had brought me here to hatch. Besides, she sometimes gets offended when I try to pay for things or don't let her pay. That's the problem of having a friend in a totally different tax bracket.

Our drinks were ready in under a minute and we rejoined Eric and Matthew back at the table. It was still shaking along with Matthew's leg, but not as badly as before. Maybe the caffeine was working its way out of his system.

"Hey, Bryan, did you get a Vanilla Caramel? I've never had a Vanilla Caramel. Can I try it? I wanna see what it tastes like."

And maybe not.

"Matthew," Eric said, all big-brother-sternly. "I said you could come here with us if you stayed calm. So far, you've stolen my drink and annoyed half the people here with your motormouth. Keep it up and it's the last time you hang with me and my friends."

"Sorry," Matthew said, chastised. I felt bad for the kid. I'd been known to hit a good sugar buzz once in a while myself back when I was his age. Still, if I was half as annoying on sugar as Matthew was on caffeine, I would like to think someone would have sat me down and gagged me.

"Sorry," Eric said to us.

I just shrugged. There wasn't anything to really apologize for, but whatever. I had every intention of being on my best behavior. Eric had just referred to me as his "friend." It was about time I started treating him that way too, wasn't it?

There were two open seats at the table. One was a chair beside Matthew, while the other was a space on the small wicker love seat next to Eric. As much as I was trying to get used to us being "friends" again, I felt the love seating was more appropriate for him and Sam.

When Sam sat beside her beau, I couldn't help but notice how they were perfectly framed together by the wicker back of the seat. I hate to admit it, but they kind of looked cute, sitting there, sipping their drinks . . . or what Eric had left of his drink.

"Okay," Sam said, calling the meeting to order. "I think we're all worried about Hope and Drew, right?"

Eric nodded.

I shrugged. "I'm worried about *Hope*."

"You'd be worried about Drew if you knew what he did last night," Eric said. Then he finished off his drink. He didn't say anything else. I mean, come on! You don't say something like that and leave a person hanging.

"What?!" I asked.

"Okay." He looked around to make sure no one could hear him, then leaned forward. The three of us leaned in as well. "All night. Barry Manilow. On shuffle."

"Eeeeee," Sam and I said. Matthew just looked confused.

Let me explain. Drew's mom? *Total* Fanilow. She took us to a concert way back before Drew and I knew what we were getting ourselves into. The emotional scars took years to heal. If Drew was reopening old wounds, that meant things were serious all around.

"So, we agree something has to be done, right?" Sam said.

"Why?" I asked. "If they want to get back together—"

"Hope's gone at the end of next week," she reminded me. "And they can't even be in the same room. If they don't deal with it now, they might spend the summer apart and miss their chance to get back together."

The logic was flawed, but I did get what she was saying. I wasn't so sure that Hope and Drew did belong together, but, quite frankly, that wasn't my decision to make. And while some might say that it wasn't our business to interfere . . . well, as Sam kind of said earlier, that's what best friends are for.

"So, what are we going to do to get Hope and Drew back together again?" She turned to me with an expectant expression.

"And you're looking at me, why?" I asked. "This is your scheme."

"No," Sam said. "My scheme was to get you here so I could go along with your scheme. You know I suck at this."

"Sam said suck!" Matthew announced. Loudly.

I couldn't help it. I burst out laughing while Eric hung his head. Faux Hippie Dude shot us all a look then slammed his MacBook shut and huffed out of the place. Two coffeehouse vultures dove for the empty seat, nearly smashing their laptops into each other in the process.

"You tricked me," I said to Sam. "I only signed on to this thing because you said you had a scheme."

"And I refer to my previous statement," Sam said. "You *are* my scheme. So what do you want to do?"

I was flabbergasted. Actually flabbergasted. I had never been flabbergasted before. It was quite the odd feeling. Somewhere beyond shocked, but not quite dismayed.

"I don't even know where to begin," I said. "Why are you putting this on me?"

For some reason, Eric decided to chime in at that point. "I think we should—"

"Not now, babe," Sam said, gently placing her hand over Eric's. "We're not done yet." She turned back to me. "I am beseeching you. I would get on my knees if I thought they cleaned this floor with any amount of regularity. I need your manipulatively evil and brilliant mind on this."

"Okay," I said. "But I'm not quite there yet."

"You need more ego stroking?"

"No, I'm good," I said. "Just not ready to commit to an idea. In the meantime, I defer to Eric."

A brief flash of shock—or flabbergast—crossed Eric's face when I turned to him. He quickly recovered. I guess he was emboldened by my generous attempt to include him. "Why don't we re-create their first date?"

So much for that.

"I was kind of kidding about *The Parent Trap* earlier," I said to Sam.

"Uh-huh," she said, supportively squeezing her boyfriend's hand under hers. We both knew his plan was lame, but she was trying to be the good girlfriend. This? Was going to be fun to watch. "That's one possibility," she said. "Do you know what they did on their first date?"

Eric was looking at me, like I should know the answer or something.

"What?"

"Do you remember?" he asked.

"No."

"Well, it was a thought," Sam quickly said. I had a funny feeling that she knew exactly what Hope and Drew had done on their first date. Not that Sam knew Hope back then, but I'm sure it's something they've talked about. That's what girls *do*. Just as I'm equally sure that Drew never ran his date plans by Eric even though they did know one another back then. Because that's what guys *don't*.

Sam turned to me. "Got anything yet?"

"You could always force them together," I said. "Lock them in the observatory until they make up. I hear that kind of thing's worked before on people."

"I was thinking of something a little more . . ."

"Devious?"

"Subtle."

"Oh," I said. "I'm going to need some more time."

"Excuse me," Matthew said, raising his hand like he was in school. "I don't get it. *Why* are you trying to make Drew get back together with Hope?"

"Not now, Matthew," Eric said.

"It's okay," Sam said, turning to the little guy. "When two people are meant to be together, I think you should do everything in your power to help them stay together."

Matthew seemed to consider that for a moment. Then he turned to me for some reason. "Why do you think Drew and Hope belong together?"

"Hey, this one's on her," I said, lifting my Vanilla Caramel Java. "I'm just here for the coffee."

"Me too," Matthew said, staring longingly at my drink.

"Matthew!"

"What? You're all being weird. Whenever Dad tries to force me to do something, it's, like, the last thing I want to do."

I smacked my coffee down on the table. "And there it is."

"What?" Sam asked. She knew I was on to something.

"What?" Eric echoed with a look of confusion. He was still a few steps behind.

"We don't do anything to force them back together," I said, liking my scheme even more as it came out of my mouth. "You know they both expect us to try something. At least Hope does. So, we do nothing."

"Nothing?" Sam asked. "That's your big scheme?"

"No," I said. "That's not right. We do, do something. We do everything in our power to keep them apart over the next two weeks. Don't let them see each other. Don't let them talk to each other. That way, neither one of them will be able to do anything to make the other one any madder than they already are. By the time Hope's ready to leave for New York, they're going to be dying to get back together, if only to say good-bye. Then, we let nature take its course."

"I *like* it!" Sam said. Eric was nodding his head in appreciation as well.

Of course, it was possible that by keeping the two of them apart that long, Hope might actually go off to New York without seeing Drew one last time. Then they'd have the rest of the summer to get over each other. I didn't necessarily consider it a flaw in the plan.

"But we have to make sure they have time together before Hope leaves," Sam said.

Drat. Foiled again.

"There's always the observatory," I said.

"Or we could always just have a good-bye dinner for Hope and Eric," Sam suggested. "If we need an excuse."

"Well, that's a possibility too," I said. "Let's see where things go. But I still like the observatory idea."

"We'll hold that as a last resort," Sam said. I don't think she was being serious. Can't imagine why. "And thank you, Matthew," she added. "I owe you one."

"Can I come to the good-bye dinner?" he asked.

"No!" Eric said.

He continued buzzing, undaunted. "How 'bout another coffee?"

I looked down to see that my Vanilla Caramel Java was a lot emptier than I remembered it.

"Matthew!" we all yelled.

The Vagina Monologues

"Sorry we're late," Sam said with more enthusiasm than I could muster. She, Hope, and I made our way down the side aisle of Hall Hall, threw our stuff on some chairs, and hopped onstage. Everyone was standing in a lopsided circle. We slipped in between Jason and Tasha, exchanging apologetic smiles for disrupting the group's grand design.

"I always expect some stragglers in the summertime," Mr. Randall said. "Looks like one of you isn't quite awake yet."

"Almost there," I yawned, though nothing could have been further from the truth.

Phase One of our little scheme to keep Hope and Drew apart required Sam and Eric to coordinate their schedules to make sure there weren't any accidental run-ins during the week. This is why on Tuesday morning I found myself, once again, getting up before the crack of bloody dawn to begin my day.

Sam called Hope the night before suggesting that we all get together for breakfast to go over the monologues we'd chosen. Hope said she wasn't in the mood, but she eventually agreed.

I liked the idea because I couldn't pick among a few choices and I knew they could help me make my final decision. I *didn't* like the idea because it meant that I had to wake up way early, pick up Hope, and meet Sam in Santa Monica for breakfast. Which is why I was still sleepy when we got into our morning workshop. And to top it off, we were starting the day with improv.

I was in *no mood* for improv . . . or anything that required me to think.

(*Aside:* "Improv" refers to improvisational exercises. It's acting without a script. Like *Whose Line Is It Anyway?* or Nick Cannon's *Wild 'N Out*.)

"Here's the deal," Miss Julie, aka Ms. Blackstone, aka the daughter of the most famous man in modern theater, said. "We're going to start with a movement exercise. Everyone come up with an animal you want to portray. You're going to walk across the stage as that animal and we have to guess what animal you are."

Seemed simple enough. I was mentally going over my best "mooing" sound when she added, "Silently. You can't make a sound. We have to guess solely from the way you move."

Okay. A little harder, but not impossible. At least I didn't have to come up with dialogue. I was still wiping the sleep out of my eyes.

Miss Julie started us off by lumbering into the circle waving her arm in front of her from side to side. Several students yelled out "Elephant," while Jimmy Wilkey did one better by shouting, "Pachyderm!"

Me? I stood quietly as she continued walking toward Holly and tagged her to cross next. Not surprisingly, Holly chose a preening peacock to strut across the stage. This one took us slightly longer to figure out, largely because once she started wafting her hands out from her butt most of us broke into stifled hysterics.

The game continued as everyone got his or her chance. We went through snake and rabbit and chipmunk and a rather impressive impersonation of a camel with two humps. Usually, I prefer to go last in these things, but with every student chosen I lost the chance to do easier animals. We continued with giraffe and frog and an unsightly slug. (That one was Belinda, which made us all laugh.)

When Gary stepped into the circle, the entire class yelled, "Monkey!" before he even made a movement. He laughed and shook his head before moving forward with a rather convincing display of a flamingo. That boy had balance. Too bad he balanced his way over to me, making it my turn in the circle.

I guess being sleep deprived put me in a playful mood, because I went with skunk and started out by turning my fanny toward Sam and making it look like I was spraying her.

"Bryan!" she screeched, smacking my butt.

"Dog!" someone yelled out, which told me more than I wanted to know about her pet.

I crawled into the circle on all fours acting like my tail was in the air. "Bobcat!" "Coyote!" I feigned fear of predator and turned and sprayed again. "Scorpion!" Maybe I really was too tired because it was taking way longer than anyone else had. I was stuck in the circle as more and more incorrect animals were shouted out. As a last resort, I went with a Pepé Le Pew act, sure to entertain *and* get myself out of the circle.

Holly chimed in with "A sick walrus."

I shot her a look.

"A Labradoodle!" Sam burst out.

"Exactly," I lied, tapping Mr. Randall in. As I took my place back in the circle, I heard someone mumble, "I *said* dog."

Okay, that was *way* more difficult than it should have been. I continued to watch my friends and enemies as their animal choices got more and more exotic. We wound up going around the circle a few times, but thankfully, no one forced me to go again.

Once we were warmed up, we worked on voice projection. Mr. Randall and Miss Julie sat at the back of Hall Hall while the students took turns modulating the volume of our voices to make sure we could be heard. Considering how many of us were onstage, the lesson was fairly time consuming.

Finally, it came time to announce our monologue choices.

Mr. Randall had us take seats in the audience while he asked us—starting with the sophomores—which monologues we had chosen. It wasn't as easy a process as one might expect. There was a fair amount of overlap, caused by the fact that Mr. Randall had lent out his book of monologues to some of the juniors and sophomores and everyone kept picking the same pieces.

This wasn't usually a problem when we performed in class. There were only so many monologue books out there. And there were only so many parts that Orion Academy students wanted to play. (Usually, we chose wealthy yet mentally unbalanced characters. . . . I guess most of us could relate.) But with Hartley Blackstone coming to critique us and choose two students for his acting program, everyone wanted to *shine*. And that was going to be hard to do if we all performed *To be, or not to be*.

Once everything settled down, it became immediately clear that the seniors were all taking this way seriously. There was no overlap. No typical monologue choices. None of us had gone to Mr. Randall's big book of monologues for our choices.

I already knew that Sam had spent most of the night going through every monologue she could find online as well as through her own personal play collection in search of the perfect piece. She finally settled on the sarcastic and sardonic lesbian trapped in Hell, Inez from Sartre's existential classic *No Exit*. (*Aside:* The play deals with the idea that "Hell is other people." So true.) Clearly, Sam was going all out for this. In pure Sam fashion she already had the piece memorized when we'd sat down for breakfast.

Hope was doing a comic turn as Kate, the female lead from *The Taming of the Shrew*. It was a good choice. Hope was very much like the strong-willed character. It would definitely play to her strengths. At least, it would play to the strengths of the usually brash and bawdy Hope Rivera. The moody and sullen friend that was still mourning over the end of her relationship wouldn't have a chance.

Considering that Hope had chosen "sloth" as her animal choice onstage, I was beginning to worry that her mood was going to affect her performance on Friday. This was getting serious. Hope was *not* the kind of girl that let a guy get in the way of her chances at an opportunity like this.

As for me, I chose Tom from *The Glass Menagerie*. It's a drier piece than I would normally go with, but I thought it was the kind of thing Blackstone would like.

The rest of the seniors were doing a variety of pieces I knew well enough, along with a couple from plays I had only heard of in passing. Based on the selection alone, it really did seem like Jason was going to be the one to beat with his monologue from *The History Boys*.

Holly Mayflower made her followers, Alexis and Belinda, go first so she could be the last one to announce her monologue. Both Hope's stepsisters had chosen a piece from *Medea*. Considering that Alexis pronounced it like the word "media" instead of meh-DEE-a, I figure Holly had probably just handed them the monologues she wanted them to do.

When it came time for Holly to announce her monologue, I swear I heard a drumroll in the background. But maybe that was just my imagination. Or maybe she had a drummer from one of her dad's bands stationed outside the theater. The girl is known for spectacles.

She stood up in her row, took a deep breath, and announced,

"I'll be performing the part of the sensual and emotionally divided character Ivy from Jamison Montrose's groundbreaking play *The Mayflower Maxim*."

Heads all around the theater were turning to their neighbors as confused whispers filled the air. Hope and I looked right at Sam, who was a veritable walking Wikipedia of theatrical history. She just shrugged and shook her head. She'd never heard of *The Mayflower Maxim* either.

Sure, we all knew about Jamison Montrose. He was the new wunderkind on the Broadway scene and the heir apparent to Hartley Blackstone's throne. His play *Stop!* had just won the Tony for best *everything*. And he was in the pre-rehearsal for his supposedly revolutionary new musical *Go!* But even with everything about the guy in print lately, *The Mayflower Maxim* was a new one to me. And it was slightly bothersome that Holly's last name was in the title.

"*The Mayflower Maxim?*" Mr. Randall asked. "I've never heard of that play." He looked to Miss Julie, who shook her head like Sam had.

"It hasn't been produced yet," Holly said. "Jamie is . . ."

". . . a friend of Daddy's," Sam, Hope, and I whispered in unison along with Holly.

"Figures," I mumbled.

My mumbling was lost in the cacophony of voices protesting Holly's monologue. Holly was going to preview a new piece by Jamison Montrose—I'm sorry, *Jamie*—in front of Hartley Blackstone. Even if the monologue was crap, he'd probably be impressed by her connections. And really? *Ivy?* In

The Mayflower Maxim? Were we supposed to think this monologue wasn't specifically written for her: Holly *Mayflower*? She'd brought in a ringer of a writer to write her a ringer of a role. Combine that with her natural talent and she was even more of a threat.

"Aren't you going to say anything?" Jason asked Sam.

"What would be the point?" Sam asked with a shrug.

Besides, everyone else was already saying enough.

"Now, hold on," Mr. Randall said, raising his hands to implore the raging students for quiet. "Hold on. If—"

"Mr. Randall," Holly said, waving a hand. She cut him off just as he managed to regain order. "Is there something wrong with choosing an unproduced piece?"

"Well, it's not that, exactly," Mr. Randall said. "But—"

"No, I get it," Holly said magnanimously. Holly is very good at magnanimous. It's *genuine* she has a problem with. "It's just . . . this piece really spoke to me, you know? I didn't realize everyone would be so threatened by it."

Mr. Randall nodded in understanding . . . because he was understanding what she wanted him to understand. Holly knew she'd cause a stir when she announced that she was doing a piece that—let's be blunt—must have been written specifically for her. I'd be surprised if we ever heard of this play actually opening. But Mr. Randall had always let us choose anything we wanted for monologues we performed in class. We were usually encouraged to seek out alternative sources for materials, like novels, songs, and poems. I've been hard-pressed to find any performance that matched the emotional resonance of Tasha Valentine's dramatic reading of the list of ingredients in a Twinkie. I remember even seeing a few tears in the room by the time she had gotten to sodium stearol lactylate.

"We've always been free to do scenes or monologues from whatever sources we've found during the school year," Mr. Randall reminded us all, and let us know the direction his decision was about to go. "This program will be no different. Holly, you may use the piece."

This was met by a collection of groans.

Holly was on top of that too. "No, Mr. Randall. I'll be fine. I'm sure I can pick something else out. And don't worry at all about it cutting into my rehearsal time. I don't need as much prep time as other people."

"Oh, for crying out loud," Sam said softly. Then, she added loudly, "Holly, do the damn piece. You know you're going to, anyway."

Holly regarded our group with practiced innocence.

"Why, thank you, Sam," Holly said. "I never expected you to be on my side."

"Oh, I'm *full* of surprises," Sam replied with a smile.

"I can't wait for you to see it," Holly said.

Sam's smile was still frozen tightly in place. "Neither can I."

Noises Off

We broke for lunch after Mr. Randall finished recording our monologue selections. Not surprisingly, no two people would be reciting the same monologue, although Alexis and Belinda would be performing the same character. And I couldn't *wait* to see that.

In spite of—or maybe because of—the fact that their mom is a bitter, washed-up actress, neither of Hope's steps had ever set foot on a stage before. The two of them preferred to spend their life in the audience, commenting on the action rather than taking part in it. Can't say I blame them. It's easier to talk about people than to be talked about by people.

Figuring we could get in some extra rehearsals—and keep Hope away from Drew—Sam arranged for us to lunch in her mom's classroom. Anne's room was locked during the summer, but she gave her daughter the key. Hope stayed behind to talk to Mr. Randall for a minute as Sam, Jason, and I split off from the maddening crowd and wound our way through the empty halls.

"It's cool that your mom will let us use her room," Jason said. I tend to forget how convenient it is to have a parent (or pseudo-parent since she's not *my* mom) on staff. "We can really use this time to get in some good work."

Sam shrugged, blushing. "It balances out how annoying it can be for my mom to be around all the time." I always find it funny when Sam acts like she's annoyed that Anne works at the same school she goes to. They're like the closest mother-daughter act this side of Mama Rose and Gypsy . . . okay, bad example.

Once inside the empty room, the three of us pulled chairs up to Anne's desk and brought out our lunches. While we ate, Jason took a *one-hundred pound* Shakespeare anthology out of his bag and slammed it down on the desk.

"I hope you don't mind," Jason said as he heaved the book open, "but I kind of found a scene for us last night."

Sam and I looked at each other. Jason was certainly *eager*. That was not really a surprise. But I think we both were a little wary that he was jumping so far ahead with our scene. We hadn't even started working on our monologues yet.

"What scene?" Sam asked tentatively.

"I read through *Twelfth Night*. There's a problem with the play. Different characters keep running in and out of all the scenes, so it's hard to find a good four-person scene. I tried to cut together a few scenes but no matter what I tried, the best I could come up with would leave at least one of us with about a line and a half. I hope you don't mind, but I thought maybe we should do a different play."

I looked at Sam, waiting for a reaction. All she did was nod at him to go on. We usually had some of our best debates over what scenes we would do for class. Even when we both agreed on a piece, it was far more interesting to argue the merits to make sure we were choosing the right one. I know. We're weird. But sometimes a good battle of wits can be fun if you've got a similarly armed opponent. We'd never really worked on scenes with Jason before. I'm guessing she didn't want to scare him off by being too opinionated.

"I flipped through *A Midsummer Night's Dream* and found a really great scene with the four main characters that should be fun to do. I made copies." He handed us some pages he had stuck in the back of his book.

"Wait a minute," I said. "You went through two Shakespeare plays *and* picked your monologue last night?"

"I was excited," he explained. "I couldn't sleep."

When I can't sleep, I lie in the dark staring at the ceiling.

Jason? Studies Shakespeare texts.

"I know this scene," Sam said after a quick perusal. "It's kind of an obvious choice, but it shows some range. I'm in."

I barely glanced at the pages. "Then I guess I'm in too." If both Sam and Jason liked it, I doubted that I'd find anything wrong with the scene. It was *Shakespeare*, after all. Since Sam wasn't up for a debate, I figured I wasn't going to start one. It would be inappropriate to fight in front of Jason. Actually, I was just afraid to lose. He clearly knew his Shakespeare, whereas I knew how to count the cracks in my ceiling with only the moonlight to see by.

We all have our talents.

Before we finalized the decision, Sam remembered that we weren't a trio. "We'll just have to see what Hope—"

"CAN I *HELP* YOU WITH SOMETHING?" Hope's voice boomed from the hallway, causing us to jump out of our chairs. Aside from the shock of the unexpected yell, it was also a surprise to hear Hope raise her voice, considering her mood of late.

The three of us looked up to the doorway to see Alexis and Belinda breathing heavily with their hands pressed to their hearts . . . or the spaces their hearts would have been had they actually had hearts. Figures, the one thing that would bring her out of her silence would be the steps.

"Scare us to death, why don't you!" Alexis shot back.

"Maybe next time," Hope threatened. "If I catch you eavesdropping on my group again."

"We were just coming to talk to you," Belinda said. "To see if you needed a ride home later."

"And you couldn't wait until after lunch?" Hope asked. "We're not leaving for another three hours."

"We were just trying to be helpful," Belinda said.

"Yeah. Last time we do that," Alexis added as she grabbed her twin by the arm and stormed off.

Hope watched them leave before coming into the room and making a point of shutting the door behind her.

"What was that about?" Jason asked.

"They probably wanted to find out what we were doing so they could report back to Holly," Hope said.

We nodded. I wanted to say something about Hope raising her voice, but I didn't know how to do it without sounding stupid. I think Sam was having the same internal debate because we both kind of stood there with confused looks on both our faces.

"So, what *were* we doing?" Hope finally asked. Her tone was softer than usual, but it was nice to see her interested in something.

"Picking a scene for next week," Sam replied. I could hear the concern in her voice. If Holly knew what scene we planned to perform, she'd choose a scene specifically with the intention of showing our team up. Not that she'd have much of a chance of showing us up with Alexis and Belinda in her group, but she could try.

"Should we pick a new scene?" I asked.

"No," Sam said with absolute certainty. "I'm not about to fall into Holly's trap. We shouldn't make our choice based on what she may or may not do to sabotage us."

"Good," Hope said softly, but firmly.

"I'm with you guys," I added. "But, then again, I'm always with you."

Jason nodded his head. We were united in our selection. Or, technically, we were united against Holly. Either way, we had a scene, so we could get down to work on other things. Our monologue performances were only a few days away.

"What did we choose?" Hope asked as she joined us with her lunch. Jason and Sam filled her in on the scene while I munched on my food. It was interesting listening to them both talk Shakespeare. So much more fun than listening to Sam discuss soccer with her boyfriend.

"No more talk of scenes," Sam decreed once they got that business out of the way. "We need to focus on monologues."

"Speaking of which," I said, turning to Hope. "What did you talk to Mr. Randall about?"

"I've changed my monologue choice," she replied.

"But *Taming of the Shrew* is perfect for you," Sam said.

Death Glare! Death Glare!

"No . . . I mean . . ." There was no way Sam was going to get out of this one unscathed.

"Why did you change it?" I asked, deflecting Hope's anger. As scary as it was, it was nice to see it again. Maybe Sam and I had overreacted about Hope's mood. It could have just been normal end-of-relationship stuff she was dealing with.

"When Mr. Randall said we could do unproduced work, it got me thinking. I'm going to write myself a monologue."

"Really?" Sam and I asked in unison. This was not a good idea.

"Might as well put my mood to work for me," Hope said.

Oh no. Oh, no no no.

Don't get me wrong. Hope is an amazing writer. I had no doubt that she could create the monologue to end all monologues. What worried me—and Sam too, I'm sure—was the whole "putting her mood to work" for her part. At that moment, her mood was definitely reflected in her eyes. She had chosen the black contacts that were all pupil and no iris. Those blank eyes always freaked me out. And I was *really* afraid of what those eyes could come up with in terms of a monologue. I could easily see her putting everything she felt into her speech. That level of honesty and openness could really backfire on her, considering that we go to a school where gossip is a weapon and truth is ammunition.

Without a word, Sam and I silently agreed that it was even more important to keep Hope away from Drew that week. The last thing Hope needed was to add any fuel to that fire.

We spent the rest of the lunch hour working in silence while we individually broke down our monologues into beats. (*Aside:* That's something you do so you know where to take the proper moments. Examine the motivation for each and every line. Know when to take an action. That kind of thing.) Well, three of us were working on our monologue breakdowns. Hope was writing her own monologue on the back of her copied pages from *The Taming of the Shrew*. From what I could tell, she wasn't getting much actual writing down, but a lot of crossing things out and starting over.

Every time she scratched something else out I got a deeper feeling of impending doom.

With five minutes left in lunch, Sam put down her pencil and announced: "Okay, everyone, papers to the front of the room." She handed me her monologue. Jason looked confused, but he did the same.

"This is what Bryan does," Sam explained to Jason as I went to work on her monologue. "He's, like, an expert at scene breakdowns. Trust me. You won't be disappointed."

I felt my face going red. It was true, if I do say so myself. I had this crazy natural talent for breaking down a monologue. It was the actual presenting it onstage that I always had a problem with.

You know. The important part.

Once I was done, I handed Sam's back for her to look at and went over Jason's with him. "I think if you keep these lines together and build on the moment here"—I pointed out the passage I was talking about—"you'll have a much stronger moment. You know. If you want to. It works the other way too."

"No," Jason said. "Thanks. This is much better."

I was blushing again. I could feel it.

"Good job," Sam said, putting her own monologue back in her bag without questioning any of my suggestions. She checked her watch. "Lunch is almost over."

We all got up and left the room, making sure that Sam locked up behind us.

"I need to swing by my locker," Hope said.

"We'll go too," Sam said. "Meet you back at the auditorium, Jason."

"Okay," he said, and went off in the other direction.

"My locker's on the other side of school," Hope reminded us. "We're going to be late. You don't have to come with me."

"No prob," Sam said, grabbing Hope by the arm and pulling her along. "We'll be late together, 'cause *it's friendship . . . friendship . . . just the perfect blends*—"

A locker door slamming echoed through the hall.

"Let's cut through the courtyard," Sam said as she kicked open the outer door that led outside. "It's faster that way."

"No, it's no—" Sam grabbed me by the collar and pulled me out after them. As I crossed over the threshold, I looked back to see Eric standing by his locker and guiding Drew off the other way.

Oh.

The Forced Marriage

The brief spark of life that Hope had shown during lunch Tuesday was pretty much gone by the time we got back to the auditorium. And as the next couple days passed, I wasn't so sure that our scheme was helping out all that much either.

Keeping Hope and Drew apart didn't seem to be having an effect on either of them. Hope remained sullen and quiet. She spent all of her time working on her monologue in a new journal she had purchased solely for that purpose. Either she had a lot to get off her ample chest or she had decided to turn her monologue into a one-woman show. I wouldn't know, since she still refused to show us what she was doing or talk about her feelings with Sam.

Drew didn't seem to be doing any better. The one time I passed him in the hallway, I swear I heard the pulsing beat of the *Copacabana* coming from the headphones he had on.

Our scheme wasn't even all that much of a challenge either.

Hope went where we told her to go and she did what we told her to do. If Sam turned us down a hall we didn't need to go down, Hope followed without question. When I drove Electra at two miles an hour to school to make sure we'd be late, Hope didn't even slam her foot down on the gas pedal to make us go faster. Not that she would have done that normally, but she would have at least questioned why an elderly man with a walker was passing us on his daily stroll. It was like the only motivation she felt was for writing in her journal. I was beginning to worry about her monologue performance. Not just what she was going to say, but if she was going to be able to say anything at all.

But her monologue wasn't the only one I was concerned about. My prep was not evolving the way I wanted either. Then again, I don't know of any actor who is ever happy with his work, so maybe I was doing better than I thought.

For the rest of the week, our classwork had been focused on vocal exercises, projection, and stage presence. Anything that would help us give a better performance on Friday. The actual rehearsal of our monologues had been left for outside of school on our own. My group didn't even work on them in Anne's classroom over lunch. We all felt that it was better to do the preliminary rehearsing by ourselves so that we didn't interfere with one another's choices. Of course, we had no intention of going onstage Friday without getting other opinions.

It's a long-standing tradition in our trio that Sam, Hope, and I always preview our work together the night before any performance. Since Jason was part of our scene group, we invited him to join us. We chose to do it at my house because it was the most convenient for us. The location also helped us with a new phase of our plan to see if Hope and Drew were meant to be back together.

Sam went first, as she usually did. She'd also go last. She would go in every position if we let her. Sam likes to work a scene to death. She's not happy with a piece until the moment of her performance, and even then she wants to go back and do some things over to prove to herself that she did everything she could in the first place. I've tried to explain to her that there is such a thing as over-rehearsing, but she refuses to believe me.

Sam was amazing, as usual. Inez was a very different character for her. Usually, Sam plays the innocent ingenue. Like Dorothy in *The Wizard of Oz*. *No Exit* was a bit of a darker choice than she normally made. Inez was about as strong-willed as a pre-breakup Hope. But Sam really worked the part. She had us all shouting, "Brava!" by the end. (*Aside: Brava* is the feminine form of *bravo*. Yes, even applause can be sexist.)

"Comments? Questions?" Sam asked after a bow.

Neither Jason nor Hope had anything to say. I, however, did have a question. "Why did you start out with so much intensity?"

"This is the part where Inez finally blows up," Sam said. "I wanted to come in big."

"Yeah," I said. "But then you kept building from that moment. You might want to try opening big, then taking it down a bit and building up to the end. I think you had too many big moments. It might be better to tone some of it down. But still . . . amazing performance."

"Thanks," Sam said as she dropped beside me on the couch.

Jason went next. His performance was almost as good as Sam's. I wasn't familiar with *The History Boys*, or Jason's character, but I got what he was saying and understood the moments he was playing like I knew the play by heart. The only weakness I could see was that he swallowed some of his lines. Sam and Hope also caught that one. We all suggested that he play things out to the audience a bit more and then moved on to me.

I wish I could tell you that my performance was so good that my friends couldn't even come up with a note to give me. But, that was *far* from the truth.

"You need to ground your character in reality a bit more," Jason suggestion.

"Really?" Hope asked. "I thought he should play up the dream element. It's like he's recalling a memory, not simply narrating a play."

I looked to Sam, who was the one person I trusted most when it came to acting advice. "I think they're both right," Sam said. "You're playing the lines, not the emotion." I nodded. I got what she was saying, but I wasn't so clear on how I could translate it into my acting.

They had some more specific comments for me that I listened to diligently while I wondered how I was going to incorporate it all into my performance by the next morning. Just as I reached the point of total saturation, Sam suggested we move on to Hope.

"We can't wait to see this magnum opus of yours," I said, glad to have the focus off me. I was trying to keep the moment light, but I could tell that Sam was just as concerned as I was over what we were about to see. Hope had been keeping us in the dark on her monologue since she announced she was writing one herself. She wouldn't even tell us what the subject was, but we had our guesses. And they were all the same guess. Now that we were finally going to see it, we were on the edge of the couch in anticipation.

We all—including Jason—braced for impact.

"Um," Hope said. "It's not quite ready yet."

Sam shook her head. "Uh-uh. We always share our work the night before a scene. No backing out. That's the rule. Now go."

It wasn't that either of us were hurt that Hope didn't want to perform her piece in front of us—well, maybe a little—but Sam and I were mostly concerned. With the wounds of her breakup still fresh, we were worried Hope would get up onstage in front of everyone—most notably her steps—and pour out her heart. And *that* would not be good for anyone. Well, the steps would probably think it was hilarious, but the rest of us would be feeling varying degrees of discomfort and pity for her. And neither Sam nor I wanted any of that.

Then again, maybe Hope was writing a lovely piece about the beauty of summertime and the excitement of a future laid out before her.

Riiight.

"No," Hope said. Her voice was calm, but her tone was firm. "I want my performance to be fresh. I'm not rehearsing it at all. When I set foot onstage, I want the words to come out of me naturally. With genuine emotion."

Now I was really worried about this monologue. And Hope in general.

"Hope, you have to rehearse," I said. "You have to find a character. Block your movements. Otherwise you're just reading a diary entry, which . . . *interesting*, but not acting."

Sam and I spent the next few minutes trying to convince Hope to at least show us what she was working on, but she wouldn't budge. The scary part was that she didn't even argue with us. She just shut down and let us do all the talking, which is *so* not like Hope. I gave up when I realized we weren't getting anywhere, but Sam had one more point to make.

"You'll never get into Blackstone's program if he thinks you're just going up there and being yourself," she said.

This, at least, got a response. "Sam, there are more important things in this world than Hartley Blackstone's acting program," Hope said. I thought Sam was about to fall over on that one. "But don't worry. I do intend to play a role . . . a role unlike any other I've ever played before."

Duhn-duhn-duhn!

As if on cue, there was a knock at the kitchen door. Actually, it wasn't entirely on cue as it came several minutes earlier than it should have. Sam and I shared a knowing glance that we hoped Hope didn't catch and then excused ourselves to check on who we thought was our not-so-mystery guest. Turns out it wasn't who we were expecting. It was my not-so-mysterious mom and her best friend and business partner, Blaine.

"Thanks Bryan, I couldn't reach my key," Mom said as she came through the door loaded down by a box of doggie-related merchandise. This was almost routine around the house lately. She'd been bringing a lot of stuff home from her store so she could work on the designs in her studio. Kaye 9 may be one of the more popular stores on Melrose Avenue, but all the magic happens in a small work space that was once our garage.

I grabbed the box from her and put it down on the kitchen table, taking a peek inside to see what she brought home to work on. It appeared to be her fall line, as there was an abundance of browns and oranges in the mix. This is what I hate about retail. Summer hadn't even begun for me yet, and Mom was already focused on back to school. She even had little doggie backpacks in there . . . for their little doggie textbooks?

"Hey, kiddo," Blaine said as he came in carrying two more boxes. Even with his arms loaded down, he still managed to flip back my fedora and muss my hair. "Hi, Samilina."

"Hey, Blainerosa," Sam said.

Don't ask me. They came up with those nicknames entirely on their own.

Blaine . . . or *Blainerosa* . . . is the brains behind Kaye 9, while Mom is the heart, soul, and creative vision. That's not to say that I don't think my mom is smart. She's incredibly gifted when it comes to art and design and she may even have a little dog whisperer in her. But Blaine's the one with the business savvy. If it weren't for him, Mom would probably be stuck in a mall kiosk somewhere.

Before the kitchen door could close behind them, the headmaster's dog came bounding inside.

"Get the gate! The gate!" Mom yelled.

Sam lunged for the doggie gate that we kept in the space beside the refrigerator and the doorway, but she couldn't move fast enough. Canoodle burst out of the kitchen and into the rest of the house, leaving a trail of paw prints on the beige carpet.

"Canoodle!" Mom yelled as she gave chase.

Another dog poked her head in through the back door before it closed. Mal kind of looked in like she was asking if the coast was clear before she plodded into the room and right up to me. Mal is Blaine's Labrador, and the closest thing I have to a cousin in this or any other world. She seemed thrilled to see me, even as she glanced toward the still ungated doorway to the rest of the house. To this day, Mal (which is short for Maleficent) has never been past that threshold. Rather than appearing jealous that Canoodle had gotten to the promised land and making her own attempt at freedom, Mal just shook her head as if she had already had enough of that crazy dog.

I could relate.

Jason heard the commotion and wrangled Canoodle back into the kitchen. Once the dust had settled, further greetings were exchanged and we decided to take a snack break. As we gathered around the center island for our milk and cookies, *that* was when the not-so-mystery guest arrived.

"Hello?" Eric called out with a tentative knock on the kitchen door that sent Canoodle into hysterics. Mal looked up at me like she was embarrassed for the entire canine race.

Since Blaine was the closest to the door, he got it.

"Mr. Blaine!" Eric said in surprise.

"Please . . . just Blaine," he replied. "Mr. Blaine makes me sound like a gay hairdresser . . . and I am *not* a hairdresser."

Blaine is a man of many nicknames, but nothing about him would ever be mistaken for the stereotypical hairdresser often portrayed in Hollywood. He struck an imposing figure in the doorway, all two-hundred-fifty pounds of muscle on him. His hand swallowed Eric's as they shook. Back when we were kids, my friends used to call Blaine "Mr. Blaine." (Kind of like Miss Julie, I guess.) I always liked it, because I was the only one that got to drop the "Mr." when I called him by name. There was a time when I called him "Uncle Blaine," but that got cumbersome quick, so it's pretty much always been Blaine for me.

If my calculations are right, Eric hadn't seen Blaine since my grandfather's funeral, back when we were fourteen.

"Eric Whitman," Blaine said. "Where have you been keeping yourself?"

"I've been around," Eric said.

"He's here for Sam," I clarified, realizing I just blew our cover in front of Hope. This was supposed to look like a spontaneous visit. "I mean . . . I assume he's here for Sam. Unless you need me for something?"

"Smooth," Sam whispered as she pushed past me to give her boyfriend a kiss hello. "I told him I'd be here rehearsing."

"I got that thing for you," he said as he handed a bag to her. I guess he was as bad at the subterfuge as I was. How hard was it to come up with a noun to describe the "thing" in the bag? Especially considering there was obviously something *in* the bag and that something *did* have an actual name.

"Thanks," Sam said as she put the bag down on the table without opening it. Would it have killed her to at least *act* like she was surprised over the gift? Maybe take a peek inside? We were really blowing this one.

Thankfully, Jason helped us along without even knowing he was giving us some much needed assistance. "Hey," he said, "you want to stay and watch us run through our monologues again?"

Considering how poorly Sam and I were doing with our little charade, I fully expected Eric to stumble all over himself. Jason had jumped in and moved up our script. Sam was supposed to ask Eric to stay after we used some other stalling tactics first. But Sam's boyfriend covered like a pro. "I really shouldn't," Eric said, trying to sound nonchalant about his next line. "I left Drew in the car."

Sam, Eric, and I watched Hope perform a not-so-subtle glance out the kitchen door. There was a kind of wistfulness to the look that led me to believe that she was starting to miss Drew a bit.

"He didn't want to come in?" Hope asked.

"I told him to wait," Eric explained, following our script. "I figured you two didn't want to see each other."

"It would have been okay," Hope said with another dash of wistful thrown in.

"Next time I'll know," Eric said. Then he did something every actor dreads. He looked right at me because he knew I had the next line. He was supposed to wait for me to start speaking before he looked at me. Now, it seemed like he was waiting for me to say something.

I had to speak quickly to cover it. "You have to at least stay to see Sam's monologue."

Eric pulled up a stool. "I guess a minute wouldn't hurt. That is, if Sam doesn't mind doing it in front of all of us."

Sam? Mind having an audience? Not likely.

"I still have some things to work out," Sam said. "But . . . okay."

The rest of us got comfortable around the kitchen while Sam went through her preparations. Girl can't read so much as the title of a play without going through some warm-up exercises. Usually, it was pretty annoying, but this time I knew she was warming up with a purpose, so I didn't mind as much.

While she went through her vocal routine the three of us schemers watched as Hope watched the door. Apparently, we weren't the only ones watching.

Blaine made a move for the kitchen door. "I'll get Drew," he said. "He might want to see this too."

"That's okay," Sam, Eric, and I said *way* too earnestly . . . and too much in unison.

The room went silent for a moment. Sam hadn't even covered with vocal exercises. Everyone was waiting for one of us to explain why we didn't want Drew in the house.

Thankfully, Eric came through with an excuse. "He's on his cell phone," he explained.

"Besides, I'm ready to go," Sam said as she launched into her monologue. This time, it was even better than her first performance. Sam really feeds off an audience. I couldn't wait until the following day when she'd have all the Drama Geeks there along with Mr. Randall, Miss Julie, and most important, Hartley Blackstone himself.

As she finished, we rewarded her with heartfelt applause. Sam had taken my suggestion about varying her levels and it really added to the performance, if I do say so myself. While we were still clapping, Drew slipped inside, without bothering to knock, just like when we were kids.

Mom was the first to see him. "Drew! Honey, it's been ages. How's your family?"

"Fine, thanks," Drew said, trying—and failing—to keep his eyes off Hope.

"We should get back to work," I suggested.

"Work!" Mom exclaimed, scaring us all. "I almost forgot. I need to get that . . . thing from my studio."

"The materials order forms," Blaine reminded her.

"I know," she said. Blaine and I didn't believe her for a second. Mom could be kind of scattered at times. For instance, she was an incredibly polished and well-dressed woman. But somehow she always seemed to be missing a button. On her shirt. On her skirt. Wherever. The outfit she was currently wearing had *two* buttons missing, which usually signified that she was under some stress. Mom pushed past me and stepped over the doggie gate to head to her studio.

"Thanks for this, Eric," Sam said with a nod to the mystery

bag as she walked him to the door. Again, would it have hurt for her to give "this" a name?

"No problem," Eric said, with a kiss. "Coming, Drew?"

"Yeah," Drew said with a last glance at Hope. "Bye."

"Bye," Hope said.

"Bye!" I said a little cheerily.

Eric and Drew left without a backward glance.

"Back to work," I repeated, waving our little acting troupe in the direction of the living room. Jason led the way, but as we filed out of the kitchen, I felt a massive hand come down on top of my fedora, squishing it to my head. I decided to hang back a moment to see what Blaine wanted. It seemed the smart thing to do.

Once my friends were gone, Blaine looked me right in the eye and said, "Care to tell me what that was about?"

"What?" I asked oh-so-innocently. "We're rehearsing."

"That thing with Drew and Hope," Blaine said, crossing his arms and looking at me with a challenging eye that neither of my parents could even come close to pulling off.

Busted!

The Tragical History of Dr. Faustus

My mind was working on a half dozen different excuses that didn't sound remotely believable, even to me. There was no way I was going to be able to fool Blaine. I couldn't manage that on my best day. And, as my little display a few minutes earlier had proven, this was *far* from my best day . . . at least where scheming and deception were concerned. So, I spilled. Everything from the breakup, to Sam's and my scheme, to our earlier performance that had been meant to tease Hope and Drew without actually letting them spend time together.

When I was done, I waited in silence for Blaine to tell me what an idiot I was for going along with the plan.

This time, however, he surprised me by not prefacing his commentary with an insult and got right to the heart of the matter. "Do Hope and Drew even want to get back together?"

"Neither one of them will talk about it," I said. "But they seem miserable now that they're apart."

"Yeah," Blaine said. "That's called a breakup. They're supposed to be miserable. If they were happy, they'd be together."

"What if they're miserable *because* they're not together?"

"Better question," Blaine said. "Do *you* think they're better off as a couple?"

I wondered what *my* opinion had to do with any of this. Blaine's question had to go unanswered because the doorbell rang, providing the distraction I was looking for. "Who could that be?" I asked. "All my friends are here."

"One way to find out," Blaine said, giving me a gentle shove in the direction of the front door.

"I got it," I yelled to no one. Mom couldn't hear the doorbell from her studio. It was soundproof. She designed it that way so she wouldn't be distracted while working on her latest doggie creations. She takes her work very seriously.

"It's like Grand Central Station in here," Sam commented as I passed by the living room. When I opened the door to find Holly, Alexis, and Belinda standing on my steps, I wished that it *were* Grand Central and that I was on the next train out of town. I had no clue what the three witches would be doing on my doorstep, and I really didn't care to find out.

"Yes?" I asked, without bothering to hide my surprise. Dropping in unexpected was not the Holly Mayflower style. She usually called ahead to give one time to roll out the red carpet and lay rose petals along the walk.

"We need to see Hope," Alexis said, rather bluntly if you ask me.

"Um . . . Hope!" I called back to the living room. "Your sisters are here."

"*Step*sisters!" she yelled back.

I smiled at the girls in the doorway, waiting for Hope to come out. Or to say something more. Or to respond in some way, shape, or form.

But . . . nothing.

"HOPE!" I called out again.

"Why don't you show the young ladies into the house?" Blaine asked from behind me. For such a large man, he moved with quite the stealth. I hadn't known that I was followed from the kitchen.

"Please, come into the house, young ladies," I said as I stepped aside.

As they walked in, I could see Holly shoot a look at the twins, rolling her eyes at our modest furnishings. When I say "modest," I mean by Malibu standards. Considering that our house is only a one-floor, three-bedroom ranch style and we don't have any Picassos in the foyer, Holly probably equated my family's housing situation with that of the characters in *Rent*.

Not that Blaine caught the look, mind you. It was only meant for me.

I didn't bother to introduce Blaine as etiquette might demand. As far as I could remember, he never would have met Holly before. Maybe the twigs, but I wasn't sure. Either way, I didn't think it would be important for him to know who they were, and I was fine not bothering to explain it. I guess he caught on to what I was up to since he didn't introduce himself either. He did watch me the entire time with an expression that suggested I was committing a major faux pas.

Pinocchio gets a tiny cricket as his conscience. Me? I warrant a two-hundred-fifty-pound bald black man.

I showed the girls into the living room where all rehearsing had stopped and posturing had begun. When I had breezed past the room to get the door, Sam and Hope had both been lounging on the couch while Jason prepped to do his monologue. Now, the girls were both standing with their arms folded in front of them. They were prepared for war. Poor Jason looked confused. Like he was aware of the tension, but not sure why it was there.

"What are you doing here?" Hope asked with more venom in her voice than the situation demanded. It was odd, considering her general malaise of the past few days, but strangely good to hear. The old Hope was back. At least, for the moment.

"We need the car," Alexis said, getting right to the point.

"I have it tonight," Hope said. "That was the arrangement. I get Thursdays so you two can have the weekend."

"I know it's a lot to ask," Belinda said, "but if you could get someone to drive you home, we could really use it."

Hope looked over the nicer of the two twigs. Belinda is the real one to watch out for. She's all sugar while her twin is the spice. Belinda has a way of forcing you to give in to what she wants simply because you'd seem like an ass saying no to her.

Not that Hope cared about that. "No."

"We need it to get ready for Mom's party," Alexis said.

"Party?" I asked. That? Was a mistake.

"You didn't know?" Holly slipped in the question in a tone suggesting that I was clearly an idiot for being unaware of the social event of the season.

"None of us are going," Hope said.

Belinda looked genuinely shocked. "I thought your dad—"

"Yes. He talked to me," Hope said. "And I told him I'm not going. Now, if you don't mind, we are trying to work here."

"We still need the car," Alexis said.

"And you're still not getting it," Hope replied. I couldn't believe that Hope was actually fighting over the pink-and-purple Mini-monstrosity. Then again, I didn't think this argument was over a car at all.

"Fine," Holly said, plopping herself down on my couch. Funny. I didn't remember inviting her to stay. When you're Holly Mayflower, I guess formal invitations don't matter much. "Since we have to cancel our plans, we might as well hang here. I'm sure you guys could use some help with your monologues."

"Ha!" Sam laughed. "Not a chance."

Holly looked over her competition. "Not ready to show anyone yet? I understand. Some people need to polish right up to the last second. While others . . ." She let her sentence hang.

"While others," Sam said, "have trouble realizing just how much work they still need."

Now, normally, I'm the least confrontational in the bunch and would have stopped this before Holly even wormed her way into the house. But I was having too much fun watching Sam go toe-to-toe with Holly. I was also waiting to see how long it took for Hope to lay a smackdown on her steps. I guess Jason felt the need to rush in and be the gentleman, though.

"I'll be going home soon," he said. "I like to get a full eight hours' sleep before a performance. Hope, I can take you home if you want." Damn Jason and his theater rituals. We were spoiling for a good fight. Then again, that was still a possibility. Hope looked like she was about to kill him for giving her steps the opportunity to take the car.

"The car is mine on Thursday nights," Hope repeated. "That was the deal." At this point, even I was getting uncomfortable. I'm all for standing your ground, but she didn't live that far from me. Any one of us could have driven her home.

Alexis pulled out her cell phone and hit the speed dial. "If you want to play it that way." Once the phone connected, Alexis said, "Mom. She won't budge." There was a brief pause, then she handed the phone to Hope.

Knowing better than to let the phone hang in the air, Hope put it to her ear. She didn't say anything, but we could all hear her stepmom's voice on the other end. We couldn't make out what she was saying, but it was certainly shrill.

Hope didn't say a word, but we could all hear her teeth grinding. The noise was even scaring the dogs. In the kitchen!

Eventually, the voice on the other end died out and Hope flipped the cell phone shut, probably wishing she could do the same thing to her stepmom. "Fine," she said, reaching into her purse. She pulled out the car keys and threw them at Alexis. Belinda managed to snatch them out of the air in an impressive move that saved her sister from a big red welt on her cheek.

Pity.

"Looks like somebody got up on the wrong side of the breakup this morning," Holly said as she stood. "This is why relationships are overrated. They never end well. Or they don't end at all, which is just as bad."

"Sounds like justification for someone who's never had a long-term boyfriend," Sam said.

"Oh, I've had plenty of long-term boyfriends," Holly said. "Just, none of them were mine."

I showed them to the door, but Holly wasn't done yet.

"By the way," she said to Sam, "where *is* your boyfriend tonight?"

I intervened before things got ugly. "He was here earlier," I said, opening the door.

"Hmm," Holly replied. "Wonder where he is now?"

"Probably with Drew someplace fun," Alexis added.

"Maybe we can catch up with them," Belinda threw in for good measure.

Holly and the twigs left on that final note. I think Hope and Sam were about to fight over who got to slam the door behind them. In the end, Blaine took hold of it and closed it gently. I was too busy formulating a new plan.

"So," I said, trying to break the remaining tension. "What's this party their mom is throwing?" Notice how I didn't refer to the woman as Hope's stepmom. We tried to refrain from any acknowledgement that there was a relationship between Hope and the woman.

"DVD release party," Hope said. "It's the twenty-fifth anniversary of *On Angel's Wings*."

"*On Angel's Wings*!" Blaine screeched uncharacteristically from his spot hovering in the background. "I *love* that movie!" Then, he hit us with the familiar quote that was—I kid you not—etched into the glass door on the front of Hope's home. "*One voice is enough to beat back the devil when it's the voice of an angel.*"

What can I say? It's a big door.

"Yeah," I said. "Hope's dad is married to Kara Bow." That's a stage name, by the way. We don't know her real name and don't really care to find out.

"How did I not know that?" Blaine asked with an accusatory glare in my direction.

"It's not that big a deal," Hope said, uncomfortably. She hated talking about her stepmom's past success . . . emphasis on *past*.

On Angel's Wings was this movie musical that Hope's stepmom starred in when she was a teen. It's the story of a fallen angel named Sylvia Angel (seriously) who needs to find her way back to Heaven through the power of song. All the while, the devil tries to keep her on Earth by posing as a recording artist and pretending to fall in love with her. It's kind of a rip-off of *Xanadu* but without the credibility of having Olivia Newton-John and Gene Kelly in the cast. (*Aside:* If you've never seen *Xanadu*, put this book down right now and go rent it. The movie is cheese-tastic!)

"So, when's the party?" Blaine asked.

"Tomorrow night," Hope said. "And that's exactly why I didn't want to give Alexis and Belinda the car. Everything for the party is already done. Kara hired a team of party planners. The steps just wanted the car so they could go clubbing on Sunset with Holly. Last time they went together, Holly hooked up with some random guy and forced Alexis and Belinda to take a cab home!" She ended her rant by calmly telling Blaine, "I can put you on the guest list for the party . . . if you want."

I've never seen Blaine so excited, yet at the same time, he managed to maintain his composure and not *look* like he was totally excited. Just another reason why he is the coolest adult I know. "If it wouldn't be too much to ask," he simply said.

"No problem at all," Hope said as she grabbed her bag. "You can go in my place." We said our good-byes, and Hope and Jason left in his car. Sam, who had borrowed her mom's car, was still hanging around.

"Your mother's been gone a long time," Blaine said once everyone was gone. "I'd better go check on her."

"Yeah," I agreed. "She probably forgot what she was looking for."

Blaine nodded ruefully and left the room.

As soon as he was gone, I hopped on the couch beside Sam and announced, "New scheme!"

"I'm tingling with anticipation."

"We've been doing this all wrong," I said. "We don't need Hope to be miserable. We need her to be mad. That's when Hope gets all decisive."

"True."

"And who can bring her from zero to insane in point-five seconds?"

"Alexis and Belinda."

"Exactly," I said. "So how insane do you think Hope would be if one of her steps was moving in on Drew?"

"In. Sane. But isn't that like making some kind of deal with the devil?"

"Like you said about Hope earlier. We don't have to *tell* the girls what we're doing. All we need to do is set up the situation. I have complete faith in Alexis and Belinda to be able to take it from there."

"And what if it backfires and Drew does hook up with one of them? Or *both* of them?"

"Okay. Didn't need *that* picture, thank you."

"I didn't mean at the same time! Eww!"

I shook the image from my brain. "Drew can't stand either of them. Never could. So we don't have to worry about it. Then again, that would prove one way or another whether or not his relationship with Hope is truly over."

Sam considered what I was saying. "Remind me never to make you angry."

"You know I only use my powers for good," I said.

"Yeah, but whose definition of 'good' are you going with?"

"Point taken."

The Crucible

Sam and I put our scheme on hold Friday morning because we didn't need anything to distract us from the auditions. I was nervous enough. I didn't need to be working on ways to manipulate people. Besides, we were too busy on the ride in trying to get Hope to show us her monologue to worry about anything else.

"No," Hope said for the tenth time as we turned onto Breakwater Lane.

"But, Hope, don't you want to run it by someone just once?" Sam asked. "Just to make sure it sounds the way you want it to."

"I can hear myself just fine," she said.

"You know an audience appreciates things differently than you hear it in your head," I insisted. "That's basic acting, Hope."

"It's not ready yet," Hope said.

"We're pulling into school," I pointed out the obvious. "How much more time are you planning on taking?"

"As much time as I need," she said, putting an end to the argument. I'm sure Sam was ready to go another few rounds, but I had other things on my mind. As we walked to the auditorium, the real worrying began for me.

I don't remember ever being so nervous about a performance before. I actually felt a little sick to my stomach. I didn't think throwing up onstage would impress Hartley Blackstone all that much. Then again, considering his long résumé, he'd probably seen much worse before. Not that that thought was helping.

As soon as we stepped into Hall Hall, Sam, Hope, and I split up. We were going to use every second possible to continue preparing.

We weren't the only ones.

The Drama Geeks were all spread throughout the auditorium sitting, standing, or pacing in whatever space was available. Mr. Randall had clearly known we'd all be early, as the doors were open by eight o'clock, even though our teacher was nowhere to be seen. Not that any of us were looking for him. We were all too busy in our own worlds, going over our monologues for the last, second from last, third from last, and however-many-more-from-last times we could fit in before Hartley Blackstone arrived.

I went over my lines in my head, only checking back to my script occasionally. If I didn't have them down yet, no amount of last-minute cramming was going to commit them to memory.

I knew this from experience. I had them almost all memorized, except for a couple lines in the middle I kept dropping.

Most of us were only holding on to our scripts and checking back to confirm a line or two. From what I could see, only Alexis seemed to be studying her script like all the words were foreign to her. At the same time, she seemed the least concerned of everyone. Even her sister—who was sitting right beside her—had her eyes firmly closed as her lips silently ran through her part.

It's always interesting to watch how other people prepare for an audition. That's what this was, basically. We'd given up any pretense of it being an acting exercise or simply another facet to the Summer Theatrical Program. This was, quite simply, the most important audition of our lives.

No pressure.

So, why did I keep drifting out of my own rehearsal to watch everyone else when I was supposed to be going over my lines? I couldn't really help myself. Living theater was all around me.

Sam was going through her vocal warm-ups. Jason was doing some stretching. Those two usually did the most preparation out of everyone. And it showed in their performances.

Tasha Valentine was sitting with her eyes closed listening to her iPod. She looked to be in a state of relaxation that I was quite envious of. Meanwhile, Jimmy Wilkey was at the total opposite end of the spectrum, pounding Frappuccinos in between opening and closing his script as if he expected the words to change every two seconds. If ever there was an example of what Eric's little brother would eventually grow into with his own caffeine addiction, it was Jimmy Wilkey.

Holly was filing her nails, as if she wasn't concerned in the least. She probably wasn't either. That's just one of the reasons I both hate and admire her at the same time.

And our darling Hope was sitting with her new journal in her lap, rewriting her monologue . . . only five minutes before Hartley Blackstone was supposed to arrive.

Oops. Scratch that. Julie Blackstone was walking down the center aisle with a man who could only be her father at her side. I mean, of course he was her father. He looked exactly like all the photos I've ever seen of Hartley Blackstone.

Everyone in the auditorium stopped what he or she was doing to watch Hartley Blackstone make his entrance. And a grand entrance it was. The man swept into the room, standing tall with perfect posture. His head was held high in the air. His eyes were focused on the stage and did not waver. Not once did he bother to look at the students openly gaping at him.

We were speechless.

Let me pause for a moment to explain what a unique experience this was. Celebrities are nothing new to us here on the left coast. Heck, several of the Orion Academy parents are major movie stars in their own right. (Not mine, mind you.) We see famous people all the time walking their dogs along the beach, going for coffee at Starbucks, or just sitting at a red light on the PCH with their babies in their laps. (Okay, I only saw that once. And, oddly enough, it was right outside a Starbucks.) Celebrity sightings are nothing new, even to the most jaded of us. But this? *This* was Hartley Blackstone, the king of Broadway. The man who created more stars than the big bang.

We were all suitably impressed.

Miss Julie introduced her father to Mr. Randall and we continued to watch as they exchanged a few words. I can't imagine I was the only one trying to read their lips. I failed, but you have to give me points for the effort. The conversation was brief, and the two Blackstones quickly took seats at the end of the first row while Mr. Randall waved us all to the front of the auditorium.

As one, we moved toward him, slowly so as not to look too eager, but somehow managing to appear even more excited than if we had run there. We filled in the seats around the Blackstones, careful not to get too close for fear of coming across as too pushy. Even Holly, who had made a beeline for a seat in the front row, kept a few empty spots between her and the theatrical genius.

Noticing that the auditorium seemed to be leaning a bit house right, Mr. Randall took a few steps over toward us to address the students. He said a few words about Mr. Blackstone and his career. To be honest, I don't think I heard anything more than a dull buzz. I was about to audition for the one and only Hartley Blackstone. Who cared what my teacher had to say at the moment?

Sorry, Mr. Randall.

I guess the formal introductions were done, because everyone around me suddenly burst into applause. I joined them as the master thespian stood up and gave a half bow. Instead of moving up beside our teacher, Mr. Blackstone mounted the small staircase that took him onstage. Although pretty much all of us were still seated house right, he stood front and center to address us.

"The theatre," Blackstone announced before taking a long, dramatic pause.

(*Aside:* While we're pausing, you may have noticed I switched up on how I usually spell "theater." You see that I'm spelling it "theatre" here. Technically, either one is correct, though the "er" ending is traditionally American while "re" is usually European . . . or American Pretentious. I don't know, but there was something about the way Blackstone spoke that made the latter spelling seem more appropriate.)

My, but he was taking a long, dramatic pause.

"The theatre," he said again as if we weren't hanging on Every. Single. Word. "Is a cruel mistress. One day, she can be a painted whore with her rouged face and her come hither expression showering you with her love and attention." *Oh my.* "And the next, she can turn her back on you, leaving you cold and alone in the silence of a disenchanted audience. Why any of us would choose this existence is beyond even the best scholars." Personally, I think it has something to do with money and fame. (And maybe a bit of a selfish narcissism that craves the attention. But I'm no scholar.) "Yet, time and time again, we do," he continued. "We answer the call of the greasepaint and are mesmerized by the beckoning stage lights. It is who we are. It is . . ."

He looked out at us like he was waiting for something. Meanwhile, we were waiting for the rest of his sentence. Sam,

Hope, and I shared a glance. We weren't sure if he was a lunatic or a genius or both. Either way, he was Hartley Blackstone, so we did what was expected in this situation: We applauded.

The auditorium echoed in boisterous applause. I was pretty sure we weren't the only ones who didn't have an idea what he was talking about, but it didn't matter. We were about to perform for the chance to be accepted into his summer acting program in New York. If he wanted to stand there all morning while we applauded, we'd do it, if only to increase our chances.

And, okay, Alexis was too busy laughing to actually clap, but what did she know about theater . . . or *theatre* for that matter.

After several bows, I guess he'd had enough. Blackstone raised his hands, like an orchestra conductor, and silenced the room. "Let the auditions begin," the artist said before descending the staircase. When he reached the bottom step, his daughter stood and joined him as they walked halfway to the back of the auditorium and took seats in the middle of the row.

"Thank you, Mr. Blackstone," Mr. Randall said as he stepped back in front of his class. We were all trying to focus on our teacher, but our heads kept twisting back to see what Mr. Blackstone was doing. As one might expect, he was just sitting there waiting for us to start.

"All right," Mr. Randall said, checking his watch and then looking to the back of the auditorium. "We're running a couple minutes early, but do I have any volun—"

"Me!" Hope shot out of her seat, putting way more enthusiasm behind her waving hand than I had ever seen from her before. Certainly more enthusiasm that I had seen from her all week. Sam and I looked at each other as our friend pushed past us to get to the aisle. We were not ready for what was about to happen.

At this point, I should mention Hope's choice of apparel for her scene. We don't usually dress in costume for monologues. And, if you didn't know Hope, you might not have realized that she was, in fact, in costume. While it was true that she was still sticking to her almost all black Goth-Ick style of dress, it was the name brands plastered across her clothing that tipped me off to what she was up to and the exact subject matter of her monologue.

Hope was dressed in black Hollister jeans, a black Hollister T-shirt, and a black Hollister baseball cap. I knew this because each piece had a colorful logo emblazoned on it to make sure you caught the name. Her contacts were a shade of gray that seemed quite familiar to me. In fact, there was a definite air of familiarity in her entire guise—one that matched a certain ex-boyfriend who shall remain nameless.

Before Hope could mount the stage, we heard the rear door to the theater open.

"Sorry we're late," Coach Zach called out as he walked in with the soccer team.

The soccer team?

"What are *they* doing here?" Hope yelled.

"They always come to see our performances during the summer program," Mr. Randall said. "Just like we always help with their scrimmage."

Bedlam.

Pure and utter bedlam.

This was not some performance. It was an audition. A fact that the majority of students found the need to remind Mr. Randall of, at a rather increased volume. It took about a minute for Mr. Randall to regain some control. He had managed to bring us to a small roar as the soccer team filled in rows in the center of the house.

"We can go if it's a problem," Coach Zach said before the guys sat.

Mr. Randall was torn. "Well—"

Mr. Blackstone cleared his throat, bringing utter silence to the room. We all turned in his direction. "This is theatre," he reminded us. "It is meant to be performed in front of an audience. If your students are unable to present their monologues in such a manner, then I do not feel that they would be right for my program."

That pretty much put an end to that.

The soccer team silently took their seats.

Without another word Hope walked center stage and looked out toward the audience. Sam and I both clearly saw her glance in Drew's direction. We were both shaking our heads and mouthing *no* to her. She could not do what she was about to do. I still had no idea what her monologue was about, but she was *not* going to do an impression of Drew. It would've been bad enough to do it in front of the Drama Geeks, but to do it in front of the soccer team and Drew himself? That would be a nightmare.

She wouldn't do it.

She couldn't do it.

Could she?

"Hi, my name is Hope Rivera," she said. Then she took a silent beat that about matched Blackstone's earlier dramatic pause in length. It was so bad that Mr. Randall leaned forward like he was about to check on her. I guess he figured she was suffering from stage fright or something. I almost thought she was too. I've never seen Hope look uncomfortable before—in *any* situation, much less onstage. From my seat, I could see a dozen different emotions flashing on her face during the length of her pause. Fear. Indecision. Anger. Love?

Sam and I looked at each other again, silently wondering if we should say something.

Hope finally found her voice. "I had originally intended to perform a piece that I had written myself. However, I'm not quite happy with it yet. So I've decided to go with a monologue from the nurse in *Romeo and Juliet*."

I doubt that Mr. Blackstone could have cared less about the change in program. I, however, was thrilled that she had used some restraint. Still, I was dying to hear what she had been working on almost all week. If only because I suspected that it might give us a clue what Hope and Drew had broken up over.

Hope launched into her monologue. It was the same one she had performed in our acting final in drama class at the end of the school year, so there weren't any real surprises. It was a rather lackluster way to start things off if you ask me. Not that she wasn't entertaining. No one does agitated older women better than her. Even though we had all seen her do the same performance a couple weeks before, Hope had managed to find a different approach to the character to keep it fresh. Considering that she was dressed like a guy probably brought a fresh approach to the character too.

"And . . . scene," Hope said as she ended her piece. Even though we don't applaud for one another in an audition, I could tell that most of the people around me were impressed. Even Belinda was smiling in appreciation.

I can't say the same for Hartley Blackstone.

"That was certainly some character work," the auteur said. "Not necessarily *good* character work, but there really is no such thing as good character work if you ask me."

"Excuse me?" Hope said from her spot on the stage. Her defenses were already up.

"Let me ask you this," Blackstone said. "You have the opportunity to audition for a world-renowned theatre program, and you settled on a character piece? Something with broad comedy and no nuance whatsoever? What possibly possessed you to think that was a good idea?"

"Juliet's nurse is one of the classic theater roles," Hope reminded him.

"True," he ceded. "But all the mugging and the exaggerated gestures. Do you really consider that serious acting?"

"No," Hope said. "That's why it's called comedy."

But Blackstone hadn't heard her. "Though I guess with your body type, you won't be landing the role of leading lady any time soon."

"And what *exactly* is wrong with my body type?" Hope asked. If there hadn't been a dozen rows between them I would have feared for our guest's life. I swear I saw Mr. Randall's career flashing before his eyes. But the fire in Hope's eyes was exciting to see.

"I will grant that it was an effective performance, if ill-advised," he said. "Hardly worthy of my program, but better than average for a high school production. Thank you."

Hope's mouth opened, but nothing came out, which is . . . unprecedented. I could tell she was just as confused by his criticism as I was. Though he was incredibly rude to the point of offensive it almost sounded positive at the end. At least as far as her performance as a high school student was concerned. Hope looked a little shell-shocked as she came down the stairs and took a seat beside Sam and me. Neither of us said anything to her. We didn't have a clue what to say.

"Who'd like to go next?" Mr. Randall asked.

Not surprisingly, there were no takers.

"Anyone?"

No one.

"Okay, then," he continued, looking down at his clipboard. "Ms. Valentine."

It's rare that Tasha exhibits outward emotion. She's usually rather even-tempered. But I could feel the stress and fear emitting from her like waves from the Pacific were crashing over the PCH and up the bluff to take us all out as she stepped onto the stage.

Dramatic, no?

She looked out at her judge, jury, and executioner and began her monologue.

And thus the carnage began.

Sticks and Bones

"Boring." "Flat." "Uninspired."

These were the nicest words that Blackstone used in his critique of Tasha's performance. He went on for a while about how she made the same choices over and over and over again. Personally, I didn't think her performance was nearly as repetitive as his criticism of it.

As the morning wore on, his vocabulary got more interesting, but not any nicer.

"Bromidic." "Prosaic." "Abysmal."

One by one we took stage and one by one he tore us to shreds. The guy made Simon Cowell look like Mary Poppins. It got so bad I could even see the soccer team cringing. I could be wrong, but it's possible that Blackstone may have even started making words up halfway through the morning because he'd run out of insults.

"Banausic!"

Jason was the first student to actually earn more positive notes than negatives. Mr. Blackstone found the "performance as a whole quite moving," but thought that Jason "relied too much on subtleties of movement that barely made it past the audience in the first row." Then he went on for quite a while on the difference between acting for a large auditorium versus a small space, picking apart Jason's monologue for examples. All the while, Jason was stuck onstage.

But I remind you, that was the positive critique.

He got right back into form when Mr. Randall sent a row of sophomores at him like lambs to the slaughter that ended memorably with Missy Weinberg's interpretation of Carnelle from *The Miss Firecracker Contest*. I think we all knew it was going to be a disaster when she walked onstage with a CD player.

The monologue started out okay, but it quickly devolved into a hot mess. I guess Missy knew that her acting alone wasn't going to be enough because on the last line she hit the music and broke out into a tap routine that didn't quite fit in with the mood of the piece. We were all slumping down in our seats by the end, waiting for the worst.

Blackstone took another long dramatic pause before breaking out in a self-satisfied laugh. "Dance: Ten. Looks: Three," he said with what sounded to be a fair amount of pride in his *Chorus Line*–inspired critique. "Acting? Even worse." Hers were not the first tears of the morning.

Our teacher cleared his throat. "Mr. Blackstone, I would prefer that you refrained from commenting on how you perceive the students look."

"Mr. Randall, she is playing a character in a beauty contest. I am merely extending a criticism that is appropriate to the chosen role."

Missy picked up her CD player and made her way back to her seat. Her friends were there hugging her and shooting evil looks at the man we had all respected only a short time ago. Actually, scratch that. It wouldn't have been so painful if we all didn't still respect his opinion. It was the man behind the opinion we were growing to hate.

The lowlight of the morning had to be Jimmy Wilkey, our intrepid stage manager who had never acted before in his life. It was a massacre. *Way* too ugly to repeat here.

But I'll try.

It started with the performance.

"I'll be doing Eugene from *Biloxi Blues*," he said.

And we're off.

Jimmy launched into the monologue at breakneck speed. His movements were just as frenetic. Racing through his lines, he missed every nuance of character. Every moment. Every chance to breathe. It was like watching theater cranked up on speed . . . or espresso, more likely. The words all meshed together as he tripped over his speech racing to the end. Or, almost the end. He ran out of breath before he could choke out the last word.

But what killed . . . what *killed* was the innocently open and almost eager expression on his face when it was over. Jimmy had no idea how truly horrible his performance was.

He was about to find out.

"What the hell was that?" Blackstone exploded, his New York accent coming out for the first time all morning. The carefully constructed theatrical facade cracked for the barest moment before he recovered. "Mr. Randall, if this is the kind of talent you wish to place on display for me, well, I simply cannot understand what is it you expect me to do here today. That was . . . there are no words. No words!"

And yet, Blackstone continued to go on for another minute with words you wouldn't find on any Orion faculty–approved vocabulary list. The only reason I suspect Jimmy did not collapse onstage under the weight of his critique was because he honestly had no interest in being an actor.

Even so, I give the guy props for being able to take such harsh criticism without crumbling.

Thankfully, we all got a little comic relief when Alexis stepped onstage soon afterward. Her "performance" could only be described as tragically delicious. Without even bothering to introduce herself, Alexis launched into her monologue from *Medea*. Or should I say *attempted* to launch into her monologue.

"Women of Corinthia," she said. "I mean . . . Corinth. Women of Corinth!" Then a long pause. "I would not have you . . . have you censor . . . cen*sure* me," she continued. "So I have come here . . . come here . . . supercilious!" She froze. Looked out at Blackstone. Then at Holly. Then up to the heavens. Back to Holly.

"Fuck it," she said and walked off the stage and right out of Hall Hall, hopefully never to be seen again.

"Finally," Blackstone said. "Someone please thank her for saving me the trouble."

Her twin sister, Belinda, on the other hand was surprisingly good in her monologue. Not only did she get the words right, she clearly understood what she was saying. Blackstone still ripped her apart, but she also seemed to take that better than anyone else had so far. Having never acted onstage before, I guess she was just happy to get it over with.

That left Sam, Holly, and me for last.

"Mr. Randall," Holly said. "I would be happy to go next."

"Okay," our teacher said. Since there were only three of us left, it wasn't exactly noble of her to volunteer now, of all times. I could only assume that she didn't want to have to follow Sam's performance. Not that Holly would ever admit that, mind you.

I had no doubt Holly's performance would be fine, but it couldn't come close to the acting she was doing by just walking up onstage. She stood tall and moved with an air of confidence that no other student had since Hope first stood before Blackstone. Of course, it's possible that it wasn't an act at all; maybe Holly was really that poised. Not that I could imagine what that kind of confidence was like.

Holly performed the role of Ivy like it was written for her—which, we all knew it was. I've got to give her credit. She was near perfect as usual. Sure, I could sit there and pick apart her performance: how she played too much to the audience and didn't internalize things as much as she should have. But that would be petty of me. Besides, I figured Mr. Blackstone was about to do just that.

"Very nice," he said. That was the first time he had ever started off his critique with a positive comment. "This young lady is clearly the reason my daughter brought me. You all could learn a thing or two from her . . . Miss Mayflower, is it?"

"Yes, sir," she said demurely . . . I mean, *really* . . . demurely!

Let me wrap this up because I can't sit through it again. He was positively glowing in her review, but he did point out that some of the parts were forced, like I thought. He suggested she take some of the passion out of her piece and replace it with more subtle emotion. I'd like to see that from the emotionless automaton myself. Oh, now I *am* being catty.

He also suggested that she might consider adding a few pounds because her small frame was positively diminutive onstage. HA!

Holly left the stage with the same look of confidence that she had when taking stage. Sam's name was called next.

"Figures," Sam mumbled as she passed me. It was either going to be her or me, so I guess it did kind of figure. That meant I was going to be next. And last.

Great.

I was so worried about my own approaching dance with death that I hardly heard Sam's monologue, but what I caught was full of her usual brilliance. No one, not even Holly, can match Sam for pure energy when she takes stage. She becomes the character. It's like I almost forget she's my best friend when I'm watching her. She's that good.

Apparently Blackstone thought so too. "Now I see why Mr. Randall saved these two young ladies to go together," he said. "An interesting study in acting techniques, I must say. In many ways, your performance was like Miss Mayflower's. You put every ounce of passion into your piece. Too much, at times. Consider holding back more. No need to force your audience to accept you in the part. Turn out to the audience more too. The few small moments you did have are almost too internalized. But, overall . . . impressive. I am glad your teacher kept you two young ladies for last."

"Actually," Mr. Randall said, "we have one more."

Great, *again*.

Everyone's eyes were on me because they knew I was to be Blackstone's final victim of the day. I stood, slowly, shaking like I was on a sugar high. Slipping past Hope, I stepped out into the aisle and made my way to the stage, willing myself not to trip over my own feet. I tried to match Holly's air of confidence, but I think I probably looked somewhat like I had smelled some bad fish.

"Fedora!" Sam whispered as we passed, reminding me that I had forgotten to take off my hat. I quickly pulled it off my head and handed it to Sam as I mounted the steps and took center stage.

It was one of the smaller audiences I'd ever performed for, yet one of the most nerve-racking at the same time.

"Hi," I said out to the auditorium. I couldn't look at Blackstone. I was too nervous. Focusing on Sam or Hope only reminded me of what they'd been put through. For some reason, my eyes locked on Drew, of all people. "My name is Bryan Stark, and I will be performing the part of Tom from *Glass Menagerie*."

"That would be *THE Glass Menagerie*," Blackstone called out. "Always use the *full* title of the play."

"Sorry," I mumbled. *"The Glass Menagerie."*

"And don't mumble," he added.

"Sorry," I said loudly and with something approaching clarity. I paused and refocused my attention back at Drew, then launched into the monologue. I started out heavy, so I pulled it back quickly, toning it down a notch. I paused dramatically at the point I had rehearsed, then kind of lost it in the middle, and may have dropped a line or two, but I think I recovered nicely. I did pretty well to the end, until I stumbled on the last two words and actually saw Drew cringe. Never a good way to end a monologue, but at least it was over.

That is, the part where I had control was over.

I waited to be torn apart.

"Thank you," Blackstone said with a curt nod.

I waited for something more.

Nothing came.

That was it? Where was my critique?

The confusion on my face must have registered all the way back to the cheap seats. I could tell that it was mirrored in the faces of most of the students staring at me standing alone center stage while Blackstone ignored me so he could share a laugh with his daughter over something. Hopefully, not me.

Mr. Randall was apparently just as confused about the snub. "Um . . . Mr. Blackstone, don't you have anything more to say to Bryan?"

The auteur looked up as if he had momentarily forgotten that we were there. He seemed particularly surprised to see me still standing onstage.

"No," he said simply. "Not really."

Then he went back to conferring with his daughter. At least she had the common courtesy to shoot me an apologetic shrug, for whatever good that did me.

Mr. Randall cleared his throat. "Mr. Blackstone," he said tentatively, "are you sure you don't want to critique Bryan's performance like you did with the other students?"

Blackstone looked annoyed by the interruption. *So sorry that my abject humiliation is cutting into your day,* I thought as I shuffled from one foot to another. "There was nothing there for me to critique," he said simply.

What the *hell* was that supposed to mean?

"Now, if you'll excuse me," Blackstone addressed all the students as he made his way out of the row. "Thank you, all . . . or, thank you *some*. I cannot honestly say that I would like to thank you for all that I saw onstage today. I will be back next week to make my final decision. But I will say that I am most interested in seeing more from the two young ladies who performed last." Actually, *I'd* performed last. "The gentleman who did a piece from *The History Boys* and the young one who had a physical presence somewhat reminiscent of a monkey—you need to watch that, my young fellow." Gary is never going to live down his role in *Wizard*. "Yes. If we had callbacks, those would be my choices based on today's performances. But since your teacher has asked that everyone continue to be kept under consideration, I will say that the rest of you . . . keep trying. Who knows? You could surprise me next week." Then he laughed like he was making a joke.

He left Hall Hall without another word.

Me? I was still standing center stage trying to ignore the Drama Geeks and soccer players in the rows in front of me. All of them were turning their attention to different points in the auditorium to keep from having to look me in the eye. Drew was the only one with the courage to keep his focus on me. Too bad I couldn't look at him in return. I could actually feel the waves of pity coming off of them all. Well, pity mixed with relief that they hadn't been left standing onstage like me.

Les Misérables

You know how in zombie movies all the living dead come shuffling out of the cemetery, or the woods, or the fog with the same glazed looks in their eyes, moaning in despair, with maybe even a little drool coming out of the sides of their mouths? Yeah. That's pretty much what we all looked like coming out of Hall Hall when Mr. Randall dismissed us for lunch. Actually, he kind of dismissed us for the day, suggesting that we could either come back to the auditorium later to work on our scenes or we could go somewhere else entirely. My group was still too numb to actually formulate any thought so we went to eat and then decide on a game plan.

En route to the pavilion, Eric came up behind us and grabbed Sam. He didn't bother saying anything. He just held her. This earns him even more points from me than anything he'd ever done before. The rest of us were stuck standing trying to mind our own business, until Drew made a move toward Hope.

"I can't do this," she said.

He simply nodded and continued to the pavilion. After a couple more seconds of awkwardness while Eric and Sam kissed, the rest of us left them behind and went for lunch.

If ever there was a time when it was easy to tell the soccer team from the Drama Geeks, it was in the Kenneth Graham Pavilion that Friday afternoon. The soccer players, while respectful of our trauma, were talking, joking, and pretty much living like it was a normal day in Malibu. The Drama Geeks? Not so much.

Everyone was so stuck in their own worlds that there were pockets of total silence mixed in with the soccer guys' conversations. With the exception of Holly, who never met a critic that she bothered listening to, most of us were still going over what Blackstone had said about our performances.

Correction: I was going over what he *hadn't* said about my performance. What did he mean by not giving me a critique? Was I so good that there was nothing he could criticize? Somehow I doubt it. That left only one option.

That I was that bad.

Hope, Jason, and I grabbed a table along the back wall of the pavilion. Sam joined us a few minutes later, while Eric went to the other side of the room to sit with Drew and their soccer friends. We didn't bother to say a word as Hope made room for Sam beside her.

Eventually, the silence really did become deafening. I was so lost in my own thoughts that I totally tuned out everything around me. I guess that's what made it so much more shocking when the world came crashing back into focus, thanks to Hope.

"Who the hell does he think he is?" Hope blurted out, scaring half the pavilion.

I guess her outburst was kind of the verbal equivalent of a starting pistol. It signaled the end of the moping and the start of the righteous indignation. Every one of the Drama Geeks started griping about their critiques, their friends' critiques, and even their enemies' critiques. It was bordering on mass hysteria that I'm pretty sure scared more than a few of the soccer players. But *everyone* had something to say.

Everyone but me, that is.

Hope was all, "What's wrong with being a character actress? Character actresses are finally getting respect nowadays. Look at *Hairspray*. Look at *Ugly Betty*. Hell, I have a much better chance of getting work than that beanpole Holly."

At the next table, I heard Tasha going all out. "Flat? Flat! I'd like to flatten him!" This coming from a vegan who respects all life no matter how small . . . or creepy crawly.

Even Sam and Jason, who both had received mostly positive criticism, were engaged in comparing their notes trying to decipher what moments they had blown and which ones had worked.

But me? I had nothing.

And I wasn't the only one aware of that. Don't think I didn't see the pointed looks in my direction coming from the other tables. From people who would turn away the moment they saw me seeing them. Then, there were my own friends, who were so busy griping about their own perceived slights that they weren't even bothering to notice that I was not part of the conversation. Even Hope, who'd hardly put two full sentences together over the past week, was rambling.

Part of me—a *big* part of me—suspected that they were running on like that because they didn't want me to engage. They didn't want to have to deal with how I had been snubbed. They couldn't even come up with anything to say to me.

It took a lot for me to climb out of my despair spiral. "I couldn't have been worse than Jimmy," I finally said, not realizing it was out loud. I quickly checked to make sure that Jimmy hadn't heard, but he was across the room chugging on a bottled Frappuccino.

"Of course you weren't," Hope quickly said.

"But even Jimmy got a critique," I said with a low voice. "He was horrible and Blackstone managed to find some things to say to him. None of it good, but still."

"You weren't that bad," Jason said.

"Thanks."

"I mean—"

"It's okay," I said, cutting him off. I really didn't want to hear what he had to say. There was only one person who could help lift my mood. Oddly, she was somewhat quiet at the moment.

I turned to Sam. "What do you think I did wrong?"

Sam took a moment to consider her answer. I guess she was about to say something when her eyes suddenly closed into tight slits and her entire body tensed. That could only mean one thing: Holly was walking up to our table. I turned to see her standing behind me with Belinda.

"Wasn't Blackstone amazing?" she asked. "That man can cut right to the heart of a critique, can't he? Such a refreshing change from the norm around here."

"Do you want something?" Sam asked.

"A spot in Blackstone's program," Holly replied. "And, if I read the room right this morning, I'd say I'm almost a lock."

"I'd say you were something else entirely," Sam replied. "But is there a point to you talking to us right now?"

"Alexis took the car," Belinda blurted out to the table.

"Is she bringing it back?" Hope asked.

"How should I know?"

"You're twins," Hope said. "Don't you have some kind of psychotic link?"

"I think that's psychic," Jason said.

"I think she was right the first time," Sam mumbled under her breath.

"Anyway," Belinda said, turning to me, "Bryan, can you give us a ride home?"

I wasn't exactly sure how to answer that. Considering Hope's house was on my way home, a ride wasn't a problem at all. But I was more concerned about Hope's reaction to me doing her step a favor.

"Can't Holly take you?" Hope asked.

Holly sighed. That deep sigh must be a Mayflower family trait. Her sister, Heather, is an expert at it. "I told you she was going to be a hard-ass."

"Hope," Belinda said. Her smile never faltered. "You're going to need a ride home, anyway. I thought we could save on the gas. Holly would have to go like a mile out of her way."

"Perish the thought," Hope said. "But I'm not actually going home. We're all going out."

Once again, this was news to me. I have to say that my friends and I are very good at the ambush lies.

"Where?" Holly asked.

Hope, Sam, and I looked at each other. Frozen. So much for our talent with the ambush lies. Our minds were so full of Blackstone that we couldn't come up with anything.

"My place," Jason volunteered. "We're going to rehearse our scene. But we need to get out of here. You understand."

"Of course I do," Holly said, all sweetness and light. "If Blackstone said about me what he said about you guys, I'd want to get out of here too."

Okay. Considering Blackstone said nearly the same thing to her that he said to Sam, I wasn't exactly sure what she was getting at. Sam, however, took it extremely personally and was ready to throw down. "What's that supposed to mean?" she asked.

"I was just making a comment," Holly said. "The guy was kind of mean. Especially to you, Bryan."

How sad is it that the first person to acknowledge this out loud was Holly Mayflower?

"If I were you," she said, "I'd go right back to the auditorium and demand to know just how bad he thought you were."

Ain't she great, folks?

"He's already gone," I mumbled.

Both Sam and Hope looked about ready to leap over the table and throttle Holly on my behalf. Or to throttle Holly just for the heck of it. Either way, there was about to be some throttling.

"Thanks, anyway," Belinda said, pulling Holly away. I wasn't sure what exactly she was thanking us for. All that we'd done was exchange some open hostility, but I give her credit for being smart enough to get her friend out of there before the bloodshed. A catfight between Sam and Holly would be fairly even, but once you threw Hope into the mix . . . it would get ug-o-ly.

Still, it was nice to see these brief flickers of life from Hope lately. It was possible that she was coming out of her misery on her own.

"Thanks for the cover story," Sam said to Jason once the girls were out of earshot.

"No prob," Jason said.

"You don't really want to rehearse, though," I said.

"No," he quickly replied. "Actually, I kind of want to be alone . . . to think."

"Yeah," Hope said dropping the remains of her lunch. "I'm done." She wasn't even halfway through her sandwich, but I knew what she meant. My own sandwich had only about three bites missing. "Me too."

Sam and Jason agreed. Ignoring any childhood warnings about children starving in other parts of the world, we thoughtlessly dumped the remains of our lunches and left the pavilion with hardly a good-bye to anyone. In our own way, I guess that's how we were going to address our critiques (or, in my case, the lack thereof). We were going to ignore them.

We split from Jason in the parking lot and I aimed Electra toward the Pacific Coast Highway, heading for Santa Monica. Please note that "aim" is the correct phrase to use here, as beachgoers are always dashing across the road to get to their cars. You have to steer carefully to miss them.

We were still in primo beach time so traffic was light. Once everyone decided to head home, PCH would be a parking lot. Granted, it would be a parking lot with one of the most amazing views in America, but a parking lot nonetheless.

The ride was pretty quiet because Hope had shut down once again. Sam and I tried to fill the silence with some banter, but neither of us was in the mood, so we spent most of our time watching the ocean pass us by. And, well, I was watching for pedestrians. In the relatively light traffic it only took fifteen minutes to get to Sam's apartment building.

As we double-parked to let Sam out, we could see her mom, Anne, standing inside the security gate going through their mail. I honked hello, but didn't expect her to come running out to greet us. A simple stroll would have been fine. Maybe even a light saunter. But the running was a surprise.

I suspect her exuberance had something to do with the small piece of paper in her hand. It looked like a photo.

"Sam," she called out. "Postcard!"

"Huzzah!" Sam said, leaning out the window and grabbing the postcard. Her use of the word "huzzah" could only mean one thing: this postcard was Ren Faire–related. I tried very hard not to roll my eyes. "It's from Marq," she said, confirming that it came from her old Renaissance Faire buddy. Sam and her mom used to do the Ren Faire circuit back before Sam started at Orion. And they're not even embarrassed about it. Heck, they're actually proud to be a part of that unique breed of characters.

While Sam read us the latest happenings on the circuit, a car honked behind us. Loudly. And with a sustained blare. There really was no need since the street was way wide enough for him to go around.

"Bryan, you'd better move," Anne said. "That's the apartment manager. He doesn't like people double-parking in front of the building. There's a spot at the end of the street if you guys want to come in for a few minutes."

"Why not?" I said, pulling forward with the guy riding my bumper all the way down the street. I smiled politely at him as I took the spot that he would have gotten had he just gone around me in the first place. Sam's small building does not have a parking lot, so they were stuck with on-street parking, in an area where spots are at a premium. I could only hope that the guy didn't find anything until he was a couple blocks away as punishment for his angry horn. I fully believe in parking karma.

We hopped out of Electra and headed back to Sam's apartment where Anne met us at the door with a trio of iced teas already poured for us.

"Thanks," we said, taking the drinks.

"Bryan, I need to borrow your height in the kitchen," Anne said before I could get comfortable.

"Certainly." I followed her into the other room. "What do you need?"

"Can you get that bowl?" she asked, pointing to a blue bowl on top of the refrigerator.

I kind of looked at her questioningly, then reached out and grabbed it. To say that it was a stretch, would be a stretch. It was certainly within Anne's reach.

"Thank you," Anne said, then she added in a whisper, "How did the auditions go?"

Ah. That explained it. She wanted to know what kind of weekend she'd be having with Sam. Their apartment wasn't large enough for her to pull me aside and have the conversation without being overheard. Hence the subterfuge.

"It was"—I searched for a word that quickly encapsulated the experience I was trying so hard to forget—"ghastly." I went with a word Blackstone had used several times that morning. It was the one most stuck in my head.

"Come on," Anne said. "Be serious." Then, I guess she saw my face, because the smile dropped from hers. "Oh. That bad."

I nodded. "Sam's critique was actually okay," I said. "But I don't think she heard any of the good stuff, so I'd be on alert."

"Are you okay?" she asked.

I had to think about that. "I'm not sure."

She gave me a pat on the shoulder before sending me back into the living room while she returned the bowl to its perch on the refrigerator. Sam and Hope were sitting on the couch.

Both of them had grins that were *way* scary. I'm talking the Joker from *Batman* scary.

"What?"

"We're being stupid moping around like this," Sam said. "We should go out and have fun. Life is meant to be lived."

I wasn't sure what had brought about this sudden change of mood, but I didn't totally disagree. Still, if she broke into *A lot of livin' to do,* I swear I would have hurled.

"We're having a girls' night out," Hope said. "You're coming with us."

I looked at them. I looked down at myself. "Um . . . I have a penis. I know neither of you have seen it and you're never *going* to see it. But I assure you, it *is* there. And it precludes me from attending any event where being a girl is specifically called out in the title."

"You done?" Sam asked.

"Yes."

"You're coming with us."

"Okay," I said. "Where are we going?"

Hope's grin actually stretched to inhuman proportions. "To the twenty-fifth anniversary DVD release party of *On Angel's Wings*."

The Goat, or Who Is Sylvia?

Hope's dad was so thrilled to hear that we were going to the DVD release party that he sprung for a limo to pick us up at Sam's place and take us to the party, which was set up in a huge circus tent right in the center of the Hollywood and Highland Complex. That's a shopping and entertainment area with stores, restaurants, a bowling alley . . . and the theater where they host the Academy Awards.

Hope and I had to make a quick dash to the Third Street Promenade to pick up a few things to wear first. We'd decided to get into the spirit of the eighties, as the party invitation had requested.

Hope went with the full-on Goth-Ick Madonna look with the lacey black skirt and tank top, fingerless gloves, and some crazy neon rubber bracelets. Just to be clear, she wasn't dressing like Madonna, she was dressing like girls who dressed like Madonna in the eighties. There is a difference.

We didn't want to swing all the way back to Malibu, so Hope had to stay with the gray contacts. They didn't entirely go with the guise, but since Hope was the only person I know who regularly matches her clothing to her eyes, we doubted anyone else would notice.

My choice was practically made for me considering my general look and body type. Hats were popular in the eighties (though mostly on girls), so wearing my fedora was a given. A tight, white button-down shirt and straight-leg black jeans were the obvious choice. Even though this ensemble only served to emphasize my lack of musculature, it like, totally fit with the look I was going for. Radical, fer sure. Oh, and the best part—the *best* part—was the pencil-thin tie I found with a keyboard design. *That* made the entire outfit.

All Sam had to do was go into the back of her mom's closet to pull a few things and voilà, she was a vision in acid-washed denim. There was no doubt we'd be reminding Anne for years to come of what she had in her closet. And we now had the photographic evidence as proof.

The limo was the best part of the pre-party prep. I'd been in limos before. And this certainly wasn't my first Hollywood party. But there's something particularly exciting about the combination of the two; stepping out of a black stretch limo and onto a red carpet among the glitterati. It is indescribable.

But I'll try to do it justice.

The limo pulled in at the end of a line of limos and we pressed our faces to the glass to see what was in store. Kara had spared no expense in the party. There was no doubt in my mind that she and Hope's dad were footing the bill for this extravaganza. The studio behind the release would have probably just done a small in-store appearance with Kara signing copies of the DVD for a few dozen of her more ardent fans. Certainly they wouldn't think that the amount of money they'd make on the movie would justify the expense of a huge party that partially shut down Hollywood Boulevard.

On Angel's Wings was supposed to be Kara Bow's breakout role. The problem was that the movie was only big in a cult way and she was so tied to the character that nobody ever saw her playing any other part. She had a few poorly received movies after it, and quickly faded into obscurity. Unfortunately, with all her success behind her, Kara sort of got emotionally stuck back in the eighties, kind of like that mom in Bowling for Soup's song "1985."

She did name her daughters for a character on *Dynasty* and the lead singer of the Go-Go's after all.

Even though we knew that Hope's stepmom had a bit of a hopelessly devoted following, we had never in our wildest nightmares expected such a turnout for the DVD release. Don't get me wrong. *On Angel's Wings* was a massive cult hit with incredible kitsch value. Blaine's reaction alone was clearly evidence that a certain segment of the Hollywood community would come out to support it. But this response was way more than I'd expected when we finally got to the red carpet and stepped out among the throngs of flashbulbs.

I'm not one for name-dropping, so let me just say that before we even reached the party tent, we passed a pair of anorexic, coke-addled actresses, a closeted gay action-movie star and his secret boyfriend, and a celebutante heiress in the midst of a sex scandal. There were also a fair number of washed-up eighties celebrities. It was like the current and future casts of a celeb-reality show all on one red carpet.

Hope's dad, the famed celebrity defense lawyer, Martin Rivera, had clearly called in more than a few favors to stock the party with A-listers. From what I could see of the guest list so far, it bore no small resemblance to a rogues' gallery from TheSmokingGun.com.

Then, there were the goats.

Before I take you into the party, I have to tell you about the goats. See, an army of goats plays a pivotal role in the climax of *On Angel's Wings*. (Don't worry, I won't even *attempt* to explain it here.) So, someone—probably Kara—decided that goats should have a pivotal role in the party. And that's why the red carpet ran along a petting zoo filled with more goats than I have ever seen in my life.

Not that I've seen all that many goats in my life.

"Uh-oh!" Hope said as she stopped us ten feet from the entrance. Her mood was immediately lifted by the tackiness of the spectacle, as I'm sure Sam had intended when she'd had the idea to come to the party.

"What's wrong?" Sam asked.

"I've peaked too soon," Hope said. "We haven't even gotten inside and I've found my highlight for the evening. The one thing that even a phalanx of goats cannot beat."

"Do tell," I said.

"There," she said, pointing to the sign over the door.

I guess it was all the flashbulbs that had kept me from noticing it before. A huge, two-story-tall cutout of Kara Bow looking as she did in the promotional poster for the movie was stationed in front of the entrance to the tent. To get inside, you had to walk under an arch that was—well, there's no delicate way to say this—formed by her legs. But the *real* highlight was the banner that the fifty-foot-cardboard woman was holding. It read ON ANGLE'S WINGS.

"A perfect example of why people should not rely on spell-check alone," Sam said.

"Oh no, didn't you hear?" I said. "*On Angle's Wings* is the sequel. Her twin cousin, Tri Angle, has to solve geometry problems to get back into Heaven."

We all shared a raucous laugh as we entered the party.

That laugh was cut off as soon as we were inside. The place was packed with the hottest celebs around, all dressed as if they were experiencing an eighties flashback. You couldn't swing a dead career without hitting someone with an entourage. But who would be the first person we saw as soon as we crossed under Kara Bow's legs?

Drew.

Confirming once and for all Walt Disney's words of wisdom immortalized in song and annoying animatronic children: It *is* a small world, after all.

"That's just the perfect topper to my day," Hope said, though it didn't come out sounding nearly as harsh as it could have. Our plan was starting to work. She was obviously softening to Drew, and prime for Phase Two of our scheme.

Maybe his being at the party *wasn't* such a small world coincidence, after all.

The two of them stared at each other across the crowded room. But neither of them was willing to make the first move. Eric was beside Drew, trying to get his attention, while Sam was busy distracting Hope.

"Your dad is waving frantically," Sam said, pointing over to the stage.

Hope and I turned to see Mr. Rivera. He was dressed in a simple yet elegant suit of a style that could not possibly have been any older than last year. I wouldn't refer to his waving as "frantic," but Sam was trying to distract Hope so I'll give her a pass on that one.

"Didn't really get into the theme of things, did he?" I noted.

"He's only willing to indulge Kara so far," Hope said. "Usually about as far as his own reputation goes."

"I should go say hi," Hope said . . . and then she did.

Once Hope was gone, Drew stopped staring and made for the bar. Eric, meanwhile, came right up to us.

"What are you doing here?" Sam and Eric said in unison. Speaking of unison. Eric was coincidentally dressed in matching acid-washed denim. He and Sam looked like they were ready to start some hair metal band.

"I didn't know you were coming," Eric said.

"It's a party for Hope's stepmom," Sam said.

"Exactly."

Sam was forced to concede that point to Eric. "Why didn't you say anything about it earlier?"

"We just got the invitation this afternoon," he replied.

Showing her usually exemplary insight, Sam turned to me for the explanation. "Bryan?"

"Remember when you and Hope went into the dressing room so she could try on outfits for tonight?"

"Yeah."

"And remember how I offered to hold your bags for you while she changed?"

"I was wondering why you did that," Sam said. "You never want to hold our purses for us when we shop."

"Yes. I'm a guy. Do I have to keep reminding you of that?" I said. "Anyway. While I had Hope's bag, it's possible that I used her cell phone to speed dial Alexis to make sure that Drew wasn't going to be at the party since we were now going. You know, so there wasn't any awkwardness."

"Thus ensuring that Drew would immediately be invited to the party," Sam said. "Brilliant." She raised a hand to give me five.

Unfortunately, Eric was a few steps behind. Not that it was his fault. "I thought we were supposed to be keeping them apart."

"Oh, honey," Sam said. "I forgot to tell you. New scheme." Sam filled him in on what was up while I scanned the room for the evil stepsisters. I only found the glowing red hair of their fear-mongering leader, Holly, holding court over a bevy of admirers.

She must have the heightened senses of a meerkat or something because she like *felt* me staring at her and looked up. Her flirtatious smile faltered for a moment, before she turned it back up on high and gave us all a little wave.

After the three of us waved back, Sam turned her attention exclusively to Eric. Between prepping for the auditions, and Hope's situation, Sam and Eric hadn't spent all that much time together over the past week. Knowing that they needed their space, I made my way over to the bar, where I met up with Drew, who was nursing the last of a martini. They never card at events like these, so it's pretty much an open bar free-for-all, which explains how Drew Barrymore was in rehab by the time she was thirteen. I ordered a soda . . . with ice . . . and a little stirring straw.

It's not that I'm a total Puritan when it comes to a celebratory glass of alcohol or anything, but if I got back to Sam's house with liquor on my breath, Anne would kill me. And then she'd make me call my mom to explain why I wasn't allowed to drive home. Nope. It was safer to stick with soda. Besides, Blaine was possibly somewhere at the event and his reaction would probably be even more severe than Anne's.

He'd take great pleasure in finding some way to embarrass me.

Drew, meanwhile, made like a male version of the similarly named Barrymore and ordered up his second apple martini.

"You know," I said, "there's a fine line between a couple drinks at a party and starring in an episode of *Degrassi* about underage alcohol abuse."

Drew kicked back his drink in one gulp. "I'll keep that in mind."

Now that I was standing closer, I could see Drew hadn't exactly taken the eighties theme to heart. He was wearing a Hollister T-shirt, an Abercrombie & Fitch baseball cap, and what appeared to be American Eagle jeans. He was a veritable United Nations of guywear.

"Where's your costume?" I asked.

He tapped a pair of Ray-Bans that were resting on the rim of his hat. How very Tom Cruise of him.

It's hard to say that Drew and I stood in silence at the bar, since the venue was pretty rollicking at that point. But, he and I apparently had nothing to say to each other. I guess he was still mourning the loss of his relationship while I was trying to figure out my place as Hope's friend and his former best friend. Either way, our silence was one of the more pleasant conversations we'd had in a while.

Leave it to Drew to go and ruin it. "She doesn't have to run away from me every time she sees me."

"I don't really tell Hope what she does or does not have to do."

"All I'm saying is you can share that information with her," Drew said. "I'm not asking you to tell her to *do* anything." He ordered another martini and we glared at each other while the bartender made it. Drew's eyes were already slightly hooded so I could tell the drinks were having an effect. I guess we were so intent on staring each other down, neither of us noticed the large hand that came into the picture until it intercepted the freshly poured martini.

"Thank you," Blaine said as he tipped the glass to his lips.

Both of our jaws dropped upon seeing him. Blaine had taken the eighties thing on full force. He was dressed up like Mr. T, complete with ten pounds of gold chains around his neck and a Mohawk glued to his head.

"That's not my drink," I stated clearly and for the record.

"Whoever it belonged to, it's mine now," he replied, raising the glass in silent toast. "Now, where is Kara Bow? I have something I want her to sign for me."

I tried very hard not to wonder what exactly he wanted signed.

Thankfully, he got his answer quickly. The band stopped playing, the lights dimmed, and a smoke machine started spewing dry-ice clouds into the room.

Blaine took another gulp of the drink that formerly belonged to Drew. "This looks promising."

"Ladies and gentlemen," a disembodied voice echoed throughout the tent. It sounded very much like the voice of God from *On Angel's Wings* (aka George Hamilton). "Please welcome onto the stage a woman who sang her way out of the depths of Hell. Miss Sylvia Angel!"

Blaine let out a war whoop as everyone burst into crazed applause.

Alexis and Belinda stepped through the fog from the back of the stage. Never before did I realize how much they resembled their mother. I think it had something to do with them being dressed *exactly* like her character from the movie.

Alexis was—suitably—the fallen version of Sylvia Angel, dressed in a red leather pantsuit and a wig with hair sprayed so high that one could single-handedly blame her for global warming. On the flipside, Belinda was Heavenly Angel in a flowing yet incredibly short white skirt and off-the-shoulder white top. Her hair was gently feathered to the back of her head.

Hope stood beside the stage trying her hardest not to laugh. Her father had an arm around her, beaming up at the stage with pride, like he missed out on the joke. Hope wasn't about to fill him in on it.

As the Twin Twigs of Terror flanked the stage, the lights dimmed even more. Somewhere in the background, someone struck the first chord of Kara's lone hit song from the movie: "Open Up Heaven's Gates." And a huge spotlight lit the rafters at the top of the tent.

Sam and I locked eyes from across the room. No words needed to be spoken. Nothing could be said that would beat the visual. I swear to George Hamilton that as the opening notes rose to a crescendo, Kara Bow came floating down from the top of the tent on a shiny silver chain. . . .

But wait! We're not done.

She got *stuck*. Halfway between the rafters and the stage. Just hanging there. Swinging . . . ever so slightly.

It was *awesome*!

Alexis and Belinda were jumping up and down, trying to reach their mother, but only managing to swat at her feet. The tech crew was running around yelling for a ladder while alternately trying to fix the control board. In the ensuing commotion, one of the goats from outside snuck into the tent and made his way to the buffet table.

Sam, Hope, and I locked eyes across the room. We were all thinking the same thing. As if on a silent count we began singing "High Flying, Adored," from *Evita* while we enjoyed the performance.

Unfortunately, Hope's dad quickly ran to Kara's aid. He calmly picked up a chair and carried it onstage for him to stand on. He then grabbed her legs and lifted her body so that she was able to unhook herself. Within a minute she was down on the stage and breaking out into song.

The performance wasn't *nearly* as good as the entrance. Not that I was listening. Once the goat had been wrangled—after demolishing the dessert table—I turned my attention to the throng of partygoers who were busy ignoring Kara's performance and nearly dropped my drink.

Standing with his own bevy of admirers was the last person I ever wanted to see: Hartley Blackstone.

The Critic

"That was beautiful," Sam said, running up to me after Kara's song was over. "A truly stunning performance unlike anything I've seen onstage."

"And I almost missed it," Hope added. "This is, by far, the high point of the crappiest week ever."

There was a lull as they waited for me to respond. But I couldn't. Blackstone was just standing there with his daughter. Laughing. Like he hadn't destroyed a few dozen teens' dreams only hours earlier.

"What's wrong?" Sam asked.

I nodded in the man's direction.

"What is *he* doing here?" Hope asked.

"Carrying his torment through the weekend?" I guessed.

"No. I mean . . . he wasn't on the guest list. I know. My dad forced me to help send out the invites."

"Holly," Sam said with a shrug. "She probably made sure

that he'd gotten a personal invitation. Hand delivered. By a stripper."

I *knew* she wouldn't just sit back and rely on her talent to get a spot in his program.

In unison, the three of us turned toward Holly's table. I guess Alexis and Belinda had joined her right after the performance. And while Holly still had her admirers drooling on her every word, the other girls seemed to be focused on one male in particular: Drew.

"No freakin' way!" Hope said as she stormed over to the table.

"That worked faster than I thought it would," I said.

"Not if she winds up in jail for killing the steps," Sam said. We shared a brief laugh, before realizing it wasn't so much a joke as an inevitability, and hurried over to the table. We passed Eric as he was making his way there to join his best friend. He was wise to quicken his pace along with us.

"Oh hell, the gang's all here," Holly said as we reached the table a mere moment after Hope.

"I just wanted to come over and congratulate my *sisters* on such a stunning performance," Hope said. I could see Drew trying to shy away from the girls, but Alexis and Belinda had their arms intertwined with his and were keeping him locked tight between them. "My favorite part was when Belinda was jumping up and down after Kara, and flashing the entire audience her Hello Kitty panties."

"You know what they say," Alexis chimed in. "If you've got it, flash it."

Ugh. Some people really need to leave the banter to the professionals. Still, she was doing her damage by snuggling up closer to Drew.

"Clearly a policy you've taken to heart over the years," Hope said. "Is there any guy who hasn't seen your underwear?"

"Drew hasn't," Alexis said. "But maybe we can remedy that situation later."

Oh. Hope had walked into that one. And I was reassessing Alexis's banterability.

"Hey . . . no . . . I'm not . . . It's just . . ." Drew tried to pull out from their clutches, but he could not break free of their grasp, which is ridiculous because the two of them together weigh about as much as a paper clip. And they kind of resemble a paper clip too.

"Don't worry," Belinda said gently while she continued to hold tightly. "We're just playing around. The wounds are still fresh."

"You want to talk wounds," Hope said as she took a step toward the steps.

Eric interceded before anything untoward could happen. Not that it stopped them from their verbal jousting over poor Drew. Rather than enjoying the experience, the guy just looked like a wounded bird. I didn't get to enjoy it either, due to the voice suddenly speaking in my ear.

"Now's your chance," Holly Mayflower said, leaning closer to me than I honestly felt comfortable with. I hadn't even noticed her getting up from her chair and shaking off the random guys that had been surrounding her.

"My chance for what?" I asked.

"To find out what Blackstone really thought of your performance," she said, tilting her head in his direction. Hartley Blackstone was over by the bar, ordering a drink. It was the first time I'd seen him on his own since I realized he was at the party. Not that I would have done anything about it had he been available earlier.

"Leave him alone, Holly," Sam said, immediately on guard once she realized there was a side conversation taking place.

"What?" Holly asked. "I think Bryan deserves a critique. Everyone else got one. Don't you think Bryan deserves to hear what Blackstone thinks?"

In my defense, I knew at the time that I was playing right into Holly's perfectly manicured hands, but I couldn't help myself. I looked at my best friend with accusation in my eyes. I wanted to hear what she had to say to that.

"Oh, please," Sam said, backing down. "I'm not going to play this game. Bryan, Hope, let's go."

"No," I said. "I want to talk to Blackstone."

Sam put a hand on my shoulder. "Bryan."

I shook her off and pushed past her before she could stop me. "I want to hear what he has to say."

I continued to maneuver my way through the crowd, regretting my spontaneous decision every step of the way. I couldn't back down now. I was committed. There was no way I could veer off and run out of the tent like I wanted to. At least, not without coming off like a fool. Holly would have a field day with that one. Besides, it was already too late.

Blackstone had been handed his drink and he turned around to face me right as I stepped up to him.

I pulled my fedora from my head and twisted it in my hands. "Pardon me, sir," I said, feeling a bit *Oliver Twist*. "I don't know if you remember me from earlier today . . . at Orion Academy? I'm Bryan . . . Bryan Stark?"

"Bryan Stark," he said, searching his memory banks. "I think I once had a financial planner by that name."

Great. There's one possible future occupation if the acting thing doesn't work out.

"Bryan Stark?" he asked again. I wasn't sure if he wanted me to fill in the blanks or not. I gave him another couple seconds. Honestly, I was in no rush. "*The Glass Menagerie*? Tom, right?"

I nodded vigorously. "Yes."

"I'm not so good with names or faces, but I never forget a performance," he said with a laugh.

"Good," I said with a little more enthusiasm than I had intended. "That's what I wanted to talk about. My performance."

"What about it?"

"Well, that's . . . that's kind of what I was wondering. You left without giving me a critique."

"Yes. I did."

I glanced back at my friends and enemies. They were too far away to hear what was being said, but they weren't even bothering to hide that they were staring right at us, watching for reactions.

"Um . . . could you?"

"Could I?"

"Give me a critique?"

He took a sip from his drink.

"Not really," he said.

"Well, why not?!" Yeah. I took a page from Hope on that one. Particularly with regard to the volume level. If the room hadn't been loud with conversation, I'm sure my voice would have echoed through the tent. By their reactions, I think Sam and Hope *did* manage to hear me several tables away.

There was one person whom I had no doubt could hear me. Alexis had sidled up to the bar to order herself a drink and eavesdrop. Now when I looked back, I could see that Drew was physically holding Hope back so she didn't interrupt to kill her sister.

I focused back on Blackstone in time to see the man shrug off my question. He actually shrugged! Though he did manage to tear himself away from his ever-so-interesting drink. "There was nothing there for me to critique."

"Dad," Miss Julie said as she came over to us. I guess she heard me yell too. "Maybe we should take this conversation—"

Blackstone waved her off. "Nonsense. This young man has asked for my opinion. My opinion must be given."

Any other time I would have snickered at his comment. I would have rolled my eyes back at Sam and Hope. I would have done any number of things to make fun of his obnoxiousness.

All I did was twist my fedora some more.

"Bryan," he said. "Some people are born with talent. They have a natural ease on the stage. As if the theatre is in their very blood. Others can be taught. They'll never be as good as those born with it, but with time, they will be acceptable. Your stage manager, Timmy, was it?" I didn't bother to correct him. "That boy does not have even an ounce of talent in his overly energetic body. And yet, with the proper teacher, and years and years of training, he could learn to make a passable game show host or some such."

I did not like where this was going.

"But, in my many, *many* years in theatre, I've come to learn that there is another breed of being," he continued. "One where it's not about talent. It is not about learning. It's about connection. With you, there is no connection. You move through the part moderately well. You remember most of your lines. But watching you . . . it's clear that you never turn off your brain. You don't have a feel for the role. It's like I can see the wheels turning when you play a part. I can read it on your face. It says, 'This is where I need to look sad.' And 'This is where I should take a step.' 'This is where I need to remember my next line.'" He laughed at his little joke . . . again. I'm so glad *he* finds himself amusing. Even Alexis wasn't smiling.

"The part you are playing is all in your head," he continued with a condescending finger tapping on my forehead. "No matter how much training. No matter how much you work at it. It will never be here." He laid a hand down on my chest. Somehow, I didn't think he was talking about my rib cage.

"But—"

"No," he said gently. "I've seen it before. I've seen it in some of the hardest-working actors I've known. It's not meant to be. You will never be an actor."

"Dad."

Blackstone addressed his daughter. "It's best that the boy learn now. Rather than wasting his life pursuing a dream that will never come to fruition. . . ."

I could hardly hear him any longer. There was only one voice in my head: my own. It was saying, "Don't cry. Don't cry. Whatever the hell you do, do *not* cry in front of everyone."

Then, it said something *far* more useful.

"Run."

And I ran.

From the bar. Toward the exit. Passing Kara Bow taking photos with a trio of goats with angel's wings strapped to their backs.

My mind blocked out most everything Blackstone had said, focusing on one line.

You will never be an actor.

Over and over it repeated as I ran. The tears were flowing freely and without restraint.

Out the tent. Past the goats. Down the red carpet.

A stable full of limos were herded together at the end of Highland. Every one of them looked exactly the same. Black. Stretch. Not a white limo in the bunch to make it easier to find the one I came in.

You will never be an actor.

I ran from limo to limo looking in the front window for our driver. It was a pointless exercise. Hope had dealt with the guy. All I'd seen was the back of his head. And I couldn't even remember what that looked like.

You will never be an actor.

I made it to the end of the stack of limos, still with no idea where the hell our driver was.

I heard Hope and Sam yelling my name. They were running toward me. Hope's cell phone was pressed to her ear. I heard an engine start nearby. I ignored them and went to the idling limo. It was ours. Hope had called the guy, telling him we were ready to leave.

"Are you okay?" Sam asked.

"What did that man say to you?" Hope asked.

"I can't . . . I don't . . ." I could barely speak between the sobs. I got in the limo, slid across the seat, and looked out the window, so my friends could not watch me cry.

The limo ride back to Sam's was painfully silent. They didn't ask me anything else. My friends knew I didn't want to talk about it. I didn't want to think about it either, but they couldn't keep me from doing that.

I wondered if Blackstone was right. Or maybe he was a bitter old man who just didn't understand my talent. Or maybe he had gotten me confused with someone else. *Timmy*, for instance.

But I knew. Somewhere deep down inside me, I'd always suspected. But never put it into words. It was why Sam was so hesitant to be in my group. Why Mr. Randall always focused on my lines whenever he worked with me. Never really getting into a discussion of my performance.

I was never going to be an actor.

Babes in Toyland

The weekend passed in a blur of misery and Chubby Hubby ice cream (my comfort food of choice). My friends called, several times, but I wasn't in the mood to speak to them. Between their voice mails and e-mails, it was clear that Alexis had done what she was best at . . . spreading the news far and wide. Both Hope and Sam had heard about what Blackstone had said. And even though both of them made it clear in their voice mails that the man was one hundred percent wrong, I swore I could hear it in both of their voices that there was a small percentage of them that may have agreed.

But that might have just been my paranoid mind at work. I was beginning to doubt everything I knew. Blackstone had turned my entire world upside down and sent me into a depression spiral that lasted the entire weekend.

Monday morning found me lying in bed staring at the ceiling.

It had been a rough night of tossing and turning while I tried to shut down my brain. Just like the two nights before. No matter what happy thoughts I put there, or how many stupid sheep I tried to count, nothing could switch off what Blackstone had said.

Don't get me wrong. I've always known I wasn't the best actor in the world. Not even the best actor in Orion. But could I really be *that* bad? I was one of the leads in the school show this past year. Granted, I was Scarecrow #2; the one that *didn't* have the solo. But I figured that was because my singing has never been the strongest. But acting's my thing. I've been involved in theater since kindergarten. Sure, I never had leading roles, but I was always out there as a supporting character. You'd think someone would have said something by now.

Or would they?

There was a light tap at my door. "Bryan, you're going to be late," Mom announced from the hall.

I moaned something noncommittal.

The door opened a crack. "Time to get a move on."

Moving on was the last thing I was prepared to do.

Maybe it was the lack of sleep. Or maybe it was the general malaise, but I fell back on the old excuse I hadn't used since elementary school. "I don't feel so good."

The door swung open, and Mom flew across the room. Her hand was on my forehead before she sat down on my bed. "You do feel warm."

The benefit of having a mom who is a bit of a hypochondriac is that all I have to do is plant the seed of doubt and she's ready to call an ambulance. On the flip side, she does tend to hover when I'm *really* sick, which can get annoying. Sometimes you just want to be miserable watching the soaps alone.

"Is it your head?" she asked. "Your stomach?"

"Yes," I moaned.

"Okay, you get some rest," Dr. Mom said as she rose off the bed. "I'll make you a cup of herbal tea."

"Thanks," I said as she left on her errand of mercy. Mom wasn't into the whole Granola Earth-Mother thing, but she swore by herbal tea almost as much as some moms believed in the healing power of chicken soup.

I heard footsteps approaching a minute later. It was way too fast for Mom to have made the tea already, and Dad was still in South Africa checking his blood diamond mines or something. There was only one other person who would be at our house this early in the morning.

"Good morning, faker," Blaine said as he dropped down onto my bed. The springs squealed against his weight as I bounced like a ship at sea in the midst of a tempest. I would have much preferred Mom with the teapot.

"I'm not faking," I whined from under my covers. "I am genuinely depressed. Therefore, I am taking a mental health day."

Blaine sized up the general mood and quit with the jokes. "You want to talk about it?"

"Not particularly."

"Fine," he said. "But you know you have a choice. You can either hide from your problems like a baby or confront them like a man."

"Thank you." I stuck my thumb in my mouth and pulled the covers back over my head, choosing Option A.

"Uh-uh," Blaine said, pulling the covers back again. "I said hide from your *problems*. Not from me. Now, get up. If you're not going to school, then you're helping out at the store today."

"Summer!" I cried. "I want my summer!"

"Work ethic!" Blaine retorted. "Responsibilities!"

Now he was being unfair. I help out at Kaye 9 all the time. I'd been putting in overtime there since way before child labor laws would have permitted. Okay, dressing up stuffed dogs in designer outfits isn't exactly the same thing as working in a sweatshop, but it still wasn't the safest of working conditions. I once got a nasty paper cut from a sale sign.

"I'm going to need that photographer's eye of yours today," Blaine said.

I yawned. "The camera's on the dresser."

"I didn't say I needed your camera. I said I needed your eye."

The fear of what exactly Blaine wanted to do with my "photographer's eye" got me up right quick. I was worried that if I didn't move, Blaine would just take the eye and leave the photographer behind.

I'm kidding.

Mostly.

Mom arrived with the herbal tea as I was getting out of bed. Before she could say anything, Blaine announced that I would be joining them at the store. Knowing better than to question Blaine on the care and feeding of her own son, Mom turned around and exited my room with him.

"You could've left the tea!" I called after them.

Knowing better than to keep Blaine waiting, I dressed quickly, and grabbed a fast breakfast and a reheated herbal tea. Then we all piled into Blaine's truck and made our way to Melrose Avenue. En route, I sent a text message to Hope's cell telling her that I had to help out at the store and apologizing for missing rehearsal. A few minutes later, I received a message back asking, "R U OK?"

I didn't respond, because I wasn't sure of the answer.

Once we got to the store, Blaine had me start out by moving around boxes in the stockroom. I had the distinct impression that this was some kind of punishment for lying to my mother about being sick when I wasn't. I'm not embarrassed to admit that I don't really have what one might consider a body that was built for moving boxes. Scaring off crows? Sure. But manual labor and I were not exactly old friends.

Speaking of old friends, my time in the back room did net a bit of a surprise when I opened a dusty box and took a peek inside. "I forgot all about this."

"What's that?" Mom asked as she came into the back room carrying an armload of merchandise.

I pulled the framed picture out of the box. It was a child's watercolor painting of a dog strutting a runway wearing a designer gown. The Kaye 9 logo was hovering above the dog's head. It was a pretty good for a piece of artwork done by a ten-year-old.

The picture had hung behind the register for the first two years the store was in business. It would probably still be there, but Mom hired some high-priced decorator to redesign the store once it started turning a profit. The first thing he did was throw out the picture. Luckily, Blaine had saved it from the trash.

"I always meant to take that home," Mom said. "I'd wondered where it got to. Why don't you leave it by the back door and we'll bring it with us when we leave?"

"Okay," I said, leaning the picture against the wall. It really was an impressive-looking piece, especially considering the age of the artist when it was painted. My eyes kept going back to it as I moved the rest of the boxes.

Once Blaine confirmed that I had moved every box in the back room, he had me work the register for a while. That was cool because I got to hang with the assistant manager, Flora. She told me all about her trip hiking around Machu Picchu in Peru. A pretty impressive trip for a woman in her eighties.

By the time I rang up my third sale of Mom's most popular new item—beer for dogs imported from the Netherlands—I was getting a little tired. And hungry. It was almost lunchtime. Since the store was empty, I figured Flora could handle the register herself, considering it was her job and all.

I took five to go in the back where Blaine and Mom were huddled over the books.

When Mom saw me approaching she quickly, though subtly, closed the book they were going over. Like I had any idea what the numbers would have meant. I don't know why they were being so secretive. Maybe it was a doctored second book and they were illegally laundering money for the mob through the store.

And maybe I have *too* vivid an imagination.

"Run out of things to do?" Blaine asked.

"I'm having trouble figuring out what exactly you needed my photographer's eye for. The register looks the same as always."

"I'll explain all while we pick up lunch," he said.

As we walked to the restaurant where Mom had already put in an order, Blaine spent an inordinate amount of time talking about how beautiful the day was. It was beautiful, mind you. Not a cloud in the sky. But since it was exactly the same as the day before, and the day before that, and the day before that, I couldn't imagine why he felt it was topical. Unless he was stalling about something. Only after we had picked up the food did he finally bring the subject around to what I hoped was the reason he had gotten me out of bed and assigned me the forced labor.

"How's your mom been lately?" Blaine asked.

Still didn't see what this had to do with my eye. "Fine."

"Does she miss your dad much when he's away?"

Oh no. My parents were getting divorced! It figured. All Dad's traveling for work finally came between them. Not that they ever seemed to have problems when he was in town. Actually, they were almost adorably cute together (blech). But still, it had to be hard on the marriage. They had finally decided to give up. And Blaine was the one who was having this discussion because he's good at breaking news to me.

"I guess," I said. "She does seem better when Dad's around," I continued. "And they talk all the time on the phone." I was hoping if I could sound positive enough, he wouldn't tell me.

"Has she been stressed much? About work?"

Questions about work didn't exactly fit into my divorce scenario, but once an idea is lodged in my brain, it's hard to make it leave. "Not really," I said. "Actually, she's been kind of excited lately. I've even woken up a few mornings and she was still up from the night before working in her studio."

Blaine finally smiled, which I took to mean that this conversation wasn't going to be about divorce. Good. I have enough friends with parents who are happily separated to know that it isn't the end of the world or anything, but still, I like my parents together . . . when they are together.

Blaine stopped us in front of the store. We could see Mom and Flora laughing about something at the register. For some reason, we weren't going inside yet. I didn't say anything. We had gotten salads and sandwiches, so it wasn't like our food was going to get cold.

"Kaye 9 has been doing really well lately," he said.

"I've noticed more of Mom's designs in the tabloids," I said. The first time one of Mom's creations was seen on a celebrity dog in *Us Weekly*, orders for that same outfit quadrupled overnight. Now, it was common practice for us to go through the supermarket rags to see if there were any other shots of her clothing on celebrity pooches so we'd know to stock up.

"We're making pretty good money," Blaine said. "And you've probably noticed how busy we were this morning."

"It has been more hectic than usual," I noted. Some people might not think that a clothing boutique for dogs would get a lot of foot traffic. Those people obviously do not live in Los Angeles.

"Now that you're a senior, Bryan"—oh, we were finally getting to the point of the day—"your mom is going to need you to step up more."

"You know I'm always here when she asks me to come in."

"Stepping up doesn't mean doing what you're asked to do," Blaine said. "It means doing things without being asked."

I got what he was saying, but I didn't have a clue what it had to do with my present situation.

"Now, I don't know what's going on with you right now and why you feel like you have to hide in bed from it."

Oh, that's right. I never told him. Whoops. Odd how manual labor took my mind off my troubles. At least for a while.

"But I do know that if you wanted me to know, I'd know," Blaine said. "I trust that you're man enough now to deal with it like an adult."

"Yes, sir," I said. I don't often call Blaine "sir," but it seemed fitting.

"Now, what do you think of my window?"

Whoa! Did I miss something or did our conversation just veer off in another direction entirely?

I looked at Blaine, then at the window in question. Actually, it was two windows: one on either side of the entrance. Blaine changes the window dressing every month. June's theme had been, fittingly enough, the Dog Days of Summer. It wasn't an original title for the window, but it sure was an original design. He'd taken several stuffed dogs and placed them in Mom's beachwear. But instead of putting them in a beach scene, he had bought a bunch of stuff at Staples and put them in an office setting. It was almost like he was making fun of businessmen who had to work all summer instead of taking a vacation with their pet pooches.

"It's pretty kick-ass," I said.

"Yes," Blaine said. "That it is. And I want you to remember that when you do yours."

"My what?"

"Your window," he said. "I'm letting you do the windows this month."

Stunned.

"But . . . nobody does the windows but you," I reminded him. "Not even Mom."

"If I'm going to expect you to step up, I'm going to have to trust you to be able to do things for me."

Oh, God, Blaine's dying.

"Stop looking at me like that," Blaine said. "I'm not going anywhere." Did I mention: scary psychic? "It's just a window. And I don't want to see any stupid Fourth of July themes. Be original."

I examined the store window from every angle for a good half hour before getting down to the real work of deciding what would go in it. Getting to do the windows was a big responsibility in Blaine's world—a fact that Flora reminded me of several times once I was back inside. I think she was a little jealous. The one time she moved one of the dogs only a few inches in the display, Blaine had been so upset that he didn't speak to her for a week. For someone usually so calm and rational, even Blaine has a little drama queen in him.

I spent the next hour going over the store inventory to see

what materials I had to work with. I already knew the stock pretty well, but I had never really put it all together in my head before. Thankfully, we had a plethora of stuffed animals from Fleischman Bros. Animal Emporium in the back that I could use as my mannequins.

After an hour that got me absolutely nowhere, my stomach reminded me that I still hadn't eaten. I grabbed my sandwich out of the mini refrigerator and sat down in the stockroom for a lunch break. Two bites into my sandwich, my eyes fell on the watercolor painting leaning by the back door. It really was a nice piece of art. You could tell it was painted by a child, but that didn't mean it wasn't quality.

My sandwich was forgotten. Inspiration had struck.

I grabbed the painting and ran out to the front with it. Blaine had spent the last hour dismantling the old window display while I had searched for the new one. I leaned the painting in one of the empty windows, then ran outside. The picture really popped in the natural light. I imagined that it would look even better when it wasn't resting against a plastic fire hydrant.

After another five minutes of staring at the window, Blaine joined me out on the sidewalk. "You might be onto something there," he said.

"I think I am," I said as I dashed into the store and to the stockroom.

I loaded my arms down with every single puppy mannequin that we had and brought them out to the selling floor. One by one I took the dogs around the place to find the most adorable and childlike outfits that would fit them. Little footie pajamas. Puppy-size sports uniforms and cheerleader outfits. Even a beanie with a propeller.

I placed one of every dog toy Mom stocked in the window stage right. There were squeaky toys and chew toys and interactive toys. I even left the plastic fire hydrant in and covered it with puppies. It was the doggie equivalent of the best Christmas morning ever in that window. I briefly considered breaking out the holiday decorations and going with Christmas in July as a theme, but that seemed too obvious. Blake was expecting originality here. I needed something *different*.

In my exuberance, I had used all of the puppies in the window on the right. I didn't notice that until I went back outside to see how it was progressing. The window showed the best dog party *ever*, but the other window sat empty. I could see Blaine watching me from inside. I gave him the biggest smile ever when I found my answer.

Running back inside, I grabbed a stuffed Jack Russell puppy and stripped him out of his denim overalls. He was one of the articulated animals, which meant I could pose him, and I did. I placed him in the empty window on the left, sitting on his rear and looking over at his friends. Alone.

I swear, you could see the sadness on his face at being left out. I felt almost cruel for taking him away from the party . . . until I reminded myself that he was an inanimate object and had no actual feelings.

I finished off the windows by hanging the painting in the crazy toy-filled window and going back outside to see how it looked. The poor little naked puppy was so sad over by himself while all his friends were at play.

I couldn't imagine anyone walking past the window without feeling guilt about neglecting their own dogs. My window would totally drive up traffic into the store if only to ease the consciences of the dog owners that shopped on Melrose Avenue.

If only I had brought my camera!

Blaine came out to join me as I snapped pictures with my phone. He took a good long look at the windows. I don't think I breathed the entire time. Finally, he nodded his head in appreciation. Sometimes a silent critique can speak volumes.

While we were standing there, a mother walked up to the window with her small child in a stroller. She stopped to see what we were staring at. I could see the child's tiny face as it turned from one window to the next. Back and forth the little head twisted as he took in the scene I created.

The little guy reached out to the poor little lonely puppy. Then he burst into tears. The woman soothed the child as Blaine held the door for her so she could go into the store to shop.

Once she was inside, Blaine and I regarded each other in silence.

It was entirely possible that the kid had just wet himself. Or that he was hungry. Or a dozen other possibilities. But my mind was focused on one explanation only.

My window display had made a small child cry.

Success!

Merrily We Roll Along

I slept well Monday night. Not because I had forgotten a single word of what Blackstone had said to me, or because the success of my window design altered my mood in any way (though I did do a spectacular job). I think the sleep came because I'd hardly been able to close my eyes since Friday. Exhaustion finally took hold and I was out shortly after *Access Hollywood* ended.

Which meant I woke up a tad earlier than usual. As I stared at the ceiling for the fourth morning in a row, I tried to psych myself up for going back to Orion. It wasn't easy, but when I pushed all logic aside, I convinced myself that there was a chance I could change Blackstone's opinion of me by doing some impressive scene work.

My monologue could have been a fluke. I wouldn't have been the first actor to let the pressure affect his performance. I did want to get into Blackstone's program, badly. If I could somehow manage to push through my insecurities, I could do a stellar scene, forcing Blackstone to reevaluate his critique and see me for the talent that I possess.

Was I being delusional? Quite possibly. But it got me out of bed.

An hour later, I pulled Electra into the Orion Academy parking lot right behind Sam and Anne. We exchanged awkward greetings, deciding to avoid the elephant in the lot since it wasn't the best way to greet each other after several days incommunicado. (A rarity for us, I assure you.)

While Anne drove off, I subtly glanced at Sam's neck to confirm that she was still wearing her unicorn necklace and, therefore, had not slept with Eric. She was. And she hadn't. "Have a nice weekend?"

"Please stop doing that," she said.

"Doing what?"

"Checking to see that I've got my necklace on," she said. "I'm sorry I ever told you what it would mean when I took it off. Any time I see you after I have a date with Eric, you're always looking at my neck like you're the Vampire Lestat getting ready to take a bite. It's annoying."

So much for subtle. "Sorry," I said.

"That's okay," Sam said, letting me off the hook. I could tell she was going for gentle in light of my meltdown the other night.

"What's the latest on the Hope/Drew situation?" I asked.

"Still morbid. Still depressed."

"Still 'Can't Smile Without You'?"

"That's what Eric says," Sam replied. "There was a glimmer of hope with Hope, though. We spent an hour on the phone bitching about Alexis on Saturday. But by Sunday, she was back to cold and aloof. She still won't tell me what she and Drew are fighting—or *not* fighting—over, but I think she's softening to the whole idea of talking to him again."

"Here she comes," I said as the purple people eater pulled into the lot. I guess the monstrosity of a car had sufficiently snacked for the morning, because only Hope and Belinda got out of it. Not that Alexis would have made a proper meal for any vehicle, no matter how small.

The girls split in different directions as soon as they were out of the car. I braced myself for Hope's full-throated defense of me as she walked up. Just because Sam was tiptoeing around the subject didn't mean that Hope wouldn't be all offering to kill Blackstone to avenge me or some such. Have to say, I might have been willing to take her up had she offered.

"Hi," Hope said.

"Hi," I replied.

"You okay?"

"I guess."

Hope nodded.

That was it?

No screaming in righteous indignation for me? No bold statements of solidarity? Not even one little, tiny death threat?

Man, this breakup with Drew really was affecting her.

But since she'd opened negotiations . . .

"Look," I said, "I'm sorry I bailed on rehearsal yesterday."

Sam put up a hand to stop me. "Don't even. Blackstone's an ass. I don't blame you for not wanting to come in."

I took a deep breath. The next part, I'd rehearsed on the way over. It was difficult, but it had to be done. "I wouldn't blame you if you don't want me in the scene anymore. I don't want to ruin—"

"Uh-uh," Sam said. "No way. We're a team. You are not backing out. I don't care how bad your acting sucks. We're stuck with you."

My eyes went wide. *"Et tu, Brutè?"*

"Me too, you no-talent hack," she shot back.

"Diva!"

"Drama queen!"

"Holly Mayflower!"

"Now, that was cruel and uncalled for," she replied.

"And they say I'm the weird one," Hope added.

"Feel better?" Sam asked me.

"No, but we can go inside," I said. Actually, I did feel somewhat—well, not *better*, but not as bad. Sam and I live by the credo that we can survive anything, so long as we have the ability to joke about it.

"Where's Alexis?" I asked Hope as we went inside.

"She bailed," Hope said. "Hasn't been back since Friday. Don't think she's coming back at all."

Okay. That did make me feel a *little* better.

"Oh, I almost forgot," I said. "Blaine let me design the windows at Kaye 9."

"Get out!" Sam said, giving me a congratulatory—and painful—punch in the shoulder.

"Nice!" I said, rubbing my arm. As we roamed the halls to all of our lockers I filled them in on the story of my window design, embellishing details only when absolutely necessary. I accompanied the tale with visuals, showing them the pictures I'd taken with my phone.

"Ohhh," they said. "Ahhh."

"And the window totally made a small child cry," I added.

"Congratulations," Sam said as we reached the auditorium.

"Thank you," I said, almost forgetting that I was supposed to be miserable. Reality slammed me right back into place as soon as we stepped into the auditorium.

All eyes were on me as we walked down the aisle. And not in a good way either. Whispered conversations and awkward glances followed me every step of the way. It could only mean one thing.

"Alexis really is good at what she does," I said as we reached the front row.

"Sorry," Hope said. "I should have warned you."

"Everybody knows?" I asked. I knew Alexis was good with the gossip, but I never thought she was *that* good.

In answer to my question, Jason came up to me and said, "Screw him. We've got work to do."

It was one thing for Sam and Hope to support me. They were my best friends and all, so it was kind of an unconditional love thing. But Jason's response was entirely unexpected and quite appreciated. My mood was momentarily lightened, until I saw the daughter of the dream destroyer enter from backstage.

Miss Julie faltered a bit in her step when she saw me. She gave me a solemn smile, like she was trying to apologize for her father, but didn't know exactly how to say it. I smiled back in the most reassuring way that I could. I doubt she bought it.

I doubt anyone bought my brave act. Then again, considering how bad I apparently am at acting, that shouldn't be a surprise.

The only person who didn't seem to know what was going on with me was Mr. Randall. Either that, or he just had larger concerns at the moment, as I was about to find out.

"Everybody up onstage," he said, clapping his hands together twice.

Never before have I seen a group of students so reluctant to take the stage. It was as if we'd all been taken over by those zombies again. Then I remembered that I wasn't the only one Hartley Blackstone had destroyed with his criticism the other day. Mine was just the most vicious.

Lucky me.

"Come on," Mr. Randall cheered. "I don't want a repeat of yesterday. Energy people. Energy." Boy, he was really pouring it on. Our teacher wasn't easily excitable. So, for him to be cheering and clapping . . . well, something had to be up.

I got into position beside Sam while the rest of the group continued to lurch their way onstage. "Tell me it wasn't this bad yesterday."

"Worse," she replied.

It was the most miserable group of actors I'd ever seen. And I have to say that I was kind of annoyed. I was supposed to be the one getting all the pity. I mean, I was the only person told that he was never going to be an actor. How dare they be all selfish and self-absorbed!

"All right, let's start with some movement exercises," Miss Julie announced with way more enthusiasm than I felt was necessary. Then again, considering how we were all moving during the exercises, I guess it didn't hurt that someone in the room showed some energy. The rest of us . . . well, it looked like we were preparing for the next zombie uprising.

And lurch, one, two, three. Moan, one, two, three.

After fifteen minutes of stilted movement, Mr. Randall gave up and had us sit on the stage floor so he could fill us in on the day's schedule. In the morning we'd split up to work on our scenes in the different rooms he'd assigned us. "And the afternoon will be spent helping the soccer team prep for tomorrow's Soccer Clinic and Scrimmage," he said.

A collective moan rose from the zombies.

"Hey," Mr. Randall said, "they support us. It's only right that we support them too."

No one bothered to remind our teacher that the last time the soccer team supported us we were all embarrassingly critiqued to shreds in front of them.

"Here's the deal," he continued, assigning us our roles for the afternoon and the following day.

The Soccer Clinic and Scrimmage is this, like, *huge* event for Orion Academy. Kids in youth soccer camps from around the area come to learn the basics from our star players in the morning. Then, in the afternoon we all get to watch a scrimmage between the Orion Comets and our rivals, the St. James Knights. It's a total fair atmosphere that's usually kind of fun. But considering it meant taking time away from our rehearsals, we were, understandably, less enthused than usual.

And some of us were as incorrigible as a Von Trapp child.

Holly pulled Mr. Randall aside after he dismissed us to go to our rehearsal rooms. Sensing trouble, my group hung back to listen in. "Mr. Randall," she said. "Gary, Bel, and I would like to be excused from helping out with the scrimmage."

"I'm sorry, Holly, but you know that's what you signed on for when you joined this program," Mr. Randall said with teacherly diplomacy. "It's the same every year."

"Yes, but we don't have the chance to audition for Hartley Blackstone every year," Holly reminded him.

"If I excuse your team, I'll have to excuse all the teams, Holly," he said.

"No, you don't," Holly said. "I think Hart made it pretty clear who he was interested in." When did he become *Hart*? "You only have to excuse those groups."

"Holly, everyone has an equal chance at being accepted into Mr. Blackstone's program."

"I'm sorry, Mr. Randall, but that's just not true," she replied. "I think if we focus on putting our best work forward for Hart, then it will only serve to make Orion Academy look better as a theatrical training ground."

Only Holly could make selfishness look magnanimous.

I couldn't entirely disagree with her. Largely because I

wanted the extra rehearsal time. Blackstone had made it fairly obvious that he was most interested in seeing Sam and Jason, and I was a part of their team.

"Holly, your team can continue working through lunch if you choose, but everyone is to meet back in the auditorium at one. Now, go make use of the time that you have."

Holly looked properly chastised, but I'm pretty sure that her devious mind was working on Plan B even as I grabbed my things and accompanied my team to Anne's classroom. I figured I had a lot to catch up on, having missed yesterday's rehearsals.

Once we moved all the desks to one side of the room to give us some floor space, Sam quickly ran me through the blocking. As I had expected, they laid out the entire scene in my absence. If you ask me, it was pretty stilted. At one point, they had me walking through the scene for no reason other than they needed me out of the way. So there I was, walking aimlessly and looking at the sights. I would have said something, but considering I had bailed on them I didn't really think it was my place. Besides, who was I to question the people who had a future in acting?

"I brought this to help set the mood," Jason said as he pulled out an iPod boom box and hit play. Forest sounds filled the room.

"Sound effects?" Hope asked.

"Only for inspiration," he explained. "We won't actually use it on Friday."

"Good to know," Hope said.

"I think we're ready to start," Sam said once we'd gone over all her notes for me.

We all took our opening positions and began the run-through. As usual, Sam already had her part memorized. Hope and Jason only had to rely on their scripts occasionally, while I had my head down, reading, the entire time. I would have been better prepared if I could have managed to look at my script once over the long weekend.

The scene from *A Midsummer Night's Dream* that Jason had picked took place in the forest where most of the play is set. It came after the fairy creature Puck enchanted Jason's and my characters so that we thought we loved Hope's character instead of her best friend—whom we *really* loved—who was, naturally, played by Sam. It's all about mistaken identities, misplaced loyalties, and good old-fashioned jealousy. Comic gold, I tell you.

So, why couldn't we find the funny?

"That didn't feel right, did it?" Jason asked when we were done.

We all slowly shook our heads, but didn't really say anything. It wasn't exactly one of our best performances.

Actually, scratch that. It was totally lame.

It was clear what had happened while I was gone. Sam, Hope, and Jason each had something they wanted to prove with the performances. They didn't bother to think about the scene as a whole. It was nothing more than a series of moments for each of them to shine. Sam had chosen specific beats to push, while Jason had his own matching agenda. And Hope . . . well, Hope was just miscast.

There's no question that Hope is a great actress and she will be able to perform any role when she gets older. But right now, her strength is with her personality: big and brash parts. She kept trying to be bold when she was supposed to be shy. I get that she had something to prove to Blackstone, but I wasn't sure this was the time to be taking chances.

Naturally, I didn't say anything to anyone. Who was I to criticize? I just kept walking through my part and doing what I was told.

And I was told a lot.

"No. Say it like this."

"No. Do it like this."

"No. You should let me really smack you in the face. It looks more real."

But I wasn't the only one. While Sam, Hope, and Jason were criticizing me, they were also critiquing themselves. There was more self-doubt and more second-guessing than I had ever experienced in one rehearsal. To think that the opinion of one man—and granted, he is a theatrical genius—threw us all into such a tailspin was certainly saying something.

Then again, it kind of made sense. We do go to a school where everyone who auditioned for the spring show was cast in a major part so that no one felt left out. Growing up in Malibu, my friends and I do tend to be sheltered from any real criticism. Even Mr. Randall's critiques during class are couched in positive comments to ensure that no students—and more important, no parents—are offended to the point where Mr. Randall's job would be in jeopardy. Maybe that's why everyone was taking the criticism so badly. That, combined with the fact that these auditions meant so much . . . well, I guess we were all feeling the pressure.

"I hear David Beckham's going to be guest referee tomorrow," Jason said at the end of our last run-though.

"I wonder if Posh is going to show," Sam said.

"If she does, I imagine the paparazzi will be out in force," Hope added.

They looked at me. Waiting for me to add a line. "Then we'd better make sure we look especially good tomorrow."

Obviously, we'd found our chosen method for dealing with the pressure.

We were going to ignore it.

Crimes of the Heart

I can't believe I got bathroom duty. Then again, I couldn't have come up with a better metaphor for the week I was having. At least I wasn't alone. Sam was stuck with me as we escorted the kids through the small forest between the soccer field and Orion's main campus on bathroom runs throughout the morning. It's not like they could really get lost. It wasn't really a forest so much as it was a large patch of trees. Still, we didn't need any kids taking a wrong turn and wandering off the bluff. At least Sam kept us entertained by leading us all a rousing rendition of *Heigh-ho, heigh-ho, it's off to pee we go*.

The Soccer Clinic and Scrimmage was an even bigger event than the one last year. Parents, Orion students, and assorted guests were all over the place among the actual kids from soccer camp that the event was intended for. I guess it was true that David Beckham was coming for the scrimmage part because the paparazzi was set up before we'd even arrived that morning. I would have preferred to spend the day rehearsing, but there was no doubt the soccer team needed the extra hands. Kids were running around everywhere. And they all had to pee like a dozen times each before we'd gotten through lunch.

When we reached the bathrooms, Sam and I took a quick head count to make sure none of the kids was eaten by a coyote on the way through the woods. Nope. All there. We let them go in on their own as there was only so far that the escorting was necessary.

"Let's run lines," Sam said while we waited. Leave it to her to try to wring a rehearsal out of every minute.

"I don't have my script," I said.

"You don't have the lines down yet? Bryan, we go on in two days. You *have* to get them down." Her intensity level was somewhat disturbing, though understandable.

I shied away from her. "I will. I promise."

"Sorry," Sam said. "I'm getting a little stressed and feeling out of control."

"That seems to be going around," I said as a pair of stragglers made their way out of the trees. Jimmy Wilkey was escorting a familiar young face toward us. They were passing a Frappuccino between them.

"Hi, Sam! Hey, Bryan!" Eric's brother, Matthew, said as they reached the rest area. "This is such a great day! I'm having the *best* time. And I got to meet your friend Jimmy. He walked me here and let me have some of his Frappuccino, which was really nice. And I made sure I thanked him like Dad always tells me I should do. He's a pretty cool dude."

Probably the first time anyone had ever called Jimmy a cool dude.

"Oh, Jimmy, you shouldn't have done that," Sam said, taking the bottled coffee drink out of Matthew's hands and handing it back to Jimmy.

"I'm sorry, Sam. I didn't know. Matty said that it was okay. But I guess I shouldn't believe everything I hear. Especially from a kid. That's good advice in life, you know. I guess I am too trusting. But I'm really, really sorry, and I won't do it again."

Yep. Eric Whitman's brother was totally going to grow up to be Jimmy Wilkey. I took a particular amount of pleasure in picturing that.

"Don't worry, Jimmy," Sam said, trying to hold back the laughter like I was. "It's not that big a deal."

"Okay, thanks," Jimmy said. "I mean it. Thanks. Sorry."

Jimmy vibrated back to the soccer field, finishing his drink on his own.

"How's your plan going with Hope and Drew?" Matthew asked. He was bouncing up and down on the balls of his feet.

"What? Your brother's not keeping you in the loop?" I asked.

"I ask, but he always tells me to shut up."

I looked at Sam. "That's not nice."

"Well, I do talk a lot," he admitted.

Oh.

"I saw them together on the field earlier," Matthew added. "Well, they weren't *together*, together, but they were together. On the same field. But I didn't expect to see them there, you know. Weren't you going to keep them apart?"

"We've moved on to Phase Two," I said. "It's progressing quite nicely."

"Cool," Matthew said.

"Cool," I agreed.

While Matthew joined the rest of the bathroom contingent, Sam asked, "What is going on with our scheme? Do you have any plans for Hope and Drew today?"

"No need. The twigs can handle it on their own from here." I pointed to the parking lot. "Check it." Alexis was trying to pull something out of the back of the purpmobile, flashing her butt to all passersby. I guess one of the perks to ditching the Theater Program was that she didn't have to help with the Soccer Clinic and could come late for the game.

"Looks like Drew's going to have his own little cheering section," Sam said.

"That should annoy Hope enough on its own," I said.

"Are you sure?" Sam asked. "Because we can always have something ready to go in reserve."

"Boy, you are stressed."

"I know," Sam said. "Aside from being worried about everything I do, I'm afraid that Hope being all morbid and depressed is going to affect her performance. And that won't be good for any of us."

"She pulled it together for the monologue," I reminded Sam. "She can do the same for the scene."

"I'd feel better if we could get her and Drew back together," Sam said. "I mean, I think they should be together for themselves, but—"

"But if we get a better scene out of it, then it helps all around," I filled in the blanks. "Gotcha. And trust me. Alexis has got our backs."

We watched as our unknowing ally flagged down a guy to help her pull whatever it was out of the back of the car. If she worked Drew even half as much as she was working the guy, we would have nothing to worry about. Hope would never stand for that crap.

Once the last of our charges was out of the bathrooms, we performed another head count to make sure none of them had been flushed out to the ocean, and returned to the soccer field.

We had a few more round trips to the bathroom before the teams started to set up the scrimmage. Alexis still hadn't made an appearance and we were worried that we might miss it whenever it came. Each time we went back to the field, we saw Hope and Drew actively trying to keep their eyes off each other. I wasn't sure that either of them wanted to get back together, but it was clear to me that the period of estrangement was getting old for them.

"We hereby turn bathroom duty over to you," I said to a pair of tenth graders upon returning from our final bathroom trip.

"Thanks," they moaned. Hey. I had to miss the game for bathroom duty back when I was a sophomore. Not that I normally minded missing a soccer game. But this one promised to have quite a show with it.

The opening act began as Alexis came through the trees.

She was wearing tight blue short shorts and a silver bikini top. The matching blue shirt she had tied around her waist hardly provided any additional coverage. To say she was decked out in our school colors would be an overstatement. Scantily clad in them would be more accurate. But, just in case you missed her, she was holding a huge, professionally rendered sign above her head. She looked kind of like a ring girl from a boxing match. You know, the ones who hold up the signs announcing what number the round is. But instead of a number, the sign read GO, DREW! YOU CAN DO IT!!!

I suspected that the same sign shop made it that had been responsible for the ON ANGLE'S WINGS banner.

"What is she doing?" Sam asked. "Hope is so not going to be threatened by that. Look at Drew. He's totally embarrassed." His red face was evident all the way across the soccer field.

"This is what happens when you work with amateurs," I said. "Come on, let's do damage control."

We had to weave our way through the kidlings who were all gaping, openmouthed, at Alexis's display. Even though she was wearing more than they'd normally see on the beach, there was something out of place about it on a soccer field teeming with children.

"I can't believe I'm pseudo-related to *that*," Hope said when we reached her. Alexis was spreading herself out on the first row of the bleachers, leaning back to collect some rays and show off her emaciated body while she waited for the game to begin.

"I just can't believe she'd so blatantly make a move on him

right after you broke up," Sam added. "You'd think she'd at least wait until you'd left town for the summer."

"Yeah, she's good," I said.

"Good?" Hope scoffed. "Are you out of your skull? Drew's not going to fall for that crap."

"Well, it's not like he's ever had a cheering section before," I said. "I mean you hardly ever look up from your journal during a game."

"That's because he hardly ever has field time," Hope said.

"All I'm saying is that Alexis is making a big deal out of supporting him. Any guy would like that."

Sam nodded her head gravely, like she was agreeing with me. Okay, I admit we were being a bit cruel, but we needed to get things moving along. Hope was heading to New York in four days.

Drew was totally helping us out by playing into the act. Even though he was clearly embarrassed, Drew couldn't take his eyes off Alexis. Neither could the rest of the soccer team. *Both* soccer teams.

Coach Zach apparently realized what a distraction she was going to be during the game. He hurried over to Alexis and convinced her to cover up with the shirt she had tied around her waist. She agreed quite willingly. I assume because she didn't want to create a scene.

Riiight.

Once Alexis was looking a little more demure, Coach Zach sounded the air horn announcing that the scrimmage was set to start in a few minutes. As the kidlings scrambled for seats in the middle of the bleachers, my friends and I casually strolled over to the place on the end that had somehow become our usual spot. Hope clearly wanted to move us closer to Alexis, but there was no way to discreetly do that so she settled in beside us. Her eyes hardly left her stepsister the entire time. Even when David Beckham took the field—to the screams and adoration of the crowd and paparazzi.

The scrimmage began with both Eric and Drew in the game. That wasn't unusual for Eric since he was a starter, but Drew didn't usually get any play until we were up by a few points. Speaking of unusual, Hope was oddly vocal from the opening kickoff . . . or whatever you call it in soccer.

Sam, on the other hand . . .

Her eyes were closed and her lips were silently moving. "What are you doing?" I asked.

"Running lines," Sam said.

"But your boyfriend's playing," I reminded her.

"It's just a scrimmage. He'd understand."

"Yeah, but—"

"Where's Holly?" Sam suddenly asked. Her back went stiff as she eyed the crowd.

"What?"

"Holly?" she said. "I just realized . . . I haven't seen her all day."

"Belinda and Gary are missing too," Hope added. "I haven't seen that twig since I left the house."

"Unbelievable!" Sam said. "They're rehearsing. They snuck away for stage time. She was specifically told that we were expected to help out here. I hate how everybody at this freakin' school thinks they are exempt from the rules."

I weighed our options. It was kind of a dumb rule that we were all expected to watch a game that wasn't even part of the regular season when we had a huge audition on Friday. (Well, Blackstone had made it clear that as far as he was concerned, *I* wasn't auditioning for anything, but that's not the point.) Either we could stay at the game and continue our Hope and Drew manipulation or we could go off and rehearse too.

Like there was a choice.

"Let's get Jason and go," I suggested. Our scenemate was sitting on the other side of the bleachers with some of his friends who were neither soccer players nor Drama Geeks. (I know. There are a few of them at our school. The non-joiners.) Jason looked like he was into the game, but I was pretty sure a rehearsal would take precedence.

"No," Sam said. "I don't want to leave Eric's game."

"But you have no problem watching it with your eyes closed?" I asked.

"It's a matter of degrees."

"We can always rehearse after," Hope suggested.

"I promised Mom I'd go home and help her study," Sam said. "She's got a big test tomorrow and she's freaking out about it."

"Your mom is freaking out about a test?" Hope asked.

"That I'd like to . . . uh-oh." My eyes were diverted to the field. "Drew's getting pulled."

"Why? What happened?" Hope asked.

I shrugged. I hadn't been paying attention. I suspect it wasn't something good, since Drew had to pick himself up off the ground before he could leave the field. Alexis didn't even give him a chance to sit. She was on him as soon as he reached the bench.

"Unbelievable!" Hope said, though I personally thought it was not only believable, but expected.

"Why are you so bugged?" Sam asked.

"Are you kidding?" Hope asked. "How would you feel if Holly made a move on Eric?"

"But you broke up," I reminded her. "Technically, Drew is fair game."

"Doesn't mean I want to see him with that she-devil," Hope said. "Look at her! She's touching him!"

"Well, his hair was hanging down in his eyes," I said. "Did you expect him to brush it away himself?"

"He should be watching the game," Hope said.

No sooner had she said it than her words were proven true. A St. James player gave the ball a killer kick that sent it sailing over the field toward the benches. The crowd roared in warning as the ball continued its deadly arc, smashing into the back of Drew's head, and sending him crashing to his knees.

Alexis was stunned, as he, quite literally, fell at her feet.

Hope was up in a shot, rushing to his side. Sam and I shared an excited, though concerned, glance as we followed. That Hope had reacted so quickly was a good sign. That Drew had fallen so hard, was not. The crowd was up on its feet checking to see that he was okay.

Coach Zach was already down beside Drew as we reached them. "How many fingers?" he asked.

"Two and a half?" Drew guessed as his eyes focused on the coach's hand.

Coach Zach didn't like that answer. "Drew!"

"Well, did you want me to count your thumb?" Drew asked. "Technically, it's not a finger. It's a thumb."

"He's okay," Coach Zach announced to the gathering crowd. "A smartass, but okay."

Hope, Sam, and I each let out a sigh. We were all so concerned about Drew that it took a moment for us to realize we were only inches away from David Beckham. Well, Alexis had noticed. She was already making goo-goo eyes at him, forgetting all about Drew.

"Unbelievable," Hope said again, which brought Alexis back into reality.

"Oh, you're okay," she said, holding out a hand to help Drew up.

"Step off, hose-beast," Hope warned with a growl, actually scaring Alexis enough that she did back away. Hope held out her own hand for Drew. "Come on. We're going to put some ice on that."

"I'm okay," Drew insisted as he took her hand and stood up.

"I said we're putting ice on it," Hope said. "Now!"

"Okay," Drew agreed.

Game play resumed as Hope and Drew headed for the main campus. It was the last Sam and I saw of them for the day.

I Love You, You're Perfect, Now Change

"And how are my two best friends in the world on this fine and dandy summer morning?" Hope asked as she met Sam and me outside of Anne's classroom Thursday morning.

"Oh, dear, she's finally snapped," I said. We were all prepared to hunker down and work our scene to death all day. Mr. Randall had told everyone not to even bother checking in at the auditorium so we could get right to work. We weren't going to have enough time to psychoanalyze Hope of Sunnybrook Farm. No matter how much fun that could've been.

"Just happy is all," Hope said. "Alexis has lost her car privileges for the next month."

"How'd that happen?" Sam asked.

"She was caught with my private journal in her bedroom. She'd already been warned twice this year about stealing my stuff."

"You don't seem too broken up over the invasion of privacy," Sam said.

"It wasn't my *real* journal," Hope said, fingering the flash drive around her neck that held her most intimate writing. "It was *The Book of the Dead Puppy Poetry, Volume Six*. And I wouldn't say that Alexis *stole* it as much as I may have accidentally *left* it under her pillow after I got home from Drew's last night."

Sam and I looked at each other with raised eyebrows. We were both glad to hear that her mood had something to do with Drew. I noticed that her clothes had a more playful Goth-Ick look to them. She was wearing a black tank top with a flowing black skirt and a rainbow-striped scarf tied around her waist like a belt. Even her contacts were a cheerful shade of blue.

"You were at Drew's last night?" I asked.

"Getting back together?" Sam asked.

Hope recoiled at the suggestion. "Hell, no! We were . . . finding closure."

"Closure?" I asked with a smirk.

"Laugh at my vocabulary if you want," Hope said. "But we needed it. After we left the game, we got to talking and it all sort of came out. Everything we weren't dealing with since our fight. We are much better now. Dare I say, I think we can even be friends."

I *hate it* when all the good stuff happens offstage. "Congratulations," I said.

Sam didn't seem as ready as I was to accept defeat, though. "But your fight?"

"Was stupid," Hope said. "And not really about what we were fighting over. It doesn't matter. We've moved on."

"But you and Drew—"

"Work better as friends," she insisted.

"But—"

"Let it go, Sam," Hope said. "You're taking this harder than I am. Come on, we've got work to do."

Hope started setting up the room for our scene, forcing us to join in or look like slackers while she did all the work. Sam clearly wanted to discuss the great Hope and Drew friendship pact further, but Hope had shut down the line of inquiry. I wasn't all that broken up over it either. I found myself surprisingly happy to hear that Hope and Drew were moving on.

When Jason joined in a few minutes later, the subject was effectively dropped for good. We had some serious rehearsing to do.

"Okay, let's try this again," Jason said as he hit play on the nature sounds machine.

I'd like to say that the day off had helped us clear our heads. And that Hope's improved mood had added to the performance. But while Hope was markedly more into the scene than she'd been the other day, the group was still floundering. Jason and Sam were still under- and overplaying moments. Hope was bringing too much broad comedy to the role. And I was still dropping lines . . . among other problems.

We all knew it wasn't working, but none of us could make it right.

No matter how many times we ran through it, the thing just didn't *feel* good.

Actually, it felt like crap.

"I need a break," Sam said as we entered the second hour of rehearsals. "I'm going to get some drinks from the pavilion." She looked at me. "Come."

"Yes, ma'am."

As soon as the door was safely closed behind us, Sam said, "I don't think it's over."

"Of course not," I said. "We've still got the rest of the day to rehearse. It'll come together."

"Not the scene," she said. "Though that's been pretty crappy. I meant Hope and Drew. She did a one eighty on her mood too fast."

"She says she found closure," I reminded Sam.

"Please. They're destined to be together."

"Or," I said, "they've been dating for years and have known each other most of their lives. It's only natural that they continue the friendship."

"Don't quash my buzz," she said, rubbing her hands together. "I feel like our plans are coming to fruition."

"Mwa-ha," I said. "Ha."

"We just need to come up with a new phase," she said. "I think the Alexis thing has run its course."

"Sam, it's over," I said as we reached the pavilion. "Why are you obsessing?"

"Because Hope's our friend," Sam said. "Don't you want her to be happy?"

I grabbed a couple drinks out of the refrigerator and handed them to Sam, then grabbed a couple for me to take. "Does this have something to do with Eric?"

"What?" Sam asked. "Why?"

I'd caught her totally off guard by the question. Have to say, I was a bit surprised by it myself. I hadn't made the connection until that moment. "He's going away," I explained. "For the rest of the summer."

"But if I get into Blackstone's program, I'll be a train ride away," she reminded me.

I didn't want to ask the question, but I had to. "And if you don't?"

"If I don't?" she asked like it was the first time she'd considered the possibility. "Then, I'm still here and he's gone."

"Have you guys talked about that?"

"We've been more focused on me getting into Blackstone's program."

"So that would be a no."

Sam played with the cap on one of the bottles, nervously twisting it off and on. "I don't know where things stand with us," she finally said. "We've only been going out a little over a month. Are we exclusive? Will we see other people while he's away? Will we agree to be exclusive while he secretly dates other girls that I won't know about because he's three thousand miles away?"

"Since Drew and Eric are best friends," I said, reasoning it out, "and if Drew's still going out with Hope while she's away in New York, I'm guessing part of you thinks that will be an example to Eric that he should stay true to you while he's gone as well."

"Wow," she said. "That makes me sound stupid, selfish, *and* insecure. Impressive."

"No," I insisted. "You're not any of those things. Well, maybe insecure. But that's a normal relationship thing. Happens all the time on TV." Since I don't have any actual relationship experience myself, I've got to go with what I know. "Tell Eric you want to be exclusive. I haven't seen him with anyone else since you two started going out. He'll be fine with it."

"I can't bring it up," she said. "He's got to bring it up. Otherwise I look desperate."

"You'd rather look insane by forcing Hope and Drew back together?"

"Please stop making logical arguments," she said. "It makes it so much harder to ignore reality."

"So, you'll talk to him?" I asked.

"One thing at a time," she said. "Let's see if we can get me in this acting program, then I won't have to deal with it."

"I guess ignoring your issues is kind of a way to deal with them."

"Always," she said.

We switched to a lighter subject for the walk back to Anne's classroom. I suggested she consider releasing an album for younger kids titled *Off to Pee I Go* and that got us started on a whole slew of inspirational bathroom songs for infants learning to potty train. We were laughing quite freely by the time we returned to Anne's classroom with drinks for everybody.

The laughing stopped when Hope announced, "Mr. Randall says we're up for some stage time."

We should have been happy to get the chance to rehearse in front of our teacher onstage, but that didn't seem to be the consensus. We weren't ready to show anyone what we had. Whatever *that* was. I think we were all a little embarrassed when we entered the empty auditorium and saw him sitting alone in the front row.

During the school year, Mr. Randall usually leaves us on our own to work on scenes. I guess he realized how much was at stake so he was sitting in with all the groups to watch a run-through and then give his advice. Notice I didn't use the word "critique" there. Yeah. I've come to realize that our favorite teacher never critiques us, so much as tells us what we're doing well and what we could do better. Rarely does he ever tell us when we're doing something wrong—aside from not speaking loudly enough or dropping a few pages of text.

I don't think I was the only one that wasn't ready to start up again. Even with our short break, we were all exhausted, both emotionally and physically from the earlier rehearsals. But we would try to do our best for him, considering.

With little fanfare, we got up onstage and performed the scene for our teacher, just as we had dozens of times before in class over the years. The only difference was we weren't waiting for a grade from him. What was ultimately at stake was much more important than that. At least it was for Sam and Jason. And maybe even Hope. There was still a chance she could dazzle Blackstone in spite of his attitude toward character actors. I was pretty sure that I was far out of consideration.

But I don't think any of us would have been helped by the performance we'd just given.

"I see Mr. Blackstone's criticism got to you guys as well," Mr. Randall said with a sigh in his voice. "I had hoped if anyone would be immune . . ."

It would be what? His prize pupils? His star students? He certainly hadn't stuck up for us much during the critiques. I knew I was being unfair, but that's what I was thinking at the time.

Hope, on the other hand, spoke her mind.

"It would be who?" she asked. "Us? And why is that? Because I'm *dying* to hear from another person who thinks I can only play character parts! Glinda the Good Witch, my ass!"

There was a long silence in the auditorium. For Hope to have an outburst like that was certainly not unusual. For her to direct it at a teacher, on the other hand . . .

"I'm sorry," she finally said.

Mr. Randall was looking at us in that way that you can clearly tell he was trying to figure out what to say. Or, more specifically, *how* to say it. We get that look from the teachers a lot around school. They have a tendency to fear honesty with the students since any one of us could probably get them fired in between calls to the stylist and the therapist.

"I know Mr. Blackstone's criticisms were harsh," he said.

"But, let's be honest, you're all going to hear much worse outside of Orion. This school is set up to be a safe environment for the students. Sometimes, it may be too safe. I'm not saying I agree with everything that Mr. Blackstone said, but I think you all needed to hear it. If only to learn how to accept criticism. So far, no one has dealt all that well. Instead of rallying, you've completely fallen apart. I have to admit, I expected more from you guys."

He let that sink in for a moment.

"So, enough of the teen angst?" I said.

"More than," Mr. Randall agreed.

"We'll work on it," Jason added. Hope was nodding in agreement.

"I can give you the stage for another half hour," Mr. Randall said, getting up. "I suggest you make good use of your time."

"We will," Sam promised as we watched our teacher go.

If only we had a clue where to begin.

Into the Woods

I guess we were all thinking about the best way to proceed because there was a lot of quiet going on in the auditorium. I could feel our half hour slipping away as we stood in silence, like we were in the play *Act Without Words*. (*Aside:* Which is pretty much what the title indicates.)

Jason was the first to speak.

"This can work," he burst out with a kind of frenetic excitement as he moved about the stage. "All we need to do is make some choices . . . give it some direction. We've all been too afraid to do what we know we have to do."

"Where did he come from?" I asked.

"I guess he's found his muse," Hope said. "And she is on speed."

Apparently she was on speed and had a death wish, because Jason turned to Sam and said, "Maybe you can take it down . . . just a notch. At the point where you're calling Hope a puppet. I think the scene was starting to get away from us there."

"And maybe you can pick it up a bit," Sam said. "You kind of mumbled through the opening line. It didn't give me much to work with."

Jason stopped. "I don't *mumble*."

"No," Sam backtracked. "I just meant that you've got to—"

"Get past the first row?" Jason asked, echoing Blackstone's critique of him.

"I didn't . . . I was just saying—"

"Speaking of getting past the first row, what was with that pause you took?" Jason asked.

"What pause?" Sam asked back. I knew exactly what pause Jason was talking about. In the middle of the scene, there was a moment of silence that was kind of . . . prolonged.

"The one that lasted five minutes," he said.

Okay, maybe not *that* long. But not all that short either.

"Very funny," she said. "I was working through some internal . . ." Her face fell. I think she realized that what Blackstone had said to her was right. Sometimes, she takes moments that are so small, the audience doesn't know what's going on.

If we kept this up, it was bound to spiral out of control. "Look," I jumped in. "Let's move past the moments. We have to consider the entire scene. I don't think it's working. Maybe we should choose a different one."

"Like what?" Hope said.

Trouble was, I didn't have any suggestions. All I knew was that something was wrong with this scene. I had no clue what alternate one could work for us.

"I think you'd make a great Puck," Sam suggested.

Hope spun on her. "Meaning what?" she asked, like there was any doubt. Puck was the trickster, the fool. Depending on how you played him (or her, if you want), she/he could be very big with the broad comedy, which *was* Hope's specialty.

"She just means we might want to go with a scene that plays to your strengths," Jason said. "To all of our strengths, I mean."

Hope filled in the blanks. "No. You mean you want me to be the comic relief."

I was still going for peacekeeper. "You do usually—"

"And what if I want to stretch a bit?" Hope asked with no regard for the peace whatsoever. "Try something new? I'm getting a little tired of everyone just assuming Sam and Holly are the only ones up for the girl's spot in Blackstone's program. I have as much of a chance of impressing him as anyone."

I went with my calm voice. "I don't think anyone—"

"Oh, please," Hope said. "Sam and Jason have been going around all week like we're holding them back. Why do you think they blocked the entire scene while you were out on Monday? Did they even give you a chance to contribute to the blocking?"

"Hope!" Sam said. "That's not fair."

"No, it's not," Hope said. "But it's obvious—"

"Obvious?" Jason jumped in. "You want to talk obvious? Let's talk about your larger-than-life choices."

"Guys, we don't have time for this," Sam reminded them. "We have to get some work done. I'm not about to lose my shot at this program 'cause you guys can't get it together."

"See what I mean," Hope said. "*Her* shot. Like it's a guarantee."

It was one thing to exhibit this kind of naked backstabbing aggression when Holly Mayflower was around. It was another thing entirely when friends started turning on one another, as Sam, Hope, and Jason had all quite literally managed to do. Me? I was in the center of the three of them, looking at those backs that had turned.

And don't think it was lost on me that none of them were criticizing my performance. I guess Blackstone really had said it all last week.

"This is stupid," I said. Mr. Randall would be so disappointed to see that this is how we'd reacted to his pep talk. "We're not going to get anywhere in our scene if we don't work together."

"Now, there's the best idea I've heard all morning," Hope said.

I had no clue what she was talking about. "Hope?"

"I'm done working together," she said as she stormed off the stage and out of the theater.

The rest of us stood in silence for a moment. "Humph," I finally said to Sam. "You were the one who wanted her to be the old Hope. Personally, I think we would have gotten further with her when she was morbid and depressed."

"Is this funny to you?" Jason asked. "Just because you don't have a shot at Blackstone's program doesn't mean you shouldn't take this seriously. I thought you actually cared about your friend over there."

Usually, my attempts at humor are better received. "What are you talking about?"

"Never mind," Jason said, before taking a page out of Hope's book and storming off, stage right.

"What the hell was that?" I asked, but I got no response from Sam.

I get that the pressure had been building. We'd all been tip-toeing around these issues like cats on a hot tin roof all week. But for that explosion . . . well, it was just so unnecessary.

And Sam was still disturbingly quiet.

"Do you know what he was talking about?" I asked. "About me not caring for you?"

"No," Sam said in the least reassuring tone ever.

"Sam."

"He doesn't think you're taking this seriously when you make jokes like that," Sam said.

"Yeah, but that's what we do," I reminded her. "We make jokes. It's how we deal."

"Some people don't like jokes all the time," Sam said. "Sometimes the stress doesn't let people see the funny."

"You don't need to stress," I said. "You know you're good. I'm the one that got ripped to shreds by the country's foremost authority on acting, remember?"

"And just because Blackstone said some nice things about me, I don't have anything to worry about?" Sam asked. "Don't you get it? You have options. You can do whatever you want when you get out of here. Go to whatever school you get into. Orion is it for me. I spent my grandparents' money on this place. I have to do everything in my power to make sure I get a full scholarship if I want to go to college. Do you know what kind of help getting into Blackstone's program would be for me? So I'm sorry if I don't feel like joking right now. I have too much riding on this scene."

Suddenly, I didn't feel like joking either. There had been something nagging at the back of my mind for the past week and a half. Something that I needed the answer to. And I needed it right now. "If we weren't best friends, would you have agreed to do this scene with me?"

"What?"

"You heard me," I said.

"Don't be an idiot."

"I'm not an idiot. I want to know. With so much riding on this for you, would you have chosen me to be in the scene?"

"Blackstone—"

"I'm not asking about Blackstone," I said. "I'm asking about you. When you made that joke the other day about me sucking as an actor . . . did you mean it?"

"Well . . . I wouldn't say you *sucked*."

A ten-ton truck slammed into me, right there, center stage. My entire body felt like it had collapsed, but somehow I managed to stay on my feet, while Sam realized what she had just said.

"Bryan. Oh, God! I'm sorry. I didn't mean—"

She moved toward me, but I pushed her away.

I didn't say anything. I calmly collected my things and made my way up the aisle. Then, once I was sure that Sam was not watching . . . I ran.

Out of Hall Hall and into the halls of Orion Academy.

My fleeing footsteps echoed through the empty halls as I passed classroom after classroom. I veered to the right when I heard the soccer team in the pavilion. Figures they'd break for lunch early the one time I was looking for someplace to be alone.

I burst out the doors and headed for the parking lot. Electra was waiting for me, but I couldn't get in. I was in no condition to drive the winding Malibu roads. The last thing I needed was to hit a corner too hard, roll off a cliff, and land in a gully below.

I wasn't ready to be found. I had to go somewhere Sam would never in a bajillion years think to look for me. If she even bothered to look for me, that is.

I ran for the trees. Following the well-worn path, I was heading for the one place I knew I could be alone: the soccer field. With the team munching away, I had at least a good hour to be by myself. That would give me more than enough time to calm down so I could drive safely out of there.

I twisted my way through the trees. The promised land opened up before me. Never in my life had I been so happy to see a sporting field of any kind, much less the one sport that had become the bane of my existence.

I was home free.

Until I nearly ran right into Drew at the edge of the tree line.

Beyond Therapy

There was a moment of confused hesitation. Like we had both been caught doing something we weren't supposed to be doing.

"What are you doing here?" he asked.

"What are *you* doing here?" I asked back, hoping that my eyes weren't all wet from the tears that I was trying to hold back.

"I needed to get the ball," he said, holding up his soccer ball.

"Noooo," I said with a little more childlike petulance than I intended. But he *had* invaded my private spot. Not that it had ever been my private spot before. Not that he didn't have more right to be there than I did, considering he was the soccer player and I was the . . . well, I wasn't sure what I was anymore. I used to think of myself as an actor-photographer. Now I wasn't even a hyphen.

"What are you doing *here*?" I asked. "The rest of the team's at lunch."

"I wanted to get in some more practice." He walked to the center of the field bouncing the soccer ball off his knee as he went.

Great. I was having a total breakdown, and Drew chose this time to be all gung ho about his game. Why couldn't he just be a quitter like Alexis? Leave it to Drew to show a commitment to something he loved. I *so* did not need that at the moment, so I turned and walked away.

"Why are you leaving?" he asked.

Like there was an easy answer to *that* question. As such, I deflected it. "I think we're still in that period where as Hope's friend I'm supposed to hate you."

"You've hated me for years. Why should today be any different?"

"I never hated you. I just don't like you. There's a difference. Hating is more active."

"And you haven't done anything active in years."

"Exactly."

"Well, why don't you try something active for a change? I could use a goalie."

I looked over at the big net he was facing. Was he actually suggesting that I, Bryan Stark, engage in physical activity? "You're kidding, right?"

"It's not much of a challenge to kick the ball into an open net."

"And you think I'd be more of a challenge than empty

space?" I asked. With my life falling apart around me, self-deprecating wasn't that hard.

"You're not *that* bad," Drew said.

"I think Coach Zach would disagree," I said. "I did nearly maim him in gym class last year."

"Okay, baseball was never your sport," he said. "But you used to be pretty good at soccer. You were one of the top guys at soccer camp."

"In fifth grade!"

"Bryan," he said. "I could really use the help."

When someone who you can hardly have a civil conversation with lays himself bare before you (not *that* way) and asks for your help, how can you say no?

"No," I said.

"Bryan!"

"Okay. Fine." I took position in front of the net. I still had my own issues to work through, but maybe some strenuous exercise would help me put things in perspective. Little did I know there wouldn't be all that much exercise. Drew's first shot at the net went wide and missed the huge target by a good five feet. We both watched as it rolled off into the woods behind me. It came to a stop at the foot of an oak tree.

After about ten seconds with neither of us moving, Drew yelled, "Go get it!"

"*You* kicked it!"

"Bryan!"

"Okay. Fine," I said, again. Since I was closer, I guess he did have a point.

I went back and retrieved the ball, then threw it out to him and took position back in the net. The next shot came directly toward me, but I missed it. Score one for Drew. I spent the next few minutes blocking—or attempting to block—goals. I don't know if I was really good or if Drew was that bad, but I made more grabs than I would have expected.

Neither of us spoke while we played, which was nice. It gave me time to think. But I wasn't exactly thinking about what Blackstone or Sam had said. I was thinking about Drew. I know. Weird. But it was kind of related to what I was going through. Drew had been playing soccer for about as long as I had been doing theater. And if this practice was any indication, his abilities with a soccer ball were about on par with my stage work. I mean, really, I shouldn't have been stopping that many goals.

After a while, I started to work up a sweat, which I don't really like to do. When the ball sailed past the net another time, I yelled, "Time!" and took a seat on the field. Drew was clearly annoyed with me for stopping, but didn't say anything about it. He ran to retrieve the ball and joined me on the grass beneath the net.

"Thanks," he said as he sat. "I really need the work."

"I can see that," I joked.

The silence that he responded with told me I had touched a nerve.

We sat in that silence for a while longer, before I finally said what I had been thinking.

"How do you do it?" I asked.

"Do what?"

"This." I waved my hand out over the soccer field. "Your best friend is David Beckham in training and you're"—I looked into his gray eyes and faltered—"not."

"Thanks," he said, tugging at the blades of grass around him. "Sorry I made you exercise. I didn't know you'd be all insulting about it."

This was not going the way I had intended. "No. I'm not trying to be mean. I'm just . . ." I paused to gather my thoughts. "I was at Mom's store the other day and I stumbled across that picture you painted for her. You remember the one? That you gave her for the grand opening?"

"How can I forget?" he said. "She had it hanging over the register for two years. How embarrassing."

Just wait till he saw it in the store window.

"You're an incredibly talented artist," I said. "Amazing. But you're not doing it anymore. Instead, you're focused on soccer. Do you really think you're going to be a professional soccer player when you get out of school?"

"You really thought I was amazing?"

"Drew. Focus."

"Okay," he said. "Well, what about you? Do you really think you're going to be a professional actor when you get out of here?"

Leave it to Drew to hit the head on the nail with the first try. "Apparently not," I said.

The silence returned.

This time, Drew was the one to break it. "I heard about

what that guy said. Blackstone?" Thank you, Alexis. I swear that girl gets more hits than Perez Hilton. And she doesn't even use Twitter. She gossips the old-fashioned way: person to person.

If he pulled that "it's just one man's opinion" crap, I think it was entirely possible that I would lead him through the trees and push him off the bluff.

But Drew was much more eloquent than that.

"That sucks."

"Succinct, yet accurate."

"But was it that big of a surprise?"

My eyes bugged out. I started searching for the quickest route to the bluff.

"No," he quickly added. "Listen. It's like you asked me about being a professional soccer player. I know there's a slim chance." I gave him a look. "Okay. It's never going to happen. But that doesn't stop me from enjoying the game. Did you really think you were that good? Is this a total shock to hear?"

"I knew I wasn't as good as Sam," I said. Apparently, Sam knew it too . . . and more.

"Maybe you're so upset because you kind of believe what Blackstone said?"

"Oh, God!" I burst into tears. I didn't care about how it looked. Drew had seen me cry before. My grandfather's funeral a few years back had some real good crying going on.

That didn't mean Drew was comfortable with it. "Oh. Okay. I wasn't prepared for that."

"Why not?" I asked through the free-flowing tears. "You know how much acting means to me."

"Really?" he asked. "Acting?"

"Hello! Have you met me?"

"If you had said how important 'theater' was to you . . . that I'd get. You've loved theater since forever. But the acting part? I don't know. It never seemed all that big a deal."

"What does that even mean?"

"It's like me and soccer," he said. "I like being part of a team. I enjoy the cheers of the crowd. And, you have to admit, I look damn good in my soccer uniform." I gave no reaction to this comment. "But when it comes down to the actual playing . . ."

"Yeah, but—"

"Don't you theater people have some kind of saying like, 'Those who can, act. Those who can't, direct'?"

"That's an insult," I explained. "A joke."

"It makes sense to me. You're a good photographer. So, obviously you've got an eye for setting a scene. And you're always telling people what to do."

"I don't tell—" You know what? I didn't even bother to finish the sentence. Neither of us would have believed it, anyway. "But acting—"

"Is the only thing you've tried in theater," he said. "So what? You can't act. There are like a hundred other jobs you can do. For me it's play soccer or coach. And I'm not a sidelines kind of guy. So what are you whining about?"

I wouldn't say that I was *whining*. I prefer "introspective complaining." But he did have a point. Maybe I'm not an actor.

There are other things I can do. And director-photographer does have a nice flow to it.

Imagine that. With one simple phrase, Drew had totally lifted my mood and solved my entire identity crisis.

Okay, that was a lie. I was still miserable. But I wasn't quite as miserable as I'd been when I got there. I needed some time to myself.

And maybe to hatch a scheme.

"Thanks," I said getting up. "I still think you should get back into art, though. You can do that along with soccer, you know."

"We'll see," he said. "You up for some more practice?"

"Not really," I said.

"I get that," Drew said. "Later."

"Later," I said as I walked away.

Now that I was considerably calmer, I got in Electra and drove cautiously out of the parking lot. I'd considered going back to the theater to talk to Sam, but I wasn't ready yet. And I'm not all that sure she was ready to talk to me either.

It wasn't like I was abandoning my team by leaving. They'd already abandoned me. Both Hope's and Jason's cars were gone from the parking lot before I got to Electra. They may have given up, but I hadn't. The scheme forming in my mind was already going full force. I just needed to get home to work it out.

Before Dawn

Canoodle was bouncing all over the kitchen before I even walked through the door. You can imagine how she greeted me once I was inside. I gave her a rub behind the ear, and a brief bit of attention, but pushed past her before she was ready to let me go. I was on a mission. I didn't even stop for a snack, which is highly unusual for me.

I ran to my room and grabbed my copy of *The Riverside Shakespeare*. It wasn't as big as the book that Jason had brought to school earlier, but it was still a rather large tome, and one of the definitive collection of old Willie's works. To get me in the mood, I loaded the soundtrack to Baz Luhrmann's version of *Romeo + Juliet* into my CD player and began to brush up on my Shakespeare.

Our scene wasn't working. That much was painfully clear. Not just because we were all still reeling from Blackstone's critiques—though that *was* something we were going to have to deal with. No. It was because it was the wrong scene for our talents. (Or my friends' talents. I, apparently, didn't have any.) The only way we were going to have a chance with Blackstone was to choose a different scene. And to do that, I had to begin by considering the strengths of my team.

Hope needed comedy, but she wanted drama. That was going to take some doing.

Jason was a great actor, but broad comedy was not his strength. He was better with more straightforward roles.

Sam was absolutely amazing and could perform almost any role. The problem would be convincing her of that. And finding that perfect role for her to perform.

I scanned down the table of contents. The tragedies were too heavy to learn in one night. The histories, as one might suspect, had too much history involved. Blackstone could very well decide it would be fun to throw in a little quiz after we finished our scene. No. We'd have to stick to comedy,

Starting with our chosen selection, *A Midsummer Night's Dream*, I quickly flipped through the pages of the play. I wasn't reading every page, just checking to see what characters were in which scenes. When I came to a scene with four parts, I grabbed a Post-it note off my desk and bookmarked the page. Once I'd gone through the entire play, I went back and skimmed the scenes so I could get a quick read on what they were about.

A Midsummer's Night Dream didn't work. None of the scenes matched our talents or our needs. I immediately moved on to *Twelfth Night*. Jason had said something about scenes where one of us wouldn't have much to do. That was one of my goals. Now, I just had to meet the other criteria.

I found a scene toward the end of the play that was even more perfect than I had imagined. Technically it was a five-person scene, but that didn't matter. It would work beautifully.

I ran down to my mom's studio and fired up her copier, making several duplicates of the pages: one for each of my scenemates and a few for me to work on myself. Once that was done, I went back to my room and got to work.

I started by looking up the play online and learning all that I could in the time I had. Even though we had examined *Twelfth Night* back in sophomore year, I didn't have automatic recall on these things, so I needed to refamiliarize myself with the text. The play is about an identical twin brother and sister (scientifically impossible, I know) who each think the other is dead when they wash up on the shores of a distant land. The comedy comes from the people who keep confusing them for each other, even though one is male and the other is, obviously, female. The scene I chose was the revelation at the end where their identities come to light and the day is ultimately saved.

Once I understood the scene, I tore it apart and put it back together. I made notes in the margins, wrote in questions for myself, and cut the scene to shreds, marking out the beats, units, and all those other things we'd learned during script analysis classes. Then I grabbed a clean copy of the scene and wrote down my ideas for the blocking. If we were going to do what I had in mind, we were going to have to stage the scene perfectly.

All this work took way longer than I'd expected. It was almost time for Mom to be home. Normally, I would have waited for her before I headed out, but we didn't have a moment to waste. I grabbed my cell phone and made for the back door.

I hit Hope's name on the speed dial as I reached the kitchen. Canoodle came bounding up to me as it rang. I gave our four-legged guest more some attention as Hope came on the line.

"Hello?"

"It's me."

"About frakking time," she said. "We've been calling all afternoon."

Oops. I guess I was so into my work, I hadn't noticed the phone vibrating when they called. Or the messages on it either.

"Sorry, I was . . . involved," I said, pulling myself away from Canoodle so I could write Mom a note. "You haven't talked to Sam, have you?"

"I'm with her right now," Hope said. "She called me when she couldn't reach you. Did you forget you were her ride home today?"

Oops, again. I'd have to apologize when I saw her. Actually, I think we all had some apologizing to do.

"And Jason?" I asked.

"He's on his way over," Hope said. "We really need to get in some serious rehearsing."

"Just what I had in mind," I said as Canoodle barked to

remind me that she was in the room. "I'll be right there." As she rubbed against my leg, inspiration struck again. "Wait. No. Better idea. Meet me at school."

"School's closed," she said.

"Just meet me there," I said. "And pick up a pizza on the way. I'm starving." I hung up the phone before she could respond. It was rude to cut the conversation short like that, but Hope would never have let me go otherwise.

Oh, and I would have gotten the pizza on my own, but I had another stop to make.

I gave Canoodle another good rub behind the ears to thank her for being there. Then, I grabbed a set of emergency keys from the drawer beside the sink and made my way out to Electra, and, ultimately, to the headmaster's house.

My detour took a bit longer than I'd expected, but I still made it to school before the rest of my group. The sun was already dipping toward the ocean as Hope pulled up in the pink-and-purple nightmare on wheels. It was quite entertaining watching Jason unfold himself out of the backseat. I had yet to ride in the matchbox car. Seeing Jason, who was about my height, struggling to get out told me that I wouldn't be hopping in any time soon.

As we gathered by the school entrance, there was a moment of awkwardness among us all, but mostly between Sam and me.

"I'm sorry," she said. "Of course I want you on my team. I will always want you on my team. I will always need you on my side."

As apologies go, that one was pretty good.

"No matter how bad I suck?" I asked. Leave it to me to spoil a nice moment.

"No matter how much you suck," she agreed.

"Good," I said. "Then, here." I handed them the pages I had printed out on the copier in Mom's studio. We could have spent another hour apologizing for the stupidity of the day, but we had for more pressing issues to deal with.

"What's this?" Jason asked.

"Our new scene," I said. "With some notes on blocking I marked down."

They all looked skeptical as they perused the pages from our *Twelfth Night* script.

Sam, the speed reader, was the first to notice the discrepancy. "This is a five-person scene," she said.

"It's okay," Jason said. "Antonio only has two lines. We can cut them or reassign them."

"No cutting," I said. "I'll be playing Antonio."

"That still leaves four other parts," Sam said.

"Not since you'll be playing both Viola and Sebastian," I said.

"You want me to play a girl and a guy?" Sam asked.

"The plot revolves around the fact that they're identical twins," I explained a fact that she already knew. "You can pull it off."

"And what about the rest of us?" Hope asked.

This was going to take some finessing. I was about to screw Hope over, but it had to be done.

"You're going to be Olivia," I said.

"I've only got a few lines," she said.

"Yes, but it's the kind of part you've been wanting to play," I reminded her. "She's a noblewoman."

"But. I've. Only. Got. A. Few. Lines."

It had finally happened. Hope and I were going to have a serious conversation.

"You know I adore you," I said. "And I know you can play any role that you set your mind to. But let's be honest. Blackstone has already made his decision. There's nothing you can do tomorrow to convince him of what I already know. This is going to come down to Sam and Jason versus Holly and Gary. We need to help them win."

I waited for a response. When she didn't say anything, I got in a final dig. "As Sam's best friends, don't we owe it to her to make sure she beats the crap out of Holly . . . figuratively speaking, of course."

"I have no problem with Sam literally beating the crap out of her," Hope said.

"So you're in?" I asked.

"I'm in," Hope said.

"Don't worry," I said. "You'll still get your moments."

"Oh, I know," she said.

I turned to Jason.

"I'm in too," he said.

I turned to Sam.

"I'm not so sure," Sam said, totally spoiling the momentum I was trying to build. "Don't get me wrong. I love that you guys are willing to do this for me. And, Bryan, I appreciate all the work you put in . . . but if I'm going to be both Viola and Sebastian in this scene, you've got me talking to myself. I can't pull that off."

"Yes," I said. "You can. You just have to trust me."

"I do trust you," Sam said. "But I'm not so sure I trust myself. We do this tomorrow."

"Would I let you look stupid?"

"Yes," Sam said, finally allowing herself to crack a smile and relieve some of the pressure. "Okay. But how are we supposed to block the scene when the stage is inside and we're locked out here?"

I looked at her with a raised eyebrow.

"We are *not* about to break into school," she said.

"Not at all," I replied, pulling a set of keys out of my pocket. "I have the keys."

I knew that watching the headmaster's dog would come in handy at some point. (Okay, well, I hadn't *known* it, but I had hoped.) After I filled my friends in on the detour I took through the headmaster's house to search for the keys to school on the way over, Hope grabbed the pizza out of the car and we slipped inside.

I've been at school before when there was no one left in the building. Being among the last out after a show or coming in on a Saturday for rehearsal is always fun. It's like we have the run of the place. But being there when we weren't supposed to be was a kind of rebellion that the four of us didn't normally take part in.

I guess Sam was right when she said the students at this school acted like the rules don't apply to them. And, for once, we were acting like our classmates.

After a quick dinner, we got to work breaking down the scene and discussing the situation. We read through the piece a couple times to get a feel for the words. As I suspected, Sam already had some of the lines down from when we read it sophomore year. (Told you she was a freak.)

Jason and Hope had a harder time committing their new lines to memory, but by midnight, they were doing pretty well. I made sure we spent enough time working on character and building our parts that the lines became second nature since we were focused on the meaning of what we were saying more than the actual words.

The late hour wasn't a problem since we had each used Hope's cell phone reception to call our parents and pull the old "I'm spending the night at a friend's house" routine. We were pretty sure none of our parents would follow up with each other, though Sam's mom is always an unknown element when it comes to parental responsibility. As for my mom, I guess she was just happy to hear I was hanging out with Jason. I do have an inordinate amount of female friends.

After midnight we went over the blocking. That was the real challenge.

"Told you I'd look like an idiot talking to myself," Sam said with no joy in her tone.

"That's because you're not committing to the shift," I said. "It has to be decisive. You break character. You become the new one. It has to be fast. And it has to be complete." I snapped my fingers. "Viola." And snapped again. "Sebastian." Snap. "Viola." Snap. "Sebastian."

Hope and Jason joined me as we snapped and chanted, "Viola. Sebastian. Viola. Sebastian . . ." while Sam shifted the physicality from one to the other with each snap. We did that until it became second nature for her. Then, we did it some more.

We helped facilitate the change in characters by pulling some set pieces out of storage for her to move between when changing from male to female. Crossing behind a pillar would serve visually as the transition. Add to that some good old-fashioned suspension of disbelief and we were halfway to our scene.

But the work wasn't done yet.

"No, Hope," I said gently. "You're too haughty. Olivia is prim and proper, but she's also vulnerable. She's worried about looking like a fool while at the same time she'd never permit anyone to play her for one. Got it?"

"I think."

"And Jason, you need to play to the house," I reminded him. "Tomorrow, choose a seat four or five rows behind Blackstone and play the scene to that seat. Imagine someone in that seat and keep reminding yourself that they need to see and hear everything you do and say. 'K?"

"Okay."

"All right," I said. "Let's try this again."

We ran through the scene once more, taking my latest notes into consideration. It was better, but not perfect. "Let's run it again," I said. "Oh, and does anyone have any suggestions for me?" I wasn't really worried about my performance because I only had a couple lines, but I didn't want my friends to think I was just being critical of them while I thought my performance was perfect.

And, wouldn't you know, they picked my two lines apart. *Actors!*

By four o'clock we were all pretty tired. We camped out in the set storage room on some old couches and mattresses that parents had donated to the shows over the years. Those of us with cell phones set the alarms to make sure we woke with plenty of time to freshen up and get outside before we were found inside where we weren't supposed to be.

Hope found a daybed along the back wall of the storage room, and I curled up on a mattress on the floor beside her. Sam and Jason spread out on a pair of couches on the other side of the room. We probably could have pulled everything together, but we were all too exhausted. We pretty much collapsed where we were.

Maybe I was overtired, but my mind was racing so much with our scene that I couldn't shut it down to get some rest.

I wasn't the only one.

"Bryan," Hope whispered.

"Yeah," I whispered back. I couldn't hear Sam and Jason from where we were, but I didn't want to wake them if they had managed to nod off.

"In case things get too crazy tomorrow," she said. "Or, later today, I guess . . . I just wanted to say that I think we've got a great scene. You done good."

Wow. It was so unlike Hope to give a nice compliment like that. Not that she never had a kind word or anything, but her compliments were usually couched in a joke. No one could backhand a compliment like Hope Rivera.

"By the way," she said. "I should kill you for your little scheme to force me and Drew back together, but I'm in a forgiving mood lately. So just know that you're on probation, if you should ever think of doing something like that again . . ."

She let the end of that threat hang in the air. I should have known Hope wouldn't just compliment me for my stellar directing. I also should have expected that Hope would have been onto our scheme from the start.

Considering her "forgiving mood," I couldn't help but ask, "Any chance you'll let me read that monologue you wrote last week?"

"Nope," she replied, rolling over. "I shredded it."

I settled into sleep, secure in the knowledge that it was quite possible we'd never know exactly what it was that Hope and Drew had been fighting about. And, honestly, I didn't really mind.

Awake and Sing!

Morning came quickly, considering we didn't have much night left by the time I finally nodded off. I woke up before my alarm rang, staring at a different ceiling than I had been the rest of the week.

I was more nervous for this audition than any I'd ever had before. Even more than I'd been for the monologues last week. My fears weren't for myself. Blackstone had made it pretty clear that I was out of consideration. No. I was nervous for my friends. I wanted Hope to have her moment to shine. I wanted to see Jason move up to the next level in his acting. And I wanted Sam to do nothing less than give a performance that Blackstone would be raving about for years to come.

It was a lot to ask from one single scene, but we'd put in the work. Why not hope for the best?

Our cell phones started beeping in unison. We all reluctantly got up and made our way to the bathrooms to freshen up as sunlight filled the empty halls. We did the best we could with our clothes. Sam had a change of outfit in her mom's book closet, and Hope had a different shirt in her locker. Jason and I rifled through the ill-equipped costume closet for new shirts, but they all smelled old and musty so we just stuck with what we had worn the day before. I was sure people would notice, but there was very little we could do about it.

After grabbing breakfast from the vending machines, we locked up the school and sat in Electra to wait for someone to come by and open it up for us. It didn't take long. Not five minutes after we set up camp in the parking lot, Mr. Randall pulled up beside us.

"Looks like some people are ready to get a jump on the day," he said.

He had no idea.

Back in school, we dropped our books back in the auditorium and finished our breakfasts.

There was a nervous energy among our group. Excitement mixed with fear.

"We should run the scene one more time," Sam suggested. "Before everyone gets here." Hope and Jason were nodding their heads in agreement, waiting for me to make the decision.

Have to say, I kind of like this directing thing.

"No," I said. "We ran it enough last night. It's good. I don't want us to go second-guessing everything now and screwing it all up. We'll be fine."

I don't think they were entirely convinced, but they didn't push the issue. I was glad, because I was already questioning everything I had told them to do the night before. I didn't want to start changing things over and over again until we were forced to stop. The time for altering the scene was in the past. Now, we just had to trust ourselves. And I had to believe that I hadn't totally screwed my friends' chances.

We went through a few warm-ups together, but took our seats as people started arriving. The Drama Geeks filled the auditorium with a nervous energy as they came in for audition day. Everyone got there early and just about all the groups split off around the auditorium to squeeze the last remnants of rehearsal time out of their scenes.

Not my group. We sat in our seats silently going over our lines and blocking. Keeping ourselves focused and calm. There was no extraneous chatter. No conversation at all. Our unusual behavior drew focus from our classmates, but we ignored them as well. There was no one else in our world but our characters and our scene partners.

Leave it to Holly Mayflower to totally invade without an invitation.

"Giving up already?" she asked as she came into Hall Hall only minutes before we were scheduled to begin.

Sam ignored her.

Hope did not.

"Holly," she said. "I have just now achieved my moment of Zen. Don't make me ruin it by knocking you on your bony ass."

Holly chuckled. "Hope. You are always good for a laugh. But seriously—"

"Holly," I said, interrupting her. (Something I've never done with her before.) "Save it. You're cutting into our prep time. Enough with the stupid games. It's time to let your acting speak for itself."

"Excuse me?"

I gave her a wave of my hand. "You are dismissed."

She laughed in her own dismissive way. "Bryan, it takes a lot of courage to go onstage after what Hart said about you. I just wanted to stop by to wish you all good luck."

Jason gulped in the cool morning air. The guy was freakish about his rituals and Holly had just committed the ultimate sin: Never wish anyone good luck in a theater.

"We don't need luck," Sam said. "We've got talent . . . and a kick-ass scene."

Holly's group left without another word, but Gary did look back to roll his eyes like he knew his scene partner was crazy. We shared a quiet laugh with him and then went back to our sustained silence. Well, after we took a minute to convince Jason that our scene wasn't cursed because of Holly's wishes of luck.

Mr. Randall posted the scene order on the callboard at precisely nine o'clock. Guess he wasn't anticipating any volunteers today. Everyone ran up to see how things were going to play out, but we continued our calm preparations and waited in our seats. Holly's team did the same.

Once the mad rush was over I got up to look. I guess Gary was elected for his group, because he made his way over as well. We arrived at the list together, almost like two gunslingers meeting at high noon. All eyes were on us, like they were expecting a showdown.

According to the order Mr. Randall had laid out, everyone else was going to be our opening acts. He had mercifully chosen my group to go last. Holly's group was the one before ours. I guess we weren't the only ones who thought the decision was going to come down to Sam and Holly.

When Gary and I turned back to the auditorium, we were surprised to see that everyone was still watching us.

"I think they're expecting some macho male posturing," I said to him.

"From us?" he laughed.

I laughed too. We weren't soccer players, after all.

"Break a leg," I said.

"Break two," he replied.

With smiles on our faces, we rejoined our teams and told them when we'd be performing. My group was relieved. Holly looked annoyed. Which only made us feel more relieved.

Mr. Randall got up and said a few things to us before we started. Mostly focusing on how proud he was of all of us for the hard work we'd put in over the program. He tacked on a bit about dealing with criticism at the end and adapting it into a performance. It seemed about a week too late, but it was still appreciated.

Thankfully, he'd also mentioned that Coach Zach wouldn't be bringing the soccer team around this time. A combined sigh of relief washed over the room. It ended abruptly when Hartley Blackstone arrived with his daughter trailing behind him. Mr. Randall barely spoke to our special guest as things got under way. I'm guessing he was a bit peeved at the way Blackstone had thrown the entire program into a tizzy. I threw a smile my teacher's way to let him know his students appreciated the support.

Tasha's group went first. I did not envy them for having to set the tone for the day, but they carried it off pretty well. They'd chosen some obscure scene from a play I'd never heard of, in which Jimmy was supposed to act like a crazy person, tripping over his words and manic in his actions. I wouldn't say he was particularly convincing in his role, but his frantic energy was working for him instead of against him. That way, he wasn't distracting from his teammates' performances.

When they were done, Mr. Randall led us all in a round of applause. This was unusual for scene work. We didn't usually clap at the end. I think he was trying to find a way to combat Blackstone's negativity. I guess we all kind of sensed that, because our applause was more boisterous than the scene deserved.

Blackstone waited for us to die down before he spoke.

"Interesting choices," he said. "Good that you played to the strengths. Thank you."

The stunned expressions of Tasha's group were mirrored in the faces of all the students in the auditorium. As far as we knew, that was possibly the nicest thing the man had ever said in his life. It certainly had to be the briefest. I wondered if this was the same guy who had been there a week earlier.

No dummies, Tasha's group fled the stage before he could say anything else.

The next group consisted of three sophomores doing a scene from, believe it or not, *Miss Julie*. When they were done, our Miss Julie chimed in, along with her father, to compliment them and we all moved on to the next scene.

It quickly became clear that they were just working in anticipation of the final two scenes and the clash between Jason and Gary and, more notably, Sam and Holly. That's not to say that there wasn't some really good scene work being done onstage. Gary's best friend, Madison Wu, was particularly impressive with her Lady Macbeth. But the energy in the room just seemed to be building toward the last scenes of the morning.

It reached a plateau when Holly's group took to the stage.

"I'm Holly Mayflower," she said. "And these are my scene partners, Gary McNulty and Belinda Connors. We will be performing a scene from *A Midsummer Night's Dream*."

What a coincidence. I guess Alexis and Belinda *had* been eavesdropping outside our rehearsal the day we picked our original scene. Holly was going to be so disappointed when she learned that we changed to *Twelfth Night*.

Holly opened the scene with a monologue from early in the play that segued into a scene from the end surprisingly well. She was playing Queen Titania, who had fallen in love with Gary's character while he had the head of an ass (long story). Belinda filled out the scene playing a few random fairies all rolled into a one-role part.

I'd love to say that Holly tanked. That it was a nightmare. But watching her and Gary up there together was really something. As much as I wanted to credit it to Gary's fine acting, I knew it was just as much Holly. Even Belinda was pretty good with the limited material she had.

The applause that came at the end was genuinely enthused. As was Blackstone's commentary. "Quite impressive," he said. "Quite impressive, indeed." He went on to compliment their individual performances in more detail than he had given any other scene critiques earlier. I took this as final confirmation that his choice was going to come from the final two scenes. He even went on at length about the quality of Belinda's performance, which he referred to as "an unexpected gem."

I was so caught up in the excitement of the performance that I almost complimented Holly as we passed when my group took stage. But Holly's smug expression of self-satisfaction stopped any praise that was about to come out of my mouth. I did give Gary a nod of approval. It was clear to me that he was going to be running things once we seniors graduated next year. His smile seemed to double in size when he acknowledged my silent appraisal.

Then. It was our turn.

My group took our positions onstage. As we had agreed, Jason stepped forward to introduce the scene. When he mentioned that Sam was playing the parts of both Viola *and* Sebastian, there was an audible gasp from the audience. I couldn't see Holly's face from where I was standing, but I imagined quite an entertaining reaction there. I wish I could have enjoyed the moment more, but it was time to do our scene.

I was the first to speak. Once I got my two lines out of the way, I stood off to the side and watched the scene unfold. Sam managed her first transition from male to female effortlessly, passing behind one of the two columns we'd left onstage. She came out the other side with an entirely different character just as we'd rehearsed.

Usually, I hated to be in scenes where I didn't have much dialogue. I never knew how to stand there and react in character to what I was hearing from the others. I would always try to project what I was thinking, by nodding in agreement, or scowling, or smiling broadly. In many ways, I was acting with my face, expressing my reactions with no actual feeling behind them. Exactly what Blackstone had been talking about.

This time, I didn't bother listening to the other characters at all. I was watching my friends perform. Any reactions I had were subdued and they were entirely my own. It may not have technically passed for acting, but that wasn't my focus at the moment.

It's kind of crazy watching a scene I'd directed. Jason, Hope, and especially Sam were off and running and I could do nothing to stop them. Not that they needed stopping. Each of them was doing exactly what we had rehearsed—finding their moments and making them their own.

Sam made small adjustments in her movements to differentiate between Viola and Sebastian.

Jason tapped into Orsino's strength to be commanding in his own presence on the stage.

And Hope found the subtleties of a noblewoman, while still bringing her own power to the character.

No matter how good the scene was—and it *was* a good scene—I couldn't stop worrying. About the next line. About the next movement. I was standing in the middle of the scene with absolutely no control over the situation. I had to trust in my actors, to trust in my *friends* to follow the notes I had given them.

And they did.

And it was beautiful.

I didn't need the fierce applause at the end of the scene to know how good it was.

But after the week I'd had, it was certainly nice to hear.

"As wonderfully impressive a performance as the previous one," Blackstone said as the applause died down. "Quite a daring choice to perform both the roles of Sebastian and Viola, Miss Lawson. The way you differentiated between the two characters . . . and the transitions that you made were so . . . so . . ." He snapped his fingers to exemplify his point. It was all we could do not to laugh, considering how we'd practiced those transitions. "Brava."

Sam was beaming. She grabbed my hand and gave it a squeeze of thanks. Personally, that was the only critique I needed, but we weren't finished yet.

"Mr. MacMillan," he said, turning his attention to Jason. "You really brought me into your performance. Opening it up to the entire audience. And Miss Rivera, I was happy to see you break out of your character-part tendencies for a moment somewhere in the middle of the scene."

Sam grabbed hold of Hope's hand before she could react. I suspect it would have been a more visual response than a verbal. With her hand held firmly by Sam, Hope demurely dipped her head in a nod as if she had appreciated his comment. Of course, everyone else in the place knew that her simple move was laced with sarcasm, and got a kick out of it on its own. For a girl known for her bluster, she can do subtle really well.

We all expected him to ignore me like before, but he surprised us all by going, "Mr. Stark you managed to refrain from being a distraction as you stood off to the side. So, that's an improvement."

It was all I could do not to laugh at the pompous—

"What did you think of the staging?" Sam asked before I could finish my thought. She looked at me with a wink. "The direction of the scene?"

Blackstone nodded his head. "There were some nice things in there," he said almost dismissively.

For Blackstone, that was high praise, indeed. He mostly waved it off like it was nothing. And it probably shouldn't have really meant anything to me to hear it, but it did mean something.

It certainly did.

All's Well That Ends Well

We broke for lunch while Blackstone made his decision. Even though we joked about him going all *American Idol* with a "You're going to New York! And you're going to New York!" I could tell Sam was tense. She didn't even try to play with her food. She merely sat in silence, waiting until it was time to go back to Hall Hall.

"Hey, it's going to be fine," I said. "That was some of your most amazing work ever. Seriously. Whether or not you make it into Blackstone's program, you did your best today. No doubt." And in my mind, there was none. Sam had a future in acting, no matter what Blackstone decided. Sure, it would be easier for her if she got into his program, but aren't people always talking about how it's the struggle that makes artists better at what they do? It wasn't like there was a whole lot of struggling going on at Orion Academy. Drama? Yes. But actual real-life, hard-core struggle?

Don't make me laugh.

"What was up with that guy being all positive?" Jason asked. "That was a crazy one eighty."

"Maybe he was harsh because he knew we needed to hear it," I said. "He gave us the criticism to help us prepare for the scenes." Okay, I was being all Little Bryan Sunshine, but I was still working off the buzz from our performance.

"And maybe he was back on his meds today," Sam suggested.

We laughed harder than the joke required, but I think we were all enjoying the relief that the most hellacious Summer Theater Program ever was finally over.

Almost.

The entire pavilion went silent when Jimmy ran into the room. Even the soccer team shut up to hear what he had to say.

"He's ready," Jimmy announced.

I don't think the Drama Geeks have ever moved faster in our lives. We were back in Hall Hall in a shot, without a second thought to the food we'd left behind on the tables. Some of the soccer players came along to see what was up. Naturally, Eric and Drew had tagged along. I don't think any of us minded. In fact, I was pretty sure some of us even appreciated it.

Hartley Blackstone was already standing center stage while we filed into our seats. He waited until the room was dead silent before he spoke. "Students of theatre," he said. "I know that this last week was difficult for you. But I think you will all agree that you are now better for it." Well, I doubt that we'd *all* agree, but I wasn't about to correct him. "That is certainly true for the actor I've chosen for my program. Mr. Jason MacMillan, I look forward to working with you in New York this summer."

The crowd went wild for Jason. Even though we had kind of expected it, the announcement was still exciting to hear. As our group cheered him on the loudest, Gary leaned over to pat Jason on the back. I was pretty sure that Gary was thinking "next year" to himself while he did it.

Blackstone waited for us to calm down again before he continued. "Now, for the actress, I faced a more difficult decision. Throughout theatre history, leading ladies have often been the most challenging roles to fill. And that was no different here. From the early days of the divine Miss Sarah Bernhardt in Europe, through the evolution of the American Theatre . . ." Oh my God. He was actually going to take us through the history of modern theater before he announced who got the female spot. Clearly, the man loved to hear himself speak. But I'm pretty sure I wasn't the only one who was sick of hearing what he had to say. He continued to ramble on for so long that I almost missed it when he finally announced . . .

"Miss Holly Mayflower."

What?

I couldn't have heard that right. But the choice was confirmed when she actually *stood up to take a bow*.

Sam was all noble, clapping for her rival along with everybody else. Though, I have to admit, the applause in the auditorium was significantly less enthusiastic than it had been for Jason.

Me? I showed solidarity for my sister by sitting on my hands, along with Hope. Childish? Yes. But we were okay with that.

Even Eric was too busy consoling Sam to bother clapping. Again, earning him major points with me. At some point, I was going to have to stop counting and just admit that he was a good guy. Not today, mind you. But at some point.

Once the noise died down again, Blackstone had a few closing remarks before he swept out of the theater. Hopefully, never to be seen again.

Miss Julie then got up and suggested we spend the rest of the afternoon playing more improv games. The sophomores and juniors took her up on it, but we seniors were pretty much burnt by it all. Not to mention that my team was exhausted. It was time for summer vacation to begin. I went home to take a nap.

When I woke, I checked to see if anyone wanted to do that good-bye dinner Sam and I had talked about. Hope already had plans with her dad, which was no surprise. And Sam wanted to spend the evening with Eric so they could give their relationship a name before he left. She was still reluctant about bringing up the whole "exclusive" thing, but I told her that she didn't have to worry. Eric was too good a guy to not want that with her.

I know. I was going soft. But it really was way past time for that.

With nothing better to do, I hopped online to check out the gossip sites for pictures of celebrity dogs. I wanted to focus on helping Mom out more, like Blaine had suggested. Maybe some of her designs would be featured and I could give her an update on what to stock up on.

Color me surprised when I stumbled across an unexpected little entertainment news tidbit. It seems that Mayflower Music was getting into the movie business. And the first film that Anthony Mayflower—Holly's dad—was set to produce was going to be directed by one Hartley Blackstone.

Now, logically, I know that movie deals take forever to put together. And there *is* such a thing as coincidence. But I also know, without a shadow of a doubt, that Holly's father bought her way into the program.

So much for Holly relying on her talent alone. The girl is a Mayflower after all.

I debated calling Sam to tell her what I had found, but what would be the point? Sure, it might reassure her about her acting, but it would also remind her that in our world, no matter how talented she was, there were some ways that she just couldn't compete.

And don't go pitying Sam too much here. My parents can't afford to throw around movie deals for me either.

Since there was no one I could really tell about the Mayflower manipulation, I went back to trolling the gossip sites. On the third site I checked, I found a shot of a three-time celebrity divorcée on the beach with a pair of Welsh corgis wearing outfits from Mom's summer swimwear line. When I called Mom, she didn't even give me a chance to say anything before telling me to meet her and Blaine at our favorite restaurant on Melrose for dinner. She hung up before I could ask what was going on.

I made my way through the traffic and met them an hour later. I'd barely sat when they told me their exciting news. All the extra work they had been taking on lately had been for a very specific reason that had nothing to do with my parents getting divorced or Blaine dying like I had feared. Kaye 9 had grown so popular at the Melrose Avenue location that they could afford to buy a space at Malibu Colony Plaza. Before the end of summer, they would be opening Kaye 9 Malibu right next to the coffeehouse where Sam, Eric, and I had hatched our scheme. It truly was a space worth watching for an exciting new endeavor.

Which meant that I was going to have to start helping out getting the new place ready, bright and early on Monday morning.

My summer vacation was barely going to last one weekend.

But first, Sam and I had to see our friends off Saturday morning. I was in Electra by seven o'clock, picking up Sam and riding out to the Santa Monica Airport. Eric's dad had finagled the corporate jet for a private excursion. Not that it required much finagling since Mr. Whitman owned the corporation. The jet was going to fly Eric and Matthew out to New York, where they would then take a train to the Hamptons to meet up with their mom and her girlfriend. Hope was able to hitch a ride on the jet to spend the summer with her own mom—and Suze—in New York.

It was a morning of so long, farewells, auf Wiedersehens,

and good-byes. Sam couldn't hold back the tears, and I swear I even saw the eyes of her newly exclusive boyfriend, Eric, getting a little moist.

Drew was there too. He and Hope shared a moment saying good-bye for what was likely more than just the summer. In the end, I was pretty sure that those two would always be friends, but maybe a little distance would help with that for now.

We watched the plane take off from the airport's observation deck and stayed until it was a little dot in the sky. With all our friends gone, it looked like it was just going to be Sam and me alone for the summer.

Well, maybe not totally alone. Drew was right there beside me.

And . . . scene.

About the Author

Paul Ruditis writes for teens and people who think like teens, creating both original novels as well as books and comic books based on some of his favorite TV shows and movies. To find out more about the books Paul writes and the shows he watches visit paulruditis.com.